A LONELY DANCE

Also available from Selina R. Gonzalez:

THE MIRAVELD CHRONICLES
A Thieving Curse (Book 1)
The Dragon Prince's Heart (Book 1.5)
A Fated Quest (Book 3)

THE MERCENARY AND THE MAGE
Prince of Shadow and Ash (Book 1)
Staff of Nightfall (Book 2)
Servant, Mercenary, Brother Vol. I (Book 0.5)
Servant, Mercenary, Brother Vol. II (Book 2.5)
Bells of Winter (Book 3 – novelette)
Or get all five books in one in
The Mercenary and the Mage: The Complete Series

THE MIRAVELD CHRONICLES

A LONELY DANCE

SELINA R. GONZALEZ

Paperback ISBN 978-1-957499-02-4
Hardcover ISBN 978-1-957499-03-1

Published by Wyvern Wing Press
www.WyvernWingPress.com
www.SelinaRGonzalez.com

To everyone who has wondered if
or been made to feel that
they aren't worth loving.

May love find you and remind you
that you matter.

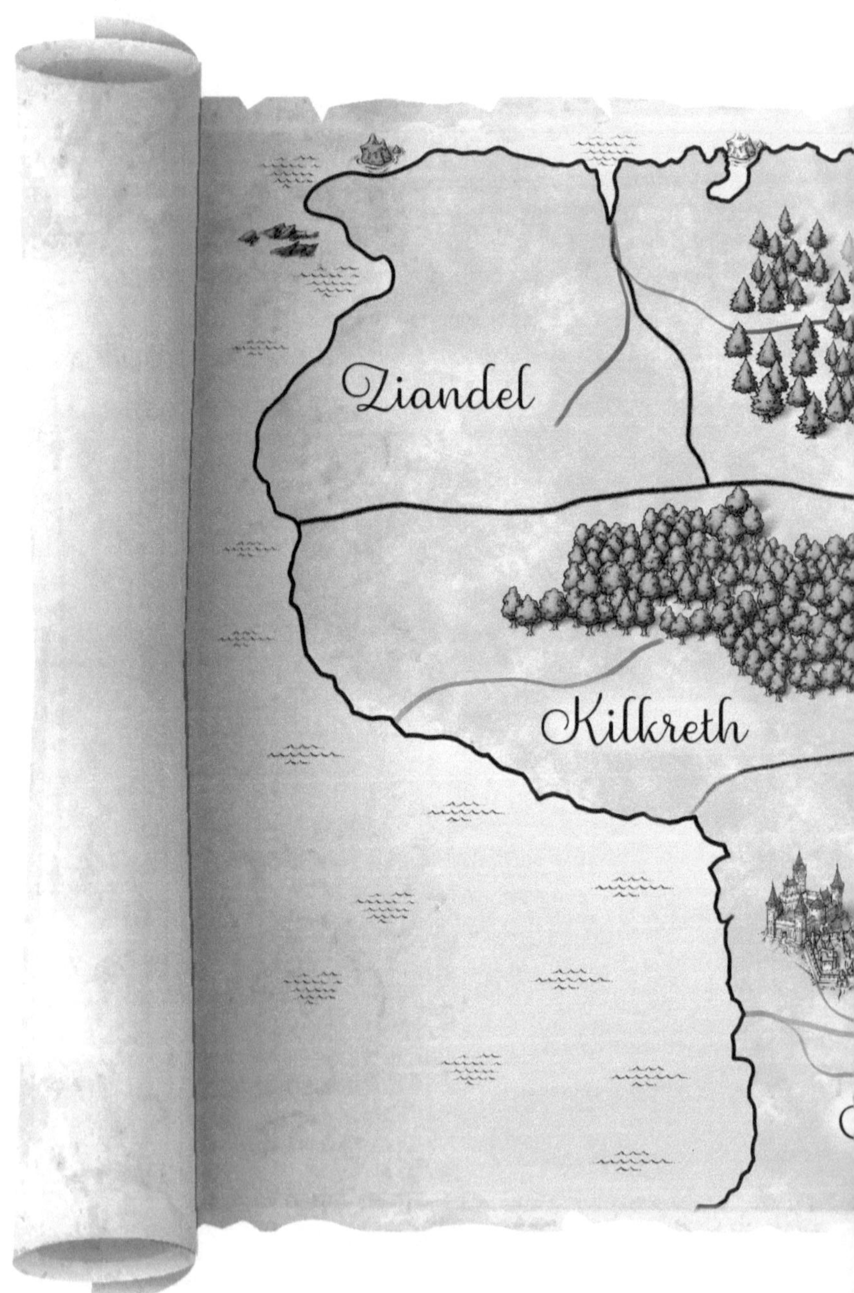

Ziandel
Kilkreth

Talland
Great House
Aedyllan
Rethali
Royal
Palace
Eynlae
Rethalyon

Ilara's Tattoos

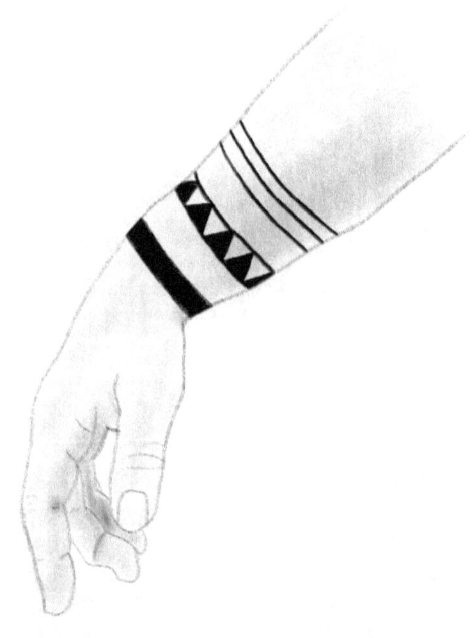

The Talland Great House

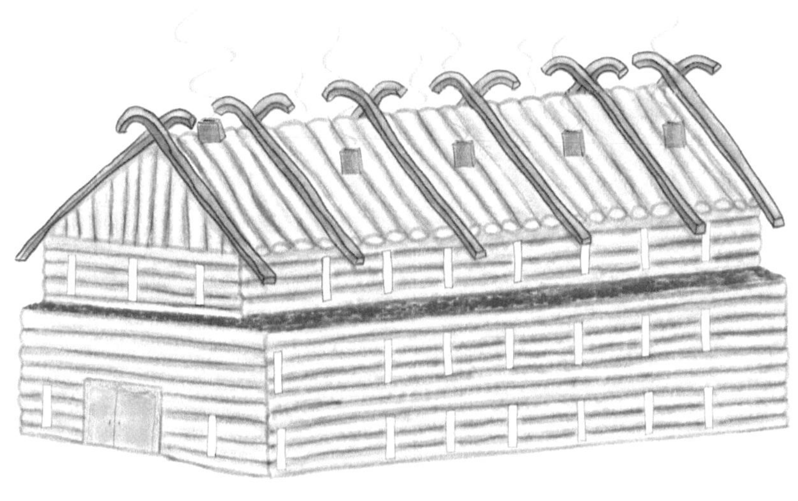

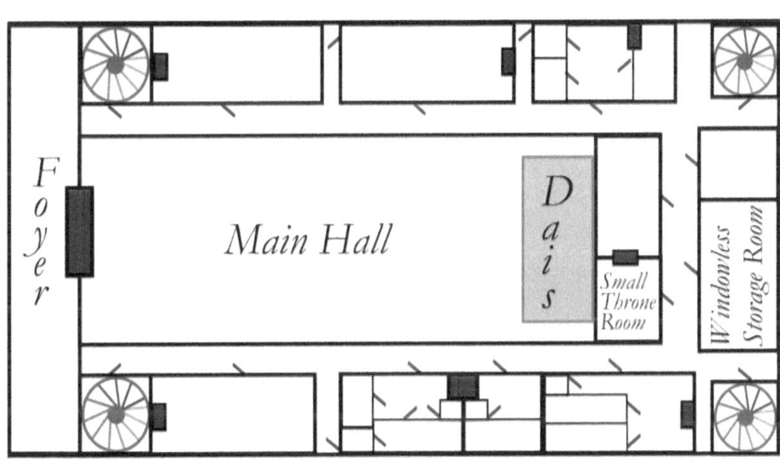

First Floor   ■ fireplace   stairs   door

1

Beware the visitor who arrives on the night of a new moon.

The evening the man with gold hair and emerald eyes arrived at the Talland Great House, the distant stars kept watch alone.

While elsewhere in the royal residence servants prepared a guest room for the stranger, Ilara glanced through the distorted glass of her bedchamber's narrow window at the growing darkness of the summer night. Moonlight was pure, their legends claimed, and only those concealing evil intentions arrived at a house or conducted important business on a night when the moon took her rest.

"His name is Earl Domhnall Halkon; he's a nobleman from Kilkreth," Papa had explained in their brief conversation about the stranger. "He's traveled far and is wearied, and I will never let it be said the King of Talland has forsaken our time-honored tradition of hospitality out of fear of a superstition."

But baseless superstition or sacred truth or perhaps a bit of both, it didn't matter. The ancient proverb repeated like a tolling bell in her mind.

A sharp prick snapped Ilara out of her thoughts as the pin of a brooch pierced the wool of her mulberry overdress and jabbed into her thumb.

"Moonless winter," she muttered as she inspected her

fingertip. To her relief, it wasn't bleeding. Still, it felt like another warning to be careful of the newcomer.

Other kingdoms didn't share Talland's reverence for the moon, so it was unlikely a nobleman from Kilkreth would know to avoid arriving at a Tallander's home on the night of a new moon. Besides, they couldn't afford to turn away a wealthy foreigner when Talland was suffering a famine caused by a fierce ice storm that spring. The food shortages had gotten worse as summer progressed, exacerbated by the reduction in foreign trade ever since the Kilkrethian merchant guild had fractured the previous year. A Kilkrethian noble might have connections that could facilitate increased trade.

Regardless of motive, Mama would have agreed with Papa. Her mother had always made people feel welcome. If she were alive, she would want Ilara to do the same.

Still, a sense of foreboding coiled in her gut.

Taking a deep breath, she secured the brass brooch at the base of the right shoulder strap of the overdress. The long sleeves of the yellow linen underdress were fitted down to her wrists, where a bit of the tattoos on her right wrist peeked out. She ran her fingertips over the three strands of blue and red beads that curved down between the two wolf-engraved brooches, double-checking that they weren't tangled.

A whine preceded a head of soft, fluffy fur bumping against her hand. The sled dog yapped and whined until Ilara scratched the red-brown fur between her perky white ears.

"Are you nervous, too, Nika?" Ilara murmured.

Nika closed her eyes, her pink tongue lolling out as she wagged a bushy tail.

Ilara laughed. "You don't care about superstitions, do you?" She nudged the dog away with a sigh. "But you are excellent at covering my dress in fur."

Picking off the white and reddish fur, she walked over to her vanity. A glance in the mirror reassured her that the intricate braids crowning her head and trailing down over the rest of her loose black hair were still presentable. They'd grown a little frizzy throughout the day, but Kiri had woven them well.

With a nod, Ilara picked up her crown, a thin band of silver in a rough half-circle set with a pearl to represent the full moon, and tucked the ends into her braids. She only wore it for important functions—or when meeting a visiting foreign noble for the first time. Then she strode out of her room, Nika padding along at her side.

The door across the hallway opened, and Kiri burst out of her own room. A wide smile lit up her youngest sister's face, reminding Ilara of their mother with a bittersweet pang.

"Ara, you look beautiful!" Kiri's smile turned mischievous. "You're sure to enchant Earl Halkon."

"Enchant...? What are you talking about? It's tea with a foreigner, not a courtship proposal." Although nothing Ilara said ever dimmed her sisters' baffling obsession with her nonexistent love life. A couple weeks ago she'd spent ten minutes in polite conversation after dinner with Olyn, son of the Head of House Vellroch, and Kiri and Meelah had been devastated there wasn't more to it than that.

In fairness, talking to Olyn *was* part of Ilara's secret assessing of eligible Tallander bachelors, but he hadn't captured her interest.

"You might change your mind when you meet him," Kiri said in a singsong voice, drawing Ilara back to the present moment.

"Wait, have you seen him?"

Kiri sighed. "No, but Meelah glimpsed him from the balcony above the hall, and she claims he's so handsome you could swoon!" She put the back of her hand to her forehead and sank against the wall with a dramatic sigh.

Ilara fought to maintain a serious expression. "You're thirteen; you don't need to be swooning over anyone."

"You could, though." Kiri straightened with a wink. "You're twenty-one and that's—"

"If you say old, I will have no choice but to tickle you until you take it back."

"And mess up our braids right before meeting with a foreign nobleman?" Kiri touched her own plaits, woven over her dark hair. "I think you won't."

"Hm, maybe after tea."

"What are we doing after tea?" Meelah's voice asked behind them.

Ilara grinned over her shoulder at her other sister. "Tickling Kiri as punishment for slander."

"A serious charge with a fitting punishment. What's the false claim?"

Before Ilara replied, Kiri said, "Never mind that. Ilara says she isn't interested in the handsome Kilkrethian."

Meelah shook her head like Ilara had done something horribly disappointing. "Oh, wait until you see him."

Ilara raised her eyebrows. "Sixteen is also too young for swooning, you know."

"Please." Meelah waved a hand. "Swooning is a waste because you don't get to remember anything that happens. You can't see his eyes widen with concern or feel his strong arms lifting you up—"

"How old is this nobleman, anyway?" Ilara asked as they walked toward the stairs at the front end of the Great House, past the various antlers, pelts, weapons, and intricate carvings adorning the long wood hallways. She hadn't even wondered about the Kilkrethian's age until her sisters started getting harebrained notions of romance.

"Too old for me," Meelah groaned.

"You know who isn't too old for you?" Kiri asked, her voice overly sweet and innocent. "Kotan."

"Shut *up*." Meelah lightly shoved her baby sister's shoulder as they reached the top of the spiral staircase.

Nika made a sound that sounded rather like *aw-wah-aaauuuurgh* at the girls and wriggled between them. The dog didn't like it when her humans appeared to be mean to each other.

"You like Kotan?" Ilara knew little about the young man, except that he was a couple of years older than Meelah and the son of the recently appointed Head of House Nockstoll.

"I think he's handsome," Meelah said with a delicate sniff. "Beyond that, I haven't decided."

As her sisters' teasing and laughter and the gentle flicker of the candles filled the wood stairwell, the knot of worry in Ilara's stomach dissipated.

Papa was waiting for them outside the door to the sitting room on the first floor. His sled dog, Chari, a fluffy female with black and white fur who was getting too old to do any actual sled pulling, sat next to him.

"Welcome, girls." Papa's warm greeting eased Ilara's nerves further. The geometric tattoos on his wrists peeked out from under his sleeve as he adjusted his crown, a thick gold circlet set with a single aquamarine, atop his dark, braided hair.

"Does this earl have the connections to increase our trade with Kilkreth?" Ilara inquired.

"I don't know, but I'm hopeful." Papa squared his shoulders, his expression settling into an air of regal impartiality that was both kind and intimidating.

"Is he a bachelor?" Meelah chirped up.

Papa blinked. "Pardon?"

"Might he court Ilara?" Far too much excitement colored Kiri's tone.

"Such questions." Papa's amused gaze met Ilara's for a moment. She'd used to wish she'd inherited his gold-flecked amber eyes instead of Mama's dark brown ones, but ever since Mama had passed, she'd grown to love her eyes. "I don't know anything about him, and Ilara doesn't need to get married any time soon unless she wants to."

Girls were often married by her age, but Ilara didn't care. She wanted to marry, yes, but she hadn't yet met a man who made her feel like their hearts called to each other—that was how Mama had described falling for Papa. Ilara was content to wait. Besides, Papa once half-jokingly admitted he wouldn't mind if it took her another ten years. Not that the court knew any of that—at least three of the House Heads seemed certain their sons had a chance.

"Our purpose tonight," Papa continued, "is representing Talland and making a good impression. Do remember that Kilkreth's nobility is more stratified and formal than ours." He sent a warning look at Kiri and Meelah before turning his stern expression on Ilara. "Ara, no business over tea." With that, Papa opened the door and led them into the sitting room.

Ilara suppressed a sigh. Just because she preferred being direct and efficient in royal meetings didn't mean she didn't enjoy conversation or wouldn't honor their traditions. Tallanders didn't discuss business matters when offering hospitality—to do so implied the welcome was contingent on a favorable outcome, and true hospitality expected nothing in return.

Of course, Tallanders also believed that a gracious host was more trustworthy, and a polite guest demonstrated honorable character. She wondered if hospitality was truly unconditional when used to evaluate a potential business partner.

However, all thoughts of trade and hospitality fled her mind as the man sitting in an armchair near the fireplace stood to greet them.

The Kilkrethian nobleman was the most foreign-looking person Ilara had ever seen. Tallanders were a hearty people. They needed to be to survive Talland's fierce winters and work her clay-rich soil or live along her rugged coast, which faced a petulant sea. Accordingly, Tallanders tended to be short and stocky, with skin tones from tawny to sun-beaten brown.

But Earl Domhnall Halkon towered over Papa. Slender and graceful, he reminded her of a willow tree. He wore dark trousers under a shimmering cream-colored tunic of silky fabric that clung to his lean muscle. Silver vines embroidered onto the narrow green cloth belt at his waist caught the light from the small fire and the scattered candles.

His hair wasn't just blond, it was gold. Pronounced cheekbones and a sharp jaw defined a pale face cuttingly handsome. But his eyes captured her.

His irises were emeralds melted into liquid. Ilara had always thought saying someone's eyes sparkled to be a mere expression, but as he smiled—a tilted curve of gentle lips—his eyes glittered.

"Good evening, Earl Halkon," Papa said with a slight incline of his head.

The Kilkrethian bowed deeply. "Good evening, Your Maj—"

Nika and Chari's growls interrupted him. The dogs crouched and laid their ears back, their hackles rising.

"Nika!" Ilara hissed, breaking out of her momentary trance. "What's wrong with you?"

"Chari!" Papa frowned down at the dogs. "Stand down."

Chari glanced at him, only to return to growling. Papa's furrowed brow matched Ilara's confusion. Neither dog had growled at a guest in years. Nika snapped her jaws as she moved in front of Ilara.

Papa grabbed Chari's scruff. "I apologize—"

"Oh, no. They're simply being loyal and protective."

Halkon extended a hand toward Nika.

Normally Ilara would trust Nika, but the dogs were acting strange. "I don't think that's a good idea—"

"It's all right, pup." Halkon wiggled his fingers, and Nika lay down with a whimper. Chari backed away, ducking her head.

Crouching down, Ilara looked into Nika's ice-blue eyes. "What has gotten into you?" She stroked the thick, soft fur on the dog's head. Nika whimpered and tucked her snout under her forepaws. "I'm sorry, but what did you do, Earl Halkon?"

"A Kilkrethian dominance trick," he replied with a nonchalant shrug. "I have a way with animals. A magic touch, you might say. I can teach you. If you like."

That made her curious. She gave Nika one more rub and stood. "I would be interested, yes."

"I didn't know Kilkrethians had such an affinity for animals," Meelah said. Hopefully Halkon wouldn't notice the smitten look in her eyes.

The earl nodded. "Something I understand we have in common, as animals are also important to Tallanders, none more so than your noble sled dogs."

More of the tension in Ilara's back eased. It was easier to trust someone who was kind to animals.

"I hope you won't judge our hospitality on the uncharacteristically overzealous protection of said dogs." Papa smiled apologetically.

"Oh, don't worry. I've heard they can be a bit stubborn, can't they?"

Ilara laughed. "You have no idea. Sometimes I think Nika believes *she's* the princess."

"Speaking of princesses, allow me to introduce my daughters." Papa motioned to each of them. "The youngest, Princess Kiri, then Princess Meelah, and my eldest and heir, Crown Princess Ilara."

She offered a small curtsy.

"It's my pleasure and honor to meet you, princesses." Earl Halkon gave another bow. "I thank you again for your hospitality, King Onak."

"It is my honor as king. Shall we?" Papa motioned to the armchairs and couch arranged around the fireplace. He took the armchair to the left of the fireplace across from Halkon's, and Ilara sat in the armchair to his right. Her sisters took the couch across from the fireplace, separated from Halkon by an empty armchair.

"How were your travels?" Ilara inquired as Nika curled up by her feet.

The earl settled back in the armchair, something almost indolent in the way he kicked out his polished boots. "Pleasant, particularly through your lovely forests. The trees are very old here."

An odd observation that Ilara didn't know what to do with, but thankfully, she was saved from replying as three servants entered. They distributed elegant ceramic cups filled with warm, spiced tea. She murmured her thanks to the older man who served her, and he gave her a small bow and smile.

Ilara held fiercely to their sacred teachings that the crown existed to serve the people and believed that servants were as much her people as the House Heads. Besides, the royal Great House wouldn't function without them. So she watched with distaste as Earl Halkon didn't acknowledge the young woman who presented him with his tea, as if the beverage had appeared at his will. To hide her frown, she wrapped her hands around her steaming cup and lifted it, breathing in the scent of clove and cinnamon and berries.

Her earlier wariness returned. *The moon isn't keeping watch. It's a night to conceal false intentions.*

"Speaking of animals and trees, I hear you have excellent hunting here," Halkon said.

Papa and Meelah engaged him on the subject, much to Ilara's relief. She'd lost her taste for hunting after her mama died on a hunting trip. Some Tallanders judged her for it, but at least Meelah's stunning skill in archery distracted most people from Ilara's lack of interest.

Thankfully, the topic shifted to architecture and the weather and other subjects, and a couple of hours passed, if slowly—particularly since prior to the Kilkrethian's unexpected arrival, Ilara had planned to spend the evening with her best friend. She'd promised Ryn she would still visit her after this meeting, and it was lasting longer than she'd like.

The servants had replaced and taken their tea long ago, and now Ilara had nothing to occupy her. But Domhnall Halkon was quick to smile and had an easy, musical laugh, so despite her initial fears, the evening was enjoyable.

"And where is Princess Ilara's husband or suitor?" Halkon asked, his brilliant emerald eyes fixing on her. "Surely such a beauty has one."

The unexpected bluntness of the question brought heat to her cheeks. "No, not presently."

"Truly?"

"It's not something we're worried about." Papa's stiff demeanor was that of a king restraining his displeasure. "Nor is it a matter typically discussed with strangers."

Halkon switched his focus to Papa. "Ah, forgive me. I only meant to make conversation. Although I'm surprised you're not more concerned about who will rule in the unspeakable event something should happen to you."

Ilara bit her tongue to stifle an indignant snort as all notions of the night being enjoyable shattered. "Daughters have full inheritance rights in Talland. I will be reigning queen with or without a husband. I have no need to rush such an important decision."

Halkon offered a chagrined smile. "My apologies, Your Highness. I fear my journey and exhaustion have had a poor impact on my manners. Kilkreth has different laws, but I spoke out of turn. I respect your wisdom in giving such a weighty matter consideration."

His sincerity made holding on to her annoyance difficult. She nodded. "It's forgotten."

Halkon made a sort of half bow, still seated in his chair. "Thank you." He turned his attention to Meelah and Kiri and chuckled softly. "I fear I've bored the little one."

Sure enough, Kiri had fallen asleep on the arm of the couch, and Meelah looked close to nodding off herself.

"I don't wish to keep the princesses from their sleep," Halkon continued. "Or say anything else I wouldn't when well-rested. Perhaps we should adjourn for the night, Your Majesty?"

Papa nodded. "An excellent idea." He stood. "We shall speak more tomorrow, Earl Halkon."

Ilara and Meelah stood as well, while Kiri slumbered on.

Halkon bowed toward Papa. "Wonderful, Your Majesty." He turned to Ilara and bowed again. "It was a pleasure to make your acquaintance, Princess Ilara."

She offered a diplomatic smile. "The pleasure was mine, Earl Halkon."

"Please." He waved a pale, elegant hand, his gaze locking with hers. "I've never cared for the name Halkon. Domhnall is perfect."

Domhnall is *perfect.* Ilara blinked rapidly, her mind oddly sluggish. She must have been more tired than she'd realized.

"Pleasant dreams, princesses." Domhnall ambled out of the room, where he was greeted by a servant who had been waiting with the utmost patience to escort him back to his guest chamber.

Papa scooped up Kiri, even though she was getting far too big for him to carry. Despite Ilara's concern, he conveyed the half-asleep Kiri up to the third floor and laid her in her bed. Papa kissed Kiri's temple while she kicked off her shoes.

In the hall, Papa stopped Ilara with a hand on her arm. "Are you all right?"

"Why wouldn't I be?"

"I miss her, too," Papa whispered. She loved that he knew her well enough to recognize the hunting talk would have reminded her of Mama.

Ilara hugged him, resting her cheek on his shoulder. "I know. I'm fine. Are *you* all right?"

"Yes." He kissed her hair. "Sleep well, Ara."

"You too, Papa." She pulled away. "I'm looking forward to discussing trade with Earl Halkon."

Papa shook his head, but he was smiling. "My driven, clever girl. I'll see you tomorrow." He patted her arm and turned down the hallway.

Ilara let Nika into her room and fetched a candle. The dog whined when Ilara left and drew the door closed before the dog could follow.

"I'll be back soon," she whispered. With entertaining the Kilkrethian over, she could finally spend some time with her best friend.

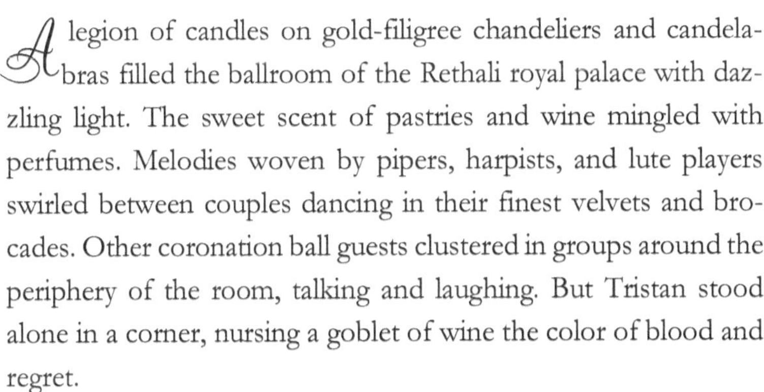

2

legion of candles on gold-filigree chandeliers and candela-bras filled the ballroom of the Rethali royal palace with dazzling light. The sweet scent of pastries and wine mingled with perfumes. Melodies woven by pipers, harpists, and lute players swirled between couples dancing in their finest velvets and brocades. Other coronation ball guests clustered in groups around the periphery of the room, talking and laughing. But Tristan stood alone in a corner, nursing a goblet of wine the color of blood and regret.

He'd found the one place in the ballroom that wasn't illuminated, where he could hide from the nobles' looks of pity or judgment. Unfortunately, his hiding spot had two choices of scenery—the barren corner of the stone walls or the dance floor.

An opening between other couples afforded him an unobstructed view of King Alexander and Queen Raelyn as they danced. Candlelight glittered on their bejeweled crowns and highlighted the matching crimson of Alex's sash and cloak and Raelyn's dress.

A year ago, Tristan's most pessimistic prediction for his future was that he would be in a loveless arranged marriage, devoid of the companionship he longed for.

Now, on the dance floor, Raelyn gazed up at Alex as if he were her entire world. Alex leaned down and brushed a kiss against the tip of her nose, and Tristan dropped his gaze to the goblet in his hand.

The reality of his present was far worse than he'd have ever imagined. Watching his former betrothed be so entirely in love with his cousin was a pain he couldn't find the words to articulate.

Love, it seemed, was not something Tristan deserved. Once, he'd held a feeble hope otherwise—the desperation of a stupid boy who thought if he performed well enough, his father would be proud of him. A fool who'd imagined if he could determine what sort of man Raelyn wanted and be that man, she would love him.

In the end, it was for the best that Raelyn had found Alexander first. Because Alex was warm and kind and innocent and good, and Tristan…

His hand trembled as he lifted the goblet toward his lips, and wine splashed over the rim. He stared at the burgundy liquid dripping off his knuckle.

Tristan's hands were stained with blood.

The room pressed in around him—the music suddenly discordant and too loud in his ears, the air too hot from the gathered crowd, the light from the legion of candles too bright. It didn't matter that he'd be seen if he left his refuge. He needed to get *out*.

He tried to edge along the walls, but refreshment tables and chairs for weary guests forced him into the open. Everything in him screamed to hurry, but running would draw attention. Besides, princes always carried themselves with composure—

Except Tristan wasn't a prince anymore.

He wasn't anyone anymore.

And it was partly his own fault.

Something caught him—a suntanned hand squeezing his upper arm and stopping him, yanking him out of his morose thoughts. Tristan went rigid as Prince Gareth, Queen Raelyn's beloved older brother, stepped in close to his side.

"If you can't keep your anger off your face," the Eynlaean prince hissed, "you shouldn't be here. I won't let you ruin this."

"I'm not angry, and I don't want to cause any trouble." At least, he wasn't angry with Alex and Raelyn. Well, maybe a little with Alex. "And actually, I was on my way out until you interrupted. I don't feel well."

Gareth snorted. "Sure."

Tristan tried to pull his arm free, but the prince didn't loosen his threatening grip. "Have I done something wrong? Today?" he amended, well aware of his past failings.

"I…suppose not." Gareth worked his jaw and finally released Tristan's arm. "To my surprise."

Tristan fixated on the glistening silver thread on a random noblewoman's skirt. "I don't know what else I can do to prove that I'm loyal and mean their Majesties no harm, Your Grace."

He genuinely didn't know. All of his attempts to be helpful had been declined with suspicion. The game was fixed against him. When he offered advice or service to Alex, everyone assumed he was either scheming or trying to grovel his way into Alex's good graces. Of course, he *was* trying to earn his way into Alex's good regard, but did that make his actions any less good? Yet when he hid in his room, staying out of Alex's and Raelyn's and Gareth's way, the rumors claimed he was plotting in secret or avoiding his cousin out of petty bitterness. He couldn't win.

Gareth harrumphed. "I'd be more inclined to believe you if you hadn't tried to kill Alexander."

"That was before—" Tristan stopped himself and took a steadying breath. There was no point arguing; Gareth wouldn't listen or care. "If you'll excuse me, Your Grace." He bowed and strode away without waiting for a response.

Some guests sent furtive glances his way as he wove around them, others outright stared, and more than a few whispered. He tried to ignore the looks of suspicion, derision, curiosity, sadness, or gloating. All he needed to do was get to the side door. Thirty paces, and he'd be free.

Then a head of dark curls blocked the door from his view as a young woman stepped directly into his path. Her lips were painted a warning shade of red and her pale cheeks were pink with excitement. "Forgive me for being so forward, but may I have this dance, my lord?"

Tristan's mouth pinched as he tried to pull his flustered thoughts from his foiled escape to the confounding woman blocking his way. "With me?"

She stepped closer and batted her eyelashes. He realized he knew her—or at least had seen her before. Lord Larson's youngest, maybe? What was her name? The young woman ran her fingertips over his chest, making him feel unbalanced.

"I heard you saved the queen's life, risking your own," she murmured in a husky voice.

His cheeks warmed as he pulled her hand away from his chest. "I'm also a nobody now, my lady." Best let her know up front, in case she thought he was still rich and important. He'd hate to get slapped because she felt lied to.

She tilted her head. "I heard you're a royal advisor."

Tristan snorted. "Someone failed to inform me." Or, more accurately, last time he'd offered Alexander his knowledge, Alex had told him, "Should such a need arise, I'll send for you." That had been two weeks ago.

"Well." The noblewoman shrugged. "It's just a dance." She snatched his goblet away and handed it to a passing servant. "You have a face worth gazing at for a dance."

The air in the room grew hotter and thicker, stifling him. In the past, he'd softened or completely avoided interactions like these by bringing up his future Eynlaean wife. It had helped him not fall for someone else before his bride arrived. But now that bride hung on the arm of his cousin.

"Never mind." The girl took a small step back, and Tristan became aware that several nobles nearby were staring at them, probably because he had been standing in silence for far longer than was polite or normal. "I shouldn't have interrupted you."

"Of course I would be honored to dance with you," Tristan said hastily. "Lady…"

"Florence," she supplied with a giggle.

"Shall we?"

Tristan took Florence's hand and led her onto the floor as the musicians switched between pieces. She ran her fingers teasingly up his arm before setting her hand on his shoulder. As he placed his hand against her back, she watched him, her lips puckered into a teasing pout as she moved in close. A reckless side of him that had apparently drunk too much wondered what she would do if he kissed her right then. She was practically begging him—if he wasn't misreading the situation.

Cold reality doused him. Based on his interactions with Raelyn, he wasn't good at reading women. The music started, and Tristan recognized the tune—a circle dance. Relief warred with dread as they shifted to join a circle, with the women on the outside and the men on the inside. He wouldn't be with her the entire song, as circle dances involved spinning the female dancer to the male on the right until she came all the way back around the circle.

But the changing partners meant he'd have to face several women, and flames knew how any of them would react to having to dance with him. But at least it would make it easier to resist Florence's flirting. Surely he didn't really want to kiss some random girl.

No, a voice whispered. *You aren't sure if you want to kiss her because you still crave Raelyn's kiss.* Tristan concentrated on the swaying steps of the dance. He hardly knew Raelyn, too, if he was honest, and she wasn't his any longer. But every time he thought he'd let her go, he found himself haunted by her kiss and wondering…what if? What would his life be like right now if she had married him instead?

"You know," Florence said, "I haven't seen you with a beard before. It suits you."

Tristan fumbled for a response. He couldn't admit *I haven't cared enough to bother with shaving since Alexander's hearing three weeks ago.* Before he could devise a reply, it was time to shift, and he spun Florence on as a middle-aged woman with a dark complexion spun in front of him. Her, he recognized. He smiled politely at Lady Otmere, who returned the smile with clear hesitation, as if she didn't know what she thought of him. The next woman scowled.

This had been a terrible idea.

He concentrated on the steps and numbing his emotions. After this dance, no one was stopping him from leaving the ballroom. He would go to sleep and not have to think or feel for a few hours of dark relief. The music dipped again, signaling the change. He spun the woman away and reached for the hand of the next woman…

And froze on the dance floor.

Across from him, Raelyn paled and stopped dancing. "Tristan." She blinked, then resumed the dance—as well as she could while Tristan continued to stand immobile. "If you don't know the steps," she whispered, "you should leave the floor."

"I know the steps," he muttered, trying not to look at her eyes like sapphires or her golden hair curling against the curves of her neck and shoulders.

"Then do them."

Begrudgingly, Tristan took her hand and placed his other hand featherlight on her back. They moved through the dance, and he felt her stiffen as the steps brought them closer. *Your affection…feels like punishment.* The memory of her words made him wince. The rigid collar of his tunic strangled him. He wanted to stride off the floor, but that would be treasonously rude.

Thankfully, he spun her away and moved on to another woman, and he realized he'd scarcely been letting himself breathe. Another partner change, and Raelyn moved out of his periphery. With the next change, Florence spun back to him.

"Miss me?" She winked, and her gaze darted to his lips.

Fine. I need to get my mind off Raelyn, anyway. Tristan let his voice drop, low and personal. "Actually, I did." As his hand found her back, he pulled her in closer than was necessary or proper.

Florence inhaled sharply, then giggled. "My, you are strong." She tilted her head back as her skirts brushed against his legs. "Strong and handsome."

"I can see what you're thinking, beautiful. Do I taste as good as I look?" The suggestive flirting tasted sour and foreign on his tongue, but it was too late to take it back.

"Cad." Florence blushed, but her hand swept up from his shoulder to the side of his neck.

Some part of Tristan's mind told him this was insane, that she didn't care about him and likely was playing with him or drunk. Was the scent of wine on his breath or hers? Maybe neither of them was in full control.

"So serious." She lightly bit her lower lip. "Have a little fun."

Why *shouldn't* he have some fun, a bitter part of him demanded. The last few weeks had held nothing but misery. What did he have to lose? He was already the villain.

As the dance ended, he spun Florence around, then drew her

back. Her sultry eyes met his. On impulse, he pressed his lips to hers.

Her kiss was messy and wet. Florence giggled as they separated, her face flushed. "Kissed by royalty." She curtsied, still giggling.

A hollow, unsatisfied feeling spread in Tristan's chest. So not just some innocent fun she was after—she'd used him for bragging rights to her friends. *Like how you used kissing Raelyn to hurt Alexander?*

"I'm not royalty anymore." The words came out almost in a growl. He gave a curt bow and left the dance floor, his stomach roiling as he headed for the exit.

A hand on his shoulder stopped him before he reached the door. Tristan's groan was cut short as his gaze landed on the royal signet ring on pale, elegant fingers, then traced up the black sleeve to Alex's hard expression. Raelyn stood next to him, glaring at her husband.

"Alex," Raelyn murmured, "it was only a circle dance—"

"Tomorrow," Alex said, "we discuss where I'm sending you."

Where he was... What was left of Tristan's control disintegrated. He shrugged Alex's hand off. "Sending?"

"You're not staying at the palace any longer. I'll find somewhere for you to go."

"Worried she'll change her mind?" The words tumbled out before Tristan considered them. He'd definitely had too much wine.

Alex made a low sound that was almost a snarl. Tristan's hands went cold. *We made a beast king.* But no. Raelyn said the twelve years Alex had spent cursed hadn't made him a monster. If there were any good people in the world, Raelyn was one of them. She wouldn't misplace her trust.

"I'm worried I'll change mine and do something I'll regret," Alex bit out.

Raelyn took Alex's hand. "I'm fine. He didn't do it on purpose." She glanced at Tristan, as if confirming he hadn't orchestrated their dance. "I wasn't expecting it, and it was uncomfortable, but I'm fine. He didn't do anything wrong."

Tristan nodded gratefully, yet Alex's tight jaw said, *perhaps not this time, but you're far from innocent.* Or maybe that was only what Tristan was thinking.

"All right, Rae. But it's still past time we decided what to do with him," Alex said quietly. "I'll send for you in the morning, Tristan."

"As you desire, Your Excellency." Tristan bowed low and worked to keep his tone level. "I am your servant." He bowed to Raelyn. "Your Majesty."

Whispers followed Tristan as he made his way out of the ballroom. He shouldn't have attended, no matter how questionable it would have looked. No one wanted him there. At least, no one other than an intoxicated young woman who had wanted some bewildering sort of bragging rights for having kissed him.

His mood grew darker as he slunk down silent halls dimly illuminated by sparse candles, his boots whispering against the scarlet carpet. This cursed palace and its red everywhere—red brick exterior, red carpets, red on Alex's and Raelyn's clothing; red for blood, as if the entire palace had conspired to mock his guilt. He should have left Rethalyon with Father.

He slammed his bedroom door behind him. *No.* He didn't want to see Henry ever again after what he'd done.

After Henry had cursed him, as Tristan had wiped away tears of pain, he'd asked if there was a way to break the enchantment. Would his father remove the curse after Alex's hearing? Henry had laughed.

"If there's a remedy, I'm not telling you. If that hex suffocates you for

trying to speak ill of me, you'll deserve it. You brought this on yourself, you worthless excuse of a son."

Tristan fell onto his bed and kicked off his boots, staring at the dark-blue canopy stretched over the bedposts.

"My father," he whispered to the empty room, "is a—" His throat constricted, as if a hand had closed around his neck and squeezed. The choking sensation passed, and he curled into a ball on his side.

A monster.

3

The small candle in Ilara's hand cast juddering light across the wooden floors as she made her way past courtiers' rooms to Ryn's. A couple of patrolling guards bowed to her, but otherwise, the halls were empty, dark, and silent. The members of the court were likely all asleep, and the servants had departed to their own nearby homes and lodges for the night.

The Great House was rarely so still. The five ancient clans, known as the five Houses, each controlled a region of Talland, and each one appointed a representational Head of House to act as the official liaison between the monarch and the noble families of their House. Every Head and their spouse and children lived as guests in the monarch's Great House—although they often left to visit their own estates—and composed Talland's royal court.

Since Ryn's father, Lord Rydack, had been elected Head of House Backenstoe long before Ryn's birth, Ryn had dwelled in the royal Great House her entire life, and in her own room for several years.

Ilara rapped her knuckles against Ryn's door. Despite the late hour, Ryn's answering call to enter sounded at once.

"Finally," Ryn said, beaming. She placed her book near the lantern on her bedside table as she shifted to the side and patted the bed. "Come on!"

The door clicked shut behind Ilara, and after she'd extinguished and set down her candle, she flopped on top of the green blanket beside her best friend.

At twenty, Ryn was a year younger than Ilara. With her similar fawn-brown complexion, freckled face, and narrow eyes, visitors sometimes mistook Ryn as one of the princesses. Although, considering Ryn had a rectangular slimness in contrast with Ilara's wide-hipped, softly plump build, and had dark chestnut hair to the princesses' black hair, the confusion might have been more because Ryn and Ilara had been inseparable since they were babes. They'd spent much of their childhood doing each other's braids and getting up to mischief, such as hiding under bear rugs in the great hall to scare hapless passersby.

Ilara poked Ryn's side. "So? How did it go?" Despite her attempt to stay quiet, her voice pitched higher. "You finally got to have an actual tryst *alone*, and I want to know everything!"

Ryn shoved Ilara's prodding finger away from her side with a laugh. "All right, no need to torture me. I'll talk!

"Lorik took me to the meadow by the pond, and he packed an impressive spread of fresh bread and a delicious seal stew he spent all day making himself."

"Himself?" Ilara raised her eyebrows. "He probably made a nuisance of himself in the kitchens."

"I can only image the disapproving scowl Maleen must have worn the entire time," Ryn agreed. "And he was so nervous I wouldn't like it. Although his nerves may have been due to his mother giving us an earful before we left. He turned red clear to his hair—she would not stop telling him to be respectful and on and on. I was worried he'd be too scared to kiss me again."

"And was he?"

Ryn pulled her blanket up over the lower half of her face. "He kissed me." She hid behind the blanket with a little giggle, then threw it down. "Oh, blessed moonlight, we kissed until I was drunk on him. And…" She turned her head and pulled back her hair to uncover her right ear, and candlelight glinted on metal.

Ilara couldn't hold back her squeal. "He proposed!"

"He did." Ryn's dimpled smile stretched wide as she brushed her fingertip over the cuff hugging the center of the shell of her ear.

Flattened bronze wires formed an illusion of encircling her cartilage twice before twisting up and down into small spirals. It was simple and uneven, as engagement cuffs often were.

"We want to get married before summer ends; that should give us enough time to plan without waiting too long, because we're both ready. I keep touching the cuff. Part of me can't believe it—I'm so happy I could burst!"

"I'm thrilled for both of you!" Ilara hugged her friend tight, and Ryn squeezed her back.

Ryn filled her in on all the details of the evening and Lorik's proposal. They lay side by side on the bed, staring up at the wood ceiling, since during the summer, the heavy drapes that went over the posts to keep the occupants warm in winter were put away. Ilara didn't know how late it was and didn't care. She had nothing scheduled for the morning, so she planned on sleeping in late to make up for it.

"Anyway." Ryn elbowed Ilara's side. "Now I get to hear all about this handsome Kilkrethian, right? What's he like?"

Ilara considered. "He's egregiously tall, alarmingly blond, and annoyingly captivating, despite assuming I need a husband to rule. But he quickly apologized for his assumption."

Ryn rolled onto her side to face Ilara. "Captivating, hm? Does that mean you like him?"

"No." She sighed. "Other than the fact I just met him, some-thing about him seems…off. Nika and Chari growled at him—it was so strange."

"They never do that."

"I know! And then he somehow made them back down. It was unsettling, although perhaps once he explains the trick it won't seem so odd." Ilara's mouth pulled to the side. "Besides, he's…so handsome it's hard to look away. Even if someone like that were interested in someone like me—"

"A *princess?*" Ryn gasped. "How could anyone like a princess!"

Ilara rolled her eyes. "I was talking about appearance. It's all right, you don't have to argue," she added before her friend started. "I love this body, apple cheeks, round waist, small chest, and all. I don't need anyone's approval. That doesn't mean a man who looks like Halkon would be interested. Maybe I'm judging him too harshly or being shallow myself, but like I said, something about him feels wrong. I don't trust him."

Ryn yawned. "Maybe you'll feel differently tomorrow."

"Perhaps," Ilara allowed. A yawn escaped. "Although I hope he's trustworthy. Between you and me, Father and I are more worried than we're letting on. By autumn, the shortages will be worse than last time." Sorrow speared her heart.

The last devastating ice storm had been over six years ago, and it had taken Mama. It'd come in the winter, only delaying planting, but losing Mama had nearly destroyed Papa. He'd often secluded himself in his room; his mood had turned volatile, melancholy or bad-tempered by turns, and he'd struggled to perform his kingly duties.

At fifteen and carrying heavy grief herself, Ilara had barely known what she was doing as she'd worked to appease the House Heads and run a kingdom almost on her own. Thankfully, Papa's mind had recovered, and Ilara hadn't been forced to become queen prematurely. He still had the occasional bad day—the ice storm that spring had sent him into a malaise that had lasted two days—but he ruled with the same commitment and fairness as he had before Mama's death, except that he included Ilara more often in his monarchial duties.

Ryn rubbed Ilara's arm and leaned her head on Ilara's shoulder. "It's going to be all right, Ara. And I'm here for you if you need to talk."

She nodded, her throat tight. How she would have survived the loss of her mama and her papa's disengagement without Ryn, she didn't know. "Thank you," she whispered.

They lounged in silence for several more moments as her eyelids grew heavier. At last she shook herself and got up. "If I don't want to fall asleep at the dinner table tomorrow, I should go to sleep."

"Oh, but I'd have so much fun teasing you about it."

"What a friend you are." Ilara lightly shoved her friend's shoulder before relighting her candle from the lantern. "Congratulations again, Ryn."

Pink crept back into Ryn's cheeks as she touched the ear cuff. "Thank you."

Ilara stumbled through the dark to her room, her candle burning low on its pewter base. Her thoughts wandered to Earl Halkon. Something hid behind that charming exterior, but what?

Part of her hoped when she awoke, it would be to learn he had left in the night. But another small, insistent part of her wanted to stare into those enticing, jewel-like eyes and run her fingers through his silky gold hair...

Wait, what?

She was overtired; that had to be it. Her half-asleep mind had confused itself with Tallander proverbs and handsome faces. After a good night's sleep, Halkon would be an ordinary man. Not perfect. Not sinister.

Only when Ilara was drifting off did she realize something, and she couldn't understand how she hadn't noticed it before.

Earl Domhnall Halkon, wealthy nobleman from Kilkreth, had brought no retinue.

Not even a single servant.

4

Once, when he was fourteen, Tristan had gotten into a fistfight with a lord's son over a disagreement while gambling with dice. Henry had called him into a private throne room like an unruly subject on trial. Tristan had been required to beg for forgiveness from his own father on his knees. Impervious on his throne, Henry had claimed the formality was to build character and serve as an example of how Tristan should treat his future subjects. It had been humiliating.

How unfortunate and somehow fitting that Alexander had unknowingly picked the same audience chamber.

As Tristan dropped to one knee on the crimson carpet before an enthroned, crowned Alexander, he clenched his teeth and lowered his head—more to hide his face than out of deference. *You don't hate Alex,* he reminded himself. *You hate Father—Henry—for his lies and belittling.*

At least Raelyn's throne next to Alexander's stood empty. Alex had insisted on placing a throne for his queen in every audience room. Eynlae afforded queens a more active role in governance, and Alex thought Rethalyon would benefit from doing likewise. Apparently, the queen would not be involved in this matter. Whether she chose not to attend, or Alex didn't want her there, at least Tristan didn't have to face her.

However, Jasper Walters, Alex's steward—who had helped Alex escape Henry twelve years ago—observed from a corner of the room near the throne, his hands clasped behind his hunched back. Tristan wasn't well enough acquainted with the man to know if his serious expression was judgment, hidden laughter, or something else.

"How loyal are you?" Alex asked without preamble.

Tristan's brow furrowed. "What? I mean—very, Your Excellency."

"What would you do for me?"

"I have told you. Whatever you asked, my king." And yet Alex never believed him. Tristan ground his teeth. Resentment was a splinter he couldn't find to remove, so it kept wheedling deeper under his skin.

Alex regarded him, his lips pursed. "I admit the idea of granting you a sham title and a cottage with a leaking roof on a plot of land small enough you can walk the perimeter in an afternoon is tempting."

Tristan's spirits fell further. Walters gave a delicate cough, drawing both cousins' attention. The older man's mouth pinched downward.

"But that wouldn't be just or merciful, as I want to be," Alex said. "So I won't."

Some of the tension in Tristan's shoulders eased, even as he marveled at the steward's brazen yet subtle chiding. "Thank you, Your Excellency."

Alex strummed his fingers on the arm of the throne. "I have something else in mind. But it requires trust."

"You can trust me, Your Excellency. I swear." The eagerness that seeped into his voice wasn't dignified, but he couldn't help but leap toward the scrap of hope that this was his chance. For weeks he'd been seeking a way to make himself useful, to feel like he still had a place, a home, a future, even after everything he'd done. Despite the bitterness he sometimes experienced toward Alex, he longed to have a positive relationship with the only family he had left.

"Good." Alex gave a small nod. "I'm making you my ambassador to Talland."

Tristan blinked, grateful for years of hiding his emotions from his father so he could cover his confusion and hurt. Him? Ambassador? Alex wanted to…send him away? To distant *Talland*? Ugh. A freezing, miserable, unrefined kingdom in the north—which was almost the extent of Tristan's knowledge of Talland.

"I'm sending delegates to nearby kingdoms to represent me and explain what happened," Alex continued. "The Court and I agreed a simple message wouldn't be enough. I'd also like to strengthen relations between Rethalyon and Talland, as I've noted that trade between our kingdoms has fallen to almost nothing in the last few years."

Tristan could have told him that if Alex had accepted his repeated offers to help with the transition of the crown.

"I've decided to send you." Alex rested his chin on his fist. "You will stay with the Tallander court to—"

"I know what an ambassador does," Tristan cut in. "But—"

"You've been trained in diplomacy. I imagine you've learned about Talland. You have the knowledge, and if you are truly loyal, your support of me will be impressive." His cousin leaned back in his throne. He looked irritatingly comfortable in it. "And you'll be out of the kingdom for at least a couple of months, until either you return with new trade agreements, or I call you back."

"Your Excellency, please." Tristan swallowed against his rising panic. Rethalyon was his home. Alex's return had destroyed much of Tristan's understanding of the world and had taken his crown and title, his betrothed, his future, and his father. Surely

Alex wouldn't take his home, too. "I swore to serve you, and I intend to keep my word, but I asked to remain in Rethalyon. That was my *only* request—"

"Then you put your hands on my wife."

"It was a dance!" His fists balled as he resisted the impulse to rise to his feet. "Are you going to exile every man who danced with her last night?"

"Not every man is you."

Tristan huffed but inclined his head. "I apologize, my king. Perhaps I should have bowed out when Her Majesty was my next partner. I feared it would appear disrespectful to abandon my queen on the dance floor. I meant no harm, and being her partner was unintentional. Please believe me."

Alex observed him in silence as a bead of sweat slipped down Tristan's cheek. At last, the king stood and walked forward to crouch in front of Tristan. "You once ordered Raelyn to tell you the truth."

Tristan clenched his jaw while shame burned in his stomach.

"So tell me the truth, on your life. Do you love my wife?"

"No." It was the truth, more or less. Love was too strong a word for simple attraction and questions of *what if*. Love was the way Raelyn had risked herself to protect Alex. He didn't know what that kind of love felt like—he feared he might not be capable of it.

Alex frowned and tilted his head, his eyes narrowed. "Do you desire her?"

Tristan bit his tongue. Directly lying to the king was tantamount to disloyalty. Henry had been keen to remind him of that every time he forced Tristan to confess to a failure or mistake. He dipped his head, unable to look at his cousin as he admitted, "A small part of me does. Forgive me, my king."

He braced himself for a blow, but it didn't come. Of course

Alex was too good to hit him.

The king stood. "I won't have the queen of Rethalyon feeling uncomfortable and afraid in her own halls. You leave tomorrow."

"I don't want Her Majesty to be uncomfortable either, my king," Tristan pleaded. "I would never act on it, I swear. I won't so much as look at her if you command it, but if I must go, I can leave the palace without leaving the kingdom—"

"And do what?" Alex asked as he settled back onto his throne. "Brood? You need somewhere to focus your energy until you forget about *my wife* and reconcile yourself to your new situation. You're going to Talland."

Alex was probably right, but that riled Tristan more. "Maybe you shouldn't send someone to represent you out of spite." He glared, battling the urge to stand instead of kneeling like a peasant, but he hadn't been granted permission to rise.

"Are you saying you would betray me?" Alex's voice rang with challenge.

Tristan shrank back. "No, Your Excellency, never. But perhaps someone else would be better suited—"

"I'm sending you."

"And what if they ask about my father? Shall I tell them he was overjoyed that you returned, free of your curse, and willingly abandoned the throne? Because that's all I *can* say." His knee ached. *Let me stand, you imbecile.*

"Get creative. Since you can say he abdicated, start there. And I'll send a letter with you. If necessary, trying to tell the truth and being unable to might be powerful. And yes or no questions can take you a long way. I know from experience." Alex took a deep breath. "If you do this well, Carbrey barony will be yours when you return. The land, tenants, title, everything."

He would return Henry's barony? The castle and its holdings had been subsumed into the royal holdings when Henry was coronated. Some lesser lord managed the estate, but the crown owned it. Alex would just...give it over?

"What does 'well' mean, Your Excellency?" Tristan didn't want to get his hopes up if Alex might yank his reward away on a technicality.

"A good working relationship with Talland would be a start. I don't know, exactly. Now, you're dismissed."

Great. No promises. "Must it be Talland?" Tristan asked, ignoring the dismissal. "Why not Kilkreth or Aedyllan? I'm more familiar with Aedyllanian customs—"

"You swore you'd do anything I asked."

Tristan bit back his irritation. "Of course, Your Excellency. I thought perhaps it would be wise to send someone who actually *likes* Talland. I visited once, briefly, several years ago. I despised it."

"Even better." A smile pulled at the corner of Alex's mouth. "Dismissed."

Oh, he wants to play this petty? I can do petty.

"Very well, Your Excellency." Tristan stood and bowed. "Before I go, I would like to note I can't bear all the blame for my desire. Raelyn kissed me back, and it was an excellent, passionate kiss. Difficult to forget."

Alex leapt to his feet, his fists clutched at his sides. The muscles in his throat tensed as his face turned crimson. "You—"

Steward Walters stepped forward with a soft "Your Excellency."

Alex pointed at the exit. "Get. Out."

Tristan bowed and backed away, guilt already creeping in over the vulgar comment. But exiling him to Talland to extol the virtues of the man who had taken his betrothed and his throne had been a low blow, too. He pulled the door open—and walked into Gareth's fist.

Pain exploded through his mouth. Every single one of his teeth ached. He stumbled and fell back onto the floor, blinking rapidly as blood seeped over his tongue and cut lips. He scowled up at Gareth and wiped his throbbing mouth on his sleeve.

"I am *so* glad I eavesdropped." Gareth shook his hand and massaged his knuckles. "I owed you that."

"I thought you were leaving, Your Grace." Tristan gingerly pressed his tongue against his teeth, relieved that by some miracle, none felt loose.

Gareth shrugged. "In about an hour."

"Prince Gareth," the king said with a sigh. "You attacked my ambassador."

"He hasn't left yet; he's not an ambassador yet." Raelyn's brother crossed his arms. "Which, by the way, is a terrible idea."

"I'm bitter, not treasonous." Tristan touched the cut on the corner of his mouth and his fingertip came away with a dot of bright red blood.

"It's a pity the rest of your father's talismans have already been destroyed," Gareth said casually. "Ensuring you can't speak against Alexander would have been useful."

Tristan flinched. It didn't matter that the stones had been smashed at Alex's command weeks ago. The taunt brought the memory back, the sting of betrayal and the agony of the curse taking effect.

"That is quite enough, Prince Gareth." Alex's words whipped through the air, startling Tristan.

Gareth's mouth fell open as he snapped his head toward the throne.

"I ask that you, as my brother-in-law, refrain from insinuating I would even *consider* using dark magic." Alex sat rigidly on his throne, but his face had paled.

Ah. For a moment, Tristan had dared to think Alex was

defending him. He pushed off the ground, his pulse rising. He needed out of the tiny room and away from these people who hated him. Unfortunately, Gareth still stood in the doorway.

"You're blocking the exit, Your Grace, and I've been ordered to get out." He'd meant for that to come out more polite. Some ambassador he would make.

Gareth lifted a brow and uncrossed his arms, his hands fisting.

"Gareth." A hint of warning sounded in Alex's tone. "Please don't punch any more of my subjects."

The prince's eyes narrowed. "No more, no. Just this one. He deserves more. We both know it."

Tristan licked blood off his lip. Between being humiliated, exiled, referred to as a subject—although that was accurate—punched and threatened, and the odd, constricted feeling growing in his chest, he was getting testy. He wasn't sure he'd be able to stop himself from returning a punch if Gareth threw another.

Alex sighed. "Your anger is understandable but not excusable. Tristan has been pardoned—"

"Not by me." Gareth jabbed his index finger into Tristan's torso. "You. Hurt. My. Sister. Her wrists are scarred from *you* ordering her bound; do you know that? She—"

"I forgave him," Raelyn's warm voice interrupted. She pushed Gareth aside and entered the little throne room, and Tristan stumbled back to give her space.

She looked lovely, wearing a sky-blue dress that accentuated her small waist. He quickly lowered his gaze to his boots.

"Alex, you didn't tell me where or when you were meeting with Tristan."

Her husband cleared his throat. "I know he makes you nervous… I thought it would be easier."

The words stabbed Tristan's chest. The list of the ways he had done Raelyn wrong was indeed long. "I apologize again, my queen.

If I could do something more than apologize, I would."

"I can think of some things," Gareth muttered. "Personally, I'd like to start with binding your hands behind your back, stringing a rope around your neck, and making you walk for four days straight. Maybe barefoot."

Tristan's shoulders hunched. He couldn't change that he had treated Gareth and Alex and even Raelyn as prisoners, although he liked to think if he had known the truth, he would have done things differently. He also feared he *had* known; he'd just been too hurt to believe it.

When he'd discovered Alex was alive, he'd believed Alex's accusations against Henry were disgusting lies. Then Raelyn, *his* bride, had spurned him. He'd been furious.

Now the fury had dulled, leaving shame and guilt in its wake. He'd let his anger control his actions again, and he hated himself for it. But wanting to stop, to do the right thing, was so much easier than actually doing it.

"Gareth," Raelyn said softly. "Be kind. If Alex and I can forgive him, you can. I'm sorry, Tristan. Gareth holds grudges easily."

Gareth and Alex had both attacked Tristan, and a swipe of Alex's dragon paw had nearly killed him. Neither Gareth nor Alex had apologized for their actions, but Raelyn had. Repeatedly. For betraying him by falling for Alex, for speaking unkindly, even on behalf of others. But her apologies stung. He didn't deserve them.

"Technically," Gareth said, rubbing his chin, "Alex officially pardoned Tristan. I'm not sure he *forgave* him."

Tristan's anxiety spiked as he glanced at his cousin. The mingled irritation and amusement on Alex's face didn't make him feel any better. Tristan bowed to Raelyn. "If you'll excuse me, Your Majesty, I need to prepare to leave for Talland."

He squeezed past her and hurried away. Being sent to Talland wasn't what he wanted.

But it was better than he deserved.

Tristan sent for a trunk but packed it himself. He needed something to keep him busy, or he'd lose his mind. Fury built in him with every item he shoved into the trunk. For the last twelve years he'd lived in the palace, and before that, he'd spent almost as much time in the palace as he had at Carbrey barony.

Halfway between his large oak wardrobe and the trunk, he stilled, his fingers tightening on a mauve shirt. He wanted to forget, but the memories came back anyway. Being excited as a child to spend time with his cousin only to feel lonely because Alex was closer to the other courtiers' children. Away from the royal family, Henry would complain about the king and the queen—his sister—and their "mishandling" of the kingdom, but Alex was a model son. At the palace or at the barony, it was always *"Is this how Alex would behave? Alex would have done it correctly."*

"It's not Alex's fault," Tristan reminded himself through gritted teeth as he added the tunic to the trunk. How warm would he need to dress? Talland had harsh winters, but would it be cold in the summer? Rainy like the day Henry had lied to his face twelve years ago, telling him that Alex was dead…

Tristan hadn't cried. Even if he hadn't already hated his cousin, Henry would have mocked his tears. And he'd believed Henry's story that the late queen had performed sorcery on the wicked prince. Maybe he'd wanted to believe it because it meant Alex finally wasn't better than him.

Except he still was. After Henry's coronation, the comparisons became worse. *"If Alexander hadn't transformed into a monster and I hadn't been forced to kill him, he would never have spoken out of turn!"*

Tristan pulled out a stack of clothing at random and slammed the wardrobe door. As much as it terrified him to leave the familiarity of the palace, it wasn't really leaving home. Maybe he'd never had a true home.

The thought hurt like a knife through his heart. If only he could go back to before all this happened; before he fully understood what a villain his father was, before the façade cracked and everything fell to pieces… So many little moments where this all could have been avoided.

If Alex had never found Raelyn in the mountains, if they hadn't fallen in love, if Tristan hadn't hunted down the dragon, he and Raelyn would be wed, and he'd be…

He was kidding himself if he thought he'd be happy. Maybe less miserable.

A small, intrusive voice whispered he should have used the love spell instead of surrendering it to Raelyn, who had then used it as evidence against Henry. Worse, he wondered what would have happened if he had used it in the great hall when Henry put a dagger to Raelyn's neck and demanded Tristan enchant her in a last-ditch effort to keep the throne.

Tristan shuffled around his room, packing more odds and ends, but the activity couldn't deter his thoughts. The heartbreak and fear in Raelyn's eyes as he'd started the incantation still plagued him. He'd done the honorable thing in attacking Henry. He'd been right when he said he couldn't live with knowing Raelyn didn't choose him. And if Raelyn had never met Alex, then Alex would still be cursed and in hiding and Henry would still be getting away with murdering his sister and his brother-in-law and cursing Alex.

So why did he sometimes wonder what it would have been like to be loved by Raelyn, when she was so happy with Alex and justice had been done? He didn't deserve to have any woman look at him the way Raelyn looked at Alex, least of all Raelyn.

But he longed for it all the same.

Tristan shut the trunk and sank onto his bed as his pulse throbbed behind his temple. The headaches had kept coming since he'd discovered Henry's lies. The physician said he was fine, just stressed. He massaged the center of his forehead and closed his eyes.

No, getting away would be good, even if it was hard. He could leave behind all the pain of his past and his own misdeeds. It would grant him a reprieve from Alex and his ridiculously perfect…everything. The man was married, yet the ladies of the court swooned every time he smiled. *Ugh.*

Plus, he'd get away from Raelyn and her perfect…everything. Tristan laughed bitterly and opened his eyes. Clearly, they deserved each other. And Tristan…he deserved to be exiled to Talland to suffer. He lay back on the bed, still massaging his forehead. It could be worse.

He could have been banished, like Henry. Alex could have banished him *with* his father. Perhaps that wouldn't have been so bad. Where was his father? Had he found work somewhere? Wheedled his way into a court? Was he starving in a gutter? Dead? He hated that he cared.

Henry had been a villain and raised Tristan to be the same. There had even been a moment at Alex's hearing after Henry pulled his dagger when Tristan had feared his father would kill him.

The palace had never been home, and Henry had never been his father, not in any way that mattered. Alex hadn't seen Tristan for twelve years, and when they met again, Tristan had tried to kill him, among other transgressions. There was no reason for Alex to care about Tristan or want to reconcile. So why did it all *hurt* so much?

Why did some small, foolish part of him that he didn't want to acknowledge still miss his father? Why did he cling to the idea of the palace as home or hope for Alex's…well, if not friendship, perhaps acceptance? Maybe this ambassadorial mission would force him to let go and move on.

"Fine," he muttered to the empty room. "You're right, Alex. I don't belong here. But why Talland?"

5

Wet dog kisses on her cheek and pressure on her side jolted Ilara awake. Nika stood on the bed, one paw shoving down on her ribs.

"All right, I get it; you need to go out!" Ilara shifted, and Nika leapt down, talking in her own manner with a whiny *arah-wah-wah-wah*. Ilara's stockinged feet shuffled across the floor as she half stumbled to her bedroom door and let Nika escape. The dog would find her way outside and back inside when she was ready.

Ilara stretched, wondering about the nagging sensation there was something she'd forgotten; some thought lost to the haze of sleep. No matter. She had more important things to worry about—like determining if Earl Domhnall Halkon had connections that would prove useful for trade, especially for importing food.

After getting dressed in a deep yellow, long-sleeved linen slip beneath a crimson wool overdress with thin shoulder straps, she sat on the stool in front of her vanity to do her hair. She'd barely touched the hairbrush when a knock sounded on her door. "Come in!"

The door opened with a quiet creak, and Kiri sashayed inside. "Good, you're *finally* awake! Oh, can I do your hair?"

"I'd love that," Ilara said as she handed over the brush. Their mama had taught them all to do their traditional braids, but since Mama's passing, Kiri had become obsessed and learned the most intricate plaits. She said she felt like Mama was with her when she braided.

"Papa was disappointed you weren't at breakfast. Earl Halkon asked about you." Kiri grinned mischievously as she got started on Ilara's hair. "So Papa sent me to make sure you come to lunch."

"Is it midday already?" Ilara glanced at the thin window of foggy glass. She hadn't intended to sleep in *that* late.

"We'll have just enough time for me to do some more intricate braids to impress the earl."

Ilara rolled her eyes. "I'm not trying to impress him, Kiri." She considered. "Well, I might want to impress him, but not like that; more impressed with what Talland has to offer, so he'll be eager to trade."

Her sister shrugged as she started sectioning off Ilara's hair. "That sounds rather boring."

"Is calling me boring going to become a habit?" Ilara stuck her tongue out at their reflection in the oval mirror above her vanity.

"I called trade negotiations boring, not *you*. Why did you sleep in so late, anyway?"

"Stayed up far too long talking to Ryn."

Kiri bounced on her toes with a sound of delight. "Oh, yes! I noticed her engagement cuff. It's so exciting! I haven't been to a wedding since I was too little to enjoy it. Pass me a tie and a couple pins?"

Ilara picked up a delicate strand of leather lacing from a pile on the vanity and two slender bone hairpins from a shallow dish and handed them over. Kiri hummed as she worked, her fingers flying through Ilara's tresses as she made several thin braids from the top half of Ilara's hair. Most of the finer braids she wove together into three thicker, intricate braids. Ilara closed her eyes, relaxed as Kiri's knuckles brushed against her shoulders. Kiri shaped the braids into swirls on the back of Ilara's head, then tied and pinned them in place. A few thin braids still hung around Ilara's face. Once the large braids were in place, Kiri pinned the remaining smaller braids into a crisscrossing pattern.

"Where's your comb, the wood one with the flowers painted pink?"

Ilara fished it out of a vanity drawer, and Kiri tucked it in among the braids at the crown of Ilara's head.

"There." Kiri stepped back and clasped her hands with a wide smile. "Finished! You look just like Mama."

Ilara turned her head, watching herself in the mirror. Her mother's dark, narrow eyes stared back at her from a round face. The braids were precise and complicated, like Mama had loved to wear. Ilara's eyes misted.

"Thank you, Kiri, they're exquisite. She'd be so proud."

Kiri blushed. "Thank you. Come on! We don't want to be late to lunch."

Meelah was emerging from her own room when they entered the hallway. She praised Ilara's braids as they headed downstairs, making Kiri beam. They found Papa and Domhnall Halkon already in the hall. They were chatting amicably with two of the House Heads near the table for the royal family, which had been pushed in front of the raised dais for the meal.

The rectangular hall was positioned in the center of the Great House, and its high ceiling stretched to the bottom of the third floor. Beneath the balcony running around the hall at the level of the second floor, the walls were decorated with tapestries and carvings, with lanterns and candle sconces hung at frequent intervals. Most of the court was already present and seated at the two rows of long tables and benches. Ryn waved from where she sat between her brother and her betrothed.

Domhnall's gaze snapped to Ilara as she approached, and he excused himself from the group. "Princesses Meelah and Kiri, so lovely to see you both again." He gave a small bow as the girls giggled on their way to their seats. "And Princess Ilara." He offered her a deeper bow, and she returned the gesture with a shallow curtsy.

Something about Domhnall's impeccable poise left Ilara unbalanced, but she refused to be intimidated by a pretty face. "Good day, Earl Halkon."

"I thought we'd agreed on Domhnall, Your Highness?"

"Right, of course, Domhnall." The words were out of her mouth almost before she realized she was saying them. Ah, well, she preferred to be less formal, anyway. "I'd be pleased if you called me Ilara as well."

Domhnall's smile looked almost triumphant. "The pleasure is all mine, Ilara."

Papa appeared at Domhnall's side as the Heads of Houses Nockstoll and Kylmur joined their families at the lower tables. "Ah, good; you're here. We may begin."

Ilara hurried to her own seat, pausing for a moment when she saw the honored guest's chair placed to her right rather than to Papa's left. Papa took his seat to Ilara's left, and Domhnall sat in the seat between Ilara and Meelah. After Papa welcomed everyone and delivered a short blessing, servants emerged with the food.

Lunch went smoothly, even though Domhnall kept drawing nearer to her than necessary. Their arms or knees brushed or bumped into each other several times, and every time either of them spoke, he leaned into her space. Yet somehow, she couldn't be upset with him.

As servants cleared away their plates and Meelah and Kiri excused themselves, Ilara whispered to Papa, "Have you discussed trade yet? I'd like to join you."

"Actually," Papa said, his voice unusually soft and his gaze unfocused as he peered around her at Domhnall, "We…I thought I'd let you handle this, Ilara. I have a meeting with the treasurer I must keep."

"Oh." Ilara struggled to cover her confusion. Papa had trusted her with more responsibility over the last several years, but this was different. It wasn't entirely appropriate for her to meet with a man alone, and the discussion with Domhnall could wait a little longer. Papa almost sounded dazed. Was he having a bad grief day? He'd gotten better the last few years about telling her so she could help instead of trying to hide it.

Before she could say anything more, Papa stood, kissed the top of her head, and strode out of the hall.

"I have every confidence that you're perfect for this, Ilara," Domhnall said.

She faced him, that sense of dread creeping back. But Papa trusted her to host Domhnall and open up conversation about trade, and she wouldn't fail him.

Looking around for Steward Dessen, Ilara stood. "Shall we talk in the sitting room? I just need to find our steward to accompany—"

"Oh, no." Domhnall's hand clasped her shoulder, his thumb brushing against her skin with a shock of energy that made her gasp. "That's not necessary. We can go alone."

She smiled placatingly. "Dessen will—"

Domhnall grabbed her opposite shoulder with his other hand and stared into her eyes. Another shock leapt from his finger into Ilara's skin, and she twitched. "We can go alone," he repeated.

Ilara's stomach twisted, but then surety settled over her like a thick blanket. "We can go alone."

He sagged, as if suddenly exhausted. But then he motioned

for her to lead the way.

As they walked through the halls, Nika rounded a corner and yipped before bounding toward her. At the last moment, the dog shifted her attention from Ilara to the earl. Her fur spiked along her spine, and her teeth flashed in a rumbling snarl.

"Nika!" Ilara moved between her dog and the Kilkrethian. "Lie down!" Nika whined and obliged, but her hackles were still up.

"Seems your pet could use better manners," Domhnall noted, his tone light.

"I'm so sorry; she honestly never behaves like this."

He stepped past her, trailing his fingertips down her arm. Strangely, she was almost disappointed when his fingers only brushed against her hand before leaving her skin.

"Now, Nika." Domhnall crouched and wiggled his fingers by Nika's muzzle. "Why don't you go outside?"

Nika whimpered before running back the way she'd come, her tail tucked down.

Ilara stepped forward to go after her dog, dimly aware of an odd sluggishness to her thoughts. "Wait, what did—"

"She's fine, Ilara." Domhnall moved into her path, the crooked tilt of his lips too perfect to be anything but practiced. All the same, her heart did a strange fluttering thing. She didn't know if she mistrusted Domhnall or wanted to kiss him.

Kiss him? Moonless winter, what had come over her? She took a step away, so they weren't so close. "Um… Anyway. This way."

He stepped aside, and they continued. The door to the sitting room had scarcely shut behind them when his warm fingers caught her hand, and he tugged her around to face him.

"Ilara." He stood so close his breath brushed her hair. "You're remarkably beautiful."

Her thoughts scattered in a million fuzzy directions. "I…I am?"

Domhnall chuckled. "I think we make an excellent pair, you and I. Don't you agree?"

"Um, I—that is, I…" Why was she so tongue-tied?

His thumb stroked the back of her hand. "You agree, yes?" He leaned closer and lowered his voice to an intimate pitch. "What do you say, my lovely Ilara?" He pushed some of her loose hair over her shoulder, his fingertips brushing against the side of her neck with another, smaller shock. "Will you marry me?"

For a moment, Ilara felt detached, almost as if she were watching someone else in her body. Then everything around her snapped into clarity as if someone had doused her in ice water.

"I…marry?" She yanked free of the earl's grasp and backed away, bumping into an armchair. "Are you out of your mind? Is that why you're here? Are you trying to secure yourself a crown?"

The corner of Domhnall's mouth twitched before his features smoothed. "I simply find myself enamored by you." He closed the distance between them again. "Don't you feel a connection as well?"

She felt ill. "I just met you! And what was that? How are you doing that?"

"What?" he asked, far too innocently.

"You're tampering with my thoughts!" It sounded ridiculous out loud. She turned around. "We're waiting to have this meeting until the king can attend."

"Ah, come now; I'm sorry for making it awkward." His lips curved into an amicable simper as he slipped between her and the door and motioned toward the seating. "Put it out of your mind. Shall we see to the business at hand? I have grain I'm hoping to sell to your people, and I'd hate for my foolish heart to ruin that."

That gave her pause. She wouldn't let an easily besotted foreigner with a too-pretty face prevent her from getting her kingdom the food it needed, but… "A short wait won't ruin anything."

Domhnall seized her hand again. "All is forgiven, yes, Ilara?"

She nodded, almost on instinct. "Of course."

"Good." His grip tightened as he held her gaze, and that odd foggy feeling returned. "Let's sit and discuss, please?"

"All right."

Domhnall collapsed into the same armchair he'd occupied the night prior, rubbing his forehead as his expression pinched. Had those dark circles under his eyes been there at lunch?

"Are you well?" Ilara asked as she lit a few candles to illuminate the dim room.

"Fine, just…tired. Took more out of me than anticipated…my travels, that is." He shook his head.

She frowned, but returned her attention to a sconce. With the room more comfortably lit, she sat in the chair across from him. She was startled to see Domhnall rolling an apple between his palms. Where had he been hiding that?

"Well." Ilara cleared her throat. "You say you have grain? Did you have something in mind for trade? Our craftsmen are—"

"Apple?"

She blinked. "No, thank you."

Domhnall shrugged. "Suit yourself." He bit into the apple with a loud crunch, and Ilara gaped as juice trickled down his chin. Wiping it away with his fingers, he abruptly stood. "I'm intrigued by your people's craftsmanship. I presume this carved and painted caribou skull on the wall behind you is an example?" He pointed past her with the hand holding the apple.

Ilara relaxed a little. This she could work with. "It is one type of Tallander art, yes," she said as he came and stood beside her chair, attention fixed on the decoration. "We pride ourselves on finding usefulness in as many of the byproducts of our hunts as we can—food, clothing, art, and more."

"Indeed." Domhnall's hand shot toward her, his fingers sticky with fruit juice pressing against her lips as she gasped.

The next thing Ilara knew, she was blinking at a dim room, the candles extinguished and muted sunlight filtering through the two narrow windows in the wall to the right of the fireplace. Domhnall was gone, and she had sunk down into the armchair in a most unbecoming fashion.

Had she fallen asleep? She had vague memories of entering the sitting room with Domhnall, and…and…

And what? Why didn't she remember? Her heart pounded, her breaths coming in gasps. She needed to find Papa at once. Her thoughts were muddled, yet of one thing she was absolutely certain—Domhnall couldn't remain in the Great House.

She tripped over herself and didn't even close the sitting room door in her hurry. Papa wasn't in the hall, but Nika was sleeping on a bear rug spread before the dais.

"Oh, girl, I'm so glad to see you." Inexplicable relief filled her as she threw her arms around Nika's fluffy neck, but she'd never been happier to hug the brown and white dog in the four years she'd had her. Nika wiggled and released a short, quiet howl as she rubbed against Ilara.

"Let's go find Papa, girl."

Papa wasn't in the small audience chamber behind the hall, so she hastened to his private study next. A guard slouching against the wall near Papa's study straightened at her approach. *Thank the moon.* This hallway wouldn't have a stationary guard unless Papa was in his office. At the door, she paused as muted voices filtered through the thick wood.

"As I've mentioned twice, I'm not looking for a husband for Ilara."

Ilara pressed her ear to the door. The guard lifted an eyebrow at her but didn't say anything. Nika sat down and cocked her head with a yip. Ilara shushed her.

"With all due respect, Your Majesty, you aren't getting any younger," Domhnall said. "Ilara is a bright, capable girl, but do you want her to reign alone should something befall you? You lost your wife prematurely; surely you realize anything might happen. You should—"

"Do not presume to advise me how to rule or parent, Halkon," Papa thundered.

"I would never, Your Majesty," Domhnall said placatingly. "But it's not too soon to consider the future. We get along, yes? You like me. Give me Ilara in marriage."

"I give… What? No." There was a sound like a chair being pushed across the floor. "Earl Halkon, you've overstayed your welcome, and I rescind my hospitality."

A muttered curse. "Will you grant your blessing if Ilara agrees to marry me?"

Silence. "If Ilara wanted you, I would consider it."

Flinging the door open, Ilara burst into the room. "I don't! And you won't change my mind. I don't trust you, Earl Domhnall, because…I can't remember! And that's the problem. There's something strange going on, and I won't marry you. In fact, you need to leave at once."

Papa had been leaning forward on his desk, but now he straightened and crossed his arms. "As I said, Earl Halkon. You've overstayed your welcome. If you don't leave, you'll be escorted out."

Domhnall stared at her, surprise giving way to cold fury. "Ilara—"

"We've rescinded hospitality. Leave before we also rescind any pretense of friendliness." She lifted her chin. Nika growled at her side.

Domhnall's jaw twitched as he turned back to Papa. "Fine. Then a threat. Give Ilara to me in marriage, or there will be consequences."

Papa laughed, harsh and disbelieving. "It seems you wish to become acquainted with my dungeon."

"Last chance." The Kilkrethian smiled, but his tone was laced with poison. "I will marry Ilara. Unless you and your other daughters want to know what malice I'm capable of, you will give her to me now."

Ilara's mouth fell open. "You—"

"Guards!" Papa reddened. "Guards!"

"So be it." Domhnall bowed, but it was sloppy and mocking. "A curse upon your entire house. Your daughters' days of slumber will belong to you, but until Ilara and I are wed, your daughters' wakeful nights will belong to me."

Nika started barking. The guard from the corridor ran into the study, only for Halkon to shove him aside with a burst of colorful light that erupted from his palm. Acrid fear roiled in Ilara's stomach.

He was using *magic*.

"I'll see you tonight, Ilara." The air around Domhnall crackled and swirled with multicolored light. Abruptly the light went out, and the sorcerer had vanished.

The guards searched for him without success. Papa ordered guards posted outside Ilara's and her sisters' rooms that night, and Ilara slipped a dagger under her pillow.

Regardless of what strange magic he possessed, Domhnall Halkon would die before he touched her.

6

*I*lara stood near the foot of her bed, her eyes straining in the dark, with no memory of how she got there. Her limbs felt heavy, and an odd sweetness coated her mouth. Her fingers brushed against her dress, and she froze.

Wool. She was dressed, no longer wearing her linen night-gown.

"What…" She stumbled to the edge of her bed, exhaustion overtaking her as if she hadn't slept. Her feet ached in her…shoes?

Her head pounded as she sought an explanation. She'd gone to bed—

Domhnall. His show of magic and a threat.

No, not a threat.

A curse.

Your daughters' wakeful nights will belong to me.

She certainly felt as if she'd been awake all night, but she didn't recall anything after going to sleep. Domhnall must have tampered with her memory again.

"Stay calm," she muttered. "You're still in your room, so maybe he failed. After all, the guards—wait, the guards!"

Ilara ran to her door and threw it open. In the corridor, the six guards, two outside each princess's door, were lurching to their feet. One rubbed at his bleary eyes, and another's brow was deeply furrowed as he looked up and down the hallway.

"Report," Ilara commanded. The guards snapped to attention, all turning to face her.

"I…um…" The guard standing directly in front of her, a middle-aged man with a bit of gray showing at his temples, swallowed hard. "We fell asleep, Your Highness. We just awoke." He dropped to one knee. "I'm pleased to see Your Highness is all right. I apologize for my lapse and throw myself at your mercy."

Ilara stared down at him, then surveyed the other guards. "*All* of you?" They nodded, heads bowed. There was no chance that was a coincidence. Not when they were dealing with a sorcerer.

Across the corridor, Meelah emerged from her room. She was also dressed, and her face looked ashy.

Kiri's door opened, and her youngest sister tripped into the hall. "Ara! What's happening? I woke up standing and wearing this"—she motioned at her dress—"but I don't remember putting it on! And there's something sticky on my chin, like fruit juice, but I couldn't have eaten in my sleep…right? I don't remember anything! And I'm so tired." Her words ended in a whine.

"Same," Meelah whispered.

"Me too." Irritation welled in Ilara at whatever twisted game Domhnall was playing.

"Ugh." Meelah slumped against her doorframe. "I feel like I danced all night."

At that, indistinct memories flashed through Ilara's mind. Snippets of music, wine splashing over her tongue, a firm hand on her back, green eyes…

Footsteps hammered down the hall, and then Papa rounded the corner, breathless. His tunic was bunched in his belt, his boots were unlaced, and his hair was disheveled. Relief sank into his features.

"You're all here and fine. Nothing happened."

"Not exactly," Ilara said.

Color bled from Papa's face. "What do you mean? What happened?"

"We fell asleep, Your Majesty," said the guard, who Ilara realized with a start was still kneeling before her.

"And something happened." Kiri's lower lip trembled. "But we can't remember."

Meelah stretched and groaned. "I'm not even hungry. I just want to sleep."

Ilara hid her shaking hands behind her back. "You may rise," she said to the guard. "Papa, it's not their fault—"

"No, of course not." Papa sighed. "That sorcerer must have enchanted them."

"And taken us to some kind of party," Ilara said. "With food and dancing. But that's all I remember."

She fought to stay calm, especially as she saw Papa's growing panic. He would need her to be strong, just like after Mama died.

"We'll figure this out." Papa went to Kiri and pulled her into a tight embrace. "I promise. We'll stop him. There has to be a way."

7

When a knock sounded on his sitting room door early on the morning of his forced departure, Tristan answered, expecting a servant or maybe an armed guard to escort him out. He nearly choked when he saw Alex instead. He quickly stepped back and bowed low.

"Your Excellency."

Alex held out a sealed scroll. "Here's your letter of introduction, Baron Carbrey."

Baron? Tristan's mouth refused to move. Was Alex toying with him?

"You're going to need it." Alex waved the scroll. He also offered a folded piece of parchment. "And here's a letter for you detailing hopes and concessions for trade."

Tristan finally got his body to respond and took the scroll and letter. "I don't understand."

"Frankly, I don't either. I've lost my mind." Alex mussed his hair, but he did so only directly on top of his head, the motion small. Avoiding horns that were no longer there. "I might have been…" He worked his jaw. "Petty. And you're right. Sending an ambassador out of spite is asking for disaster."

Tristan frowned, hoping against hope. Did that mean…?

"I'm still sending you," Alex clarified to Tristan's disappointment, "but I'm giving you the barony now. No strings. It's true that what was given *can* be taken back, but I'm trying to close the rift between us. I think the best way to do that right now is give you time away from Raelyn. And away from…me. The title is a gesture of goodwill."

Goodwill? Maybe Alex *had* lost his mind.

"And to be clear: I do forgive you, Tristan."

Tristan tossed the letter and scroll onto a chair as shame made him irritable. "Are you mocking me?"

"What?"

"You must hate me. After everything…and yesterday. I thought you despised me, and I can't blame you. This kindness…it must be a trick." Tristan crossed his arms. "Honestly, I almost wish you'd punish me. Leave me in a cell for a few days, flog me, something. I was relieved you pardoned me, pleased even, but I didn't really think you would. Either you're trying to make me feel guiltier or you're setting me up to knock me down later."

Alex chuckled, which infuriated Tristan further. "If my forgiveness makes you feel guilty, that's more about you than me. I made a choice not to seek revenge. I don't want to start down that road. I don't want to end up…"

"Like me?" Tristan supplied.

"I was going to say like your father, but I suppose that works, too."

Tristan's face heated. "Yes. Always perfect Alex. My father's gone, but don't worry, you're still here to remind me. 'Alex wouldn't have—'"

"You know what, Tristan?" His cousin's hand fisted at his side. "Stop blaming me for your stupidity and cruelty."

He eyed Alex's fist. "You want to hit me? Hit me." *There's a little stupid and cruel in you, too, isn't there?* He lifted his chin. "Gareth was right. I deserve it." *Hit me. Show me you're not that much better than me. Make me pay so this guilt can end.*

"I don't want to hit you." Slowly, Alex relaxed his hand. "A manservant and a couple of guards will accompany you, for your protection and service. They—"

"You don't want to hit me," Tristan pressed. "What do you want? You want to cut my back open? How is your back, anyway?" His mouth kept talking even as he panicked, telling himself to shut up. "I heard a rumor those cuts were infected."

Anger clouded Alex's expression. "What's your problem?"

"Mine? What's yours!" He pushed the door open wider. "Don't you want to make me bleed, the way I made you bleed?"

"Gareth made you bleed. I'll settle for that."

"So you *do* want to hurt me?" Tristan held out his hands. His headache was returning, and an inexplicable wetness threatened his eyes. "Here I am."

"Well, next to you, I look completely sane." The king pursed his lips. "What's going on?"

He couldn't speak the truth, but for some reason, he couldn't stop talking, either. "Just wondering how weak of a king you are. You're a pushover. Kiss the queen, get a barony."

Alex made a sound like a growl and stepped through the doorway. "Enough."

"Or what? Are you going to growl at me again, Your Dragonness?"

Alex turned red all the way to his ears.

"It's good your feet healed so you could dance last night, or I would have had to take every dance with Raelyn."

"You're pushing me. Why?"

To see if you'll snap. To drag you down to my level since I'll never touch yours. Because I deserve to be punished. But Tristan kept those thoughts inside as he leaned his hip against the back of an armchair. "I think you're sending me away because you're afraid. Afraid Raelyn secretly liked kissing me."

"Well, now you just sound like an idiot and a churl," Alex said, his voice low. "She hated it. Surely you don't honestly think—"

"No. But I liked it." Tristan sneered, even as the words left a bitter taste behind. "I loved kissing her, tasting her, touching her."

Alex yelled, somewhere between a roar and a shout. *Come on.* Tristan braced himself. He would not dodge this. But Alex turned and drove his fist into the door with a resounding crack. The door shuddered on its hinges.

Alex clutched the sides of his head, took a deep breath, and exhaled slowly. "You leave in an hour. I expect you to send a report back within a week of your arrival."

"What?" Tristan gaped at him. "That's all?"

His cousin smiled tightly. "Twelve years I practiced controlling my temper when I had a dragon inside me that craved violence. You're nothing compared to that."

Tristan shook his head. "My father would have—" An invisible cord curled around his throat, cutting him off.

Alex's smile vanished. "Would have what?"

"Nothing." The curse wouldn't let him say it. Besides, now that his mind had caught up to his tongue, he didn't actually want to tell Alex that the few times he'd argued with Henry, afterward he'd have an unusually difficult combat training session that involved severely uneven odds and canings for the smallest errors that would leave him bruised for days.

On rarer occasions, such as after Tristan had brought Alexander back from the mountains alive, he'd hit his son himself—Tristan actually preferred that. The emotional pain was more acute, but the humiliation was done in private, and the physical pain didn't last as long.

"Whatever's going on with you," Alex said, watching him with silent questions in his eyes, "if your guilt is becoming too much to bear, or whatever it is, I hope you sort it out soon. I need a rational ambassador, not one who goes around hoping to be punched. Can you handle that?"

Tristan lowered his head. His fight was gone, his pride and anger evaporating. "I won't let you down, Your Excellency. And I…" He swallowed as emptiness carved deeper into his desperate heart. "I apologize, Alex—Your Excellency. I'm sorry."

He cringed at himself. What was he thinking? Saying such horrible things and then asking for forgiveness? He'd known what he was saying was wrong even before the words passed his lips—it wasn't a mistake to be forgiven.

"I forgive you."

Tristan sucked in a breath. Surely he'd misheard…

Alex turned away, then paused and looked over his shoulder. "But never talk about Raelyn like that again. I can't have one of my lords disrespecting my queen." He walked away, his long strides leisurely. Self-assured.

Tristan shut the door and collapsed into an armchair. What was wrong with him? He didn't even want Alex's forgiveness. He closed his eyes. No, the truth was, he longed to believe it was real. Alex seemed sincere, and that both relieved and terrified him.

What do you do when you can't forgive yourself?

8

Two knights, a manservant, four horses, and a pack mule carrying their trunks were waiting in the courtyard. Tristan emerged into the blinding sunlight, his sword buckled at his side. The morning was already hot, as was usual as summer approached its scorching peak. He might as well embrace the warmth while he could, rather than complain.

Realizing he wouldn't return for some time, he took a lingering look around the courtyard. And when he came back, he might not be welcome at the palace, maybe even be ordered never to leave his barony.

Regardless of the past or future, he wasn't leaving like a beat dog. He stood tall as he walked to his entourage. The knights and manservant bowed and mounted their horses without a word. He didn't recognize them. Probably pulled from outside the palace to avoid any potential conflicts of loyalty. Had they been instructed to spy on him?

"Tristan."

He stiffened with his hand on the pommel of the saddle. What was Raelyn doing there? He rotated slowly to face her and bowed as she descended the palace steps, holding up the skirt of her forest-green dress.

"Your Majesty." He straightened, noting with confusion that Raelyn had come alone.

"I heard what happened this morning."

He bit the inside of his cheek. "His Excellency told you?" As if it wasn't shameful enough that he'd said the words at all.

She blushed. "Um, no. I was…eavesdropping."

Horrified embarrassment mixed with amusement. "Did you learn that skill from your brother, or the other way around?" Since when had he become so bad at holding his tongue?

Raelyn's lips curved down. "You're hurting, and you're lashing out. I'm sor—"

"Please, Your Majesty." He shook his head. "You don't need to apologize to me. In fact—"

"I'm afraid this is my fault."

Tristan was quite certain his banishment was his own doing.

"I suggested making you an ambassador." Raelyn fidgeted with her skirt. "You're a man of action. It took you only moments to decide to hunt down the dragon you thought had captured me. Alex wanted to send you to a distant corner of Rethalyon to live out your days, and I had the idea that maybe, if you could do something more active, prove your loyalty, it would help you feel you still had something to offer. I thought it might make things easier for you, and…you'd still be gone. For a while, but not forever." She rubbed her arm. "I'd assumed he'd give you a choice."

For a moment, Tristan didn't know what to say. Her reasons were…actually thoughtful? He felt another twist of guilt over what he'd said to Alex, followed by another stab of resentment that Alex hadn't given him a choice.

"You're probably right that I needed a task. Thank you. And…" He cleared his throat. "I'm sorry about what I said. About you. It was wrong. I was just…" He trailed off. There was no excuse for his behavior.

"Lashing out?" Raelyn pulled her long braid over her shoulder and ran her fingers over the bumps. She did that a lot when nervous or thinking. It was cute.

Stop! He focused on the massive sapphire wedding ring on her finger.

"I am sorry, Tristan. It can't be easy… Your life was upended, too. You probably feel that your title and future and—and, well, probably me—were stolen. I'd hoped this would give you a new purpose, a fresh start. I wasn't trying to make things worse for you."

Why did she have to be so caring? It both made him feel ashamed and made him want to love her. And he couldn't love her. "Your thoughtfulness is most kind, Your Majesty." He bowed. "But I must depart."

"Be well. I hope you find some peace."

In frozen Talland? Unlikely. He began to turn toward his horse, then paused. She watched him, waiting, as if she sensed he wanted to say something else.

"I did many things wrong," he said quietly, hoping only she heard him. "I can't apologize enough for the hurt I've caused you. But I need to know…if you hadn't fallen for him, would you have wanted me to touch you? To kiss you? Or would you still have felt uncomfortable?"

Raelyn blushed. "I would have minded less."

Less. Was something wrong with him? Florence hadn't found him repulsive.

Her lips pulled to the side as her forehead wrinkled. "Women are people, Tristan. We desire to be respected, not ordered like dogs, or touched just because you can. Maybe women in Rethalyon feel differently, but I doubt it. No woman owes you herself, not even your betrothed."

That didn't align with what Henry said. But then, Henry had poisoned his own sister and never spoke of his late wife, so he was the furthest thing from an authority on women.

Tristan inclined his head. "I appreciate your honesty and insight, Your Majesty."

He mounted his horse and looked to the knights, both of whom watched him with concerned expressions. He glanced toward Raelyn, but she was hurrying into the palace, holding up her skirt so she wouldn't trip. He faced the knights.

"To clarify, there is nothing between the queen and me."

One of the knights, a towering, muscular man with his blond hair pulled back in a long tail, raised his brows and snorted. Laugh lines crinkled his tanned face, and he appeared to be in his thirties. "That's obvious."

The younger knight, a tall, lean man with short black hair and brown skin, sat in his saddle with the relaxed air of a man on holiday, his amusement poorly hidden.

Tristan's cheeks burned hotter. "Let's go."

They'd been riding for over an hour, Tristan stewing over what Raelyn had said and trying to sort through his emotions, when he realized he was being an idiot. He peered around at his companions. "I'm sorry. I don't know your names."

Ponytail chuckled. "Wondered when or if you'd ask." The big man reached into a purse at his belt and fished out a silver coin, which he tossed to the other knight. "I'm Sir Hugo Masarik. Everyone calls me Masarik."

The black knight slipped the coin from Masarik and a coin from the manservant into a pouch on his belt. He looked around Tristan's age of twenty-three, maybe a little younger, which meant he couldn't have much fighting experience.

"Sir Allyre Sharland, my lord," he said, his tone warm and

relaxed. Well, Masarik might have no manners, but at least he'd be useful in a fight. Sharland, Tristan was less sure about.

Wait.

"Sharland?" Tristan narrowed his eyes. "Like Baron Julius Sharland?" He knew the baron from the Court of Lords—a usually soft-spoken man with light skin and long black hair, who never attended palace functions. Baron Sharland had been quick to take Alex's side at the hearing and had appeared pleased with Henry's deposition.

Sir Sharland's piercing eyes fixed on Tristan as if studying him. "My father." He continued watching Tristan, and if Tristan hadn't spent the last twelve years learning not to flinch under scrutiny, he would have looked away.

"I wasn't aware Baron Sharland had a son." Nor did Tristan imagine that the baron's son would willingly protect Henry's son. He eased his right hand to his sword, his gaze darting between the brazenly rude Masarik and the possible liar Sharland.

Something odd gleamed in Sharland's eyes. "My mother wasn't fond of the court and kept me away. I'd never stepped foot in the palace before King Alexander's return. But you can take your hand off your sword. I'm who I say I am, and I'm here to protect you, not kill you."

Tristan nodded, unsure how to respond as he abashedly released his sword. Twisting about, he eyed the manservant. "And you are?"

"Remy, my lord." The man looked young, at least a few years younger than Tristan, with an overeager expression and a wild mess of mousy hair over a sunburnt face. "Remy Fournier."

"Good to meet you, Fournier." At least his manservant seemed harmless enough. Tristan turned back to Masarik. "So. What was that bet about?"

Masarik chuckled. Hopefully he was as intimidating as his

appearance suggested, and not merely a muscled jester. And hopefully he wouldn't turn that strength against Tristan. The knight jabbed his thumb toward Fournier. "Remy bet you'd know our names and wouldn't have to ask. Allyre bet you'd ask us by the end of the first day. I wagered you wouldn't ask our names until you went to introduce us and realized you didn't know them."

Tristan frowned. "Why?"

"Baron. Former prince. Rumor says you're heartless." Masarik shrugged. "Seemed unlikely you would care."

Hm. He needed to work on how others perceived him, or this ambassadorial mission would be difficult. Or had Alex specifically chosen knights that disliked him? Why would he do that? To spy? To test whether Tristan would retaliate when blatantly disrespected? This was going to be a long trip.

"How did Al—His Excellency pick you?"

"Shortly after King Alexander arrived," Sharland said, "he sent word offering a place in the royal guard for any free knights without connections to the palace. Clearly, I fit that description, and I was looking for somewhere to serve and gain more experience. I convinced my parents to allow it. Then yesterday, word came His Excellency had asked for volunteers for this mission."

Now it was Tristan's turn to stare at Sharland. He was bothered by the *gaining experience* bit for one of only two guards assigned to him on a cross-kingdom trek, but that wasn't what surprised him. "You...volunteered? Why?"

Again Sharland regarded him like he was trying to read Tristan's mind. Finally, he shrugged. "Curiosity. A chance to travel, observe another court, and serve the new king sounded like a unique experience."

Tristan didn't appreciate the way Sharland had eyed him as he said *curiosity*. His suspicion that Alexander had told the men to spy on him grew.

"Politics bore me," Masarik cut in. "But the pay couldn't be refused. Assuming we make it back alive, we'll be very well compensated. Just the money the king gave us for agreeing was enough to get my youngest sister the dowry money she needed, plus some extra, and still give me plenty to spend without borrowing from your lordship."

So Masarik was there for the money. Great.

"I'm curious if the stories about Talland are true," Fournier chimed in. "Like that everyone hunts and even the nobles live in houses of wood, and are there really white stags the size of bears? And it is an honorable, well-paying position."

Tristan nodded absently. He was traveling across Rethalyon, through Kilkreth, and deep into Talland with three men of questionable loyalty to either himself or their king, other than to the king's gold, and who might report his every move. Excellent. His head was starting to ache again.

9

A hand caressing Ilara's cheek woke her. She blinked against the dazzling torchlight, her mind sluggish. Something tasted sweet and strong on her tongue and lips.

A handsome face looked down at her, nearly stealing her breath away. The man had cheekbones and a jawline as fine as if they had been carved of marble, framed by straight golden hair. His name filtered into her consciousness. *Domhnall Halkon.* Despite his allure, something deep in Ilara's chest kicked back in fear.

Domhnall smiled, a lazy angling of his soft lips into a scandalous smirk. He held out his hand. *You trust him,* a breezy part of her mind whispered. At the same time, misgiving settled into her stomach, and yet…she was already reaching for his hand. As her fingers touched his, a tiny sigh escaped her. She stood, gazing into his emerald eyes.

"Finally warming up to me, my dear?"

Ilara didn't understand what he meant, but it seemed like she should agree, so she nodded, feeling detached.

He lifted her hand and gently pressed his lips against her knuckles. "Pick something pretty and get dressed while I wake your sisters." He swept out of her bedroom, leaving her in the dim illumination of a single candle on her nightstand.

Ilara drifted to her large wardrobe and picked out a pink

underdress and midnight-blue overdress, completing the ensemble with brooches featuring howling wolf heads carved from narwhal ivory. Then she brushed out her hair, adding only a couple of simple braids. She didn't want to keep Domhnall waiting.

She was tying on soft suede shoes when her bedroom door opened. "Are you ready yet, darling?"

"Nearly," she said, even as she frowned at his use of "darling."

When she reached her doorway, her sisters were already in the corridor with dreamy smiles on their faces.

"Come along, princesses." Domhnall led Ilara forward. "The ball awaits."

"Oh, I do love a good ball," Kiri said with a giggle. "Dancing and food and pretty clothes and food..."

"You already said food, silly." Meelah's voice sounded softer than usual.

Six guards slept in the hall, slumped against the walls. Why were they there? They usually only had a couple of guards patrolling this floor...

"Ilara, look at me." Domhnall drew her face toward him. "Ignore them." He turned away and traced a large circle in the air with his palm.

The dark corridor crackled with golden sparks, and lines of red and yellow light wove together into a giant circle as he moved his hand. Ilara watched, mesmerized and afraid, despite an odd sensation of familiarity. The circle, now filling the hall, flashed golden, and the conjured doorway opened onto a dark forest trail.

Domhnall took Ilara's hand and led them through the luminous circle into the woods. Glowing crystals as tall as Ilara's waist were spaced between the trees along the path, providing a dim teal illumination to their surroundings.

As their footsteps rustled over rich green grass, Ilara gaped at the forest. Cedars and oaks with gold bark and leaves towered over them, interspersed with maples and poplars of silver. There were gold and silver fruit trees, too, bearing plump gold peaches and heavy silver pomegranates.

The air smelled like summer, of sweet, cut grass and strawberries and wildflowers and fresh ocean breezes. Fireflies floated between the silver and gold trunks, flickering in the shadows between crystals. The delicate melody of harps and flutes drifted through the wood.

The path led to a spacious grassy clearing packed with dancing couples. Around the edges, people watched the dancers or talked around tables loaded with food and drink. A group of musicians sat to one side, providing the enthralling music. All the tables and chairs and the lantern posts surrounding the meadow were either made of wood or formed from living, metallic saplings. A full moon that appeared larger than any Ilara had ever seen hung over the scene, casting everything in a dreamy, silvery glow. The slightest breeze set the gold and silver leaves glittering like gemstones.

The dancers represented a variety of builds and skin tones, from a woman with skin like midnight to a man whose skin, hair, and eyes were all white. But they were all, every one of them, tall and gorgeous, wearing clothing embroidered with shimmering thread. Overall, they intimidated her. And Ilara rarely felt intimidated.

"Go." Domhnall dropped her hand and pressed against the small of her back. "Eat, dance, and be merry."

Kiri and Meelah drifted into the spinning couples, where they quickly found partners.

Ilara blinked. Why did her head feel so fuzzy? "I'm not sure..."

Domhnall held out a gold peach and caught her gaze. "Eat, Ilara."

She shoved the peach into her mouth, unable to refuse. As

soon as the delicious juices coated her tongue, all her concerns fell away. Warmth spread through her, and her whole body felt lighter. "I want to dance now."

Domhnall nodded, pleased. "I'll see you in a little while, my dear princess." He strode past her, the dancers parting for him as he made his way to a throne made of entwined wood vine on the far side of the meadow. A line of people stood before the throne, as if waiting for an audience.

A young man with black skin approached her, his dimpled smile welcoming. "Might I have this dance, my lady?"

"I would be delighted."

Soon they were spinning through the couples, the forest a swirl of color and light around them. Man after man asked for a dance, and she accepted each one. Sometimes she caught sight of Kiri or Meelah dancing with other men, laughing and smiling.

Ilara had just started a fast jig with a new partner when the music cut off with a discordant hiccup. The dancers stilled, and the entire meadow seemed to hold its breath.

"Lord Eldrich." Domhnall's voice was like frosted steel. She couldn't see him from where she stood near the center of the dancers, but panic filled her—only she wasn't certain if she wanted to run to Domhnall or away from him.

"Lord Domhnall," returned a more pleasant man's voice. "Which one is she? That one looks a bit young. Surely you haven't stooped so low."

"I don't recall inviting you or your lackies."

Ilara stole between restless men and women, moving toward the voices. *A bit young.* Was the stranger talking about Kiri? A need she didn't fully understand to protect her sisters thrummed through her.

"I took the nearly nonexistent magical barrier as an open invitation."

The words confused Ilara but sent a ripple of whispers and gasps through the crowd. She ignored them as she spotted Kiri near the edge of the stalled dancers. Her sister was staring at a group of two men and three women, all armed with swords or spears except for one man. Ilara cast them a curious glance before taking Kiri's hand.

"Kiri," she whispered. "Let's go."

Her sister blinked at her. "Go? Where?"

"Go home…" She trailed off. How did they get home? Where were they, anyway? The more she tried to think about it, the more her head hurt.

"Is this the lucky lady?"

Ilara looked up to find the unarmed man from the outside group advancing on her. Domhnall strode toward them as well, and Ilara pushed Kiri behind her, glancing between the two men.

"She looks awfully frightened for a human in your realm." The stranger smiled at Domhnall, the expression disingenuous. "Are you—"

"Why are you here, Eldrich?" Domhnall snapped. He stood next to Ilara, his nearness somehow possessive.

"Why are *we* here?" Ilara demanded. "Where is Meelah? What is going…" Memories crashed back into her mind, leaving her dizzy for a moment. She turned an accusing glare on the sorcerer. "I demand you return us home at once!"

Eldrich laughed. "Oh, you picked a strong-willed one. That or your magic truly is pitiful now."

Domhnall's fingers twitched at his sides. "She will marry me—"

"I will not." Ilara lifted her chin, even as she glanced around for Meelah. "And this place, this ridiculous party, the poison you've laced your food with that makes me forget, none of it will change my mind."

Domhnall faced her with a charming grin. "My dearest Ilara,

you pain me. Perhaps you'll feel better after some refreshment."

He offered her a gold goblet that he hadn't been holding a moment before. Ilara eyed the ruby liquid with distrust.

"I do wonder which will break first," Eldrich mused. "The human girl's resolve not to marry you, or your resolve not to resort to violence? I'm so certain that her determination will outlast yours, I'd consider raising our wager."

"Drink this," Domhnall said as he shoved the goblet into her hand. "Or your sister will," he added in so low a whisper, she barely heard him.

As Domhnall turned back to Eldrich, Ilara lifted the goblet to her lips, her hand quivering. But if the wine couldn't be trusted, she couldn't let Kiri or Meelah drink it.

"May I remind you," Domhnall said, a threatening edge to his voice, "that our deal only pertains to my refraining from violence against the girl or her family or countrymen, not you and your courtiers, and you are in my domain."

Ilara paused with the cool rim of the goblet against her lips. Was she understanding correctly? Domhnall had sworn not to harm her, her family, or her people?

"Get. *Out*," Domhnall snarled. "And if any sniveling member of your court enters my lands again without my invitation, there will be unpleasant consequences. Actually, spread the word. *Anyone*, from any other court, sets foot in the Gilded Court without my permission, they will suffer."

Eldrich's mouth twitched; in fear or amusement, Ilara couldn't tell. "A threat I would take more seriously if you weren't on the verge of losing your power, Lord of a dying Gilded Court. And is that a no on raising our wager? Your self-confidence is that low?"

"No," Domhnall snarled. "I'll win her and our bet."

"Then you'll add your inter-realm scrying mirror into the deal? I know you have one."

Domhnall's teeth ground so loudly it was a wonder they didn't break. "Then I want your frost blade."

"Hm." Eldrich rubbed his chin, his eyes slitted and mouth twisting to the side. "Deal. You convince the human girl, this Princess Ilara of Talland, to marry you without resorting to violence or threats of violence against her, her family, or any Tallander, and you get everything we previously agreed plus my frost blade. But if you enact violence upon or bully her with threats of violence against her, her family, or her people, or abandon your pursuit, I get everything we previously agreed plus your inter-realm scrying mirror—as well as the pleasure of knowing I was right."

"Agreed." The two men clasped each other's forearms. Lines of gold, silver, blue, and green light encircled their hands. "The deal is made."

"The deal is made," Eldrich agreed. The lights blinked out, and they withdrew their hands. "I will take my leave, then—although I imagine I'll be back in a few days to collect my winnings." He gestured lazily to his retinue, and the group wandered away through the trees.

Domhnall turned to face the dancers, his eyes flashing. "What are you all standing around gawping for? *Dance.*"

The musicians hastily began again, and a moment later, dancers paired off. Ilara grabbed Kiri's hand and drew her away from the swaying bodies.

"What is happening?" Kiri whimpered and tucked herself against Ilara's side. "I don't understand…why do I feel like I'm dreaming, but it's a bad dream?"

"Troublesome, troublesome Ilara." Domhnall sighed. "You haven't tasted your wine."

"You can have it." She threw the goblet, splashing dark liquid all over the front of Domhnall's pale green tunic and trousers.

With a grunt, he waved his hand, and colorful light shimmered over his clothes. The stain vanished. "Don't push me—"

"To what?" Ilara smiled thinly. "You have no leverage if you want to win your wager. So return us home now."

Domhnall shook his head. "Oh, no. You see, I lose if I hurt or threaten to hurt you or any Tallander. I also lose if you don't marry me, and I lose more than a bet. If I must lose, I'll do so covered in blood if need be, but you *will* be mine. So will you marry me, Ilara?"

Ilara tightened her grip on Kiri's arm as Kiri sobbed. It took her a moment to force the words past her tight throat, but a crown princess did not surrender so easily, and certainly not to a sorcerer she doubted had good intentions for her kingdom. "No. I won't be intimidated."

"Then I'll try charming you for a while longer. It shouldn't be *that* difficult to wear you down. I just have to be patient, and I have far more experience with waiting than you. Now." Domhnall leaned forward and held out two slices of golden orange, inches from their noses. "Have a bite. You'll feel better."

Ilara looked from the orange to his face. "I'm not going to— mmph."

Domhnall shoved the fruit into her open mouth, and her teeth broke through the thin skin before she could stop herself. The sweetest, most delectable orange juice she had ever tasted delighted her.

By the time she swallowed the fruit, she had forgotten all about threats and wagers. Kiri drifted away, wandering toward an overflowing refreshment table, and Domhnall bowed.

"Dance with me, my flower."

Feeling as light as a feather, Ilara let him draw her into a dance, their bodies spinning close together. All that existed was that moment, a night of dancing and music and the sweet-smelling meadow.

10

ristan's initial instinct when they stopped the first night was to hang back and let his guards and new servant make camp. Then he debated with himself. Crown Prince Tristan would *not* help with manual labor. Tristan the rejected nobody should be humble and help. What about Baron Tristan, official ambassador of Rethalyon? Anyone else in his position shouldn't be expected to assist with menial tasks, right? Yet he'd been a baron all of a day, and his ambassadorial mission was more of a punishment than an honor.

More importantly, he suspected Masarik, Sharland, and Fournier would consider him pompous if he didn't help. Sharland in particular could judge him as a baron's son himself…although he *had* volunteered to be a guard… No, Tristan would be relying on these men for weeks or months, and he needed their loyalty. Or at minimum, their acceptance.

So he removed his horse's tack, pitched his tent, and gathered firewood. He didn't miss the coins Masarik and Fournier slipped to Sharland as he erected his own tent, but this time, he didn't ask. The way Masarik had gawked at him before muttering a curse and digging into his purse said enough.

With camp made, the others settled around the campfire and dug into the dried meat and hard bread. The food wouldn't last the entire trip, but it would get them about halfway before they had to stop to hunt or buy supplies.

Tristan got his supper and hesitated. He was tired and just wanted to be left alone. Instead, he swallowed his pride and sat with them around the fire.

He'd scarcely settled down when Masarik said, "So, Carbrey. Rumor has it you're cursed. That true?"

The dried meat turned to leather in Tristan's mouth. He forced it down and nodded. To his relief, the curse didn't activate.

The big knight's eyes narrowed. "Also heard you were handsy with the queen while in the mountains, but then the story is you could've enchanted her to love you and didn't. Doesn't make sense to me. Do you like it when they fight you?"

"Masarik!" Sharland sounded shocked, but he still sent a questioning look Tristan's way.

The hard bread crumbled to bits in Tristan's fist. He'd lost his appetite anyway, his stomach threatening to push up what he'd eaten as shame devoured him.

"I left Princess—Queen Raelyn alone when I realized I was scaring her," he said quietly as he brushed breadcrumbs off his palm. Clasping his hands, he attempted to steady himself. "Did His Excellency put you up to this?"

Sharland frowned at his fellow knight. "Masarik just has a big mouth."

"Actually," Fournier said, "I heard from a guard who was in the Hall during the Court of Lords hearing that the queen said Prin—Baron Carbrey gave her a love spell charm instead of using it, which she used to prove that King—I mean, Henry had lied about using magic. That made Henry furious, and he tried to force his son to use the spell in front of everyone, but he wouldn't. I figure, well…I've seen the queen. If a man has the chance to make her love him and doesn't take it twice, he must be a good man."

Masarik rolled his eyes, and Sharland studied Tristan in that unnerving way again.

The tips of Tristan's ears burned. Fournier might be the only person in all of Rethalyon who thought well of him. "Ask Prince Gareth whether one right choice makes someone *good*." He stood. "Good night."

With that, he stomped into his tent. As he tossed and turned on a thin mat on the hard ground, he wished he hadn't stormed off or disagreed with Fournier. It would only alienate the one member of his entourage who actually liked him. Even without Tristan's surly behavior, Masarik would disabuse Fournier of any ideas about Tristan's chivalry, anyway.

But it would have been nice to have someone who believed in him.

As the days passed and Masarik and the others didn't bring up curses, Alex, Raelyn, or Henry again, Tristan relaxed. He wouldn't go so far as to say they were becoming friends, but he didn't feel the need to be constantly vigilant. Which was why, as they followed a disused trade route through a dense forest deep in Kilkreth, he'd let the others' conversation fall into the background and was simply enjoying riding in the cool evening air.

"Carbrey!" Masarik's voice startled Tristan, and he glanced back at the knight, immediately on alert for danger. Masarik motioned toward Fournier. "Tell this birdbrained peasant farm kid he has no idea what he's talking about."

Tristan relaxed. Not a threat, just Masarik getting worked up over something because the man loved to argue.

"Now, Masarik, that's uncalled-for." Sir Sharland rode next to Tristan, his reins held loosely in one hand. He was leaning back, his face upturned toward the late evening sunlight filtering through the pine boughs. "Remy hardly deserves to be spoken to like that, and anyway, you're smarter than to insult the cook."

Masarik's rigid posture relaxed. "True enough. Sorry, Remy, it's nothing against you personally, but you don't know nobles. Carbrey knows the court best, he'll tell you."

"It's *my lord* or *baron*," Tristan said tiredly, not for the first time. He'd give up, except flames knew what the Tallanders would think of him if his knight showed so little respect. "And I wasn't listening to whatever you're arguing about."

Masarik thrust a hand toward him. "See? My point is made. There is no correlation between rank and intelligence or capability, and—"

"But they're well educated!" Fournier burst out. "They run the kingdom; the Court of Lords *has* to be made up of smart, capable men, and if they were incapable or made bad decisions that hurt their people, surely the other lords wouldn't allow it!"

"The Court of Lords is full of power-mad, greedy, shallow idiots and cheats! You're a naïve—"

"Cook," Sharland said drily. "Really, what do you even hope to achieve with this argument? Mostly you, Masarik."

Masarik slouched in his saddle, and Fournier fiddled with his reins. Tristan kept quiet. This was not a disagreement he wanted to be drawn into, and for better or worse, Sharland was far more adept at calming Masarik than Tristan could ever hope to be.

"Why do you keep bringing up that I'm the cook? I'm not even a good cook."

"You're a half-decent cook, which is more than any of the rest of us can say," Tristan said.

"Thanks, I think. But why is that relevant?"

Masarik gave Fournier a hard look and then burst out laughing. "Allyre, the kid's too innocent to realize he could burn my food or season it with dirt to get back at me for insulting him."

Fournier wrinkled his nose. "Sure, and have you challenge me to a duel? No thanks."

"Challenge—" Masarik held a hand to his stomach as he shook with laughter.

Even Tristan chuckled at the thought of Fournier trying to swing a sword properly.

Masarik peered back at the manservant. "What *would* you do if I challenged you to a duel?"

Fournier's eyes widened. "I was joking! You wouldn't. Would you?" He shrank back, pulling the reins with him and making his horse snort.

The fear in his manservant's posture was uncomfortably familiar to Tristan. Leather bit into his palms as he squeezed the reins. "Don't worry, Fournier. I'd forbid it, anyway."

Sharland peered at Tristan curiously. "Why?"

"Why? Look at them." Tristan nodded between the two. "Masarik is practically twice his size, and have you ever even picked up a sword before, Fournier?"

The young man grinned. "Sure! To dust it."

All of them laughed, and the thought that maybe they might actually form something like friendship dared to take root in Tristan's mind.

"I don't approve of unfair odds," Tristan explained. "It would be a beating, not a fight, and I'd never permit it." He knew that pain and humiliation too well to wish it on anyone.

Masarik's eyebrows lifted. "Truthfully? Because—"

A low growl interrupted him, and they fell silent. Tristan halted his horse and gripped the hilt of his sword as he searched the lengthening shadows between tree trunks.

Another growl, ahead of them. Tristan drew his blade while Masarik pulled up on his right. A towering shape moved in the dark and bent a tree aside as it lumbered into the road. Tristan craned his neck back, taking in the armor-like, leathery gray skin of the massive creature.

"Troll," he breathed.

"Stay back, Carbrey!" Masarik kicked his horse forward, sword in hand. The horse whinnied but obeyed its rider.

Tristan shook his head and raised his own sword.

"No, *stay here*," Sharland said, his usual relaxed tone exchanged for one of command. "Don't get in our way!"

As Sharland drew his sword and rode past, Tristan hesitated. The knights stabbed and swung at the troll, ducking under its massive, grasping hands. Between the hulking beast, the horses, and the knights' swords, there was little space for Tristan. But if he could flank it...

He wheeled his horse to the side as Sharland landed a deep cut in the troll's side. The creature howled and stumbled back, providing more room along the edge of the path where Tristan could potentially dart past.

"I see you moving, Carbrey!" Masarik shouted as he blocked the troll's swinging arm with the side of his blade. "Stop distracting me!"

"Please, my lord, just let us handle it!" Sharland pulled hard on his horse's reins, and the steed reared backward, narrowly avoiding the downward arc of the troll's fist.

Grinding his teeth, Tristan fell back next to Fournier and held his anxious horse still. Did they think him inept?

Sharland drove his sword deep into the troll's midsection. The pack mule tied to Fournier's horse skittered as the troll shrieked, and Tristan reached over to help steady the animal. Masarik sliced through the troll's neck, silencing it, and Sharland freed his sword with a tug. The knights backed up their stamping horses just in time to avoid the troll's body crashing to the ground. In the silence following the fight, the horses' panting sounded loud.

"I could have helped, you know," Tristan said as the knights rejoined them, trying to keep his sulk out of his voice.

"Aye." Masarik nodded, serious for once. "But we swore to protect you, and we do that easier if you let us do the fighting."

Sharland pulled a cloth from his saddlebag and began wiping down his blade. "It's our job to get you to Talland and back to Rethalyon in one piece with your heart still beating."

Masarik slapped Tristan's shoulder and winked, the moment of solemnity over. "If you die, I don't think I get paid."

Well. At least there was that.

Still, Tristan's pride rankled for the remainder of the day. As he finished off his supper that night in the light of their shared campfire, he leaned back against a tree trunk and crossed his arms. "I *can* fight, you know."

The corner of Sharland's mouth ticked upward. "I should hope so. You should have had the best tutors."

"Exactly, I did. And *I'm* in charge of *you*, not the other way around"—Masarik glared at him, and Tristan hurried on—"so I don't think it logical for you to tell me not to help if we're attacked."

"But isn't that what normally happens?" Fournier asked. "Don't lords let their knights fight first?"

"Cowardly ones, maybe," Tristan replied. "I'm not a coward." He returned Masarik's glare.

"Aw, did we hurt your princely feelings?" Masarik sneered. "Listen, I only care about keeping you alive, and I fight better if I'm not worried about someone else getting their skull bashed in. Sure, you had good tutors, but when have you *really* fought for your life?"

"I faced a dragon," Tristan snapped, and immediately wished he hadn't mentioned Alexander.

Masarik threw his head back and laughed. "And lost. I heard

he batted you like a cat with a ball of yarn.”

Tristan felt his face go red.

“But don’t worry.” Masarik picked something out of his teeth. “If we need any prisoners tortured or innocent people bound, you’re our man.”

Before he knew it, Tristan was on his feet, his hand flying to his sword. His mouth opened, ready to shout, but no words followed. There was nothing he could say. He couldn’t even argue his innocence. Maybe he could assert he had changed, that he wasn’t like that anymore, but Masarik had straightened, his eyes alert and his own hand on his weapon, as if he thought Tristan likely to attack him. The knight wouldn’t believe Tristan had changed no matter what he said, and Fournier and Sharland watched Tristan as if they, too, expected him to do something violent. They’d never be his friends, and he’d been a fool to entertain the possibility.

If I’d just used that spell on Raelyn, I’d be in the palace with her right now, not here.

Immediate guilt followed the thought. Maybe he *hadn’t* changed.

“I’m going for a walk,” Tristan muttered. He strode away from camp before anyone could contradict him.

He hadn’t gone far when he realized it was too dark to wander without a torch. Despite it being late summer, the weather kept growing cooler the further north they traveled, and the night air held a slight chill away from the fire. However, he didn’t want to go back to Masarik’s taunts, so he returned slowly, picking his way over the uneven ground.

The campfire came back into view, the others still seated around it, and Tristan wondered if he could reach his tent on the far side without attracting their notice. He edged around the camp but stilled as their conversation reached his ears.

"What did I say that was untrue?" Masarik demanded.

Fournier stood, cleaning up supplies from their supper. "It's cruel to throw that in his face when he had a change of heart. If the king pardoned him, who are we to say he's still guilty?"

"Exactly, thank you, Remy," Sharland said. "You could go easier on him, that's all I'm saying. And you could apologize."

Tristan pressed against a tree, practically holding his breath. He shouldn't eavesdrop, but…Fournier and Sharland were defending him?

"I'm not apologizing for speaking the truth. And he was a prince." Masarik snorted. "Those rich high-ranking noble types are used to people going easy on them and getting everything they want. Well, not you, Allyre. You're all right."

Masarik thought that Tristan had spent his life on a bed of roses, being coddled? *As if.* Maybe that was why the blond knight hated him so much.

"You're mistaken if you believe he was spoiled," Sharland said, an odd quality to his tone. "You can't repeat this to Carbrey, all right?"

A pause, during which Tristan wished he could see the others but was thankful he had decided to listen.

"Good," Sharland continued. "When Tristan started attending the Court of Lords, my father would say, 'That poor boy. He looks at his father like a dog looks at a fickle master—unsure if he's going to get affection or punishment.'"

Something lodged in Tristan's throat. Had others in the court noticed this whole time?

"Once," Sharland said, so softly Tristan strained to hear, "when Tristan was fourteen, my father realized after a meeting that his cloak's clasp had broken off in the Great Hall. He went back for it, but Henry was still on his throne, yelling about everything he thought Tristan had said wrong, while Tristan knelt in front of him with his head bowed, shaking."

Tristan sagged against the tree, dismayed by the airing of his disgrace.

"My father said Tristan had done nothing to earn a reprimand, let alone such abuse. He ranted at length about how—" Sharland stopped, and Tristan winced. Had they realized he was listening? "How a man like that didn't deserve to have children."

"Being yelled at just for trying…" Pain sounded in Fournier's voice. "I know how much that hurts."

The sorrow that replaced the usual eager liveliness in his man-servant's tone gave Tristan the sudden urge to protect the young man. He'd be sure to never yell at Fournier. No one deserved to be treated the way Henry had treated him, especially someone so willing to see good in other people.

"Perhaps Tristan was driven to be the heartless man he was to his cousin because he couldn't afford to have a heart around Henry," Sharland murmured.

"Or he's just his father's son." Masarik grunted. "What if the Tristan Carbrey that tortured a man in front of his victim's lover and friends is the honest truth of who he is at his core, and not this man learning and growing you keep trying to claim he is? Henry Carbrey murdered and cursed his own family members, and Tristan is his son. Maybe that cruelty runs in his veins and there's no getting it out."

A grasping, heavy blackness spread in Tristan's chest as some-one else voiced the fears that stalked him. He should stop listen-ing. He shouldn't have started eavesdropping in the first place. But he felt rooted in place, his feet too heavy to even lift.

"I *can't* believe that," Sharland said with an intensity Tristan hadn't heard from him before.

"Why?" Masarik asked. "Because you won some wagers that he'd be halfway decent?"

"I have my reasons," Sharland muttered.

Fournier cleared his throat. "I don't think it's fair to judge Baron Carbrey for things his father did." Oh, Tristan was definitely never yelling at him.

"Fine; I'll stick to judging him for the things he did himself."

Sharland sighed. "Masarik…"

"What?"

"Just…at least try to remember you signed up to serve him, not mock him. You can't shame a person into changing. Besides, you're still his knight and he's still a baron, and you're meant to be serving him. For all we know, if Carbrey gives a poor report of your behavior to King Alexander, you could lose your payment."

Masarik harrumphed. "That's a fair point. I still think you're crazy for caring about him, but so be it. I can keep my mouth shut." There was a loud, overdramatic yawn. "I'm turning in. Wake me if the ambassador doesn't turn back up soon so we can make sure he wasn't eaten."

Tristan dropped his head back against the tree. He would have preferred not knowing just how much Masarik despised him, but Sharland and Fournier gave him hope. If they could defend him when he wasn't even there…maybe friendship wasn't as ridiculous an idea as he feared.

Sure, Fournier probably had built Tristan up to be a hero in his mind to feel prouder of his position as Tristan's manservant, and maybe Tristan could never live up to his expectations, but somehow, it helped.

He could almost hear Henry laughing. *You're giving a peasant boy's opinion this much weight? Pathetic.*

Shut up, Tristan growled.

With a sigh, he pushed off the tree. As he entered the camp, Sharland bolted to his feet, then relaxed.

"My lord! Good, you're back."

"Yes." Tristan forced a shrug. "And all in one piece, too, so no worries about your payment."

Sharland's brow puckered in the flickering light of the campfire. "I'd be a sorry excuse for a knight if my only loyalty to my lord was money."

Tristan tilted his head. "You may have just insulted Sir Masarik."

"I think he's mostly bluster. And he's been ill-used by nobles before. It's less about you than his own grudges."

Tristan wondered what that meant, but he wasn't about to pry into the surly knight's private life.

Sharland rubbed the back of his neck. "For what it's worth, Tri—my lord, I don't hold your past against you. I see how it weighs on you, the things you did. If you ever want to talk about…anything." He waved his hands, as if not certain what to do with himself. "I'm a good listener. At least, that's what my siblings tell me." There was an odd strain to his voice.

"You have siblings?" Tristan asked, seizing an opportunity to steer the conversation away from himself. "You didn't mention that. But you must miss them."

"I…yes." Sharland sighed as he stared out into the forest, his gaze distant. "Three sisters, and…one brother. Margot, Danielle, Jennifer, and Raoul." He looked at Tristan, opened his mouth, then closed it again with a small shake of his head. "I didn't mean to offend you, my lord. But the offer remains. I wouldn't repeat anything to anyone."

Tristan nodded, suddenly wanting nothing more than to go to sleep. "Thank you, Sir Sharland." He motioned at his tent. "Well. Goodnight."

The next morning, they all acted as if nothing had happened, which was fine by Tristan. They continued north, falling into something like camaraderie. Masarik rarely called Tristan "my lord," but he was cordial. Tristan still felt like an outsider in the group, watching the others bond over stories of their siblings or songs they all knew, but he didn't. Still, he kind of liked being around them.

The further across Kilkreth they traveled, the flatter the land became. By the time they crossed the border into Talland, Tristan deeply missed Rethalyon's hills and distant peaks. Grassy, sweeping plains gave way to the moss-covered forests of pine that covered most of central Talland. The sky seemed to have taken on a permanently gray shade, sometimes perking up to a pale blue.

But there was something peaceful about the sunlight angling through the trees, and Tristan loved walking on the moss. The villages they passed through looked more comfortable in the summer than the few he had seen on his short hunting trip, and even the wattle-and-daub houses boasted carved doorways or shutters.

He'd forgotten Tallanders were shorter than Rethalis on average. At least he would get to be tall for once. The people were friendly—certainly more so than the grumpy guide he'd had on his last visit. However, food was difficult to purchase. Famine caused by a late spring ice storm, the villagers said. Tristan tucked that knowledge away—it would be helpful when discussing trade.

Finally, around two weeks after leaving the palace, they arrived at the Great House, the Talland royal residence. He hadn't visited the royal home on his winter hunting trip, and his initial impression was disappointing.

Tristan scowled at the massive rectangular building as a misting rain clung to his eyelashes and seeped into his clothes. Despite its size, the entire Great House could fit inside half of Rethalyon's brick and stone palace and was built completely out of wood. He tried to remind himself that Talland didn't have great quarries like Rethalyon—it had forests. Still, the wood seemed less impressive than rock. He spied precious few windows in the three-story structure, all of which were narrow and made of rough, nearly opaque glass.

The Rethali palace had two defensive walls of stone, but the Tallander Great House and its surrounding collection of smaller timber or wattle-and-daub buildings with thatched or log roofs didn't even have a wooden fence. Servants in simple but neat wool and linen clothing came to greet them, winding around the chickens, goats, and pigs that roamed free.

Overall, it reminded Tristan of a glorified hunting lodge. Only the armed guards patrolling the perimeter and the two standing beside the Great House's double doors signaled this was a royal residence, but their attire was similar to that of the hunters that had accompanied Tristan on his previous trip—thin suede coats treated with oil so the rain rolled off them and hats edged in fur.

"I see you have a pleasant, winning ambassadorial smile down to an art form," Masarik said drily as they handed their mounts off to stable hands. Oddly, it sounded more like how Masarik teased Sharland and Fournier than an actual insult.

Tristan tried to smooth his expression into something more amicable as a middle-aged man wearing a knee-length moss-green tunic emerged from the Great House. Tristan bowed. "Greetings, I—"

"You're not expected." The man scrutinized him. "Who are you, and why have you come here?" A note of suspicion crept into his voice. His eyes pinched, wrinkling his tawny skin.

"I am Baron Tristan Carbrey of Rethalyon, here on behalf of His Royal Highness Alexander Tallon, King of Rethalyon." Tristan bowed again.

If he couldn't even get in to see the king, would Alex count his mission as a failure?

The man frowned. "I see. Why?"

Tristan swallowed. "His Excellency King Alexander wishes to improve friendly relationships and increase trade between our great kingdoms and has sent me as an ambassador."

"Hm. Fine." The man nodded. "I am Steward Dessen. You may wait in the foyer while I ask His Majesty if he wishes to see you. But be warned—he may turn you away."

"Thank you." Tristan and his men followed Steward Dessen past the guards and through wood doors engraved with forests and beasts ranging from caribou to unicorns.

Everything inside, from the ceiling to the floors, was made of paneled wood. The fireplace set in the center of the wall across from the entrance, which currently held a small fire, was lined with brick, but there was no stone. Tristan recalled from his previous visit that there was likely a layer of plaster between the paneled interior and log exterior of the walls for added warmth. The few windows to their right and left were narrow with thick glass, making them distorted rather than clear.

Exquisitely carved wood furniture was arranged around the fireplace and along the walls. Four engraved doors, two on either side of the fireplace, were set into the wall separating the foyer from the rest of the Great House. A massive and impressive carved wood mural of a hunt set with what appeared to be deer carved from antlers and accented with gold and silver leaf stretched above all four doors and the fireplace. A dog with thick, fluffy gray and black fur and perky ears lay sleeping in one corner.

Glorified hunting lodge.

Dessen went through the door to the right of the fireplace, leaving them alone.

"This place is cozy," Fournier said, sounding entirely too happy.

Masarik pointed at the gigantic carving. "I heard the Tallanders love the hunt. I hope we'll get to join one."

Sharland lifted a shoulder. "I've never understood hunting as a sport."

Masarik regarded Sharland with one eyebrow raised. "I may have to rework my entire evaluation of you. Carbrey, you like hunting?"

"Well enough." It was the sort of leisure a prince was supposed to partake in, and why he'd visited Talland four years ago. Henry had forced him into it to win over Baron Tarith for some vote. That short trip had been a snowy and muddy disaster, with no legendary great white elk, soaked clothes, and a night of terrible traditional Tallander coastal food—blubbery seal. Tristan shuddered at the memory.

The door on the right creaked open and Dessen reemerged. Tristan's stomach twisted. *Please see me; please agree to speak with me—*

"His Majesty King Onak and Her Highness Princess Ilara will see you."

11

*I*lara stifled a yawn as Lady Lira ended her report on the state of House Vellroch's lands. As much as she'd like to, she couldn't go back to bed, not yet. Despite Domhnall claiming that the princesses would slumber all day, they'd discovered that wasn't true—they could fight the exhaustion if they wanted. While her sisters usually chose to sleep most of the day, Ilara couldn't.

At first, Papa had delayed some kingly duties out of worry. The House Heads understood, as they were all parents as well. But after a week with no progress, the king slipped into despondency, becoming nearly as withdrawn and disengaged as he had been in the weeks following Mama's death. Just when she most wished she could lean on her papa, she found herself supporting him.

Nine days after the curse, Lady Alantha, the elderly Head of House Soken, had spoken to Lord Rydack, Ryn's father, who then sent Ryn to ask for Ilara's help. The House Heads respected the royal family, and many of them had been friends with Papa since he was young, but he had responsibilities. It wasn't easy to remove a Tallander monarch—that required a war or a unanimous vote by the Houses—but the implied threat of calling a vote was there again, as it had been six years ago.

Maybe it was true what the old Tallander proverb said: *what we call humanity in a man, we call weakness in a king.*

Still, as much as it hurt when, at times, it felt like her papa was choosing the darkness over her and her sisters and Talland, Ilara couldn't accept that he was weak or give up on him. He had a good, strong heart, and he'd return to his usual competent and caring self after they stopped Domhnall. Hopefully it wouldn't take nearly two months this time, though.

In the meantime, Ilara dragged herself to meetings, hearings, and reports or assisted with his paperwork, so her people weren't abandoned. Even if she only had the energy to assist with a few royal duties, Papa's mood shifted from ill-tempered and gloomy to engaged and calm, and he kept working after she returned to bed, which gave her hope.

"I will reduce your holding's taxes by a further seventy percent," Papa was saying. "That should help with affording more food from the coast. I wish I could do more or send supplies, but there's too little to share."

Ilara's heart sank. The ice storm had come so late in the spring. Crops had been destroyed as they were sprouting, and the frozen ground delayed further planting, resulting in failed or delayed harvests. Demand had risen for foods from the oceans, and even with Papa instituting emergency laws regulating prices, as summer turned toward autumn, many struggled to feed their families, let alone stockpile for the winter. They needed trade, but the delegates Papa had sent to the bordering kingdoms of Aedyllan and Kilkreth two months ago had made negligible progress. Ziandel was suffering a drought and couldn't have helped if they'd wanted to.

"I want reports of how the taxes are spent," Papa said. "Within a month, I expect to see evidence that it is being used to aid those who need it most."

Lady Lira bowed. "Of course. House Vellroch understands and thanks you, Your Majesty. Your Highness."

As Papa dismissed Lady Lira, Ilara hid another yawn behind her hand.

"Ilara." Papa laid a hand on top of hers on her smaller throne next to his huge one decorated with carved ivory and gold leaf. Light from the silver and antler candelabras flanking the dais flickered over his worried expression. "You should sleep."

She waved her free hand. "I can hibernate in the winter with the bears. Summer is for staying awake."

Papa's frown indicated he wasn't amused.

"The kingdom has to come first, right?" she asked, quieter.

Papa sighed and drew his hand back. "Right."

The door at the end of the great hall opened, and Steward Dessen approached the dais and bowed. "Your Majesty, Your Highness. The king of Rethalyon has sent an ambassadorial party."

Ilara perked up, but beside her, Papa sucked in a sharp breath.

"No." His fingers tightened on the arms of his throne. "No more foreigners! Tell them—"

"Wait!" Ilara tugged on her papa's sleeve. "It's not the same. Domhnall didn't assert that he was an ambassador, and he came alone, not with a party." She glanced toward Dessen. "You said there was more than one, correct?"

Dessen nodded. "Yes, Your Highness. Four, on horseback with a pack mule. I would guess two guards and a servant accompanying the ambassador, who claims to be Baron Tristan Carbrey, here at the behest of his king, Alexander Tallon of Rethalyon. He claims he was sent to improve trade." Even Dessen's voice took on a hopeful tone.

In her excitement, Ilara forgot her exhaustion. "Papa, we must speak with him."

Papa fiddled with the marriage cuff on his ear. "I don't like it. Wait, this can't be true." His expression hardened. "The king of

Rethalyon is Henry Carbrey, and his son's name is Tristan. Surely a crown prince wouldn't come to us on behalf of a new king. It's preposterous. These imposters must be working with Halkon!"

"To what end?" Ilara raised her hands in a questioning gesture, struggling to be patient with this new, paranoid version of her papa. "He's a sorcerer; why would he send someone else, have them claim to be from Rethalyon, and not know whom they are impersonating? Perhaps there was a coup, and this Alexander Tallon is more amenable to trade."

"And Tristan Carbrey would serve whoever overthrew his father because?"

Ilara shrugged helplessly. "I don't know. Why don't we ask him? Please, Papa. We should at least see him."

"Hm." Papa bit his lip. "Fine. Show them in."

A few moments later, Dessen led four men into the room. Their tunics were different, shorter than Tallander tunics and with upright collars against their necks and trim running down the middle through a line of embroidered fastenings. A light-skinned young man in the finest clothing of the group walked a few paces ahead. That had to be the ambassador, Baron Tristan Carbrey. He was sort of cute, with his messy brown hair, short beard, and strong frame, but he looked like his face had been carved out of unfeeling stone.

Two men trailed after him, knights judging by their swords and leather armor. One had lighter skin, like the ambassador, but he was older and had blond hair tied back and was built like a wrestler. The dark-skinned knight was the tallest of the group and looked reedy beside his companion's bulk. A young man with a sunbeaten tan and simple clothing followed them, likely a servant.

"Your Majesty King Onak, Your Highness Princess Ilara," Dessen bowed. "May I present Baron Tristan Carbrey, ambassador from Rethalyon." He stepped aside, and the ambassador executed a perfect low bow, his men following his example with a bit less precision.

"Rise," Papa said when the men remained bowed, an irritated edge to his voice.

"Thank you for seeing us, Your Excellency, Your Highness." Baron Carbrey inclined his head as he reached into a pouch attached to his belt and withdrew a small scroll. "I—"

"You are *Baron* Tristan Carbrey, ambassador for King *Alexander* of Rethalyon?" Papa asked.

The ambassador faltered, clearly thrown by the interruption. "Yes, Your Excellency."

Ilara lifted a brow at the repeated *Your Excellency*. This ambassador seemed ill-trained in Talland's customs—but if he could increase trade, he could call Papa *Your Grand Exalted Magnificence* for all she cared. Although she'd find it difficult not to laugh.

Papa's fingers drummed against his throne. "What strange things happened in Rethalyon that King Henry's son comes to me as an ambassador for a new king?"

She wanted to chide him for his harsh tone, but it was a fair question.

The baron took a deep breath. "My father abdicated after the miraculous return of my cousin, King Alexander Tallon."

Ilara started. "Your cousin?" The story of the monster prince had made its way to Talland over a decade ago, but she had forgotten the name. "We heard that Henry Carbrey was crowned after his sorcerous nephew turned himself into a monster. I thought King Henry had slain him?"

Papa snorted. "A return from the dead would indeed be miraculous."

"Prince Alexander was not dead, but cursed."

"Cursed?" Papa straightened, and even Ilara caught her breath.

Would Tristan know how to break a curse?

Tristan's eyes widened, his composed countenance fracturing. He thrust forward the scroll. "Your Excellency, my king wrote you a letter detailing Rethalyon's current situation. I believe you should find everything explained in the letter."

Dessen accepted the scroll and offered it to Papa. When he ignored it, Ilara took it herself.

"And why can't *you* tell me?" Papa demanded. "Trying to think of a clever lie for why your Court would crown a boy who had been a monster, simply because he returned? A plausible falsehood to explain why you serve the man who replaced you?"

As she broke open the seal, Ilara eyed the ambassador. He held up his hands in a placating gesture.

"No, Your Excellency. I swore my allegiance to King Alexander, and he saw fit to entrust me with this task. I do as my king commands. There is no scheme or deception." He motioned toward Ilara and the scroll. "Please read the letter, Your Excellency. Then I promise I will answer any questions as I am able." There was a pleading, almost heartbroken note to his voice that undermined the steely expression that slid back over his features.

"I'll hold you to that." Papa took the letter before Ilara had a chance to read beyond *Greetings to Your Majesty, the honorable King Onak of Talland…*

The Rethali knights glanced at each other while Papa read, appearing apprehensive, and Tristan stood stiff as washing that had been left out and frozen. Ilara tried to read the letter, but the angle was too awkward and the handwriting too small. A couple times Papa peered up at Tristan, only to continue reading in silence. Finally, he rolled up the scroll and set it aside where Ilara couldn't reach it, much to her disappointment.

"Forgive me, Baron Carbrey," Papa said. "Your unexpected arrival comes at a trying time, and I hope you'll excuse my misgivings about your honesty. But this is all true?"

"Yes." The corner of Tristan's mouth twisted downward. "At least, I believe so. I don't know what my king wrote, but..." He hesitated, and his gaze lowered. "King Alexander doesn't lie."

"I see," Papa said quietly.

The baron's shoulders drooped, and he didn't raise his eyes. Did something in that letter paint him in a poor light? Ilara found it difficult to believe any king would send someone as an ambassador in whom they didn't have complete faith.

"This love spell you refused to use at your father's order," Papa said. "Why didn't you? Was the princess not attractive?"

Ilara's jaw dropped as she struggled to comprehend what her papa had just said. Her fingers twitched, resisting the inappropriate urge to reach across and snatch up the letter.

Tristan's face reddened. "No, the queen is indeed beautiful. I refused to get what I wanted through dark magic. That choice is why I was pardoned."

"That and defending your cousin."

"Before you think me noble, I was sorely tempted to do otherwise." Tristan grimaced, as if regretting the words. Behind him, the blond knight gave his companion on odd, almost smug look. She wondered what it meant.

"To be tempted and not give in is perhaps more noble than to do right without ever feeling the allure of the wrong." Papa leaned back. "We welcome you into our Great House and look forward to treating with you, Baron Carbrey."

Ilara smiled. Was it too much to wish the Rethalis had a surplus of food they were anxious to be rid of?

The baron bowed again. "Thank you, Your Excellency."

"But for now, we must take our leave," Papa said, disappointing her. "I have a stack of paperwork to address, and my daughter...needs to rest. Dessen, show the ambassador and his men to one of the large guest suites."

"Thank you for your hospitality and welcome, Your Excellency." Tristan bowed again, then looked to Ilara. "Your Highness." He bowed to her, and she returned a smile.

"Come, Ilara." Papa rose and led her out of the hall, leaving their new guests behind. "You were correct," he said as they entered the corridor. "I suppose I should know better than to doubt you by now."

"Do we really want to wait? The sooner we can get a trade agreement—" A yawn cut through her words, forcing her to admit defeat. "All right, perhaps I should sleep. But you could—"

"We mustn't appear too desperate if we want a fair deal," Papa said, but he sounded oddly distracted, as if thinking of something else. She hoped that meant he had other duties he planned to tend to, and not that he was going to shut himself up in his room. Her worry for his mental and emotional wellbeing was bad enough without the House Heads accusing Papa of negligence.

She'd like to see Lord Farune or Lady Alantha deal with everything that Papa did. For all their criticism, she suspected they'd make their own mistakes. How easy it was to judge how another bore a burden one had never been asked to carry themselves.

They stopped at the simple door at the end of the first floor, just before the rear northern stairwell used primarily by the servants. After the fourth night of the curse, Papa had insisted on putting his daughters together in the large, windowless storage room with a locking door. Twice Papa tried to stay with them. Both times, he fell asleep, as did the four guards stationed outside, and the girls awoke dressed and tired.

After that, they'd left the Great House. In their tent a full day's ride away, their guards still fell asleep. Ilara and her sisters had awoken in their own rooms, and Ilara had found a note in her hand that read:

Although Papa returned to his own bedroom, the sisters remained in the storage room. There was some comfort in knowing where her sisters were when she fell asleep and seeing they were safe and together when she woke up.

Papa brushed her hair back over her shoulder, his gaze unfocused. "Your mama would be so proud of you… She'd probably have fixed this already." He tried to smile, but it wavered, and sorrow knotted in Ilara's throat.

He shook his head and kissed her forehead. "I won't let Halkon take you," he murmured. "We'll stop him. I have an idea. Stay strong."

"Always, Papa." Ilara didn't have much choice—if she broke, the House Heads might look to Meelah, and she wouldn't do that to her sister. Even if her papa had done it to her. She gave him a tight hug. "You be strong too, all right?"

"I'm trying." He squeezed her. "For you, I swear I'm trying."

Ilara blinked away tears as they separated. "I know, Papa." She turned to enter the room, then paused. "Might I read the letter from King Alexander?"

"Hm? Oh. Certainly." He handed her the scroll. "Interesting story there, although I suspect King Alexander omitted details. Probably things that reflected poorly on his ambassador."

"Baron Carbrey must have had to make some difficult decisions," Ilara noted. She couldn't imagine the stress of being a crown prince and having the cousin everyone thought was dead return to take his place.

Papa merely nodded. "Try to sleep. I'll see you tomorrow."

In the room, Ilara lit the lantern on her nightstand and changed into the nightclothes a servant had laid out for her. Then she climbed into bed and read King Alexander's letter, entranced by a story of curses, deception, and Tristan's heroism.

Even after she'd doused the lantern, thoughts of Baron Tristan Carbrey kept her awake. She couldn't help but feel for him. After his father's lies and cruelties and the loss of his status and his cousin sending him away—the letter asserted it was because Alexander trusted him, but Ilara suspected it was partly the soft exile of a potential rival—he had to feel so lost and alone.

Perhaps she should talk with Tristan. Maybe he needed someone to listen, like she'd needed Ryn to listen after her mama died. Ilara drifted to sleep, thinking of ways to start a conversation with the ambassador with a face of stone.

12

As Steward Dessen escorted Tristan and his men to a suite on the second floor, he tried to decide if the audience had gone well or poorly. Since they hadn't been thrown out and the steward assured him that the Great House servants would have their things brought up and see to their animals, Tristan decided to count it as a success.

The sitting room of their new living quarters had a couple cushioned armchairs and a small couch arranged around a fireplace on the left side from the entrance. On the right, a table was set with four chairs. Past the table and chairs, a door led to a large bedroom with two wardrobes and two four-poster beds covered in woolen blankets and furs, with a nightstand between them. Masarik flopped onto a bed with a contented groan.

"Oh, this is excellent. I suspect I'm going to like it here."

Tristan frowned but continued on as Sharland claimed the other bed. A door on the opposite side of the room, near the fireplace, opened into a cramped washroom with an empty tub. The last door, directly across from the entrance to the suite, led into a chamber with one large wardrobe, a vanity with a stool, and a four-poster bed that was bigger than the other two. All the rooms were decorated with carvings and tapestries of animals.

Another, smaller door caught his attention on the right wall of the main guestroom. It revealed an undecorated room just large enough to accommodate a small bed and compact dresser of drawers. A second door opened to a narrow passageway that connected to the hallway.

"Fournier," Tristan called, feeling a little guilty about the disparity in comfort levels even though it was perfectly normal. "I found your room."

"My room?" Fournier hurried through the master bedroom, and his face fell when he peered into the servant's chamber. "Well, good. This will be convenient. And cozy."

Tristan appreciated the young man's determined optimism. "Probably smaller than you were expecting."

His manservant shrugged. "It has a door and isn't shared. That's more privacy than I've ever had."

Tristan didn't know how to respond to that, so he just nodded.

Unsure what to do with himself, Tristan wandered around his new accommodations. He considered closing the bedroom door, then recalled servants would be bringing his things soon. Yet he didn't want to hear whatever criticism Masarik doubtless had of his performance in front of the king and crown princess.

He hadn't expected Princess Ilara to be in the throne room. She hadn't spoken much, but he assumed she must be involved in Talland's rule to warrant having a place at her father's side. Which made sense, as females had full succession rights in Talland, something Henry had mocked as folly, as he believed women were too weak to rule. But even as crown prince, Tristan had never held such an honored place. He'd stood next to his father or sat on a throne on a lower dais, never at Henry's side.

A knock on the main entrance drew his attention. Before he had a chance to respond, Fournier rushed past, practically tripping over his own feet.

"I've got it, my lord!"

It was the servants delivering their luggage. Fournier insisted on unpacking Tristan's trunk and arranging everything in the wardrobe. Tristan stood nearby, a useless overseer with little reason to be there, but nowhere else to be.

Another knock came, and Fournier dropped a shirt to race to the door. Tristan was going to need to talk to him about being a little more subdued so he didn't hurt himself or someone else.

The royal steward was back. "The king requests your presence, Baron Carbrey."

"Of course." Tristan exited his room, and Masarik and Allyre emerged from theirs as well. He caught a glimpse of chaos from what looked like Masarik's clothing bursting out of his trunk.

Steward Dessen held up a hand. "The ambassador only, if you please. You need not fear; my king only wishes to speak with your lord."

Masarik and Allyre appeared displeased, but at Tristan's nod, they returned to their room. Tristan followed the steward down the stairs to the corridor at the rear of the first floor of the Great House. A lone guard was stationed outside a door, and the steward pulled that door open and motioned Tristan inside. Dessen closed the door, leaving Tristan alone with the Tallander king in a small audience chamber.

King Onak sat in a simple throne between the door to the corridor and one Tristan guessed led to the main hall. The sleeve of his moss-colored tunic had ridden up, and black geometric tattoos on his right wrist peeked out. Tristan knew the Tallanders got ritualistic tattoos, but it surprised him that their king did as well. His dark hair was drawn back in a thick braid beneath his modest crown, and a little gold cuff glinted on the middle of the curve of his right ear.

Tristan bowed briefly, trying to ignore his apprehension. "How may I be of service, Your Excellency?"

The king watched him in silence for a long moment, his expression calculating in a way that was too familiar, too much like Henry. Tristan's heart sank down to his boots. At last, Onak spoke.

"When you arrived, I thought it poor timing, Baron Carbrey. Although I'm eager to increase trade with Rethalyon, I have more immediate concerns at present. In fact, I was going to turn you away, but Ilara insisted we speak with you."

A quick blink was the only sign of surprise Tristan allowed. Princess Ilara held such sway over her father? Onak must think his daughter more capable than Henry had ever thought Tristan to be. Maybe Ilara was the one to impress, not Onak.

The king sighed. "If you had come to me a couple weeks ago with tales of curses and spells, I might have scoffed. But now…"

Onak rubbed the side of his face and took a deep breath, clearly stalling. "As I'm sure you know, it is…difficult for a man, much less a king, to admit to weakness or failure."

Tristan frowned. "I sympathize, but I don't understand."

"My daughters are in danger." He leaned back, his eyes heavy with fatigue. "I don't know how to save them. But I believe you can help."

In danger? Help? Tension crept into Tristan's shoulders. What had he walked into?

"About two weeks ago, a man came to the palace. He claimed to be Earl Domhnall Halkon of Kilkreth. But the next day, he asked me for Ilara's hand. I refused." The king closed his eyes and swallowed hard. "Now my daughters are cursed."

Tristan's mouth hung open, fear lancing through his heart. More dark magic was *not* what he needed.

"Every night since, my daughters vanish from their room and return at dawn, recalling nothing of the night except blurs of color, music, and memories of indistinct faces. Every morning they are so exhausted they sleep most of the day."

Strange, Ilara had seemed fine…although, thinking back on it, she'd had dark circles under her eyes and her father had mentioned she needed to rest. And this curse stole her memories? That was worse than the curse that stole his voice. The poor girl.

Misery etched into Onak's face. "The guards cannot stay awake at night. Even I… I failed. Every night, my daughters are taken. I sent them miles away, but Halkon still took them. They're returned uninjured, but we don't know where they go or what happens to them." He looked at Tristan imploringly. "You're a man of honor and know about dark magic. I now believe your timing is fate. Please. Help me. Help my daughters."

Then this was the true reason Onak had allowed Tristan to stay—for a task he couldn't possibly hope to accomplish? He pulled on the edge of his tunic. "I wish I could help, but I can't break my own…condition, Your Excellency."

The king frowned. "You know someone who has broken a curse. You even know someone who has *cast* curses and have handled and experienced magic yourself."

"I fear you misunderstood. I'm not an expert in magic—"

"Two weeks, do you understand? Two weeks my daughters have been in that fiend's clutches; two weeks of worry while I don't know what he does—" Onak's voice cracked. "I can't give Ilara to such a vile man or grant a wicked sorcerer the power of being prince consort, but neither can I continue to fail to protect them. A new, outside perspective could help."

"I'm truly sorry, Your Excellency." Tristan meant it, too. The pain and love in the king's expression was so unlike Henry, his devotion to his children so clear it sent a jealous pang through Tristan. The royal family had his sympathy, but that would do them no good. "I was sent to negotiate trade, not fight sorcerers."

"Then help me, and we will discuss trade. Aid us, and Talland will be Rethalyon's loyal ally."

Tristan didn't trust the growing desperation in the king's eyes. "What if I can't?"

"Free my daughters or kill this—this sorcerer, or whatever he is, and we will work together." Onak's expression became hard as granite. "Fail, and there will be no agreements."

This couldn't be happening. He couldn't return to Alex with nothing. Yet he also couldn't break a curse and had no wish to tangle with a sorcerer. He wouldn't risk death for the sake of a barony and a scrap of praise from Alex, regardless of how his conscience whispered that maybe he should help. It didn't matter if it would be the right thing. He had no skills or insight to offer, and he wasn't the hero. If Masarik were there, he'd tell Onak that he shouldn't want Tristan's help.

He focused on keeping his tone level. "If this is your requirement for trade, I may as well return to Rethalyon now."

"My daughters are suffering, my entire house and kingdom are suffering, and you refuse to help? Perhaps you are not as honorable as I thought."

A twinge of guilt made him hesitate, but he was only human, and not even a respectable one. "Why would I succeed where you have failed? There's nothing I can do." His shame deepened, but that didn't make the words any less true. "I thank you for your hospitality, but my men and I will return to Rethalyon."

He bowed. Surely Alex would understand Onak was unreasonable, and Tristan didn't have a chance.

"Wait!" Onak reached toward him, hesitation marking his features—then his jaw clenched as a cold look settled in his eyes. Silently, he stood and strode forward, stopping just in front of Tristan.

Dread slithered down Tristan's spine, but he forced himself to stand his ground. If the king hit him, especially without witnesses, Tristan couldn't defend himself any more than he could against his father. Not without condemning himself to death. He eyed the two exits, but the guards outside would doubtless stop him if he tried to run.

"I could have you executed."

Tristan's legs nearly gave out beneath him. "Your Excellency?" He hated the way his voice cracked.

"I will do anything to give my daughters a chance. Do you understand?" The king's words were more anguished than irate. "I believe you're a chance. You and your men are foreigners, and you have experience with magic and bear a curse already—perhaps that will prevent Halkon's curse from affecting you. Or perhaps you will discover something we missed."

Onak somehow managed to look down his nose at Tristan despite being shorter. "You will help my daughters, and you will not leave the Great House's lands without my permission, or I will have you hunted down and executed."

It took a moment for Tristan to find his voice. "I'm an ambassador on an official visit sent by my king—"

"A king who doesn't know what to do with you." The side of Onak's mouth twisted up, mocking him. "Honorable you may be, trustworthy enough that your cousin didn't have you executed or exiled, but he doesn't want you in his court, or he wouldn't have sent you two kingdoms away. Tell me, Tristan Carbrey, would a young king barely in possession of his crown be able to convince your Court of Lords to care about a potential rival who was killed two kingdoms away for espionage and conspiracy against Talland's monarch?"

Tristan worked his throat, trying to respond, but his jaw had locked in place. Espionage was an unforgiveable offense from an ambassador. And Alex had already come close to exiling him and mentioned the Court didn't trust him. Who would defend him? Some might dismiss the execution as overdue, anyway.

"I didn't think so." Onak didn't break eye contact. "You will put all of your energy into saving my daughters. Understood?"

Tristan swallowed. "Yes, Your Excellency."

"Good." Onak returned to his throne and sank into it like he had no strength left. "Tonight, you and your knights will guard my daughters. They're staying in a locked room on the first floor. You will join my guards outside."

What kind of sorcerer could break three girls out of a locked, guarded room without being seen? If Tristan and his knights stayed awake, he doubted they could fight such a man. Hopefully they would sleep, and the king would realize they were powerless and recant his threat.

Tristan gripped his hands behind his back to hide their trembling. He needed Onak to think he was trying long enough to stay alive. "I will rest, then, so I can be alert tonight."

"I'll have Dessen fetch you just before dusk. Oh, and Carbrey—not a word of this to anyone." Onak flicked his fingers toward the door without looking at him. "You may go."

Tristan bowed again, glad for years of practice hiding his emotions and holding his tongue.

He had not come to Talland to be executed.

13

Tristan dragged his feet as he followed a young male servant back to his quarters. He wasn't sure if the "this" in "not a word of this to anyone" meant the sorcerer and curse or who they were guarding or the threat of execution, so he decided not to mention any of those things. Probably for the best. He didn't need Masarik mutinying on the first day.

When he entered their accommodations, Sharland was on the couch, reading a book bound in faded red leather. He looked up as Tristan walked toward his suite.

"Everything all right, my lord?"

Masarik appeared in the doorway to the knights' room. "The king made it sound like he wasn't discussing business today."

Tristan turned away from his open bedroom door. "It was…not standard business. Everyone should take a nap," he added unhappily. "We're not sleeping tonight."

"Excuse me?" Masarik's blocky face screwed up in a look of distaste.

Sharland slowly closed his book. "We're…what?"

"Why, my lord?" Fournier asked as he emerged from the main bedroom.

"Well…not you, Fournier. We're keeping watch in a hallway over night as a…favor to King Onak. Make sure no one enters or exits a room; stop anyone who tries."

If only it were as simple as that.

"Guard duty, my lord?" Sharland tilted his head. "How peculiar."

Masarik grunted. "What are we guarding? And why ask an ambassador to do a soldier's duty? Peculiar doesn't start to cover it."

Tristan was too overwhelmed to bother with reminding Masarik to mind his manners. "It's complicated. And…something precious. Just know it's vital no one gets in or out and is stopped if they attempt it."

"Or out…" Sharland tapped his forefinger on his chin. "So we're guarding people?"

Tristan winced. "Don't ask questions, all right? The king is…volatile. You want to get me back to Rethalyon? Then help me with this."

Masarik barked a laugh. "Please don't tell me we've been here all of an hour and you've already provoked the man you should be ingratiating yourself with. Worst. Ambassador. Ever." He retired to his chamber, still chuckling to himself.

Heat covered Tristan's face. He stopped himself from slamming his bedroom door. Childish tantrums would not improve Masarik's opinion of him. Why he should care what Masarik thought, he didn't know, but he did.

He hadn't failed as an ambassador. Had he? It wasn't his fault some flaming sorcerer had shown up before him and made his job more difficult than it had any right to be. He couldn't be blamed for Onak being unreasonable. And surely, once the king realized he wasn't lying and couldn't break the curse, he'd let them go.

Tristan slumped on the bed and rubbed the side of his face. He should trim his beard. It was getting long and ragged.

In another life, he would be in Rethalyon with Raelyn in his arms… He pushed that thought away. She was happy with Alex, and Alex was gentle and kind and everything Raelyn deserved. Everything Tristan wasn't. Just like Henry had always said.

He kicked off his boots and lay down, but his mind wouldn't be silent.

Could he be those things? Gentle and kind? He could try. Henry had raised him to be forbidding, controlling, and to show no weakness or mercy. Tristan had attempted to please his father, had locked away the heart a king wasn't supposed to have. But Henry had revealed himself to be a monster—cruel, not strong, with the blood of his own family on his hands. Tristan had started down the same path. Raelyn seemed to think he could choose a different route.

But Tristan had come face to face with his own darkness, and it scared him.

Was there a way back for someone who had fallen as far as he had?

His sleep was troubled, haunted by Raelyn's tears, Lucas's corpse, and Alex's screams.

Fournier woke him when servants delivered food for their dinner. Tristan ate with the others in the sitting room, but he ignored their conversation, because he had latched onto a desperate hope.

Maybe this was his chance at redemption. If he somehow *could* save Princess Ilara and her two sisters, if he could help instead of hurt, he would prove to himself he was more than the man Henry had molded him into. Then perhaps Alex and Raelyn and even Masarik would respect him. Onak might send a letter commending him, and Alex would finally trust him.

Raelyn was right. He was a man of action. And without knowing it, she'd offered him exactly what he lacked: a new purpose.

Aid the princesses, thereby earning Onak's favor and avoiding execution while proving he could be good. Secure renewed trade with Talland. When he returned to Rethalyon, he would merit walking into the palace with his head held high.

All he needed to do was defy a curse. And maybe fight a sorcerer.

No problem.

Tristan, Sharland, and Masarik followed Dessen to the princesses' door shortly before dusk. Two Tallander royal guards already stood across from the room. After Dessen left, the Tallanders sat down with their backs against the wall, their demeanor as relaxed as if they were enjoying after-dinner drinks. Maybe they'd given up. No wonder Onak was desperate. Tristan took up post standing directly in front of the door, struggling to hold on to his feeble dream he could do this and earn his redemption.

"So." Masarik leaned against the edge of the doorframe and nodded at the Tallanders. "My lord is being tightlipped. What can we expect?"

One of the guards snorted. "I recommend you sit down. Otherwise, when dark falls, you fall, and you'll get a nasty bruise somewhere."

"Whatever do you mean?" Sharland cast a suspicious look at Tristan as he crossed to the other side of the doorway.

The second guard scowled. "Everyone falls asleep. Some guards chewed rilla leaves for the stimulating properties; didn't help. The Great House and its lands are cursed. There's no staying awake, no stopping the princesses from vanishing. It's a fool's errand the king has given you." He glanced down the corridor toward a narrow window where the fading light had nearly disappeared. "You should sit down."

Masarik straightened. "Hold on. Cursed? Princesses?" He

spun on Tristan. "What in a thousand hills have you gotten us…"
He wobbled, his brow furrowing. "Into?"

"Don't fall asleep!" Tristan wedged himself into the doorframe as his vision went blurry, pushing against the wood with all his might. His head grew heavy, and his limbs turned to lead. The Tallander guards already slumbered.

"What is…" Sharland sagged, then collapsed to the floor.

"We have to…to…" Tristan couldn't keep his eyes open. "Have to…stay…" He slipped down the door as he lost consciousness.

14

$\mathcal{P}$astries of every kind, some flaky, some dripping with icing, and all looking delectable, were piled high on a table set a short distance from the dancers occupying the center of the meadow. Bowls overflowed with a dazzling variety of gold and silver fruit.

A little overwhelmed by all the choices, Ilara absently played with the fabric of her dress. She looked down in surprise at the slippery material. The light gown she wore of imported blush-pink silk had trailing sleeves and a large, flowy skirt with several layers. She didn't have any recollection of seeing it before, or anything in its style. Unease crawled over her skin.

She forced herself to pick up a plate, frowning at the beautifully carved floral pattern on the dish. Why were the furniture and plates all normal wood if the surrounding trees were silver and gold?

The more she considered her surroundings, the more the charm of the music and beauty of the full moon faded. Just then, a shadow fell over her.

"Princess Ilara." Domhnall took the empty plate and set it aside. "May I have this dance?"

Ilara regarded his outstretched palm as one would a baby ice serpent, although she couldn't understand why she mistrusted him. "I'm actually a bit tired—"

"Ilara. Dance with me."

She took his hand, her misgivings forgotten as he bestowed a brilliant smile on her. They spun across the meadow, Domhnall expertly leading her between other couples.

"I apologize for ignoring you," he said. "My people always seem to have some squabble for me to judge or some problem that requires my power. Sometimes ruling is tiring, don't you agree?"

Nodding seemed like the appropriate response, so that's what Ilara did, but it made her dizzy.

"Perhaps with someone by your side, the weight of leadership is easier to bear." Domhnall leaned down, and her heart raced as his lips brushed her cheek. "I'd like to have you by my side. Marry me."

Ilara giggled to mask her confusion. "Oh…I don't know—"

To her shock, Domhnall snarled. His fingers dug into her ribs for a moment before slackening, but it was enough. Her mind jolted, and all of her memories rushed back.

This was the worst part. The moments when she broke free and could remember everything, only to have him steal her mental clarity again and leave her grasping at smoke when she awakened in her room in the morning.

"My answer is the same." She twisted out of his arms. "No."

"Your unbending will grates on my nerves and tests my patience, Ilara." Domhnall looked down at her, his expression placid, but his emerald eyes full of rage. "I've nearly had my fill of this game, and you won't enjoy the more…cruel rules of the next round."

"You…you won't hurt me." She gulped. "You can't. You have a deal."

"As I told you before, if you don't marry me, I lose regardless. That can't happen. I'm running out of time!" He ran a finger down her jaw, and she jerked her head away with a sound of disgust. "I need our marriage to make Talland rightfully mine, and soon."

"Talland isn't mine, it's..." Realization brushed icy fingers down her spine. "You mean to kill my papa after the wedding."

"Not necessarily. After we're wed, your father can abdicate. Or I can kill him."

Ilara's breath shuddered in her lungs. "You're insane."

"Me?" The sorcerer's expression turned gloating. "You're the one who can't remember what she does at night."

Anger suffused her face. "You—you sorcerous villain!"

"Sorcery?" Domhnall laughed and conjured a silver pear. "How small-minded. Now. Give me your answer. Will you marry me?"

"No."

He gave a dramatic, exasperated sigh. "Soon, either you or Onak will break, and you will take your vows. I will not be denied. So why don't we skip the unpleasantness and get to the part where we're happily wed and helping each other rule?"

"How about you—" As he shoved the pear into her open mouth, her last clear thought was cursing herself for falling for that trick again.

Ilara awoke in the windowless bedroom, vague indignation swirling in her chest. Her sisters stood at her sides, Kiri holding a flickering torch.

The girls stared at each other. As early morning sunlight began to fill the hall and spill into their room through the open doorway, Ilara noticed the fading sweetness in her mouth, the strange gown she was wearing, the shoes on her aching feet, her exhaustion, and the body sprawled on the threshold. Probably an unfortunate guard.

Kiri sniffled, then sobbed.

"It's all right, we're home." Meelah put her arm around Kiri's shoulders and drew her in close.

"I'm tired of this!" Kiri threw down the torch, and it didn't just extinguish—it vanished midair. Her crying echoed in the dark room. "I'm so tired of this!"

Meelah made calming noises. "Hush, it's all right. Are you hurt?"

"I want it to stop!" Kiri hiccupped.

"I know," Meelah soothed. "I know."

Ilara had no words of comfort to offer. She pulled off her shoes, wincing at the blister on the ball of her right foot. "Augh!" She turned from Kiri and Meelah and threw the shoes with all her might and frustration. They hit the wall with a slap and fell to the wood floor.

The figure in the doorway bolted upright with a groan. He hunched over, moaning, then went rigid before scrambling to his feet. "Princesses…" The man's voice sounded vaguely familiar. He rushed to the nightstand and lit the lamp, then whirled toward them, nearly losing his balance.

It was Tristan, the former crown prince from Rethalyon. His hair stuck out at odd angles. His tunic was wrinkled and twisted around his torso, and drool had dried in his short beard. He took them in, wide-eyed and pale.

Ilara frowned. "What are you doing here?"

Tristan's shoulders hunched. "His Excellency asked me to guard you. He told me about…all this. He thought perhaps we could help or wouldn't be affected. But…I'm sorry, Your Highness." He rubbed his chest and winced.

"That's very generous of you to agree to help," Ilara noted. He looked so guilty, she felt sorry for him. "My father fell asleep, too, when he tried. It's not your fault."

"Do you recall anything that happened?" He kept rubbing at his torso. "I feel like I got hit in the chest," he muttered.

He had been laid out blocking the entryway... She winced. Someone must have stepped on him. She hoped it hadn't been her.

Kiri rubbed at her eyes. "No, we never remember... Who are you?"

"Oh. Baron Tristan Carbrey, ambassador from Rethalyon." He bowed, then placed the lantern on the table. Guards and Tristan's knights peered inside.

"We definitely danced." Ilara regretted how much bite her words had, especially when Tristan flinched at her tone. She wasn't angry with him, but she *was* angry. "Same thing as always. Music, food, dancing, glimpses of silver and gold, and Domhnall moon-cursed Halkon with his stupid face." If she'd had anything in hand, she would have thrown it.

"I can't recall anything more than that, either." Meelah frowned. "I don't really even remember Halkon."

"I *hate* Halkon!" Kiri crossed her arms and scowled. "My head hurts and my feet hurt, and I just want to sleep!"

Ilara went to her baby sister and gave her a quick embrace and kissed her forehead. "Go lie down. I'll send for our nightgowns."

Tristan cleared his throat. "May I see your shoes and dresses, after you're changed?" He reddened at Ilara's confused look. "To inspect. Maybe there's some hint of where you've been..." He shrugged.

Ilara nodded, weariness overtaking her. "Of course. Oh, and actually"—she motioned at her dress—"this isn't mine. I haven't seen it before. Domhnall must have given it to me." Hopefully he'd let her change in privacy. She liked to think even Domhnall's magic couldn't compel her otherwise, but she didn't remember enough of the night to know.

She wished she could talk to Tristan more, but she needed to sleep first. Maybe today, instead of helping Papa, she would visit Tristan.

15

Despite knowing the task had been impossible, shame burned in Tristan's chest as he turned to leave, only to find the door blocked by Masarik, Sharland, and the two Tallander guards.

"You." He pointed at a guard, glad for something to distract him from his failure. "Go find someone to bring the princesses their nightgowns. The rest of you get out of the way."

The guard appeared momentarily surprised before he darted down the hall. The other three men pulled back, and Tristan headed out.

"I could have done that," Ilara said softly.

He turned back to her, ducking his head. "I just…" He floundered. "You look tired."

She looked good, too. Ilara was short, her build full, with round hips and soft edges. Flames, that pink was an attractive color on her. He banished that thought. No way was he going to muck up this ambassadorship further by flirting with the heir to Talland's throne. *But mucking things up is the only thing you're good at,* Henry's voice accused.

"Are you all right?"

Tristan started. "Hm? Sorry, I was…thinking."

Ilara lifted a brow. "While staring at me? I'm not sure I want to know what you were thinking."

Someone snickered in the hallway.

"No!" He tugged on his collar. "I was thinking about my father, actually." Why did he say that? Not strange at all, and now the younger princesses were looking at him like he was crazy. "Sorry. I'm going."

Ilara's face softened. "I'd like to hear your story." She yawned. "But I'm afraid I'm about to fall asleep on my feet." She sat on her bed, and Tristan bowed and left, shutting the door after him.

"Staring at the princess made you think of…your father." Masarik rolled his eyes. "Really."

"I don't have to explain myself to you, Sir Masarik."

Masarik frowned but shut up.

"What happened?" King Onak hurried down the hall, dressed in a fur-trimmed robe and slippers. "Did you see anything? Did you…" He glanced over them from head to toe as he stopped in front of them. "You fell asleep."

"I'm sorry, Your Excellency. I tried—"

"Well think of something!" Onak moved past them and entered his daughters' room, closing the door behind him.

The remaining Tallander guard headed away down the hall.

"Wait!" Tristan straightened. "Where are you going?"

The guard—the frowny one—shrugged. "The king has stopped questioning us. He always gets the same answer. I'm going to get breakfast." He turned and walked away.

Tristan rubbed at his chest, which had started aching again. "I think someone stepped on me… I woke up on the threshold and my chest feels bruised." He tried to stretch and winced.

"Serves you right." Masarik folded his muscular arms. "You need to explain. Now."

Sharland glanced at Masarik, his expression revealing nothing. "I understand you might not be at liberty to disclose everything King Onak told you, my lord," he said slowly, "but I think we should have been alerted about a possible curse and that we were protecting the princesses. Or supposed to be." He ruffled his hair. "We decidedly failed. No offense, my lord, we all did."

"I know—"

The princesses' door opened, and Onak stepped out. "A word, Baron Carbrey."

Tristan nodded, a lump forming in his throat. He told Masarik and Sharland he would meet them in their quarters, then followed the king down to a modest sitting room with a couple of armchairs and a small fire burning in the undecorated fireplace. At least it wasn't a throne room. Surely Onak wouldn't punish him for his failure in such a casual setting.

Onak sat down in one armchair and motioned to the other. After hesitating, Tristan sat as well.

"What happened, Baron Carbrey?"

"I'm sorry, Your Excellency; I truly tried, but…I fell asleep." His face burned, and not from the meager heat of the fire.

Onak sighed. "It was too much to hope you would be unaffected, I suppose. And this morning?"

Did that mean the king was realizing he had asked the impossible?

"The door was open when a sound awoke me," he continued, "and I was sprawled across the threshold. The princesses had already returned."

"Do you have a plan going forward?"

Tristan's hope that Onak would change his mind was dashed, but he forced his disappointment not to show. "I'm going to inspect the princesses' clothes to see if I can find any hints of where they've been."

Onak grunted. "If you can ascertain something more than *outside* and *there was food and wine* I'll be impressed. What else?"

"I'll consider ways to stay awake tonight. Unless Your

Excellency believes me now that there is nothing I can do and wishes to remove this requirement—"

"No. Although I'd anticipated you'd have better insight than this." The king rubbed his forehead. "I'll speak with you again tomorrow. If you've made progress by then, we will discuss trade. You may go."

Tristan bowed, then fled the little room. Once down the corridor, he stopped and rested his hot forehead against the cool wood of a wall. How was he going to make progress? Maybe he just needed to be better rested. Eat earlier so he would have energy and not have any post-meal sleepiness.

Who was he kidding? The Great House was cursed. Why would he be able to beat that curse any more than the one that threatened to suffocate him if he criticized his father?

"Baron Carbrey?" A Tallander woman with gray hair pulled into a tight weave of braids away from her plump face peered up at him. A servant, judging by her neat but simple brown dress. "Are you lost, my lord?"

"I…" He could probably find his way, but this would be faster. "A bit. Do you know where I've been quartered?"

"Of course, my lord."

The old woman led him down the corridor, up a flight of stairs, and down another hallway to his rooms. Sharland, Masarik, and Fournier were sitting around the table in the sitting room, eating eggs and toast. Tristan slumped into the remaining chair between Fournier and Sharland, holding up a hand to silence Masarik.

"Let me eat, all right?"

Masarik grunted. The moment the food was gone, Masarik slammed a palm on the table, making the ceramic plates rattle. "Explain. Everything. Now."

After everything else, Tristan had no patience for Masarik's attitude. He fixed the knight with a cool stare, the unperturbed look of authority that Henry had forced him to perfect. "Do you have a complaint, *Sir* Masarik?" He leaned forward and rested his forearm on the table. "Because I do, *Sir* Masarik. I've been lenient. But you are bordering on insubordination, which—"

"*There's* the prince."

"I'm not a prince."

Masarik glared. "You high-ranking nobles are all the same, demanding respect you never earned and—"

"However," Tristan interrupted, working to keep his tone level, "I am a baron, I am the leader of this mission as appointed by our king, and I'm your superior, and you—"

"Oh, I can think of plenty of ways I'm superior to you!"

Angry words spilled out before Tristan could stop them. "I should flog you for your impertinence." It was what Henry would have said, but he couldn't take the words back. He didn't know how to be both commanding and good.

Fournier cowered back in his chair, and Tristan's self-loathing grew.

Masarik's jaw dropped, then he sneered. "I—"

Sharland cleared his throat, disappointment plain on his face. "May I have a word with you in private, my lord?"

"Fine." Tristan stomped to his room, not waiting to see if Sharland followed. He crossed to the narrow window, irrationally angry at it for being distorted so he couldn't see through it clearly.

The door clicked, but he didn't turn around. "I'm not going to do it," he muttered. His conscience couldn't bear any more innocent blood on his hands.

For a moment it was so silent, Tristan wondered if Sharland was actually in the room. But then the knight spoke.

"What did King Onak say, my lord?"

Tristan braced a hand against the wall and leaned his forehead on the glass. It was colder than he'd expected it to be, but it helped clear his mind. "He asks the impossible. No, he demands it. I am…I can't…" His throat closed up.

How could he admit that there was nothing but failure in his past and nothing but failure waiting for him? That he had failed as a fiancé, as a cousin, a son, a prince, and a subject, was failing as an ambassador and had failed as a liege in his words to Sir Masarik; that he was failing at being the person he wanted to be? He'd sooner die than admit aloud all the shame he carried like a millstone about his neck.

"Whatever you're not saying," Sharland said slowly, "burying it will only make it worse. If you're holding onto some…difficult feelings…holding them inside only gives them power over you. It's like closing the skin over an infected wound without cleaning it and draining the infection. It will only fester. I told you I'm a good listener, my lord. I would listen if you would speak."

"You'd think less of me. You all would."

"I'm not sure Masarik can think less of you," Sharland said simply. "But I won't. I apologize for overhearing, but the queen was right when she told you that you're lashing out because you're hurting. But you can't heal your hurt by hiding your wound and biting anyone who tries to look at it."

"Why do you care?" Tristan asked bitterly.

"Besides the fact that you snarling like a wounded animal affects me and my friends? I've seen hints that you want to be better, Baron Carbrey, to do better. I'm trying to help you. My father always told me secret shame makes you defensive and angry or afraid. It holds you captive in your silence."

Tristan turned around sharply. "What do you want from me? Do you want me to admit what a pathetic failure I am? Will that make you happy?"

Sharland's lips pinched, his expression sad. "Very well. You aren't ready yet. But with all due respect, my lord, you owe Masarik an apology. And I think we deserve an explanation of what happened last night and why."

He couldn't argue with that, but the words *you're right* stuck behind his tongue. So he nodded and gestured toward the door. They returned to the sitting room. Fournier and Masarik still sat at the table, Fournier staring at his lap and Masarik scowling with his arms crossed. They both looked up, watching his approach.

Fournier's expression was guarded, the look of admiration he usually wore dimmed. Tristan hated it, even while he thought it was probably a good thing Fournier realized he was tarnished, not the shining knight the servant had built him up to be.

Masarik watched him, a look in his eyes like he was waiting for Tristan to do something rash and cruel. Sharland retook his own seat next to Masarik. Tristan hesitated before sitting down as well.

It took him a couple tries to speak. "Sir Masarik."

Masarik jutted his chin, glaring at Tristan down his nose.

"I can think of several ways you're superior to me as well," Tristan admitted. "And I'm...sorry."

Masarik jolted.

Tristan forged on, the hardest part complete. "I never should have spoken in anger, and I apologize for not treating you with the respect you deserve. I'm not asking you to respect me as a man, but as King Alexander's ambassador and baron. Your disregard for my authority will not make a favorable impression on the Tallanders should they overhear you. Your purpose is to get me back to Rethalyon alive and in one piece. I can't return until I've done my job, and your lack of respect could very well make that more difficult. I want to treat you with the respect due a knight of Rethalyon and a man appointed by our king to aid me in this mission. I'm asking that you extend me the same courtesy and respect me as a baron of Rethalyon."

Masarik's chair creaked as he leaned back. Sharland nodded, and for a moment, something like approval pulled at his mouth— or maybe Tristan had imagined it. Fournier looked at Tristan thoughtfully.

Finally, Masarik gave a curt nod. "Maybe there's more to you than I thought, Baron."

Tristan tried to keep his relief and mild surprise at the honorific off his face but didn't know if he'd succeeded. "And you're right. You all deserve an explanation." He quickly summarized what Onak had told him about the sorcerer and the curse.

"And you agreed we would stand guard last night because…why, my lord?" Sharland tilted his head.

Tristan stared down at the table. "Because King Onak has made moving forward with any talk of trade between our kingdoms conditional on saving his daughters."

For far too long, no one spoke. Masarik broke the tense silence with a curse. "Well, then. I'm asking for an 'unexpected sorcery' bonus payment when we get home." He shoved away from the table and stood. "I'm going for a walk. And maybe to find something to hit with my sword." He did a sort of half bow. "If that's all right, my lord."

"Stay out of trouble with the Tallanders, be respectful, and be back here before sunset. We're going to try again." As Masarik started out, Tristan added, "Thank you, Sir Masarik."

"Right. Yes." Masarik shook his head and left.

Sharland leaned his elbows on the table. "You surprised me. You're learning."

"Learning what?" Tristan asked irritably as Fournier quietly gathered the remainders of breakfast onto a tray. "Learning how to handle him?"

"Learning who you are, my lord. Respectfully, you've seemed…lost. Swinging wildly from pride to self-loathing as you wrestle with who you want to be. I think you're starting to find your footing after struggling to keep your head above water for a while now. But it won't last if you don't share what troubles you."

Tristan stared the knight down, uncomfortable with the accuracy of the insight. "Don't make me lecture you on respect now, Sir Sharland."

Sharland smiled, and that rankled. "I mean no disrespect, my lord. Let me know when you're ready to talk."

Tristan looked away, unsure how to respond.

After a long moment, Sharland spoke again. "If you don't mind, I would like to get out for a bit as well. Go for a jog. I'd be back by midday at the latest."

"Of course."

Sharland bowed and departed. Tristan looked to Fournier, who had finished arranging the dishes from breakfast into a neat pile for the palace servants to clear away.

"Is there anything you would like to do? I don't need anything from you; you can have the day off."

Fournier blinked. "I…actually, my lord… I thought maybe I could talk to the servants, gather information? Maybe they know something that might help you, and they might be more likely to talk to me than you."

"Really?" Tristan rubbed his beard. "I mean, that's an excellent idea. I just hadn't expected…why?"

"You said you have to help them to accomplish your mission, and I'm here to help you." The manservant fidgeted. "And I get restless without something to do."

"Oh." Tristan tapped his fingers against his thigh. "Sure, go ahead. Just…don't cause trouble. Back out if anyone seems on edge and don't stay anywhere you're not welcome."

"Of course, my lord. Don't worry, my lord; I won't get you in trouble!" Fournier bowed, a bit overenthusiastically.

Tristan sighed. "I don't want *you* getting in trouble, Fournier. Not everything is about me," he added drily.

Fournier reddened. "Yes—no—um… I'm going to go now. My lord." He bowed again and scurried out.

Alone in the silent room, Tristan slid down in his chair, curling in on himself. Sharland was right, but he hadn't the faintest idea how to stop drifting between defensive pride and hating himself. Probably lose the pride, since at least the self-loathing was warranted.

Shame holds you captive in your silence.

Maybe he should talk to Sharland. Maybe, somehow, it would help.

Someone knocked. With all his men gone, Tristan realized he had to answer it himself, and he pushed out of his chair with only a little grumpiness.

16

$\mathcal{T}$hree servant women stood in the corridor, their arms full of colorful fabric.

"Baron Carbrey requested the princesses' clothing be brought to him for inspection?" the one in front said.

Tristan stepped aside, holding the door open. "Yes, please place them inside."

The women laid the dresses out on the couch and armchair and the princesses' shoes on the floor nearby, then left with small curtsies.

He surveyed the gowns, lingering on Ilara's pink one. His heart quickened as he recalled how she'd looked in it, so he turned to Princess Kiri's bright blue dress, which was in a more typical Tallander style of wool and linen, the brightly dyed colors a mark of their wealth.

What did he even hope to find? A miracle, maybe. He examined the blue dress, working from the bottom of the skirts up. On the wrist of the right sleeve, his fingers touched something sticky. "Eugh." He drew his hand away with a grimace, then forced himself to inspect closer.

Some clear liquid had dripped down and soaked into the sleeve. He sniffed it—pleasantly sweet, like…pear? Quite a lot of juice, too, so it must have been a ridiculously good pear. Kiri couldn't be older than twelve or thirteen; perhaps she just didn't care. Pears were a favorite fruit of Tristan's, and now that he was thinking about them, he wanted one…wait. Wasn't it late for pears this far north? He should find out when he was finished with the garments.

Kiri's suede shoes were grass stained and worn out, the soles indented at the balls of the feet and the sides weakened. Whether from dancing all night or because they were old shoes, he had no idea. A couple of fresh blades of grass were stuck to the soles.

The other two sets of shoes were the same, worn and with traces of grass. Princess Meelah's dress had a wine stain near the skirt's hem, but none of the princesses had appeared intoxicated. Tired, yes, but drunk or suffering from a hangover, no. Tristan had never heard of a drink so strong it stole your memories without getting you inebriated. But perhaps with a bit of sorcery? Maybe he could warn the princesses not to drink any wine? As if they had a choice in what they did at night, he recalled glumly.

Last, he eyed Ilara's pink dress. It was so unlike the Tallanders' style. He picked it up, glancing around. His face heated, even though he was alone. Despite the fact he was meant to be handling it, it felt inappropriate. *Stupid.* Why should it be any more awkward than her sister's dresses?

Just fabric. That's all it was. Silky fabric that slid between his fingers and was finer than any silk he'd ever handled before. Fabric that smelled of flowers, light and delicate and alluring… He scowled and searched the gown. A blade of grass was caught in the hem, but otherwise, nothing. He tossed the garment on top of the others and slumped onto the couch.

Hopeless. This entire thing was hopeless.

The ache returned behind his forehead, so he retired to his room, hoping to rest in preparation for staying awake that night. Yet he wasn't tired, and his head hurt, and his mind kept listing all the reasons he was going to fail and die until he wanted to scream. Or possibly cry, although he would never admit that. Men, after all, did not cry.

But that was according to Henry, and Henry could take all his advice and burn it. Tristan tossed on his bed and glared at the single stripe of sunlight that made it through the narrow window.

If he couldn't sleep, he had to keep his mind occupied. The door to the princesses' room had been open that morning. They'd walked through it to get their clothing. Then what?

The grass indicated they'd left the Great House. Then there was the pear fruit on Princess Kiri's sleeve…

He headed down to the ground floor and asked the first servant he saw for directions to the kitchen. The servant escorted him out of the Great House into the closest building, a wide wattle-and-daub structure with two large chimneys. The shutters of a few glassless windows were thrown open in the kitchen. However, the two huge stoves had roaring fires, and the handful of servants bustling about the tables were sweaty and eyed him with annoyance.

The servant left Tristan with a dour-faced woman of sinewy muscle pounding at bread dough in a way that was oddly intimidating. Flour accentuated the harsh lines in her face, and he couldn't tell if there were hints of gray in her hair that was pulled back in a bun, or just more flour.

He cleared his throat. "Pardon me, but I was wondering what kind of fruit you have? Specifically, do you have pears?"

The woman punched the dough. Even though she was much shorter than him, her glare made him feel like a scolded boy. "No. Don't grow here; out of season in Kilkreth; would spoil by the time it got here from any further south."

"You're certain?" That juice had to be fresh.

The baker huffed, and flour puffed away from her cheeks. "Completely. Can I interest your lordship in some other fruit?"

Clear irritation dripped from her tone. "An apple, maybe?"

"Um, no, thank you. Thank you for your time."

She grunted, and Tristan turned, nearly knocking over a heavyset man carrying a large cut of meat. The man grumbled under his breath even as he inclined his head deferentially.

Afraid to return to the silent room to be alone with his thoughts, Tristan walked around the Great House. He was circling the building a third time when he stopped. Something was off.

There was more moss than grass, and the grass—he knelt down and plucked a long, stiff blade that was a shade of pale yellow-green. The grass on the princesses' dresses and shoes was more vibrant, and the blades were wider and softer. With a frown, he walked around again, paying attention to the grass. Then he went out further. He didn't encounter any grass that matched the grass on the clothing.

Fruit that wasn't available in Talland. Different grass.

Wherever the princesses were going at night…it wasn't nearby.

It likely wasn't even in Talland at all.

17

ristan slunk back to his suite, terrified of running into the king or being summoned. If Onak asked what he'd found, he would have to determine how to tell a desperate father that his daughters were being magicked out of the kingdom every night. He had a feeling that wouldn't go over well. Worse, he had no idea how to stop it. How was he supposed to stop a sorcerer so powerful he could travel to another kingdom and return in one night? And why would this sorcerer do that, anyway?

The entire situation was confusing and overwhelming, so Tristan went to bed.

However, sleep still eluded him. He stared at the ceiling in the dim light of the narrow window, wondering if he should run. It would be the cowardly thing to do, abandoning the princesses to their vile fate, but he wasn't helping them at all. It was laughable to think that he could, as much as he wished otherwise.

Although the curse had found the princesses when they'd tried to run, the sorcerer didn't know about Tristan and his men. Perhaps away from the Great House, they'd be free of the cursed slumber. If they snuck off just before sunset, by the time Onak realized they were gone, the Tallanders would be falling asleep. They'd have to ride hard, but it could work, and they could go home.

Except it wouldn't be home. Not for Tristan.

Surely Alex would at least understand and not punish his failure…but what if he withdrew the barony, anyway? Or just sent Tristan somewhere else?

That was if they even made it back. If they were caught, Onak would kill him. The king might kill Sharland and Masarik and Fournier as well to prevent Alex from learning the truth, and they didn't deserve that. Tristan had no choice but to stay and attempt to save the princesses or convince Onak to let him go.

However, perhaps he should send the others home while he still could. The prospect of staying alone in Talland without anyone he could call an ally frightened him more than he cared to admit, but was he truly so selfish he would endanger others to be less lonely? He'd lied to them, was still lying, and they might be in grave danger. It was their duty to protect him…but in these circumstances, was forcing them to do that duty cruel? As their lord, shouldn't he protect them, too?

He tried to think of something else, anything else. Not sorcerers or death or his own selfishness and weakness…

His traitorous mind spiraled back to after he had admitted to Henry that he hadn't enchanted Raelyn, and he wasn't going to. Henry had punched Tristan so hard in the gut he had doubled over, feeling sick. When he'd straightened, Henry was holding an engraved stone and chanting something in the Old Tongue. Lines of searing heat had circled Tristan's throat, making tears streak down his face. When the stone crumbled to dust and Henry stopped chanting, he'd looked at his own son with disgust.

"If only I had a curse that would make you a worthy son. Stop crying like a maid."

No. No, no, no! Stop! Tristan pressed his hands over his ears, but the voices in his head wouldn't shut up, other voices adding to his father's and the growing chaos in his mind.

"Useless!" "Generally a blackguard." "You're the only monster here!" "You caused the death of my brother." "Surely this isn't who you are!"

"Shut up!" he screamed into his pillow. "Shut up, shut up."

He didn't remember falling asleep, but when he awoke, his face and pillow were still wet, and his head pounded. Water. He needed water. He swayed before tossing his legs over the side of the bed and shuffling to the door. Relief rushed through him when he saw Fournier sitting next to the pile of dresses, darning a sock.

"Fournier." Tristan leaned against the doorframe. "Could you find some water for me?"

"Of course, my lord!" Fournier popped off the couch, dropping his mending on top of Ilara's dress.

"Fournier?"

He paused on his way out.

"You don't have to pretend to be so eager, you know."

Fournier reddened. "I'm not… I like to be useful, my lord."

Tristan could understand that, but still, he took it a bit far. "Why?"

"Well, I'm supposed to, aren't I?" Fournier scratched behind his ear. "I'm a servant; it's what I do."

A few months ago, Tristan would have agreed and left it at that. But if Raelyn and Alex had taught him anything, it was that he needed to do better at seeing people past labels like *prisoner, woman, servant.* He shifted his shoulder against the doorframe. "But you seem like you enjoy it. Why?"

He wasn't entirely sure if he was asking because he was genuinely curious to learn more about his manservant, or if he wanted to know if there was a way he himself could be enthusiastic about serving Alex.

"I have six older brothers and sisters," Fournier said quietly. "The youngest is seven years older than me. A few of them are married and their spouses help on the farm, too. I was always in the way. Everyone else knew how to do everything, and whenever I asked for help or messed something up because I *didn't* ask, they'd get annoyed. So when the palace was hiring new servants after King Alexander returned, it was my chance to be useful. It wasn't a great job, mostly grunt work in the stables and kitchens, but then they asked for a volunteer to be your manservant on this ambassadorship, and I thought…I could prove that I'm good for something, that I can be someone." He lifted his chin and squared his shoulders. "I'm happy to do my job, my lord. Should I get the water now?"

"Right." Tristan waved in dismissal. "Yes, thank you. And Fournier…you're an exceptional manservant. Very useful and not at all in the way."

"I…am? Thank you, my lord." Fournier's pleased expression wavered. "I actually… I prefer Remy. If that's all right."

"Oh. All right. Remy." Tristan nodded, tapped his fingers on his leg, and straightened. "Anyway. Water?"

"Right! Sorry." Remy hurried to the door, spun around to bow with a rushed "my lord," and left.

"Didn't think you cared about anyone else."

Tristan jumped at Masarik's voice. Masarik stood in the doorway to the other bedroom, his burly arms folded over his chest.

"I didn't realize you were here." Tristan smoothed his shirt, trying to appear less rattled at the knight's sudden appearance.

Masarik shrugged. "I was trying to sleep. Wasn't really working, though, then I heard you talking. I figured I wouldn't like you, with the stories I've heard and how…well, I've known some high-ranking nobles, and they cared about a poor, low-ranking knight about as much as they did about dirt on their shoe. Thought you'd be the same. And honestly, sometimes you're an ass."

Tristan clenched his teeth, fighting the urge to flinch.

"But then you apologized. Some would say a noble doesn't

need to apologize to someone of a lower rank, but you did. And then…that. With Rem." Masarik waved a hand toward the door, then refolded his arms. "Maybe Allyre's right, and you're changing." After a beat, he added, "My lord."

Tristan snorted. "Yes, see, calling me my lord doesn't actually make up for the ass comment, but I'll let it go." Only because the man was right.

Masarik grunted and stomped to the couch, where he picked up Ilara's pink dress. Tristan's heart jumped into his throat. "Don't touch that."

"What?" Masarik looked at him, still holding the dress. "Did you find anything?"

"Sort of, nothing helpful, but just—they'll want those returned; put it down." Tristan stepped closer, holding his hands out like he was talking a child into gently setting aside a valuable piece of art.

The knight lifted an eyebrow. "I'm not hurting it." He rubbed the bodice between his thick fingers. "Fabric's too soft for my tastes; no holding on to it. She sure looked fine in it, though, don't you—"

"Sir Masarik!" Tristan's face flushed. "You won't speak of Princess Ilara in such a manner; now put down the dress."

"Ha." Masarik tossed the dress back onto the couch. "You have an eye for the princess, *my lord*. Did you cradle her dress while we were gone; pretend you were holding her?"

Tristan crossed his arms, his expression hardening even as the tips of his ears burned. He couldn't begin to list all the reasons a relationship between himself and Ilara was an impossibility, even if he were interested. "That's inappropriate, inaccurate, and out of turn, Sir Masarik. And I believed we'd reached an agreement that you wouldn't behave in a way that might endanger this mission."

Masarik rolled his eyes. "No one's going to hear. But fine. Apologies, your lordship."

It wasn't a sincere apology, but Tristan nodded as he straightened the pile of gowns. "I did find something, though. Wherever the princesses are going, it's not in Talland."

"Pardon?"

Tristan quickly summarized his findings.

"Well." Masarik dropped into the other armchair. "Did you tell the king?"

"Not yet. King Onak is on edge enough as it is." Maybe he should admit how unpredictable Onak was. But Masarik wasn't likely to take that well. Tristan collapsed on the couch. Was it too soon for Fourn—Remy to be back with that water?

As if summoned, Remy hurried in, a ceramic pitcher and cup in hand. He filled the cup and handed it to Tristan, and then stood with his hands clasped behind his back. "Do you want to hear what I learned?"

For a moment, Tristan wasn't sure what that meant. "Oh, the servants. Yes, please."

Remy rocked back and forth on his feet. "I didn't learn much. Mostly things you already told us, although the sleeping curse has caused a few injuries, most minor. People who leave the Great House magically fall asleep the first night, but not the second, so the magic does wear off. Didn't work for the princesses, though, since the sorcerer brought them back."

Tristan rubbed his chin, gazing off at nothing. At least if he sent his men away, the curse wouldn't follow them.

"What a strange, complicated curse," Masarik mused.

"Also, my lord," Remy continued, "I don't know if it's helpful, because it's not really about the curse, but it's about the princess. Crown Princess Ilara?"

"Go on."

Remy sat in one of the dining chairs. "The servants love her. They say the king is distraught and can't keep up with running the kingdom, that the nobles whisper when they think no one is listening that since the curse started, he's acting erratic and ignoring them. But Princess Ilara is helping with royal duties, even though she's exhausted. They said the nobles say if the king doesn't improve after the curse is broken, they'll vote to make Ilara queen."

That wasn't helpful for the curse, but it was fascinating—and potentially helpful as a last-case resort. Tristan didn't want to ruin a man who was at the breaking point due to concern for his daughters, not when he'd have given anything for his father to care that much about him. Not when the princesses were already suffering enough. But if he had to…perhaps one of these nobles would be interested to hear about the secret threats Onak was making.

"Thank you, Remy." Tristan tapped a finger against his chin. "I don't have any ideas yet, but I'm working on it. There has to be a way to help the princesses."

18

*G*entle shaking and a soft voice stirred Ilara from her sleep. "A few more minutes," she mumbled.

"Ara, you asked me to wake you two hours before sunset," Ryn said above her.

Ilara pried an eye open and then closed it against the bright glow of the candle in Ryn's hand. "I take it back, go away." She groaned into her pillow.

Ryn shook her again. "Mm, no, I have it on authority from awake, cognizant Ilara to never believe just-awoken Ilara."

A wet dog tongue licked Ilara's fingers, and Nika whined.

Ilara sat up with another exaggerated groan. "Fine. Did you bring my clothes?"

Ryn held up her other arm, a simple burgundy wool dress draped over it. "What are you up to? Since it's not helping your father this time."

"Did he do anything today?" she asked, unsure she wanted the answer.

Ryn's gaze fell. "Perhaps he worked on paperwork in his room."

They both knew that was unlikely.

"I miss my mama, too," Ilara whispered as she lifted the dress. "So much sometimes it hurts. I thought he was past this, but...at times, I see his grief and loneliness and despair coming back. I know it's because he can't stand the possibility of losing us, too, but sometimes I get angry with him for how he mourns, so all-consuming. Then I hate myself for being angry. I'm cross with the House Heads for doubting and judging him, but part of me is, too, and how can I criticize him when I know how heartbroken he is?"

"It's understandable to be upset when someone hurts you, even if they aren't doing it on purpose and are in pain themselves," Ryn said quietly. "It doesn't mean you don't love him."

Ilara gulped and met her friend's eyes in the dim light. "Thank you. I wish he had someone like I have you. I think if he could talk to someone and be honest with them, someone who isn't his child or a member of his court, it would help. Then I remember he did, and it was Mama, and—" Emotion caught at her throat. "I feel guilty all over again. At the same time, I'm worried about him. And about the kingdom."

"I know." Ryn pulled Ilara into a tight embrace. "And it's hard; I know it's hard. However, it's not your job to fix your papa. You're doing everything you can for him and Talland, and the king is doing the best he can when his mind is, in a way, sick. He'll get better. The House Heads understand, even behind the disapproval. But are *you* all right?"

Ilara squeezed her friend back, fighting tears. "I'm exhausted," she admitted. "Physically, yes, but emotionally, too. I can't do this much longer. Watching Papa becoming less himself again after all this time, hearing Kiri cry, seeing Meelah trying not to be hurt when her friends' lives go on without her, not knowing what to do. I—I wish I could ask Mama what to do."

Ryn rubbed her back, holding her tightly. She didn't speak, letting Ilara fall apart for as long as she needed to. After a couple minutes, Ilara felt calm enough to let go. She wiped the dampness from her cheeks.

"Hopefully by the time I'm dressed it won't be obvious I was crying."

"To whom? Are you going somewhere?"

"Yes, and I was hoping you would join me." Ilara grinned. "I shouldn't visit any more foreign visitors alone. Could you send someone to tell Baron Carbrey I wish to speak with him in his quarters shortly? That will give us both a few minutes to prepare."

"The Rethali?" Ryn's brows knitted together. "His quarters?"

"Shhhhh." Meelah tossed over on her bed. "Sleeping."

Ilara rolled her eyes, but still lowered her voice. "It isn't official business or proper hospitality, and obviously I can't invite him to my bedroom. Can you find someone to alert him?"

Ryn nodded and slipped out, and Ilara changed clothes. When she emerged from the room, Ryn was waiting in the corridor.

"Not business, you said. Attracted to Baron Carbrey, are we?"

"What?" Ilara attempted a scowl, but by Ryn's smirk, it wasn't convincing. "He's investigating, and I want to know if he's found anything. I also hope to learn some of what was left out of the letter from his king. If we're going to make a trade agreement with him, we should know more of his character, and that letter was oddly vague. His attractiveness has nothing to do with it."

"Ah, so he is attractive?"

"Oh, hush. Let's go by my room. I need to brush my hair. Because I'm a princess, not to impress him."

"Mm-hmmm."

Ilara made a face, making Ryn laugh, and they headed up to Ilara's room on the third floor, Nika pressing against Ilara's legs and making whiny demands for attention the entire way. The poor dog wasn't happy about how little time Ilara was spending with her lately.

While Ilara brushed and plaited the top half of her hair into two braids, Ryn read King Alexander's letter—with much gasping. "Well now I understand your curiosity," Ryn said.

Ilara chuckled. "Mm-hmmmm."

They headed down to the second floor and the Rethali's guest suite. As they exited the stairwell, two men walked toward them down the hall—the Rethali knights.

The knights paused to bow, and Ilara stopped. "You're Baron Carbrey's men?"

"Yes, Your Highness." The dark-skinned knight had a deep, relaxing voice. He inclined his head deferentially.

The blond-haired knight shrugged. Ilara wasn't sure she'd ever seen a man so large. "Well, strictly speaking, we're King Alexander's men, on loan to Baron Carbrey." Nika sniffed at him, and he gently stroked her back.

"Oh." Ilara wasn't certain how to respond to that. Did the Rethali king not trust his ambassador? Or did the knight not care for his lord?

"I'm Masarik, he's Allyre." The blond jerked his thumb toward his companion. "So…what're you visiting the baron for?"

"Masarik." Allyre laid a hand on Masarik's muscular arm. "Let's go. Your Highness." He bowed again and gently pushed on the bigger man.

"I'm just curious if she's also attracted to—"

"Masarik, behave." Allyre steered his friend past them.

Ryn turned toward Ilara, lips pursed. "Still want to see this Rethali alone?"

Ilara turned up her chin, hoping she didn't look as flushed as she felt. "I'm not concerned."

Mostly because Masarik might be making things up, especially if he *was* trying to cause trouble for his liege—although that raised questions about Tristan's character. But if the knight had told the truth, and Tristan was attracted to her… Tristan wasn't unattractive, and he didn't seem to be a sorcerer, so he had that going for him.

"Besides, I won't be alone. I have you and Nika."

"Nika doesn't count as an escort when you're seeing a man, and you know it."

"He's not *a man*, he's an ambassador and someone Papa asked to help with our Domhnall problem," Ilara protested.

"Still a man."

"You've seen Lorik alone."

Ryn laughed. "Yes, after courting him for six months. Not for lack of trying before that," she added with a wink. "And it led to this." She tapped the bronze cuff on her ear. "Are you planning on letting the Rethali cuff you?"

"Maybe I am." Ilara funneled as much sarcasm as possible into her tone. "After seeing him twice, I've decided he is the one."

Ryn snorted and knocked on the door. A young Rethali man with a toothy grin and ruddy cheeks opened it.

"Welcome, Your Highness." The young man bowed and stepped aside, holding the door open.

Tristan stood in the center of the sitting room. His fluffy brown hair was combed back, and he'd tidied up his beard. Today he wore a maroon shirt with an embroidered vee-shaped collar and short sleeves that revealed toned forearms. Ilara shooed the thought away. Why under the moon should she notice his arms? That Masarik fellow and Ryn were messing with her mind.

Tristan bowed deeply as Ilara and Ryn entered. "Your Highness, you honor me." He straightened with a smile, although his eyebrows drew in, and there was a lingering sadness in his eyes. He turned to Ryn. "And…?"

"Oh, this is my dear friend, Lady Ryn."

"A pleasure, Lady Ryn."

Ryn returned his bow with a curtsy. "Baron Carbrey."

Tristan turned his attention back to Ilara. "I understand I have you to thank for this opportunity to pursue trade with your great kingdom. I am indebted to you." He gave another small bow. "How might I serve you, Your Highness?"

"I have some questions for you. Not about trade," she added, considering his little speech.

Nika padded into the room and sniffed Tristan. He looked down at the dog, and his stiff demeanor eased. "Hello there." Nika lolled her tongue out to the side, panting up at Tristan. He looked to Ilara. "Does he want me to pet him?"

Ilara smiled. "She probably does, yes."

"Ah, a good *girl.*" Tristan scratched Nika's ear, and the dog pushed her head against Tristan's hand with a pleased expression. "A very soft, very good girl," he added under his breath as he rubbed her ears with both hands.

"She likes you."

He gave a little jump, then with a final gentle stroke of Nika's head, moved his hands behind his back, standing rigid as a soldier. "Would you care to sit, Your Highness? Lady Ryn?"

His return to formality disappointed her. She liked the side of Tristan that was disarmingly affectionate toward her dog. "Yes, thank you." She glanced back as she sat in the nearest armchair. The servant still stood by the door, keeping it open. "You may close that."

The servant sent his lord a questioning glance.

"Your Highness," Tristan said, "I wouldn't want there to appear to be any impropriety—"

"Ryn is with me, and your servant is with us. There's nothing improper."

Ryn gave her a pointed look as she took a seat on the couch, but Ilara ignored her. Tristan nodded, clearly reluctant, and the servant closed the door, then withdrew to a corner. Nika lay down on top of Ilara's feet.

"What did you learn from your search?" It wasn't strictly the reason she had come, but she was curious. She didn't see the dresses anywhere. "Did you receive the gowns?"

"Yes, Your Highness."

"And did you discover anything?"

Tristan's throat bobbed, and he lowered his gaze before he said quietly, "No, Your Highness."

"Are you withholding something from me?"

He glanced up, alarm in his wide eyes. "No…I just…nothing worth mentioning, Your Highness."

Ilara tilted her head. "First, sit, please." She'd expected him to sit as soon as she did, but perhaps Rethali custom demanded explicit permission before sitting in the presence of royalty. Tristan bowed and moved to the armchair across from her, his movements wooden.

"Second," Ilara continued, "if you think to spare me, I'm already living it. I would rather know whatever you found. Or is it my papa? Did he order you not to—"

"No. I just have nothing useful to tell you, Your Highness."

Ilara sighed. This formality was stifling on its own, but it wasn't helping him be forthcoming. "Do you mind if I call you Tristan?"

His lips parted. He blinked, then bowed his head. "If that is your wish, Your Highness, I would be honored."

"Call me Ilara, please." She smiled, trying to put him at ease.

"Oh…" Tristan froze. "I'd rather not be so bold, Your Highness."

What an odd reaction. King Alexander's letter had given her the impression Tristan was courageous and decisive, but his behavior…it spoke of a man haunted by fear and uncertainty. She had many questions, but first, she needed to know what he was hiding.

"You inspected the clothing, correct?"

Tristan ran his fingers through the side of his hair, leaving tufts behind. It was oddly endearing.

"I did," he said. "Yes, I found something, but I'm unsure what it means, and I wouldn't know what to do about it, anyway." He didn't look at her as he spoke.

"Whatever it is, you don't think you're wrong, do you?"

Tristan sighed. "Your Highness… I have reason to believe Domhnall is magically transporting you out of Talland."

He'd already figured that out?

Ryn sucked in a breath. "Out of…" She looked to Ilara, as if hoping she would deny it.

"I suspected as much," Ilara said with an apologetic look at Ryn.

The baron frowned. "I also thought perhaps he can magic his way directly into your room. That's why the locked door doesn't matter."

"He can." Ilara leaned back in the armchair. "I've seen him vanish into thin air."

"Oh." Tristan fiddled with his thumbs, his eyebrows scrunching down. "Have you told your father you've put this together, Your Highness?"

"He's already worried enough. And unfortunately, like you said, knowing it doesn't help. I don't know where we go or why he thinks whisking us away to a ball in Kilkreth or wherever he takes us will convince me to marry him."

"I'm sorry, Your Highness." Tristan blew out a breath. "At least the news didn't add to your fright."

"Fright?" Ilara frowned. "I'm not frightened; I'm tired, and I'm furious. Not with you," she added quickly as Tristan paled. He was oddly skittish for a former crown prince. "Do you have any idea how frustrating this has been? I don't think Domhnall's hurt any of us, but I don't know that, because I can't remember!

"And because of his moon-cursed magic, I can't do anything!" Now that she had started ranting, she couldn't stop. "I don't know if I've ever punched Domhnall's smug face. I can't leave myself a note saying what happened. But even if I could remember, would it matter? Or would I just have more knowledge I wouldn't know what to do with? I don't have any ideas, and I'm angry with myself for not knowing how to stop him."

Tristan stared at her, the most brazen she had seen him in their brief encounters—other than when he'd stared at her and claimed he was thinking of his father. Then he shook himself and lowered his head.

"I'm truly sorry I don't have something more helpful, Your Highness."

"You honestly *can* call me Ilara, Tristan. And please don't apologize. You figured it out faster than I did. I actually thought it rather pointless and presumptuous to ask for your assistance, but maybe Papa is right and being an outsider will be to your advantage. Thank you again for volunteering, Tristan."

"Yes..." Tristan cleared his throat, staring fixedly at the rug on the floor. Maybe he didn't know how to take a compliment— also odd for a former royal. "If I think of anything more, I promise I won't hide it from you, Your Highness."

A mixture of irritation and admiration accompanied his insistence on using her formal address. He was either very proper or very determined to keep things professional. Did he not find her attractive? Not even a little? The possibility irked her, since his square jaw under that short beard was certainly striking... Ilara pushed those thoughts down. They weren't useful.

Although there's nothing wrong with acknowledging the man is handsome.

"Is there something else I can help you with, Your Highness?"

"Actually…" She smoothed her skirt. "I had some questions of a more personal nature. If you don't mind."

"Of course," Tristan said.

"I read your king's letter." Ilara propped her elbows on her knees and rested her chin on her fists. "But it seemed to be missing some details, and it's such a story; I'd love to hear it from you. Can you tell me, in your own words? How did your cousin win over your Court of Lords? And how did you become an ambassador to Talland?"

She wanted to *see* him tell the story, to hear every intonation and catch in his breath so she could evaluate his feelings. What did Tristan think about his cousin's return and becoming an ambassador? Maybe it would give her some insight into why that Sir Masarik seemed to dislike his lord.

19

"That's…complicated, Your Highness." Tristan's voice sounded small as he fought his rushing panic. Not even the distractingly pretty, impressively capable, and confoundedly informal Tallander princess could let him leave his past behind.

Ryn leaned over to the princess and whispered, "So, he's going to persist in calling you Your Highness but then not agree to your requests?"

His face flushed. "Forgive me, Your Highness. I meant no disrespect—"

"Ah, you heard me, then?" Ryn fiddled with her ear cuff. Unlike the king, Ilara didn't wear one. Tristan wondered if they had some significance.

"I always tell you that your whispers aren't quiet." Ilara winked at Ryn, who made a face back at her. They were so casual and relaxed together, and he envied their friendship.

"It's only that I would have to leave details out, as I can't speak ill of my father." He hesitated, recalling her influence with the king. Maybe, if he ingratiated himself with her, she could ensure Onak didn't have him executed.

"But…" He licked his lips. "Yes or no questions won't hurt me. I think. So far they haven't, and Alex—forgive me." He internally cursed his slip. "King Alexander said it worked for him."

"What do you mean, it worked for him?"

Tristan frowned. "His curse prevented him from saying he was cursed or how it happened. Did the letter not explain that? I'm sorry, Your Highness; I don't know what it contained." Part of him was afraid of the answer, but Ilara wasn't looking at him like he was a monster…perhaps Alex had left out the worst parts in an act of mercy.

"Oh." Ilara shifted, prompting her dog to lift its head and nuzzle at her arms. She absently reached down to rub its ears, and Tristan fought another jolt of envy. "Well, to start at the beginning… Your father cursed your cousin to be part dragon, so he could seize the throne?"

"Yes." He decided to offer more information as an apology for his earlier cageyness. "It gave him horns and wings and a tail and claws and red eyes. The ability to shapeshift into a dragon and breathe fire came later."

"I see." Ilara seemed to consider this. "I know that your betrothed, Princess Raelyn of Eynlae, was lost on the way to the wedding. Alex saved her life, and she stayed with him until he returned her to the Rethali palace because they learned that her brother was a prisoner. Then it simply says the princess lied about what happened to her, and you went to hunt down a dragon you thought had held her captive, found King Alexander, and there was a fight during which a friend of his died, breaking his curse."

Tristan barely managed not to flinch. He struggled to comprehend that Alex hadn't blamed him in the letter. But if Alex believed the truth would make his job as ambassador harder, Tristan would gladly follow his king's lead and not admit how much of the blame he carried.

Ilara's expression pinched with sorrow. "A curse that can only be broken by bloodshed is a cruel curse indeed."

He nodded and focused on picking long strands of white dog

fur off his trouser leg. Henry had assumed the horrible antidote was his security that Alex's curse would never be broken—which shouldn't have surprised Tristan. Of course Henry, with his desires fixated on power, hadn't accounted for an act of selfless love.

"Then the letter recounted your heroism in opposing your father when Alexander made his case to your Court of Lords. Although that narrative is clearly missing details."

That…was all Alex had written? His *heroism?* The Tallanders considered him a hero—except that Ilara wanted to know what he was hiding.

Flames.

"What do you wish to know?" he asked, his mouth dry.

Ryn leaned forward. "If her brother was a prisoner, then her family continued to the palace without her? Why?"

"They thought her dead. Well. Most of them." Tristan worked his jaw. "Princess Raelyn's horse bolted in the mountains. They found her horse's body, but…Prince Gareth believed she was alive."

"And why was he taken prisoner?" Ilara asked, clearly puzzled.

"He…" Tristan shrank back. That wasn't the worst of his misdeeds, and already these questions made him want to sink into the floor. To think he'd been curious about the princess's visit. "He tried to convince me to search for her. I should have been gentler in denying his request. Gareth struck me." He stared at his lap. "I deserved it, but the treaty was in question without the princess, and a visiting prince attacking the crown prince…my father didn't appreciate it. Prince Gareth was arrested as surety that the Eynlaeans would bring a replacement bride."

Ilara and Ryn exchanged a glance. Tristan couldn't interpret their expressions, but they didn't seem favorable.

He closed his eyes. "Please understand. Our Court was demanding this marriage. There was a treaty at stake, and those mountains are full of beasts and monsters. We believed we had to set aside compassion and fulfill the treaty without her." He opened his eyes with a suppressed sigh. "That doesn't change that it was a mistake."

And that maybe, if Tristan had admitted to himself then that his father was cruel and his methods wrong, if he hadn't stomped out the part of himself that had felt sympathy for Gareth, things might have gone differently.

"So when Raelyn returned, you believed she'd escaped a dragon?" Ilara asked, her tone surprisingly kind.

Tristan nodded. "From what I understand, initially Alex kept her out of fear she would betray him and concern she wouldn't be safe in the Rethali palace." Given everything Henry was capable of, Alex had probably been right. He moved on, fighting to keep any emotion out of his voice.

"They fell in love. She returned to protect her brother, and she lied to protect Alex. My father said the dragon needed to be slain. Raelyn hadn't expected that. But my father didn't expect me to insist on leading the hunting party—or that I'd agree to take Gareth and Raelyn with me when they asked."

"They wanted to stop you," Ryn guessed.

Tristan shook his head. "She hadn't even told her brother. He wanted to kill the beast as much as I did. I'd hoped avenging Raelyn would endear me to her, and that we might bond…on what turned out to be a quest to murder the man she loved." He laughed dully. Fool that he was, he'd also hoped killing a dragon would win Henry's approval.

"It was noble of you to want to slay the dragon that had tormented your betrothed." Ilara's gentle words only made Tristan feel worse.

"What did you do when you learned it was your cousin?" Ryn asked, her eyes wide.

Why did she have to ask? Why did his stupid conscience compel him to answer?

He hesitated, unsure what the curse would let him say. "I…was informed," he said carefully, "that dragons could enchant, and if Raelyn made any unbelievable claims, it might be because she'd been ensorcelled."

"Ah." Ilara winced. "Your father told you this?"

"Yes. So when she admitted it, I didn't believe her. I'd also been told Alex was infected with evil sorcery by his wicked parents, so I thought he'd enchanted Raelyn and was lying. I was furious… So I tried to kill him. Flames, I knew he was my cousin, but I tried to kill him, anyway, even after his curse broke. And I— I made many mistakes. I hurt so many people." All of his transgressions stuck in his throat, too horrible to utter.

He wanted to hide his face behind his hands, but he forced his expression into stone as he glared at the carpet. Why he'd said that, he didn't know. Perhaps it was Sharland getting to him, making him think somehow admitting it would help.

As the silence dragged on, he risked looking at the princess. To his surprise, she didn't look judgmental or shocked. She looked…sad.

"What else did you have questions about, Your Highness?" Despite trying to keep his voice level, the words came out hoarse.

Ilara tilted her head as she regarded him. "I suppose, for now, I'm just curious. I understand pardoning you after you risked your life to defend Queen Raelyn and King Alexander against your father, and since your actions against your cousin were because you'd been deceived and then cursed, and then you willingly swore your allegiance. But after everything your father did, King Alexander only exiled him? He didn't execute him?"

"Yes, well, King Alexander is, in all things, most admirable." Tristan forced a smile he didn't feel. "He refused to start his rule with violence. I was forgiven, but not liked, so Alex sent me here."

"Oh—I'm sorry."

Tristan's gaze snapped to the princess. He'd just admitted that he'd hurt people, and she…was sorry for him? "Don't be. I'm fortunate my king is merciful."

Ilara gave him a sympathetic look. "It must have been difficult, learning your father had lied to you, having him turn on you, and then losing your position and home and adjusting to a new future."

She…understood? His throat tightened.

"You've handled it with great honor," Ryn said gently.

His shoulders hunched. "I did one or two things right after doing many cruel things. I…I'm not a hero. I just couldn't add any more misdeeds to my conscience."

The room fell silent. *Please, please, can't the princess and her friend leave?*

"So you changed," Ilara said. "You chose to be better. Admitting you were wrong and striving to change is never easy. Your king must believe in you, or he wouldn't have given you a barony and sent you as his representative."

Tristan looked up, feeling empty and wishing she was right, that it wasn't because Alex wanted him gone. "Blood doesn't wash off that easily," he murmured.

Why couldn't he keep his mouth shut? Stupid, stupid Tristan. "If you have no further questions, Your Highness, I'd like to eat something before tonight."

Ilara blinked. "You're standing guard again?"

"I promised your father I'd help, and I don't have any other ideas." A thought occurred to him, one he never would have indulged under Henry's thumb. "Unless…you have an idea of what to try, Your Highness?"

"I wish I did." With a sigh, Ilara stood, prompting her dog to get up and stretch with a yawn that showed intimidating teeth for such a friendly dog. "Well…I wish you luck, Tristan. And thank you for answering my questions." Her smile was far gentler than Tristan deserved, and yet it warmed him. "I'd like to speak with you again—perhaps about something more lighthearted."

A weak smile of his own broke through his melancholy as he stood out of deference. "I would prefer that, Your Highness. Maybe we could start with the weather."

Ilara laughed. "I hope we can find something to discuss between the mundanity of the weather and painful memories."

"I'll look forward to that," Tristan replied with a bow.

And if Ilara could be that kind and accepting when he was admitting his mistakes, he meant it.

Perhaps Sharland wasn't entirely off his horse about talk being productive, after all.

20

As Ilara and Ryn moved to leave, Nika bounded over to Tristan, making quiet yet demanding *arroo-rah* chatter as she tried to wheedle more head rubs from him. Ilara apologized and called her back. Judging by the way Tristan scratched Nika's chin and murmured to her, he didn't mind.

Ryn accompanied her to the windowless room while Ilara mulled over what Tristan had said. Her heart ached for him. He had suffered greatly and carried so much guilt… He'd looked so contrite and hopeless, as if he didn't even like himself.

She wondered about that guilt, though. Sensing how it pained him to speak of his past misdeeds, she hadn't pressed him, and she did believe if his cousin had pardoned him and trusted him, he must have redeemed himself. But perhaps whatever hurts Tristan had caused were why Sir Masarik had been so quick to say he wasn't Tristan's knight. It was disappointing to know Tristan had been cruel, and yet…a wicked man didn't suffer a guilty conscience or do the right thing in the end. At least a man with a conscience would negotiate trade fairly.

"I think I like him," Ryn said, interrupting her thoughts. "It takes strength to own your errors. And the acts of heroism keep coming with him deciding to help you." She nudged Ilara. "I take it back; maybe you can court this one."

Ilara bumped her shoulder into her friend. "What is it with you and Meelah and Kiri trying to foist me off on every foreign visitor lately? Correction, almost any eligible man my age with a decent face. Besides, didn't *you* warn me to be careful?"

"Well, Nika likes him." Ryn shrugged.

"That's true." Ilara patted Nika's side. "You would tell me if Tristan was up to no good, wouldn't you, Nika?"

Nika just panted in return.

Once in bed, Ilara kept turning over her conversation with Tristan—specifically how'd he'd seemed so shocked when she acknowledged he'd been hurt, too. As if he was used to his feelings being discarded. Her last thought before she fell asleep was that maybe he just needed someone to care.

"I had another present made especially for you, my dear," Domhnall said as he lightly pushed Ilara into her bedroom. "It's on your bed. Go on." He pulled the door shut behind her.

Nika slept on her cushion in the corner, and she didn't stir as Ilara set down her lantern on the vanity. That was all right; she would be leaving soon, anyway.

The powder-blue dress was ethereal. The fitted bodice came up to her neck and had long sleeves that hugged her arms. It had layers of a fine netting between the linen underskirt and a satiny overskirt covered by a nearly translucent top layer that had a faint shimmer. Thick embroidery-like floral patterns decorated the waistline, shoulders, and the bottom hemline. The back had an elaborate ribbon lacing she couldn't hope to do on her own—

Ilara froze, looking over her shoulder into the mirror on her vanity. The back was laced. Perfectly.

Panic rose in her chest, but a knock jarred her from her shock.

"Ilara, my dear," Domhnall called through the door. "Are you ready?"

"I…" She shook her head. "I need to brush my hair." She drifted over to the vanity, unraveling her braid.

The door opened as she began brushing out her hair, and Domhnall entered, looking her over with satisfaction. "You're a vision."

Ilara started to part it to do new braids, but Domhnall drew her hand away. "I prefer your hair loose. Come on." He led her into the corridor. "We're late. That's what happens when I let Daven talk me into a game of drinking checkers. One turns into four and then suddenly it's so much later than I thought."

Ilara was too confused to bother asking what any of that meant.

They met Meelah and Kiri in the corridor, and Domhnall led them through a luminescent doorway into a dark wood of silver and gold trees. A path brought them to a ball occupying a meadow lit by moonlight, fireflies, hanging lanterns, mushrooms glowing pale blue, and crystals as tall as her waist emitting teal light.

"May I have this dance, Ilara?" Domhnall tugged her in among the other dancers without waiting for a reply.

The layers of skirts were uncomfortable. Somehow, they were both lighter and more cumbersome than wool. Domhnall spun her, and the dress swished around her legs.

Someone tapped on Domhnall's shoulder, stopping their dance.

"What?" he snapped.

The intruding woman curtsied, her hand on a sword at her belt. "Apologies, my lord. The alerting ward you placed on the borders has been activated along the river. We're searching the area, but someone might have slipped through."

Domhnall growled something crass under his breath. "Pardon

me for a while, dearest." He grabbed a tall man dancing with a blonde woman next to them.

The man glanced over his shoulder, then quickly released his partner to bow. "My lord?"

"Entertain Princess Ilara for a while, would you?"

"Of course, my lord." The man bowed again.

"Who was stationed along the river?" Domhnall demanded as he departed with the woman wearing a sword. She was also wearing a tunic and trousers, Ilara noted distantly.

"You're looking particularly beautiful tonight, my lady." Her new partner swept her into a dance, and she forgot all about Domhnall and the woman.

The man was gorgeous. Tall, perfectly proportioned, lithe and strong. His irises were swirls of gold tones that shifted with the light, and his coily black hair surrounded his dark face like a halo.

"Are you real?" The words spilled out of Ilara's mouth. Heat suffused her cheeks as she missed a step. "Sorry, of course you are; you just…look so perfect."

He laughed. "Thank you. No small amount of magic goes into this look." His eyes widened. "That is, um…" He cleared his throat. "Do you need a drink? Or food?" He led her to a nearby table, but Ilara couldn't think about eating.

"What do you mean, magic?"

The man laughed, but it sounded frantic. "Just a metaphor." He shoved a goblet toward her. "Here."

Magic. Ilara looked around the meadow. None of this was right. Not the too-beautiful dancers, the gold and silver trees, the full moon. It was all *wrong*, but trying to figure out why was like groping for a small object in the dark. She sipped the rich wine, and her tight shoulders relaxed. Whatever she'd been worrying about, it wasn't important.

Meelah joined them, laughing and hanging onto the arm of a

young man with light-tan skin and narrow eyes, who might have looked Tallander if he hadn't been so tall. He plucked a gold strawberry off the table and held it out. Meelah bit into the strawberry, her eyes sparkling with mischief.

"Meelah," Ilara chided.

"What?" Her sister leaned her head on the young man's shoulder. "Papa isn't here to scold me." Her mouth puckered. "Why isn't Papa here?"

"Why does it matter?" The young man offered the strawberry to Meelah's lips. "We're having such fun."

Meelah took another bite, and her expression turned carefree. "Can we dance more?"

"I'm afraid you've worn me out." Her partner tossed aside the rest of the strawberry. "Rian! Come dance with Princess Meelah."

Another handsome young man led Meelah onto the dance floor. Were any of the guests over forty?

"Ilara." Domhnall's voice at her side made her turn. "Come with me." He seized her arm and drew her toward his throne. "I can sense you hiding in the trees," he called. "So you might as well show yourself."

A shadow shifted at the edge of the forest, then solidified into a young man. *Magic.* With that, Ilara's memories rushed back, and she tripped over the hem of her skirt.

"Well, my lord," the shadow man said in a scathing voice. "It seems the rumors are true."

Domhnall's grip on her tightened as he turned to confront the man. He had skin like ivory and hair white as snow. Like all the other guests, he was unnaturally attractive, but he wore a dark blue tunic that fell to the ground and was girded with a silver belt.

"Byron," Domhnall bit out. "Did your uncle send you to spy?"

Byron ignored him, his attention focused on Ilara. "How long has it been? A fortnight or so? And you still haven't succeeded at the easy task of convincing a human to wed you." He clicked his tongue. "Oh, how the mighty have fallen."

Veins bulged in Domhnall's neck. "Get. Out. Of. My. Court."

Byron grinned, the look savage. "Your court for how much longer, oh *powerful* Lord of the Gilded Court?"

There was something Ilara was missing here, something significant, and she thought if she could just understand, maybe she could use it to stop Domhnall.

"Is that a threat?" Domhnall asked, his tone deadly calm as he pushed Ilara behind him, finally releasing her hand.

"The Lord of the Shade Court doesn't trifle with threats." Byron sniffed.

"Yet if he sent you to spy, you're doing a miserable job of it."

The corner of the man's mouth twitched upward. "If he'd sent me to gather information, I'd certainly have it."

"Well then." Domhnall waved dismissively. "Go report to your lord. Deliver a message from me as well, will you?"

"But of course." Byron gave a mocking bow, no longer bothering to hide his cruel smirk. "Is it short, or will I need a pen and parchment?"

"No, no need to write it down." Light flashed out from Halkon's fingers and slammed into the intruder, fading to reveal vines binding his legs together, tying his arms to his sides, and wrapping around his head, leaving his face barely exposed.

"You wouldn't dare," he gasped.

"Tell Raith he shouldn't have violated the sovereignty of my court by sending a subject without warning or permission, and he really shouldn't have sent a spy, not even his own nephew. And to remind him who he's dealing with…" Domhnall flicked his hand, and more vines grew over the spy, covering him from head to toe except for his mouth.

A sick feeling warned Ilara she didn't want to know what was about to happen, but she couldn't bring herself to look away. Thorns ruptured out of the vines, drawing a pained shriek from Byron. Domhnall moved his forefinger in a lazy circle, and the vines twisted. Ilara stumbled backward, squeezing her eyes shut against the carnage, and clapped her hands over her ears as the man screamed.

"Oh, hush," Domhnall said. "It's over, and they're just flesh wounds. You'll heal quickly. Well…mostly."

"My eyes!" Byron screeched. "I can't see!"

"And here I thought your court loved darkness." The wicked amusement in Domhnall's tone made Ilara's stomach heave, and she fell to her knees, trembling. "Fallon, take this Shade Court debris to the border before he bleeds all over my meadow. I have a feeling he's going to have trouble finding the way." A dark chuckle accompanied this pronouncement, which did nothing for Ilara's nausea.

Even after the spy's shrill cries faded into the distance, Ilara knelt in a heap of skirts, her eyes pressed shut and hands uselessly clutching her ears. Someone touched her shoulder, and she stiffened.

"Ilara, my dearest," Domhnall said, his breath brushing against her cheek. He gripped her hands and pulled them down.

Almost against her will, Ilara's eyes opened, and she found herself looking into Domhnall's face inches from hers. "Don't you touch me." She yanked her hands out of his and pressed them against her middle.

"Ah, weak stomach?" Domhnall leaned back, giving her more space. "Here." A gold plum glittered into existence on his palm. "This will help you feel better."

"And make me compliant and forget everything," Ilara snapped. "No."

The sorcerer huffed. "If you think I have *any* patience left, you are mistaken. I told you, if I'm going to lose my wager, it will be by my choice to no longer care, not because you escaped me. Now eat the fruit before I get the urge to hurt anyone else."

Ilara glanced toward the dancing and glimpsed Kiri spinning with abandon. Domhnall wouldn't torture one of her sisters…would he? She snatched the plum with a glare at Domhnall. "You're a monster."

"You're hardly the first to say so."

She bit into the fruit and didn't fight the mist that rolled into her consciousness, obscuring her concerns. Domhnall helped her to her feet and pulled her into a dance.

"You belong here," Domhnall whispered as he held her close, the thick skirt crushed between their legs. "With me. As my wife and queen. Marry me, Ilara."

Her mind became her own again with a force that made her gasp. Could she deny him after what she had seen tonight? And yet, how could she marry a man capable of such violence? What else would he threaten her into if she allowed him to rule at her side?

"What will it take to get you to stop this?" she begged. "What else will satisfy you?"

"Ilara…" Anger flashed in those unnaturally green eyes. "I'm running out of time. I've been patient and gentle. I've spent weeks trying to woo you."

"Woo? You think this—"

"Listen to me. I need a human kingdom to house my realm, or my magic will fade, and I will lose the ability to walk between realms and will weaken. My people will be in danger. My enemies will rise. But if I can anchor my realm to the mortal realm, I will grow stronger."

She didn't understand. Her mind was clear, but he was speaking moon-cursed nonsense.

"I need your help, Ilara. I hate needing it, but I do. If you keep denying me, my methods will become harsher. Don't make me do that. Marry me."

A monster who turned her into a submissive fool every night and called that wooing? Who tortured and blinded a man and laughed? "Never."

She slammed her fist into his stomach and tore backward. Her other hand escaped his painful grip, and she spun, searching for her sisters. They needed to find a way out. Maybe if they could escape, they would be free. At the very least, perhaps she would keep her memories and could tell Tristan. He was intelligent and capable—and as loath as she was to admit it, he would be more use than her father, who was already near broken with worry.

"Meelah! Kiri!" She caught sight of Kiri laughing with a young woman by one of the refreshment tables. A dancing couple moved into her way, but she darted past them and headed for her sister.

A hand seized her forearm and yanked her around. "Apparently I've said too much." Domhnall scowled. "Accursed waning magic."

"I don't care about your magic or your enemies," Ilara said as she struggled to pry his fingers off her arm. "I'm not marrying you, and you're going to let my sisters and me go!"

"I've chosen you to be my queen. You should be honored."

"You'd ruin Talland."

With a growl, Domhnall seized her jaw and shoved several silver blueberries into her mouth, shoving up her chin before she could spit them out. She fought against the complacency that came over her, but she couldn't win.

She blinked and looked up at Domhnall. "Were we dancing?"

He ran his fingers through her loose hair. "Yes, my dear. We were."

21

ristan paced in front of the princesses' door. Two Tallander guards—a different pair than the night before—sat on the floor, watching with unconcealed amusement. Sharland had taken a seat to the right of the door, but Masarik stood to its left.

Masarik rolled his eyes as Tristan turned. "You look particularly dour. My lord."

Tristan glanced toward the window at the end of the corridor. Nearly dusk. "Would you prefer I be idiotically joyful that I don't have a plan?"

"You seem more determined tonight." Masarik lifted a burly shoulder.

"Just trying another tactic," Tristan said.

He couldn't admit that he was more determined. Besides needing to do this to save his own neck, the more he thought about his conversation with Ilara that afternoon, the more he wanted to help *her*. She had looked at him like…like she cared about him because he was a person. She didn't know all the stains on his soul, and she didn't look at him with disgust or pity, but with kindness. Although he didn't deserve it, he longed to feel the warmth in her gaze again like a parched man longed for water.

Tristan still wasn't sure what to make of her, this princess who visited him in his suite with only her friend and asked him to call her Ilara instead of requiring deference, who didn't revel in her superiority. This woman who had defiance in her eyes rather than hopelessness or terror when she spoke of suffering in a situation she couldn't control—but who also didn't hide her weakness or lie, admitting she was tired and didn't know what to do rather than posturing to maintain an image of strength. This future queen, already so respected by her people, whose words were gentle when he'd admitted to mistakes. In every way, she was the antithesis of everything he'd been taught.

A king has no time for pity, no use for gentleness. A king is firm, unyielding, merciless.

Would Henry's voice never leave him alone?

Tristan let the feeling of caring grow. It felt strange and weak and yet…right.

Maybe he had no idea what he was doing or if he could be more than Henry's son, but he knew one thing with absolute certainty.

He wanted to talk to Ilara again, and he wanted to help her and her sisters.

Because no innocent person deserved a curse.

And because helping them could be the first step toward being someone who merited Ilara's kindness…

Tristan tripped as the world fell into darkness.

When Tristan awoke, his right knee hurt, the pommel of his sword had bruised his side, his left arm tingled from sleeping on it, and the sun was rising. He stumbled to the princesses' door.

The girls stood in the middle of the room. No gentleness marked Ilara's hard expression as she turned toward him and squinted at the dim light behind him. She wore the most unusual dress Tristan had ever seen, with a fitted bodice with thick floral embroidery and a skirt that puffed out. She looked ethereal in the pale-blue gown, but it meant Halkon had taken her again.

"I'm sorry." Tristan dropped his gaze to the ground and rubbed his face. What a fool to think he'd stood a chance. "Your Highness, forgive—"

"I told you it's not your fault."

Ilara sounded more tired than angry, and when he looked up, her expression had softened.

"I'm not upset with you." She ran a hand over the large skirt of her dress. "Could you do something for me?"

"Anything, Your Highness." He'd expected wrath at his failure, and her understanding only made him more desperate not to let her down again.

"Yesterday I wasn't certain, but I know Domhnall must have given me this dress." She gripped the fabric in a fist. "After you inspect it, burn it."

Tristan blinked. "I—yes, of course, Your Highness."

"You may go." Ilara sighed. "I'm tired, and I'm afraid other than the dress, I have no information for you, other than a vague sense of foreboding."

Kiri stretched with a yawn. "I'm so exhausted. Can't he leave us alone for one night?" Her lower lip trembled, and Tristan's heart twisted.

"Princesses, if I may be so bold…" He gulped as they peered at him inquisitively. "Tonight, might I stay inside your room?"

Meelah huffed a broken laugh. "They've tried that. It won't make a difference."

But Ilara nodded. "You may try."

Tristan was nearly back to his room, a sleepy Sharland and grouchy Masarik trailing him, when a servant stepped into his path. The man gave a brief bow and looked up at him, his thin black moustache somehow emphasizing his serious expression.

"His Majesty the king would like to speak with you in private, Baron Carbrey."

Tristan's stomach clenched. *There's the rebuke.* He left Masarik and Sharland and followed the servant to the small audience chamber behind the great hall. No comfortable sitting room today. Tristan bowed low and waited for Onak to acknowledge him before he straightened. Dark circles weighed down Onak's defeated-looking eyes.

"I heard you fell asleep." There was neither accusation nor question in Onak's tone, simply resignation.

"I apologize, Your Excellency. I tried. I—"

"Have you learned anything?"

Would the truth anger the king? If Ilara herself hadn't told her father, should he? "Nothing helpful."

Onak frowned. "Have you learned something…not helpful?"

Flames. Tristan licked his lips. "Yesterday, I…"

The air in the room grew thick and rustled. The scent of flowers in bloom and ripe fruit wafted in, yet no door had been opened. In front of Tristan, swirls of multicolored light burst into existence. He lurched backward, his hand flying to his sword.

The lights flashed brighter, then vanished. A tall man with a commanding presence stood between Tristan and the king, his silken blond hair cascading down his back over a knee-length jade tunic.

"King Onak." The man, who could only be the sorcerer Domhnall Halkon, spoke in a regal voice, clear as crystal. "Have you reconsidered?"

The king stood. His hands trembled at his sides. "Guards!"

The doors to the hall and the rear corridor banged open, and a guard rushed in from either side, their swords in hand. Tristan drew his own sword and stepped forward. Halkon waved at the guard on the right, then at the one on the left. He caught sight of Tristan and flicked his hand in Tristan's direction.

A golden glow enveloped Tristan's sword, and he stopped short. It wasn't hot or painful, but the blade shone so brightly he couldn't look at it. The guards' swords were glowing as well, and they halted their attack as the light faded.

Tristan threw down the long-stemmed rose that had been his weapon. The guards stumbled backward, petals falling off the flowers they dropped to the wood-paneled floor.

This wasn't like Henry with his cursed stone talismans. This was magic beyond what Tristan could fathom. His hands quivered as he backed away from the sorcerer.

"Come now, Onak." Halkon daintily straightened his tunic. "It's terrible manners to attack your future son-in-law."

"What are you doing to my daughters?" Onak's voice trembled. "Release them!"

"I will." The smug coldness in Halkon's tone sent chills down Tristan's spine. "Once I'm married to Ilara."

"Why would I give my daughter to a man who cursed her?"

"Because you don't want anything else to happen to your daughters." Halkon inclined his head, not elaborating as if leaving the threat up to Onak's imagination. "Consider carefully. I won't ask so nicely next time." Colorful light swirled around Halkon, and he vanished from the room.

The king stumbled back into his throne. "No… No." His throat bobbed. With Halkon gone, Onak's wild gaze locked on Tristan, then darted to the stunned guards. "Get out," he growled. "Not you, ambassador," he added as Tristan turned to leave.

The doors closed, and the king beckoned Tristan closer. He wanted to run, but he drew within a couple steps of the throne and waited.

"I don't know how much time we have." Onak chewed at his

lower lip. "He came a few days after he cast the curse, again a few days later, and now again about a week after that. Who knows when he'll return? You must save my daughters *now*."

A weight wrapped around Tristan's chest and squeezed. "Believe me, Your Excellency, I want to, but I've never seen or heard of anything like this—"

"Three more days, then. I dare not hope for more, and I can't lose them. I can't."

Tristan felt for Onak, but how could he do in three days what the entire Great House hadn't managed in two weeks? "I will try, but—"

"Try, but?" The fury that twisted the king's expression and filled his voice was far more familiar to Tristan than Onak's loving dedication to his children. So much so that Tristan flinched away. "No. No more half measures from you; no *trying*, no excuses. Save my daughters in three days, or I'll have you beheaded."

Bile pushed at Tristan's throat. He dropped to his knees. "Your Excellency—"

"Do it! And don't try to run." Onak shoved out of his throne and hurried to the door leading to the rear corridor, his hands shaking so violently he struggled to turn the handle. He slammed the door behind him.

Tristan stumbled to his chambers in a haze. Sweat made his shirt cling to his back. He tripped through the door, and Masarik looked up from the couch where he was polishing his boots. Remy tossed a tunic he was folding onto the table and rushed to Tristan.

"My lord!"

"I'm fine…" Tristan waved him off, but he barely made it to an armchair before collapsing. His stomach gurgled, and he couldn't make his body stop trembling.

"By all the rivers and the seas." Sharland appeared from his room. "Are you all right? What did the king do to you?"

"Nothing." Tristan wiped sweat from his brow with a jumpy hand. "I'm fine…" He doubled over and vomited on the rug.

There was complete silence as Tristan hung his head between his knees, his eyes closed and face burning. He wanted to lock himself in his room or yell at his men to leave, but he'd promised himself he wouldn't yell at Remy… The silence dragged on as Tristan wrestled with a decision. There wasn't another choice if he didn't want to go back to being the old Tristan, Henry Carbrey's son in actions as well as name.

Finally, he straightened.

"Remy." He cleared his stinging throat. "I'm terribly sorry…could—"

"I'll take care of it." Remy rushed to the washroom, returning with wet towels and a small washbasin.

Tristan leaned his head on the back of the armchair. "I need to talk to you all. Just…a moment."

For several minutes, he focused on breathing. He couldn't think about anything else. Once he recovered, he sorted out his thoughts. By the time he reopened his eyes, Sharland, Masarik, and Remy were all sitting and watching him, waiting.

"I haven't been completely honest with you."

"You don't say." Masarik pinched his lips and glared at him.

"The day we arrived, when King Onak spoke to me in private, he gave me a choice—help save his daughters from this sorcerer, an act that would ensure trade between Talland and Rethalyon…or he would have me executed on false charges of espionage and subterfuge."

Masarik's jaw dropped.

"You didn't think we should know this?" Sharland asked, concern rather than anger lacing his tone.

"He told me not to tell anyone. Besides, I'd hoped he would realize there was nothing I could do and remove the threat and it wouldn't matter." Tristan sighed. "And, selfishly, I wanted to keep you here. As the only people I know who cared even a little about keeping me alive; the only people I know at all. But now…" He gulped. "The king has given me three days. If I run or fail to break his daughters' curse within three days, he will kill me. If the sorcerer gets his way before then, I have no idea what will happen. But Onak's threats have only been against me. You should all go home while you still can."

Masarik and Sharland glanced at each other.

"My lord…" Remy's leg bounced. "Wouldn't it be better to have help?"

Tristan gaped at him. "Don't you understand? Onak is going to kill me. Flames, he's going to *kill me*." His stomach flipped, and he pressed his hand to it. "I saw the sorcerer. He appeared in a swirl of light and disappeared the same way. He turned my sword into a rose. A rose!" He laughed like a crazed person. "I can't… It's hopeless. And if I leave with you, the Tallanders will hunt us down and probably kill us all. If you leave now while I remain, I don't think he will stop you. But I don't know what will become of you when…when…"

He was going to be sick again.

Worthless. Useless. Excuses.

Alex would figure it out.

Tristan clenched his fists, as if he could fight the voices in his mind. "I'll write a note explaining everything to King Alexander, including that you aren't to be blamed or punished. He'll probably be thrilled to hear I'm dead, anyway." He didn't care about his heavy tone of bitterness.

"You can leave my name out of the letter, my lord," Sharland said.

Tristan's whole body went still. "What?"

"I'm staying." Sharland settled back on the couch, as if that proved his words. "I might not know about fighting magic, but I was charged with protecting you and keeping you alive, and I will do my best. If that means trying to help you escape in three days' time, so be it."

Sharland had been friendly, kind even. In another life, maybe they could have become friends. Tristan couldn't let the closest thing he had to a friend die because he was a useless coward.

"You have family back home, Sir Sharland. If you stay, I can't guarantee your safety."

Sharland's jaw tightened, and something pained flashed in his eyes. "I'm needed here."

Tristan rubbed the side of his face. He should order Sharland to leave, but he couldn't help but feel relieved. "Thank you." The words came out quieter than he'd intended.

Masarik grunted. "I'm not committing to staying the full three days, but I'm not leaving yet." He eyed Tristan. "You didn't have to tell us. You didn't have to dismiss us or worry about our lives. Honestly, I didn't expect you to.

"And I don't like you much, but I don't like the idea of anyone being told to do the impossible or face death. More importantly, I'm hoping to stay around long enough to find out if you're the cruel, unapproachable prince or the man who cares about his servant's feelings and tries to save the lives of his men without consideration of his own." Masarik tilted his head. "I can't figure you out."

"Let me know if you do, because flames if I even understand myself." Tristan stared at the ceiling, then sat up with a start. "Wait. You can't stay. Remy can't get back by—"

"I'll stay." Remy looked at Tristan earnestly.

"You don't mean that, Remy."

"But—yes, I do. I—"

"There's more likely death than recognition at the end of this,"

Tristan said. Exhaustion weighed down his bones, as if he hadn't just slept the night through.

"But maybe I can help," the young man insisted. "Somehow. If I can be useful, I will be. Maybe we can smuggle you out in a couple days if you haven't figured it out. We could put you in a trunk. Or a basket—"

"I think the Tallanders would check that," Sharland said, his eyes crinkling. "But I like the ideas. You've a useful head on your shoulders."

Remy blushed.

"That settles it." Masarik grunted. "We're staying, for now."

They would stay. For *him*. Even Masarik.

"You're all idiots." Tristan rubbed his forehead. "But I'd be lying if I said I wasn't grateful to have you all here."

Sharland fixed Tristan with that unnerving stare again, the one like he was looking into Tristan's mind. "We'll do our best to help you, Tri—my lord."

Tristan just nodded, then excused himself to wash up. Although he couldn't imagine what it meant, he noted that for all of Allyre Sharland's respect and decorum, that was the second time he had almost called him Tristan.

Light rain pattered against the window in Tristan's room. He sat wrapped in a soft wool blanket on the bed. Since he couldn't sleep, he'd opened the door to the main room, where a fire burned with low popping noises. Sharland and Masarik had wandered off somewhere, and Remy was humming under his breath as he folded laundry at the table. If his death hadn't been hovering over him like a raised axe, Tristan reflected, he might have found the atmosphere comfortable, relaxing even.

He wasn't ready to die.

A knock on the door interrupted Remy's soothing humming. He admitted the servant delivering Ilara's blue dress, and Tristan reluctantly left the meager protection of his bed.

He learned nothing from inspecting the dress, other than the silky material and make were foreign to him, ruling out Kilkreth. Thankfully, the rain had stopped when he took the garment outside, and he was able to burn it. The smoke stunk, and burning it provided no insights, either.

After that, he wandered around the forest, too jittery to be still. There was something he must be missing about Halkon and this curse, but it was beyond the reach of his fraying mind. So he meandered over moss-covered rocks and between trees sprouting strange mushrooms and let the creaking of branches and cool air permeate his senses.

He had no appetite for dinner. Sharland coaxed him into eating a few bites at supper, but he shortly regurgitated all of it.

The only thing that calmed his panic was considering Ilara's strength and resolve, how she assisted in running a kingdom while her life was upended. If Ilara could be brave, surely he could, too—not because he was better than her, but because he wished he could be more like her.

For the princesses and himself and his men, he would find a way to stop Halkon.

Or he would, through no desire of his own, die trying.

22

A tapping intruded on Ilara's sleep. Her first thought was a woodpecker and the notion that if she had a rock, she would throw it at the nuisance. Then came the realization that it was not, in fact, a woodpecker, but someone rapping on the door. She sat up with a groan and rubbed her eyes. What time was it? No way of knowing in the dark, windowless room. Whoever it was knocked again.

"Princess Ilara? May I come in? It's Baron Carbrey."

She blinked. Why… Oh, right. He'd asked to spend the night in their room. "Come in."

Tristan entered and began to close the door, but she held up her hand.

"Wait. Light the lantern first?"

"Of course." Tristan crossed to the table and lit the lantern, his movements stiff and awkward. He then closed the door and sat on the floor with his back against it.

Ilara watched with amusement. "Blocking the exit?"

Even in the low lighting, she saw him redden. "Maybe it will work this time. Something has to work." He cleared his throat. "Does the light help you trust me?"

She chuckled and shifted so she was sitting with her back

against the wall. "No, I'm not worried, or you wouldn't be here. I like to see who I'm talking to."

Tristan cocked his head. "Your Highness? You—I thought you would sleep…"

"Do you not wish to talk with me?" She adjusted her blankets, trying not to be hurt. It wasn't like he owed her conversation.

"No! I mean, yes—or, that is, I…" He exhaled. "I would gladly speak with you, Your Highness."

That appeared doubtful. "You seem on edge, Tristan."

"I do?" He laughed, but it sounded tense. "I'm sorry. I'm trying to form a plan in case I stay awake."

"Oh. Any ideas so far?"

He shook his head, pulled something out of a pouch at his waist, and started to eat.

Ilara propped her chin on her fist. "What are you eating?"

"Forgive me—"

"No, it's fine!" Why was he so quick to apologize? "I only asked what it was. You don't need to share or stop or anything. Did you sleep through supper?"

"No, but I haven't eaten all day." He tossed another piece of whatever he was eating in his mouth. "I found some nuts from Rethalyon in my bag before I came down, so I brought them. I also thought maybe the act of eating could help me stay awake. It's silly—"

"Who knows what could work?" Ilara shrugged. "Why didn't you eat today?"

Tristan choked and coughed, as if the question had taken him by surprise. She couldn't imagine why.

"I, um. Out of concern for you and your sisters. And nervousness about what I'll do if I succeed in staying awake." His fingers strummed against the floor. "Not that I won't try! If I can help you, I will do it. I swear it…on my life."

A warm feeling stirred in her chest. "That's very noble of you."

He lowered his head.

Ilara searched for something to say. "You're not wearing your sword."

"Not much point, is there?"

"What?"

Tristan looked up, his forehead wrinkled. "Because…oh. You must not know." He fiddled with his little bag of nuts, his expression wavering with indecision, before he sighed. "Halkon visited your father today. I was in the room. I and some guards tried to attack him, but he turned our swords into flowers. They reverted, but long after he was gone."

Ilara felt her face go pale. "What did he say?"

"He asked for your hand."

"Can you come over here?" She unfolded her arms. "I feel like we're shouting."

"That's because you are," Meelah muttered. "Sleeping. Shh."

Ilara rolled her eyes. Tristan stood and walked closer, stopping about a pace away from her bed.

"By the moon, that's not what I meant. Here." She pointed at the floor right next to the head of her bed, opposite the nightstand.

Tristan took a step back rather than nearer. "I'm not sure I should, Your Highness."

"Why ever not?"

He tugged on his collar. "Yes, Your Highness." He sat where she had indicated and stared straight ahead.

She sighed and lay down on her side, where she could see his profile. "Do I make you nervous, Tristan?" She spoke softer, so as not to bother her sisters.

"I simply don't wish to offend you," Tristan murmured.

"Why should I be offended?"

His throat bobbed. "I have a poor record with women, Your Highness. It seems I was taught poorly how to interact with them."

Ilara couldn't help her laugh, but she quieted when she saw Tristan's tense expression. "Women are just people. It's not difficult to talk to us. In fact, I suspect if you dropped your tiring formality and relaxed, I would enjoy talking to you."

His head snapped toward her, and for a moment, their eyes met in the dim lantern light. She wondered what those eyes would look like in sunlight if she were to see them so close. He turned and rested his head against the wall.

"Habits are hard to break. My father ensured I had a healthy respect for rank. He said it would help me be a better king. Honestly, I now think he was just—" He sucked in a breath. "Nothing."

"Such an odd curse," Ilara murmured. "Can I guess what you were trying to say?"

Tristan shrugged.

She considered what he'd said. "Strict?"

"Sort of."

"Hm. Controlling?"

He nodded. "I think…some people…enjoy the feeling of power. Over anyone." His shoulders rose and fell with a deep sigh. "Can I ask you something?"

"Please."

Tristan glanced at her before speaking. She wished he would look at her without constantly looking away. It made her irritable.

"Your friend, Lady Ryn. She wore one of those metal cuffs on her right ear. So does your father. I supposed they might be related to rank, but you and your sisters don't—"

Ilara snorted. "You really don't know much about Talland for an ambassador."

Tristan's lips turned down. "If I may speak frankly, Your Highness?"

"Finally." She fought a yawn. "Please do."

He gave her an annoyed look. Rather than adding to her irritation, she found she liked that he was acting like a normal human.

"I visited Talland once, four years ago, on a hunting trip in the winter."

"While you were a crown prince? How did I not know that?"

"You weren't meant to," Tristan said with a shrug. "I joined a Rethali noble's sport hunting trip to stroke his ego and win his support for a vote for my father. We didn't tell our Tallander guide who I was, and we only spent a few days in the far southwest. It was wet and freezing, my companions were awkward around me, our irritable guide yelled at me for approaching the sled dogs, and we didn't find any large game, let alone the magical great white elk. At the time from the glimpses I saw, I judged Tallander clothing and lifestyle as rustic and found the wood buildings laughable. I scarcely gave Talland another thought after I returned home. Alex couldn't have picked a better place to send me as punishment if he'd tried."

Her mouth hung open as she stared at him. She wasn't sure if she was angry at his aspersions against her home or amused that when he finally stopped acting like a dried piece of wood, it was to insult her kingdom. He seemed to realize what he'd said, as he paled and hunched down, staring at his hands.

"Overly polite to insulting," she murmured. "What will you say next?"

"I shouldn't have…I'm so sorry—"

"An apology." Ilara shook her head and sighed. "I should have guessed." She tucked her forearm up under her pillow and stifled a yawn. "The winters aren't so bad when you grow up here. They're just a part of life. What do you think of Talland this visit?"

"Hm. Aside from curses and sorcerers?" There was actually a note of humor in his voice.

She chuckled. "Yes, aside from that."

Tristan was silent for a long moment. "It's different from Rethalyon," he said at last, "in so many ways. In the past, I thought that made it worse, but now… I was out walking today, and your forests differ from Rethalyon's, but they're peaceful. Your wood architecture has its own comfortable beauty, and it's not so cold as stone. I saw little of your people's craftsmanship and artistry on my last visit, but it's everywhere, and it's excellent. Your clothing suits you. Your climate, that is."

She lifted a brow, but he wasn't looking at her.

"Many of your ways confuse me, like your succession rights and how little you care about rank and formality and ostentation, and yet, when your servants speak well of you and you challenge everything I was taught, I wonder…if it's actually good. I think, if I had time, Talland could grow on me." He sounded almost mournful.

"I'd love to show you everything there is to adore about Talland." She smiled, but he still didn't look at her. "Anyway. The ear cuffs are symbols of engagement or matrimony. Ryn recently accepted a marriage proposal. Any self-respecting man capable of doing so makes his own engagement cuff for his intended. The patience and time invested in shaping the piece are a sign of his dedication. A jeweler is hired to make the marriage cuffs for men and women, and women's marriage cuffs often are bigger, have more swirling designs, and might be set with stones or gems or polished glass. Also, on the subject of things you don't know, the monarch of Talland is Your Majesty, not Your Excellency."

"Oh." He slid down the wall a little. "Thank you for explaining, Your—"

"Please, just…Ilara. Or nothing."

He looked at her, really looked at her. "Is that common in Talland? In Rethalyon, using titles is common. Married couples often call each other my lord or my lady. This is not so in Eynlae. Couples call each other their given names." He turned his attention to his hands on his lap. "But even in Eynlae, a baron would never call a member of the royal family by their given name."

"It is usually reserved for friends," Ilara admitted.

Tristan gave a short laugh. "I don't have friends. Do you think it's dusk yet?" he asked before she could inquire what he meant. "I didn't realize I was so early."

If he didn't want to talk about friendships, she would respect that, even though his shift into harmless small talk disappointed her. "I'm not sure. Are you lethargic?"

"Oddly, no. But I still don't know what to do."

"Maybe you should simply observe." She tried not to yawn and failed. "See where we go, what we do…" Exhaustion slammed into her. "If you stay awake…watch…and learn…" Her eyes drifted shut.

23

As Ilara's breathing deepened into sleep, Tristan's tension faded. He wished he could do parts of that conversation over, but he'd enjoyed it. Still, he needed to focus on breaking her curse, not think about her lovely low voice or the way she talked to him with friendly respect. Such thoughts wouldn't help him—

The hair on his arms stood on end as the air shifted to feel like the middle of a thunderstorm. In the center of the room, a thread of blue light twisted into being. More light in an array of colors appeared, exactly how it had just before Halkon materialized in the king's side chamber. Tristan internally cursed himself for his lack of planning.

In a rapid decision, he slid under Ilara's bed. With no better ideas, he'd follow Ilara's suggestion of reconnaissance.

Halkon stepped out of the fading lights. Tristan focused on keeping his breathing slow and quiet, and hoped his heart wasn't as loud as it felt. The sorcerer turned toward the lit lantern.

"Probably attempted to stay awake again, the foolish girl," he muttered under his breath. He lifted his hand, and a shimmering goblet appeared in his grasp.

Tristan watched Halkon's boots move to Meelah's bed. Then he went over to Kiri, and Tristan moved enough that he could see as Halkon opened Kiri's mouth and poured a little of what appeared to be wine down her throat. He shifted back under the middle of the bedframe as Halkon turned and approached Ilara.

A protective instinct rose in Tristan, but he forced himself to be still. He would watch and look for any hint of weakness. Even though that meant letting Halkon get away with whatever he was doing as he leaned over the crown princess.

Halkon tsked. "Leaving the lantern burning while you sleep, my dear? In a wood house? Seems reckless. Come, Ilara."

The sorcerer led the princesses out—past a slumbering Sharland and Masarik and two Tallander guards. After a few heartbeats, Tristan followed.

The group didn't speak as Tristan stole after them down the corridor and up the stairs to the princesses' rooms. Halkon strode forward with graceful purpose, but the princesses trailed behind him as if in a daze. It unsettled Tristan.

The girls all entered their own rooms. Halkon leaned against a wall and Tristan dodged back to the stairs, only relaxing when the sorcerer didn't follow. After a few minutes, a door opened and closed, then another. More silence. He crawled to the top of the stairwell and peeked down the hall. Halkon still lazed against the wall, making a knife appear and disappear in a twinkle of purple and gold. Meelah and Kiri waited quietly next to him.

Ilara breezed out of her room in a traditional Tallander dress of dark green and blue with strings of beads across her chest attached to bronze clasps near her shoulders. Her hair hung down her back in a single braid. She would have looked fetching if not for the drugged look in her eyes.

"What about the dresses I gave you?" Halkon asked.

Ilara glanced down at her attire, her lips pursing.

Halkon sighed. "Let's go." He shoved off the wall and pointed his palm down the hallway, away from Tristan. As he moved his hand in a circle, a corresponding circle of swirls of various colors formed. Tristan's mouth dropped open.

The sphere of light opened into a wood. But not a normal wood.

This forest had lush, dark-green grass. Fireflies flickered between trees of gold and silver. A gold leaf fluttered to the ground, glittering in the illumination of glowing crystals poking up every several feet on either side of a worn trail. Halkon strode through the opening without looking back. Ilara followed, with Meelah and Kiri drifting after her.

Tristan made another hasty decision.

He ran after them through the magical doorway.

The opening closed with a soft snap just after he entered. He darted behind a tree and forced his breath to slow. After a moment, he peered around the silver trunk. Halkon and the princesses were several paces ahead of him. He pursued, stealing from tree to tree and avoiding the lighted path.

They drew closer to the sound of strings and pipes, the beautiful music floating through the forest. Soon soft chatter, punctuated with occasional light laughter, mingled with the instruments.

Halkon led the girls into a vast meadow lit by a low, full moon and ringed by glowing mushrooms, crystals, and lanterns. Couples danced while other guests loitered around tables covered in…silver and gold fruit?

The entire scene reeked of otherworldly magic. Tristan's body buzzed with nervous energy. He watched with growing distaste as tall men with too-perfect faces led Meelah and Kiri into dances. Halkon said something to Ilara, but they were too far away for Tristan to hear over the music.

Whatever her response was, Halkon must not have liked it, because anger flashed over his face. He said something else, then left her and stalked away to the far side of the meadow, where he sat on a throne of tangled vines with normal green leaves.

Another too-perfect man led Ilara into a dance.

The party featured a variety of guests with every skin tone, but they were all similarly tall with flawless complexions and had the silkiest hair Tristan had ever seen. Their graceful movements flowed like water as they danced. He hated all of them. Even the women, whose beauty practically hurt to look at for too long. There was something not *right* about any of them.

The princesses were the worst part, though. They had dreamy, almost drunk countenances and didn't converse much, while their partners—like everyone else at the ball—looked completely alert. Meelah's and Kiri's partners sometimes pulled them close or laughed with them, but every so often Ilara's partner glanced toward Halkon, who was engaged in playing a card game on a floating table with three other guests. It was as if the sorcerer had claim to Ilara, and her partner feared overstepping.

Tristan couldn't hide in the shadows while these—beings— danced with enchanted princesses. Something had to be done, but he would be spotted in an instant among all those tall, perfect people. *Alex would probably fit in.* He pushed the annoying thought aside.

Regardless of height and features, he wore brown trousers and a simple short-sleeve gray tunic. The men all wore exquisite long-sleeved tunics trimmed with gold or silver thread and dark fitted trousers. A stupid plan occurred to him. He couldn't fake their faces and height, but their clothing…

Tristan snuck around the perimeter of the clearing, watching the men loitering near the trees. One of the shorter ones—still taller than Tristan, but at least closer—downed a goblet of wine and staggered.

Perfect.

He drew as close as he dared and threw a silver twig at the drunkard's head. The man rubbed the spot and looked over his shoulder, blinking rapidly. Tristan knelt behind a bush. The man shrugged and turned back toward the revelry.

Tamping down his frustration, Tristan chucked another twig and hoped no one else was paying attention. This time, the man approached the edge of the forest.

"Gwendolyn, are you teasing me again?" A pleased, sloppy smile came over the man's face. "Are you trying to lure me into a secret tryst, Gwendolyn?" He staggered into the woods.

Tristan leapt up and slammed the man's head into a trunk before his victim could do more than squeak.

It was awkward, and much more difficult than Tristan had anticipated, to remove the man's attire, and putting on a stranger's still-warm clothes felt wrong. He used his own belt to tie the man's hands behind his back, his trousers to bind the man's feet, and his shirt to gag him. Hopefully, when the man woke up, he wouldn't be able to alert anyone. At least not quickly.

Tristan stopped at the edge of the shadows in the woods. This was insane. Did he really think he could walk into the crowd, and no one would notice? What would they do if they realized he wasn't one of them—and they probably would?

In the twirling, swaying couples, Ilara spun with a man with long, red hair and broad shoulders. As the musicians ended a song, the man gripped Ilara's waist and dipped her backward. She giggled, but her eyes seemed distant, as if she wasn't fully aware of what was happening.

That was all Tristan needed. This curse was cruelly using the princesses, and although he didn't know how he was going to help them, he had to try.

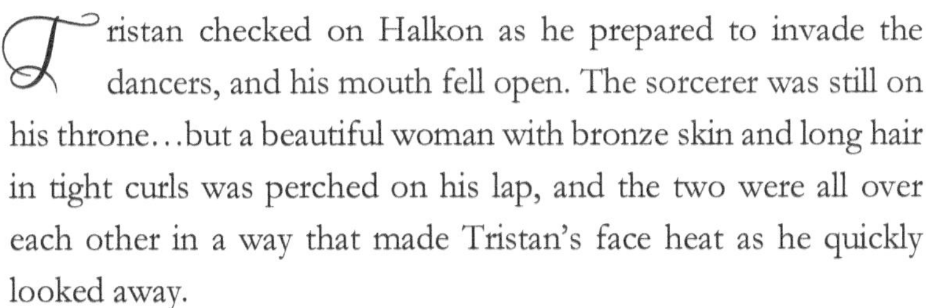

24

Tristan checked on Halkon as he prepared to invade the dancers, and his mouth fell open. The sorcerer was still on his throne…but a beautiful woman with bronze skin and long hair in tight curls was perched on his lap, and the two were all over each other in a way that made Tristan's face heat as he quickly looked away.

He couldn't fathom what that meant for Halkon's demand to wed Ilara, but at least the villain was distracted.

Tristan wove between couples, his gaze fixed on the crown princess. None of the otherworldly-beautiful people paid him any mind. He ignored his racing heart as he tapped on the shoulder of her dance partner.

"May I cut in?"

The man glanced at him, then stared. His golden eyes bore into Tristan, but then he shrugged. "Not as enjoyable to dance with a woman when his lordship won't allow any fun, anyway." He released Ilara, stepping aside and quickly taking up with a new companion.

"Princess." Tristan bowed.

Ilara gave him a weak smile that he didn't like and curtsied. "So many handsome men tonight," she said, her voice light and detached.

Tristan started. She…thought him handsome? Compared to that man she had just been dancing with? He drew a steadying breath as he stepped forward and placed one hand on her back and took her hand in his.

Ilara met his eyes. "I know you…don't I?"

"Yes." Tristan led them into the steps, attempting to match the other dancers. They needed to be as inconspicuous as possible. He drew her in closer. "Princess Ilara, it's me, Baron Tristan of Rethalyon," he whispered. "If you can wake up, come out of this—"

"Tristan." The murky look in Ilara's eyes vanished, and she tightened her grip until his hand felt crushed. He winced as she slowed to a stop and looked around. "Oh, moonlight. What—"

"No," he hissed. "Keep dancing!" He led her forward. "Dance, Your Highness, please."

She lurched after him, then resumed dancing. "Why?"

"I don't want to draw attention. I don't know what will happen if Halkon discovers I've snuck into…wherever we are."

"Oh." She nodded. "Where is he?"

Halkon was still entangled with the woman, to Tristan's mixed relief and disgust. "Distracted for now."

Ilara looked over her shoulder, then snapped her head back toward Tristan, her shock quickly morphing into revulsion. "Such a faithful, attentive suitor," she spat. "But how did you get here?"

"I don't know why, but I didn't fall asleep. I hid under your bed, Halkon appeared in your room and woke you—"

"Yes, I remember." She glanced around, and when her eyes met his again, they were dark with anger. "I remember *everything*."

Tristan missed a step and recovered, his cheeks heating after his blunder. "You do?"

"I do every time I wake up here, which always happens." She glowered, then her expression brightened. "Which means I can tell you, and maybe you will remember! Last night, Domhnall said something about joining his realm to mine or losing his power."

Tristan's stomach twisted. That didn't sound good, but it aligned with what he already suspected—wherever they were, in wasn't in their world at all.

"Wait." Ilara's voice drew his awareness back to her. "Did you steal someone's clothes?"

He winced. "I may have knocked one of the guests unconscious and stolen his clothing and left him bound and mostly naked in the woods, yes. I didn't kill him."

To his shock, she laughed. Not a detached titter, but a genuine laugh. "Clever." She sobered. "So. Do you have a plan?"

He looked away from her intent regard. "No, Your Highness—"

"Tristan, really. You followed a sorcerer through a magical doorway and stripped another man naked to help me; maybe you could call me Ilara now?"

Her teasing almost made him chuckle. For a moment, he considered giving in—but she wouldn't be so familiar with him if he had told her the truth of everything he had done, if she knew of the shadows in his soul.

"Tristan?" She moved closer as they danced. Too close. It made him want to pull her against him, just to know how it would feel.

He cleared his throat. "Perhaps we should get some refreshment, Your Highness?"

"No!" Her fingers tensed on his shoulder. "It's the food that makes me forget and become so...vapid. Whenever I wake up, he forces me to eat or drink, and then I can't remember anything again."

"Oh!" If they hadn't been dancing, Tristan would have slapped himself. "Of course. I saw him pour something from a goblet into Princess Kiri's mouth. I think he did the same to you and Princess Meelah, but I couldn't see."

"Because you were hiding under my bed." Ilara smirked.

His ears burned. "Well, yes—"

She laughed again, and he would have given anything to hear that sound over and over. "It was good thinking. If only—"

"Flames." Tristan ducked his head and pulled her closer. "Halkon is heading this way."

"Oh, moonset." Ilara bit her lower lip. "You should go. I'll pretend I was thirsty and needed to stop. You should hide and follow us back." She kissed his cheek, and time slowed as he lost all sense of anything except the brush of her lips against his skin.

He blinked and squashed the insane urge to kiss her. *No woman owes you herself.* She was only thanking him for helping her.

"Go," she whispered urgently.

Tristan released her, wishing he didn't have to, and stepped aside. He started to walk away as Halkon reached them.

Ilara giggled, but it sounded forced. "Oh, hello—"

"Don't leave on my account, boy."

A hand clamped on Tristan's shoulder, jerked him back, and spun him around. A tempest brewed in Halkon's unnervingly green eyes.

Around them, the dancing stopped.

Halkon looked over the guests, like a king inspecting his knights. "None of you thought to inform me of the human infiltrator?"

Even though he had suspected, Tristan didn't care for how the specification of *human* implied the rest of them were, in fact, not human. What did that make them?

The people around them looked down or shuffled their feet. Somewhere a woman said, "I'm sorry, my lord; I assumed you couldn't not know…"

The corner of Halkon's mouth cut downward.

"And he's wearing our clothes," a man chimed in. "I thought he must be here at your permitting, my lord. Maybe to put the princess at greater ease."

"*I* was fully aware," Halkon ground out. "This was a test. You've lost either your sense or your respect."

Several heads ducked. Tristan hoped Halkon couldn't feel his frantic heartbeat.

"Do you think me weak?" The sorcerer surveyed the crowd. "Perhaps you believe I haven't the strength to enforce my will?"

Vines exploded all around the perimeter of the meadow, growing thick as a man's waist and towering over them until they threatened to block out the moon. Several guests cowered.

"Domhnall," said a male voice, his tone conciliatory. A man with pale skin and flowing brown hair pushed aside a stunned couple to approach. "My lord. My friend. No one meant you offense."

A chorus of murmured assent followed this pronouncement.

The man drew closer and spoke in a whisper, sympathy etched into the worried lines around his eyes. "Can you afford such wasteful displays? Do you believe this will make them think anything other than that you're overcompensating? It doesn't matter if it's not true, they'll wonder."

"You're right, as usual," Halkon whispered with a sigh. "But why didn't you say anything about this?" He gave Tristan a small shake, jerking his shoulder.

The man winced. "You seemed…indisposed to be interrupted. And I assumed you must be toying with the humans." His gaze searched Halkon's face, and when he spoke again, Tristan could barely hear. "You honestly didn't sense him. Did you?"

"Tell anyone that," the sorcerer hissed, "and even you won't be spared my wrath, Daven."

A wounded expression shadowed Daven's features. "I

thought you trusted me more than that, nephew."

"I thought you knew I abandoned trust a long time ago."

Tristan gawked at Daven, scarcely noticing as the vines retracted into the ground. Daven looked the same age as Halkon, maybe even younger. But Daven carried a hint of world-weary sorrow in his eyes.

"Continue the revelry, please." Halkon made a welcoming gesture with his free hand. "I need a word with my guests." His fingers dug into Tristan's shoulder, and he snatched Ilara's hand before forcing them both over to his throne.

"Ilara, my dear." Halkon turned a syrupy smile on her. Tristan wished he would release his death grip. "Why don't you help yourself to some refreshment?"

"Not a chance." She yanked her hand free of his and crossed her arms.

Yes, Tristan preferred her like this. Henry had been a fool to tell him he should desire a meek, easy-to-control wife. That wasn't Ilara, and no one should be forced to change who they were to suit the tastes of someone else.

The fury of wounded pride crackled in Halkon's eyes. He was like Henry. He would demand Ilara's submission, even if he had to break her to get it.

"Ilara." Halkon blew out an agitated breath. "Dearest—"

"Stop calling me that!"

The sorcerer seemed unfazed by her response. "Do you have a preferred term of endearment? My sweet? Lovely? Flower? Beloved?"

"I would prefer you never spoke to me."

"That will make our marriage rather awkward, don't you think?" Halkon lifted a regal brow.

Ilara released a derisive snort. "As awkward as your philandering?"

"Ah." Halkon shrugged. "Just a bit of harmless fun. It's not as if we're married yet."

"And she's not going to marry you," Tristan spat.

Halkon's expression darkened. "*You*." He pointed in Tristan's face. "What are you doing here, and how?"

Tristan's courage faltered. "I followed you and the princesses."

"Trying to be the noble hero and save them, is that it?" Halkon finally released Tristan and lightly shoved him backward. "I don't know how you're awake, but I assure you—you can't succeed. I have chosen Ilara as my bride, and I get what I want. I don't lose." He slung his arm around Ilara and conjured a gold nectarine out of thin air.

She tried to slip away, but Halkon grabbed her shoulder, pulling her against his side, and held the fruit in front of her mouth.

"Ilara, my flower, have a bite to eat."

"I like having my mind clear, thank you." She slapped the nectarine out of his hand.

"Hm." Halkon returned his attention to Tristan. "How did you steal those clothes?"

Tristan shrugged, unsure he wanted to answer that question.

"Will I find one of my subjects dead in the woods?"

"Not dead." He shook his head. He didn't need any more murders on his conscience. Although, if these people weren't human, maybe they wouldn't count. He didn't know.

"You failed, Domhnall. I demand you let us go home and leave us alone." Ilara lifted her chin. Tristan couldn't believe she really thought that would work, but she certainly acted as if it should.

Halkon rolled his eyes. "No." He raised his hand and a gold peach shimmered into existence between his fingers. It unnerved Tristan. "I warned you my patience is nearly at its end. Eat now, and I'll let your friend return home with you in the morning, which is most generous of me."

"Don't," Tristan said, even though inside, he was screaming at the thought of being trapped in this enchanted wood.

Halkon waved the peach. Lowering her gaze, Ilara took it. Tristan's shoulders sagged as her eyes glazed over.

Halkon ran the back of his finger over her cheek. "Ilara, my queen. Will you marry me?"

She giggled, and it wasn't the unabashed, full laugh that Tristan liked. "I can't marry you…" Her brows pinched, as if she couldn't remember why.

"Your Highness, he's trick—"

"Another time." Halkon patted Ilara's head. "Go dance." He pushed her away, and she wandered forward until a man drew her into his arms.

"What's the point of making them dance?" Tristan asked, his anger barely contained.

Halkon turned to Tristan with a scowl that made his blood freeze. "Because I enjoy a party. Because I can. Because it makes them eat and drink more, which makes them more receptive to my will. Or it should," he added under his breath. He sat on his throne and tapped his fingers on the woven vines. "Now. What to do with you?"

25

ristan tugged on the edge of the stolen tunic. How foolish would it be to run? Halkon had claimed he'd let Tristan return with the princesses, but he could have lied. It was the kind of manipulative tactic Henry might have used. But even if he escaped into the woods, what then? He couldn't stay in this gold and silver otherworld, and as far as he knew, Halkon was the only way back to Talland.

The irony of *wanting* to go to Talland would have amused him if the situation hadn't been so dire.

"You're not Tallander," Halkon noted. "Who are you?"

"No. I'm Baron Tristan Carbrey of Rethalyon."

Interest gleamed in Halkon's eyes. "And you're in Talland…why?"

Well, as long as the sorcerer was asking questions, he wasn't turning Tristan into a flower, so he decided to keep answering. "I'm an ambassador."

"Then you're helping the princesses…why?" Halkon leaned forward, propped his elbows on his knees, and placed his chin on his clasped hands. "Why would a Rethali ambassador care what happens to Tallander princesses?"

Tristan rubbed the side of his neck. His heartbeat had slowed, but his muscles were still tense. "I don't have a choice. King Onak threatened to execute me on false charges if I refused.”

Halkon laughed and leaned back in his chair. “Oh, brilliant. I’d planned to feed you my food so you would forget everything and send you back as a benevolence to Ilara. But this…this is much better. I’m going to use you.”

Tristan went rigid, his breath slowing. “Use me?” He didn’t know if he could handle another curse.

“You already have one death threat dangling over your head, so let me offer something sweeter.” Halkon’s lips curled into a wicked grin. “Convince Onak to give Ilara to me in marriage, and I’ll remove your curse.”

Tristan’s mouth fell open. To be free of the curse…to not have to avoid talking about his father or carefully wording everything, to not have to choose between lying, omission, or strangling to death… Could Halkon actually *do* that?

“How do you know I have a curse?”

“I can feel it.” Halkon shrugged. “Can’t quite discern what it does, but it’s dark, angry, vengeful. My kind of curse, to be honest.”

Not being able to tell the curse’s effects didn’t engender in Tristan much faith that Halkon could—or would—remove it. But it didn’t matter. Even if he could convince Onak, he couldn’t betray Ilara.

Tristan was done playing the villain.

But that didn’t mean he didn’t know how to stay alive. “I can try, but I doubt Onak will listen to me.”

“You’re an ambassador. Surely you can be convincing. I don’t care what tactics you use, but if you succeed, I’ll remove your curse.” Halkon moved his fingers through the air, trailing glimmers of purple-blue light and shimmering silver. He flashed an intimidating smile. “Go entertain yourself, sleep, or whatever you wish to do. In the morning, you will start on your new goal. Do we have an agreement?” He stood and stepped close.

Tristan hated how Halkon towered over him. "Agreed."

"Don't disappoint me." The unspoken threat hung in the air.

With a curt nod, Tristan forced his stiff legs to turn him around. How did this flaming mission keep getting worse?

His gaze landed on Meelah, dancing nearby with a man with pale blond hair who was being rather handsy. The young princess didn't seem to notice. Tristan scowled.

If he'd been wrong to touch Raelyn—and he had been—when they were betrothed and she didn't want it, it was unjust for that man to touch Princess Meelah when she was drugged and unaware. He strode forward and cut in, stealing Meelah away.

"Princess Meelah." Tristan met her gaze, hoping, begging, for her to come out of her trance. "Princess Meelah, please wake up."

She giggled. "I am awake, silly man. Don't you love dancing?"

Tristan sighed. "Yes, Your Grace." He danced with her for two songs, by which time Meelah decided she was thirsty. He followed her to the refreshments, pleading with her the whole way.

"Your Grace, you can't drink this wine; it's—"

"Yes, Baron Carbrey?" Halkon walked up on the other side of the table. "What is the wine?" Tristan didn't miss the note of challenge in his voice.

For a moment, he debated standing his ground. But what would be the use?

"It's strong," he muttered.

"Oh, don't worry about me," Meelah said lightly. She lifted a goblet and took a long sip. Tristan's heart sank further. He walked away, unable to watch her eat and drink more of the food that stole her will and awareness.

He spied Ilara at another table, surveying the gold and silver fruit. He strode over to her. Halkon would probably show up and ruin it if he woke her up, but he still wanted to try.

"Princess Ilara."

She looked over her shoulder. "Hello…"

"Tristan." His voice came out more pleading than intended. "Baron Tristan Carbrey of Rethalyon, Your Highness. And you are Princess Ilara of Talland. You belong in Talland. Not here."

"Not…" Ilara blinked hard, and her eyes cleared. "…here."

He sighed with relief. "You're awake." But why hadn't he been able to wake Meelah? Maybe it was mentioning Talland that did it.

"Domhnall didn't hurt you, did he?" Ilara craned her neck and glanced about, doubtless looking for Halkon. "And he's letting you walk around, not enchanted?" She peered at him. "Or does his magic not affect you?"

Tristan shifted his feet, not wanting to discuss his conversation with Halkon. "He's leaving me alone and allowing me to return because I'm not Tallander." He told himself it was safer to lie when Halkon or one of his vassals might overhear. It still felt wrong. Why was being good so hard?

"Oh." She eyed him like she wasn't convinced of the logic. "What time is it?"

He shook his head. "I don't know. The moon is strange. The stars don't move, either."

"The moon…" Ilara glowered at the sky. "It's been directly overhead all night."

He nodded.

"Come to think of it, it's been full every night since we started coming here, too." Something like relief washed over her features. "Oh, that's the best news I've had so far."

Tristan frowned, baffled. "Why—"

"It means it's not our moon, or perhaps an illusion. You see, the moon is sacred to Talland. It guards our nights, and Talland winters are long with short days. Legend says the moon sees us safely through winter." Her expression fell, and she lowered her gaze. "The moon watching over our lonely dances under

Domhnall's controlling enchantment felt like another betrayal."

"Another?" He chided himself for the presumption of asking, but she answered before he could rescind the question.

"The moon didn't save my mother from dying in an ice storm off the coast." Her arms crossed over her stomach, making her look smaller and vulnerable.

He wanted to help, to ease her pain, and had no idea how. She deserved someone good and caring who could chase away the sorrow in her eyes and make her smile again. But he only knew how to hurt people.

Just like his father.

No. He could choose to try to help instead of harm. Unfortunately, only one stupid idea presented itself.

"You said the dances were lonely, but you don't seem to have had any shortage of partners."

Ilara snorted. "Dancing under magical compulsion in a strange land where I don't want to be with men I don't know, or with a maniac sorcerer determined to force me to marry him… Sometimes even surrounded by people you can feel so alone."

A pang went through Tristan's heart. Loneliness when standing right next to someone was a feeling he knew well.

"You know me," he said. She didn't, not really, but he locked that thought away.

Ilara perked up. "Are you asking me to dance?"

He bowed and held out his hand. "Unless you have a better idea of how to pass the rest of the night, Your Highness?"

The corner of her lips curved upward. "If you agree to call me Ilara, I'll dance with you."

Stubborn girl. Tristan glanced down to hide his slight chuckle. "May I have this dance, Ilara?"

"You may, Tristan." She smiled and took his hand, and he led her into a dance.

"I tried to wake Princess Meelah," he confessed as they moved through the steps. "I couldn't. I saw you before I found Princess Kiri." He scowled. "She's too young for this. Taking you and Meelah is outrageous enough, but does Halkon have no shame, enchanting a child?" The words turned sour on his lips, and he winced. "He would have gotten along well with my—" He caught himself just in time.

"I appreciate you trying." Ilara smiled. "And caring."

Tristan nodded, tongue-tied by her smile. As they circled through the beaten-down grass that served as a dancefloor, he was captured by her eyes. He'd never considered dark eyes beautiful until he saw hers. A dangerous thought. He focused on her nose instead, with its myriad of light freckles. Oh flames, why were those cute, too? The stress must have finally broken him, and he was losing his mind.

"Can I ask you something?"

Ilara's question pulled him out of his confused thoughts. "Of course."

"You've never mentioned your mother. What happened to her?"

Tristan swallowed. "She developed an infection after my birth. It seems there was little the physician could do. She died when I was a few weeks old. I've always debated if it was better that I never knew her, because I have nobody real to miss; or worse, because there's nothing there at all, and I miss the idea of her."

"I'm so sorry." The kindness and sympathy in Ilara's gaze overwhelmed him.

"What was your mother like? Only if you want to tell me," he hurried to add, feeling foolish.

"Energetic. She loved life and adored Talland. The land and the people, but especially the land. She spent as much time out-doors as she could and was more adventurous than my father."

Ilara smiled sadly. "I always admired her liveliness…and for a while, I resented it after she died. If she'd been more like my father—cautious, content to stay home—she wouldn't have gone on that hunting expedition. She wouldn't have been caught in that ice storm and have gotten separated from her party and died."

Her hand moved from the top of Tristan's shoulder to the back as she drew nearer to him as they spun. He didn't understand why she'd do that.

"I think," Ilara said quietly, "really, I was angrier with myself that I wasn't with her. She invited me, but I wasn't feeling well, so I stayed home."

Tristan remained silent, unsure what to say and sensing she needed to talk about this.

"I wish I'd made a different choice, or convinced her to wait, or…" She sighed. "But we can't change the past, you know?"

He certainly did.

"It was hard. It still is," she whispered. "Some days it hurts like it was yesterday, not six years ago. All the moments when I think she should be there, when I wish I could talk to her, and then I feel her absence.

"But I'm thankful for the time I had with her. She taught me to be determined and unrelenting and to embrace life, but also to be kind and understanding. Every memory I have of her, I treasure. And there's so much of her in me, and in my sisters. Sometimes that makes the pain worse, but usually, it helps." She drew back. "I'm sorry! I'm here talking about being glad I knew her and—"

Tristan offered what he hoped was a reassuring smile. "I asked. I'm happy you knew her. She sounds wonderful."

"Well, she was hardly perfect." Ilara laughed. "We argued and annoyed each other at times, as parents and children do…" She bit her lower lip. "I'm so sorry—I keep saying the wrong thing—"

"Don't be." They spun around, and Tristan pulled her in closer. It felt better, somehow. "I wouldn't wish my family on anyone."

"Does that include your cousin?"

He couldn't very well say *only for selfish reasons.* "No. Everyone loves Alex."

"But not you."

He didn't have a clear answer to that.

Ilara squinted at him. "I had to fight to get you to call me Ilara, but you call your own king Alex."

His cheeks flushed. "You're correct; I shouldn't—"

"Do you not respect him?"

Tristan considered the question. "I do. He's gracious yet strong. Resilient and merciful. Prone to a temper, but if he can keep that under control, he'll make at least a decent king, probably a good one. And he'll be a wonderful husband to Raelyn."

"But you don't like him."

The song ended, and they separated to bow and curtsy.

"Is this important?" he asked, trying not to become agitated.

"Just curious."

He straightened the strange, lightweight tunic and looked out at the silver and gold trees. Around them, couples began dancing to a new, slower song. "I'm trying. He took my crown, my bride, and my home. But Alex belongs on the throne, and he and Raelyn belong together. For a while, I blamed him for taking my father, too, but I'm realizing more and more…I never had my father. Honestly, I should have known. It seems stupid now that I didn't realize how cruel—" His throat closed up as the curse took effect, and he coughed and tried not to panic. The strangled feeling faded.

"Anyway," he muttered, "the fact is, those things were never truly mine to start with."

"But it still feels like a loss," Ilara said softly. "It still hurts."

He nodded, emotions tangling his tongue and ridiculous, unwanted tears threatening his eyes. Raelyn had been the only other person to acknowledge his hurt, but somehow, it felt different coming from Ilara—more understanding and without any judgment or implication he had no right to feel sorrow or pain. Ilara's sympathy meant more than he could have imagined.

"Well." He offered her his hand. "We should probably either dance or get out of the way."

26

$\mathcal{C}$lara lost count of how many times they danced. All she knew was her feet felt heavier, and her legs more wooden with each step. Her mouth was parched, and her stomach kept rumbling for food—thankfully, mostly covered by the music—but she didn't want to stop.

Sometimes she told Tristan stories about her sisters or Ryn or described some of her favorite places in Talland and why she loved them. He listened attentively, in a way that didn't make her feel awkward or silly for talking so much. His intent brown eyes focused on her, not like he felt obligated, but like he *wanted* to look at her.

Tristan told her a little about Rethalyon, and she had so many questions about their massive palace of red brick and the power held by their Court of Lords—but by the way his mouth tightened and he averted his eyes, talking about his past distressed him, so she didn't ask all of her questions.

Sometimes they danced without speaking, and those moments of quiet were her favorite. When they weren't conversing, Tristan drifted closer. The longer they danced, the more comfortable their silence and their closeness became. A hint of strong muscles shifted beneath his stolen tunic. His hand on her back was firm and confident, but not controlling or crass. It was probably foolish for a princess to fall for a dethroned prince turned ambassador she had known for a couple days, but she couldn't deny her growing attraction to him.

As the night dragged on, she rested her head against his shoulder. He smelled of musk and forest and felt strong and so comfortable and warm—until he pulled away.

"Perhaps we could…sit down for a bit?" Tristan cleared his throat. "Just a bit tired and thirsty and hungry, but…can't partake of the refreshments if I want to remember."

"Oh. Sure." She released him and turned away, weaving between couples as quickly as possible. How stupid was she? Tristan didn't even want to be in Talland and had only recently been in an arranged betrothal. He wasn't interested in her.

But then, if he didn't care about her…why had he followed them? Why was he trying so hard to help them? It didn't make sense.

Or he was simply tired and hungry, and she was overreacting due to her own hunger and exhaustion. How much longer until dawn? She sat on a stump chair near the edge of the meadow and glared up at the always-full moon that gave no indication whether any time had passed at all.

Tristan sat on another stump chair near hers with a heavy sigh. He rested his arms on his legs, and his head fell forward. "How have you been doing this every night? My feet are killing me."

Ilara was about to respond that her feet ached worse than usual when a voice behind her made her jump.

"The food and wine help," Domhnall said.

Ilara twisted around on the stump. The sorcerer stood behind her, rolling a silver apple between his palms.

"You must be famished, my dear." Domhnall held forth the apple. "Eat. It will ease your mind and your body."

"No, thank you." She turned her back to him, an angry fire burning in her chest.

"I don't remember saying please." Domhnall circled around in front of her and proffered the apple again. "Eat."

"Moonless winter take you and your fruit."

"What does it matter to you if she eats?" Tristan asked. He still sat on his stump, but he stared coldly at Domhnall. "It isn't making her agree to marry you."

Domhnall gave Tristan a patronizing, closed-lipped smile. "I have no need to explain myself to you, Rethali. Don't test my mercy."

Tristan's jaw tightened, but he kept his mouth shut.

"Ilara, you need sustenance." When she continued to ignore him, he huffed a bored sigh. "Don't make me resort to threats. It will put such a damper on our relationship."

"If we have a relationship," Ilara snapped, "it is only that of a captor and captive."

"Then be a good captive and do as you're told, and I don't have to do anything unpleasant."

Ilara hesitated. "But you can't—"

"Really, dearest, need I explain again that losing my wager is an option, but losing you isn't?" Domhnall rolled his eyes. "I haven't yet made any threats or done any harm. Do you really want to know what it will look like when I do?"

Memories of bloody vines and Byron's screams assaulted Ilara. "I'll—I'll eat it." She took the apple and stared at its dull silver surface with resentment before biting into it. The fruit crunched between her teeth. Her anger and fear receded until they disappeared.

"Eat a few more bites, dearest." Domhnall gently guided her hand holding the apple back to her lips.

She started to open her mouth but paused as she spotted a man standing near Domhnall. He was vaguely familiar, with his brown hair and square jaw with a short beard, and he looked troubled. Domhnall stepped to the side, blocking the man from her view. She ate more of the apple.

"Good." Domhnall patted her arm. "Go find your sisters."

Ilara found Meelah and Kiri quickly, as the guests were departing, and the clearing grew emptier by the second.

"Is it time for bed yet?" Kiri asked around a mouthful of food. "I do love dancing, but I'm so tired."

"Even I'm exhausted." Meelah yawned as she set down a goblet, as if proving her point.

"Maybe you've had too much to drink," Ilara joked. Maybe *she'd* had too much to drink, although she didn't recall drinking. She didn't remember any of the evening at all and felt oddly detached. As she led her sisters to Domhnall, something niggled at the back of her mind; an indistinct feeling of dread.

"Don't forget our deal," Domhnall was saying to a far shorter man with brown hair.

Ilara's sense of unease grew, and yet she couldn't bring it into focus. Her thoughts slipped through her fingers like mist.

The shorter man glanced at the girls and nodded.

Domhnall followed his companion's line of sight. "Ah, princesses, good. Time to go."

He led them through a dazzling doorway made of glittering multicolored light and into a pitch-black room. She blinked in the startling darkness.

"I'll see you tonight, my dear." Domhnall lifted her hand and gently kissed her fingers, his emerald eyes fixed on her like an adoring lover. Ilara watched him leave through the light, wanting him and loathing him at once.

The door disappeared with a snap and the light vanished, leaving them in a dark so deep there was no difference if her eyes were open or shut. Someone brushed against her.

"Sorry," a man whispered.

Ilara drew away, curling her hands into fists. "Who's there?"

"A friend."

There was some shuffling, a thud, and a muttered curse, followed by more fumbling noises. The sharp rasp of steel on flint sounded, and sparks flew to Ilara's right. After a few strikes, a lantern blazed to life, casting a yellow-orange glow on a barren wood room with three unmade beds. The man turned from the lantern to Ilara, his features sagging.

"Are you awake yet, Ilara?"

"Of course I'm…awake…" But then her mind woke up. She couldn't recall what had happened last night—other than dancing and Domhnall's face—but she recognized Tristan and understood her situation. She groaned and cursed Domhnall.

"Moonless winter." Meelah threw herself onto her bed. "I hate this. I hate that Domhnall Halkon. I hate him, I hate him, I hate him." She screamed into her pillow. Ilara wished she could help or comfort her, but she had nothing to offer but the same frustrations.

Kiri stared down at the floor. "Why does he have to take us all? He only wants you! Why can't he leave me alone! This is your fault!"

"Kiri…" Ilara winced, guilt and anger mixing at her sister's accusation.

Meelah sat up. "Kiri—"

"I'm sorry." Kiri wiped her eyes with the base of her hand. "I'm just so tired." She sobbed, and Ilara pulled her into a tight embrace.

She had no words of comfort, no reassurances like her mama would have given. She didn't know if things were going to be all right. So she just held Kiri and rubbed her back while they both cried.

A moving shadow caught her eye, and she looked over.

Tristan moved toward the doorway, looking uncomfortable. Wait…Tristan had been there—in the meadow.

"Tristan!" Ilara sniffled, still holding on to Kiri. He stopped and looked over at her. "I…I remember…a little." She wiped at her face, keeping one arm around Kiri. "You were there… You followed us. We danced!"

Tristan nodded, and for a moment, the corner of his mouth pulled up in a smile, but then his expression fell. "Yes. I managed to wake you a couple times, until Halkon made you eat that fruit again. I don't know how, maybe mentioning Talland. I couldn't get Meelah to come out of the trance. I didn't have a chance to try with Kiri."

"Fruit…" Ilara's breath caught as bits and pieces of memories returned. Not the whole night, but parts of it. The magical forest, the enchanted wine and food, dancing…especially dancing with Tristan. His palm against her back and her hand in his, the muscles under his…no, not his tunic, a tunic he had stolen. And… "Domhnall told you to remember your deal." The words came out with more venom than she'd intended.

Tristan scrubbed his hand against the side of his face. "He offered to remove my…punishment." He tapped his throat. "If I convince you or your father to let you marry him. I lied and told him I'd try so that he wouldn't force me to eat the fruit and forget."

Her heart softened. She shouldn't have been so quick to accuse him of conspiracy. He was too honest and chivalrous for that.

"I should go." He edged toward the hallway. "I need to report to your father, sleep, and form a plan for tonight."

Ilara lifted her brows. "You're going to try again?"

"I—of course."

Kiri pulled out of Ilara's arms and shuffled to her bed, where she sat and took off her shoes.

"But Domhnall caught you. I doubt he'd be happy to see you…there again." Wherever there was.

Tristan gave a half-hearted shrug. "That's something I'll have to plan for." He bowed. "Goodnight…er, day, Ilar—um, princesses." He slipped out into the dim sunlight in the hallway and shut the door behind him.

Meelah swung her feet back and forth over the edge of her mattress and nodded in the direction of the door. "What's going on there?"

"Nothing." Ilara stuck out her tongue at her sister, then yawned. She sat on her bed and debated going to sleep in her dress instead of waiting for a nightgown. They should have a dresser brought in. But no, moving in a dresser was too near an admission they couldn't beat Domhnall. She couldn't allow that.

After a servant brought them nightgowns and Ilara had given directions to be woken in four hours, she snuggled under her blankets and lay there, halfway between consciousness and dreams, thinking about dancing with Tristan.

27

"But *how* did you stay awake?" Onak asked again.

Tristan bit back another sigh and blinked to get his fatigued eyes to focus. "I don't know. Maybe it was proximity—"

"I've sat right next to her and fallen asleep."

"Well…" He covered a yawn with his hand. "I was eating." It was difficult to think about anything other than crawling into bed and sleeping. "I promise, Your Ex—Majesty," he corrected, recalling Ilara's instruction, "I will consider what I did yesterday carefully and let you know what I discover. I'll be trying again tonight, and whether or not I succeed, that should help me understand."

"Very well." Onak slumped back in his throne. "Go. I can see you're exhausted."

"Thank you, Your Majesty." Somehow, Tristan managed not to fall over when he bowed, then stumbled up the stairs to his suite. He shook his head with a grunt at Sharland and Masarik and made straight for his bed, stopping only long enough to kick off his boots before dragging himself under the covers and falling asleep.

A crash and laughter woke him. Judging by the light coming in through the flame-cursed window, he must have slept for several hours, but his heavy body wanted to go back to sleep. He should get up, though. He needed to review the day prior to determine what he had done differently than the first two nights and make a plan. As soon as he sat up, his head started aching. He groaned and leaned forward.

The laughter from the sitting room quieted, and a moment later, his door opened a crack. Remy pushed the door open and bowed.

"I'm sorry, my lord; did we wake you?"

"It's fine." Tristan's voice came out a garbled mess, and he cleared his throat. "I need to be up. And water. I need water desperately." He tossed back the covers, stretched, and threw his legs over the side of the bed as Remy scurried away.

"So you stayed awake and followed the princesses." Masarik leaned in the doorway, his bulk taking up most of the space. "How?"

Tristan rubbed sleep out of his eyes. "Don't know. Wait, how do you know that?"

"Guard heard the princess talking to the king about it between meetings in the great hall; he told a servant, so everyone knows."

"Ah." Tristan frowned. "Ilara has been in meetings today?" He was struggling just to have this conversation.

The knight grinned. "Seems she's made of stronger stuff than you."

"Pardon me, Sir Masarik." Remy waited for the knight to move aside, then brought a goblet of water to Tristan.

"Thank you." Tristan's mouth was gross, but he didn't care. He gulped down the water and handed the cup back to Remy. His stomach rumbled. "Can you get me some food? And order hot water drawn for a bath?"

"Of course, my lord." Remy rushed back out, squeezing past Masarik still looming in the doorway.

"So what happened?" the knight asked. "Where do they go?"

Tristan took a deep breath to steady himself and released it slowly. As tired and hungry as he was, he wanted to snap at the knight to be quiet, but they were finally getting along. "I'll make you a deal, Sir Masarik. You leave me alone long enough to wake up, eat, and bathe, and I'll tell you everything."

"I just don't understand why you didn't fall asleep when everyone always does."

Tristan clenched the blankets as he focused on not losing his temper. "I don't know, Masarik. I ate some nuts and—"

"Wait, the almonds?" Masarik asked. "From Rethalyon?"

"Yes…?"

"Maybe because the only food you ate yesterday was Rethali."

Tristan straightened. "You're right. The nuts were the only food I ate—well, ate and kept down. And Halkon's strange food is what makes the princesses forget…" He flopped back on the bed as his empty stomach twisted in on itself. "He cursed the Tallanders' food. I don't have any more almonds. I can't eat if I want to try again tonight." Ridiculous and embarrassing as it was, he had the urge to cry.

Instead, he forced himself to sit up. "It's fine. I'll manage." His stomach gurgled, and he gripped it with a grimace.

Masarik snorted. "Sure, and fine shape you'll be in if you do stay awake." He uncrossed his arms. "I think I still have some almonds and dried figs from Rethalyon in my bags." He walked away. Tristan stared at the empty door. Was Masarik…helping him?

When Masarik returned a few moments later, he tossed a couple small sacks to Tristan. "Eat. Then I want to hear everything."

Tristan caught the pouches and looked from them to Masarik. "Thank you."

Masarik just grunted and turned away, nearly running into Remy. "Oh, excellent." He grabbed a covered tray out of Remy's hands. "I'll take that since his lordship doesn't need it."

The lost, panicked expression on Remy's pale face as Masarik carried the tray to the table made Tristan chuckle.

"It's fine, Remy. It might be the Tallanders' food that's making everyone sleep." He held up the little sacks. "So only nuts and figs from Rethalyon for me."

"Oh. Sorry." Remy's lips twisted to the side before he brightened. "But the water should be up shortly for your bath."

After a sad meal of almonds and figs and a bath that did little to ease his tired body and aching feet, Tristan dressed and entered the sitting room. Sharland sat at the table with the other two men, playing cards. They looked up at him and abandoned their game, turning toward him expectantly.

Tristan sat in the armchair nearer the door to his chamber and fixated on the brick lining the empty fireplace. "If you're hoping for good news, I have none. If anything, what I learned is more reason for you to leave."

"Tell us what happened, my lord, and perhaps we can decide for ourselves, yes?" Sharland lifted an eyebrow and fixed Tristan with a steady gaze.

Tristan shrugged and focused again on the bricks as he recounted the night. It sounded ridiculous, but he knew what he'd experienced.

"Halkon agreed to allow me to return to Talland with my memories," he finished. "I told King Onak it was because I'm Rethali, but the truth is Halkon only let me leave because Ilara ate his enchanted fruit, and he left me with my memories only so I can convince Onak and Ilara to accept his proposal."

One of the men drew in a sharp breath. Masarik scowled, and Remy looked both shocked and confused.

Sharland pursed his lips. "You agreed to his deal?"

"I don't intend to actually attempt it." Tristan tapped his fingers on the arm of the chair. "Halkon is…vile. There's something *off* about him and his world and his perfect subjects. I don't think they're even human."

"Right, they're fae," Remy said.

Tristan stared, his mouth open. "I…what?"

Remy blushed. "Is that not what you were thinking? Fae?" He looked to Sharland and Masarik. "Doesn't that make the most sense?"

Masarik shrugged. "That's what it sounds like. Not sure I believe in the fair folk, though."

"I'm sorry… Fae?" Tristan rubbed his temple. "You're being serious?"

A deep line creased Sharland's forehead. "I'd think it would be obvious."

"How? How is fae obvious?" Tristan demanded as he tried to ignore the headache forming behind his brow.

"Well…the food, mostly…" Remy scratched the back of his head. "Didn't you ever hear the story of Sir Roderick and the fae? If he ate the food, he'd lose his mind and never find his way out of their realm?"

Masarik looked at Tristan with disbelief. "The magic doorways sound similar to what's in a lot of legends about the fair folk. Although in the stories, they're called portals."

"The stories also often describe the fae world as an enchanted wood," Sharland added.

Tristan slunk down in his chair and avoided looking at any of them. "I'd have to have been told nursery stories or allowed to read legends to know those things," he mumbled.

"Did…did you just say you've never been told a nursery story?" Bewilderment filled Sharland's voice. Maybe even a twinge of sorrow, but Tristan must have imagined that. "Surely you just don't remember."

"You must have read a book of legends," Masarik insisted. "The palace has a library."

Tristan clenched his teeth as his stiff fingers dug into the arms of the chair. He forced his body to relax. "Henry believed nursery stories were the purview of women, and that women were weak. Legends were useless tales that filled the mind with nonsense and didn't help a king rule. So no, I know nothing of the fae."

"Unbelievable," Masarik said. "The one man who wanders into the fae's realm happens to be the only one who doesn't know a thing about them."

Tristan would have liked to tell the knight off, but he reminded himself it wasn't actually Masarik he was angry with. It was Henry and Domhnall Halkon and King Onak and this entire ridiculous situation—none of which were Masarik or Sharland or Remy's fault. He looked up at them.

"Then tell me. Please. The princesses haven't made the connection, either. I don't know what I'm doing. Is there anything useful in these tales?" He tried not to let that glimmer of hope ignite, but it was the first time there had been any real chance of forming a strategy.

"Well…iron," Remy said.

Sharland nodded. "All the tales agree that both fae and their weaker, smaller cousins the fairies can't stand iron. It weakens or burns or kills or repels them, depending on the story, but it's always used against the fair folk, so there must be some truth to it."

"There are two basic rules for dealing with fae, from what I've heard," Masarik said. "You've already figured out the first one. Don't eat their food." He winced. "You already messed up the other rule."

"What?" Embarrassing panic crept into Tristan's voice.

"Don't make deals with fae." Masarik frowned. "But mostly because they're tricky. Some stories say they'll keep their word, but in a way that benefits them more than you. Some say they'll twist words to suit them, regardless of intent. Other legends say a fae can't go back on a promise or a deal, but they also bestow terrible punishments on anyone who breaks their word."

Tristan's stomach writhed. He hoped he wouldn't regret eating Masarik's almonds and figs.

"Nothing to be done about that," Sharland noted. "Perhaps avoid any further deals, though?"

He nodded, feeling oddly disconnected from his body.

"You should probably go back to bed." Remy's brows pinched and worry crept into his eyes. "You look pale, and you'll need rest if you're going to try again. We'll be quieter. Right, Masarik?"

"Aye. I'm going out, anyway." Masarik stood.

"What?" Tristan snapped back to the moment as a more immediate issue demanded his attention. "Where? Why?"

"Don't get your cape in a twist, my lord; just meeting up with some Tallander guardsmen for archery target practice. They're going to teach me their techniques." Masarik headed toward his room. "Nothing to worry yourself over. Promise I'll be on my *very* best behavior."

"I don't wear a cape," Tristan muttered under his breath. "All right. If I'm not up, please wake me an hour before dusk." He returned to his room and sank into the bed, where sleep silenced his anxious thoughts.

yn eyed Ilara with concern as they walked down the hallway. "Are you sure you don't want to go back to sleep? You look exhausted. This really can wait—"

"Moonlight, no." She didn't need Ryn coddling her, too. Papa did enough of that already. "Domhnall is not going to take spending time with my best friend away from me. We have a wedding to plan, and I promised I'd help."

"I'm not getting married until this curse is broken, so I don't know why you're so insistent we plan right now."

"Because I need *something* fun to distract me." Ilara nudged her companion as they entered the stairwell, trying to lighten the mood. Nika ran down the steps ahead of them.

"What about a Rethali who mysteriously stays awake when no one else can?" Ryn lifted a questioning eyebrow.

"Who is also an excellent dancer…" Ilara fiddled with her hair. "And who didn't want to come here and had some insulting things to say about Talland. Although he says it's growing on him, and he said a lot of nice things, too. He's confusing is what he is."

"Tristan's an excellent dancer?" Ryn opened the door to the foyer. "Are you saying you remember something from last night?"

"Quite a bit, actually. It's strange." Ilara explained the bits and pieces she could recall as they headed outside, Ryn leading the way to the spot she and Lorik had chosen for the wedding.

"So what are your feelings on Tristan after all of that?" Ryn asked as she took a stick from Nika and threw it for her.

"It's a shame." Ilara sighed, her disappointment returning. "I think I could really like him. You know, *like*. He seems honest. Straightforward. Heroic. He's undoubtedly brave. And he swore on his life to help us."

"So why only *could* like him, then?"

"I don't think he likes me, aside from his general dislike of Talland." Ilara took the twig from Nika and tossed it again. "He's so formal and stiff. He pulled away when I leaned on him when we were dancing."

"You *leaned* on him? My, my."

Ilara swatted at a cloud of gnats hovering in a patch of sunlight in the forest path. "I was tired. And he was…comfortable. But then he asked to stop dancing."

"Men are mysteries."

Especially men named Tristan Carbrey. "Speaking of men, I thought we were going to discuss *your* wedding? Nika, come. Leave the rabbit hole alone."

Nika whined, but obediently returned to Ilara's side.

"Honestly, picking the location for the ceremony is about as much as we've done, other than starting to write our vows."

"That's it?" Ilara stopped walking and caught Ryn's hand, forcing her to stop as well. "Why?"

"It's hard to think about a wedding with everything going on," Ryn said softly, her gaze on the path ahead. "Lorik asked me about flowers for the arch yesterday and I broke down crying." She looked at Ilara, and her eyes were damp. "You're supposed to be helping me. We always said…" She sniffled, and a tremble went through her.

Ilara swallowed back her own emotion. "Ryn…" She pulled her

best friend into an embrace, ignoring Nika brushing against them.

"I'm sorry, Ara…" Ryn's voice shook.

"Shhh, no, why would you be sorry?" Ilara rubbed Ryn's shoulder, wishing she was better at offering comfort.

"You're going through…everything, and I'm here crying over flowers."

"It's not the flowers," Ilara murmured.

"I'm so worried about you." Ryn eased out of her arms. The tattoos circling her wrist poked out of her sleeve as she wiped away her tears. "I'm happy about my engagement and sometimes when I'm with Lorik everything feels so right and joyful and then I remember why I don't see you as much anymore, and I feel guilty for being happy. I want to help and there's nothing I can do. I feel so scared and helpless and get so angry and sad that you're not with me like you should be, and then I realize it's so much worse for you, and I'm so selfish, acting like it's a trial for me when—"

"No!" Ilara gripped Ryn's shoulders, her heart heavy. "You're allowed to feel all those things, Ryn. It's hard on you, too, and I'd never be upset with you for being worried about me or for feeling sad. Besides, you *are* helping. You're helping me cope and feel more like myself and you deal with my crankiness from not getting enough sleep. And don't you ever, for one second, feel guilty about being happy. I want nothing more than for my best friend to be happy. All right?"

Ryn nodded, although she looked like she wanted to argue. Ilara spoke first.

"Come on." She tugged Ryn forward and they started back along the path. She had to throw the stick again to get Nika to stop walking so close she almost tripped over the dog. "Tell me what else you've decided on. Food?"

"Oh, food," Ryn groaned. "I don't want to talk about how much food is going to cost with the shortages—sorry." She reddened. "You wanted something fun, and I'm talking about shortages."

"I did ask." Ilara sighed. "I hope Rethalyon has grain to trade, but Papa says he doesn't want to consider trade until Domhnall is dealt with. He won't even let me discuss it with Tristan on my own. I'm worried about him…I did more talking in today's meetings than he did. That hasn't happened in years." She shook her head. "Meanwhile, our people struggle. What does it matter to Tallanders if this sorcerer is defeated and yet they starve?"

"He's trying," Ryn said quietly.

Ilara knew that. She also knew Papa was terrified of losing any of his daughters after he lost Mama, and that the last time he had given in to his pain and despair, he hadn't been able to think clearly, and she feared it was happening again.

"And what good is it if the people are fed now but a sorcerer takes over Talland and destroys it?" Ryn countered.

"I suppose." Ilara tossed the stick for Nika with a little more aggression than necessary. "I wish I remembered more of what Domhnall said about joining realms and his magic. Maybe understanding what he was trying to do and why would help me know how to stop him." She glanced over at Ryn and felt a prick of guilt at the heavy expression on her friend's face. "Well, that's enough of that talk. Are we close?"

Ryn brightened. "Almost there. Also, I realized I did decide on one other thing. I want my dress to be periwinkle."

"You do look good in periwinkle."

"Lorik thinks so, too." Ryn blushed. "Ah, here we are! So we're thinking the arch over there…" She dove into an explanation, asking Ilara for input, and Ilara smiled, glad for something bright and beautiful to focus on, even for a moment.

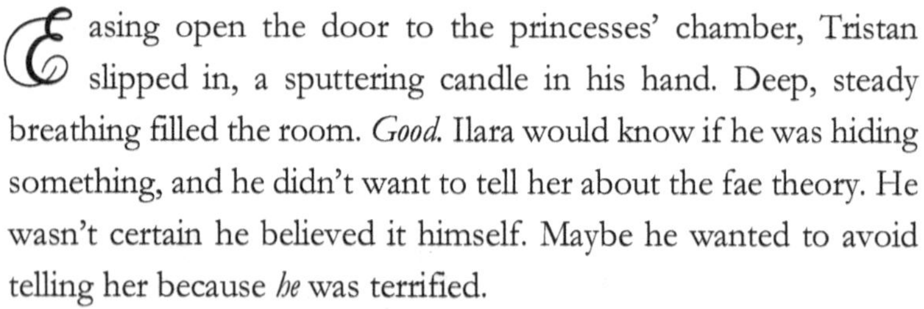

29

 asing open the door to the princesses' chamber, Tristan slipped in, a sputtering candle in his hand. Deep, steady breathing filled the room. *Good.* Ilara would know if he was hiding something, and he didn't want to tell her about the fae theory. He wasn't certain he believed it himself. Maybe he wanted to avoid telling her because *he* was terrified.

The door made a soft click as it closed. He frowned at the darkness. Should he hide under Ilara's bed again? Or stay up and tell Halkon that accompanying the princesses was part of his strategy to convince Ilara to agree to the marriage?

He'd meant to plan this all out ahead of time, but after talking to his men, he'd slept until Remy woke him—later than he should have. Tristan had scrambled to freshen up and eat a few figs before rushing downstairs.

"*Useless,*" Henry's voice taunted.

"I'll figure something out," Tristan muttered.

"Do you always talk to yourself?"

He nearly jumped out of his skin at Ilara's quiet words. "I thought you were asleep."

She propped herself up on her side. "Come over here."

Tristan obliged, surprising himself with his eagerness to be near her again as he returned to his spot sitting next to her bed.

He set the candle on the ground and rested his head against the wall.

"You don't have to do this, you know."

Tristan barely managed to stop himself from laughing. He didn't have a choice; her father had seen to that. But she didn't know that. Instead, he said, "I gave my word. On my life."

Ilara was quiet for a moment, but he could feel her watching him. "So. *Do* you always talk to yourself?"

"No." Tristan frowned. It wasn't even really talking to himself, it was arguing with the judgmental voices in his mind, but he couldn't say that. Could he?

"You're talkative tonight," she said, and Tristan shot her an unamused glare, which only made her chuckle. "Do you have a plan?"

"No." He rubbed the side of his head. "Other than an experiment. Yesterday all I ate was nuts from Rethalyon, and I stayed awake. So today I only ate some Rethali nuts and dried figs. If I stay awake again, that means—"

"It's the food!" Ilara bolted upright on her bed and slapped her forehead. "It's his strange fruit that makes us forget, and we're never hungry here since we eat there. *Of course* it must be that he did something to the food here that's making everyone sleep. Tristan, that's wonderful. All we have to do is determine how far away people *aren't* falling into an enchanted sleep and have the guards eat food from there, and then they can catch Domhnall."

Tristan watched her excited expression with a heavy heart. If only it were that simple. But he kept quiet, finding he didn't want to be the one to extinguish her hope.

Her smile faded as she studied him. "You don't seem to agree with me."

"No, I agree with trying food from outside the Great House's grounds, but…" He hesitated. "Do you remember me mentioning that Halkon turned my sword into a flower? I'm not sure it will be so easy as merely being awake."

"Oh. Right." She eased down onto her pillow, her face pinched. "There has to be a way to stop him. Or keep him from using his magic or"—she yawned—"or something."

Tristan chewed on the inside of his cheek. Dare he share his men's information? In his rush to leave, he hadn't had time to check if he had anything made of iron to bring with him to test against Halkon and his subjects. Perhaps it would be best to wait.

But Ilara was watching him with narrowed eyes. "You're not telling me something again."

She always knew. He was seriously starting to wonder if Henry *feared* how intelligent and capable women were, and that's why he'd disparaged them so.

"My men have a theory," Tristan admitted in a low voice. "I'm not sure I believe it, and if it is true, it's not great." He took a deep breath, then explained the reasoning his men had given for believing Halkon and his people were fae.

She was silent for so long Tristan finally looked over at her, heat suffusing his face.

"I know, it's ridiculous—"

"No, it makes sense." Ilara rolled onto her back and stared up at the ceiling. "I haven't thought about fairies since I was a small child. They don't feature much in our legends. Sprites and spirits are more common. But I still—I should have realized. He said his *realm*, like it's separate from our world, and he talks about himself as if he isn't mortal. And everything else… Oh, I'm so blind." Heavy, sorrowful anger undercut her murmured words.

She huffed, then rolled onto her side to look at him. "But then—the legends say they have a weakness, right? The fair folk in the stories can be bound by—oh, what was it?"

"Iron," Tristan answered. "My men say it's iron."

"Your men. So…this didn't occur to you, either?"

Tristan smiled wryly. "As I told my men, one would have to have been told nursery stories or have been allowed to read legends to know fae lore."

"Your father didn't seriously forbid you nursery stories and legends?" Ilara's chuckle tapered off as he gave her a blank stare. "That's…I'm sorry."

His shoulder blades dug into the wall at his back, and he shifted, trying to get more comfortable, but he wasn't positive whether his discomfort was due to his position or the conversation. "Well. What were the chances of fae stories becoming relevant to my life and survival, right? When have legends ever actually saved someone's life before?"

Ilara didn't respond, and he looked over, fearing he had offended her, only to find she'd fallen asleep. Tristan smiled to himself, then stiffened. If Ilara was asleep, that meant Halkon would arrive any moment. He blew out the candle and slipped under Ilara's bed.

Just as he pulled himself fully under the mattress, the air shifted, and light flashed in the center of the room. Halkon stepped through a portal, his arms full of pink fabric and a goblet clutched in one hand. Tristan practically held his breath as Halkon went around waking the princesses, starting with the youngest and ending with Ilara.

"Ilara, my dearest." Halkon's seductive tone made Tristan want to shove out from under the bed and kick the villain in the jewels. "I've brought you a new gift, since you seem to have lost the previous ones." As they walked out of the room, Halkon handed Ilara the bundle of fabric. "Do wear it tonight."

"Oh, thank you," Ilara mumbled as the little group turned out into the hall.

Tristan waited a few moments longer before following them.

Once again, Halkon waited in the hallway while the princesses readied themselves for the ball. Tristan lingered on the stairs, occasionally daring to peer over the top step and confirm that Halkon was still there, looking bored. A door opened, and Tristan peeked again as Ilara walked out of her room in a pink dress with off-shoulder sleeves and a puffed-out skirt that swished around her legs. Silvery vines decorated the neckline and embroidered leaves ran down the skirt. Her hair was partly done up in a crown of braids. She looked like a dream.

"You do look beautiful in my people's clothing," Halkon said.

Tristan shook his head and snapped his mouth closed, suddenly aware that he'd been gawking.

Ilara chuckled, light yet uncomfortable. "The fabric is so strange…and I think the back laced itself…"

"Did it?" The tug of Halkon's mouth to the side and the smugness in his tone suggested he was responsible for that. How, Tristan wasn't sure he wanted to know.

"I think it needs one more touch…" Halkon waved his hand over Ilara's head, and in a shower of glittering gold-and-green light, a delicate wreath of leaves wove into her braids. "Now you look like a queen," he said, a hushed reverence to his tone.

Meelah and Kiri emerged from their rooms, and Halkon conjured another portal and strode through. Tristan darted down the hall and dove through the magic opening, hiding behind a gold tree while he watched the portal blink out of existence.

He released a slow breath and closed his eyes. No going back. And if things went wrong tonight, there might not be any going back at all. It wasn't as if he had the prospect of a long life ahead of him unless he determined how to stop Halkon, anyway.

"I saw you, boy."

Tristan's fingers tensed against the rough bark of the tree as his eyes flew open.

"You might as well come out."

Internally cursing himself for believing he could pull off the same trick twice, Tristan pulled back his shoulders and left the meager shelter of the trees.

Halkon stood in the path with his arm around Ilara's shoulders, their skin cast in a blue-green hue from the large, glowing crystals lighting the trail. Tristan's jaw clenched. She wouldn't allow that if Halkon hadn't enchanted her. Beyond them, Meelah and Kiri were already following the path toward the meadow.

"I didn't expect you'd be foolish enough to follow me through the portal a second time. So imagine my surprise when I heard a rustle and turned to see you darting into the shadows." Halkon scowled. "I'm also annoyed, as I didn't sense you following me, and the reminder of my waning abilities has me irritated. I'm considering taking that annoyance out on you. So explain your presence here quickly, and maybe I *don't* turn you into a fruit fly and step on you."

Tristan gulped, and it took him a moment to get his mouth to work. "I hate to intrude, truly." His mind raced, searching for a believable lie. "I wouldn't be here except that King Onak desires to know more about you and your subjects. He thinks he's sending me to spy for him, but I'm actually getting him to trust me more as I guide him toward accepting your marriage proposal to Princess Ilara."

Ilara frowned at her name and peered at Tristan as if she'd just noticed him, but no recognition lit her face.

Domhnall lifted an imperious eyebrow. "Is that so?"

"Yes." Tristan shuffled his feet. "I believe Onak can be convinced if he thinks it's best for his entire kingdom, and the princess will obey her father's wishes." He had a sneaking suspicion Onak couldn't force Ilara to do anything she didn't want to, but that didn't matter. He just needed Halkon to believe it.

"I'm pleased to hear it." Halkon nodded, his expression thoughtful. "Best for his entire kingdom… I should have thought of that." He turned to go, pulling Ilara with him, but Tristan cleared his throat.

"Perhaps…if you would give me leave to dance with Princess Ilara, it would help me win her trust as well as her father's."

Halkon fixed him with a cold look, and Tristan hoped the request wouldn't undo his other lies. Sweat slid down his neck and his hands felt clammy. He met Halkon's stare, wearing the stoic mask he had learned to display around Henry and the court's constant judgment.

At last, Halkon nodded. "I shall allow it for tonight only. If I see you in my realm again, I won't be so accommodating. And you move freely about my realm at *my* permitting—don't forget that, mortal." He led Ilara down the trail, and Tristan relaxed, but only a fraction.

Mortal.

Halkon had to be fae. What other explanation was there?

he moon was wrong.

Ilara didn't know why or what it meant, but as Domhnall led her out of the gold and silver trees into a spacious meadow filled with dancing couples, something in the back of her fuzzy thoughts was convinced the moon was wrong.

Domhnall's arm slipped off her shoulders. "Dearest—"

"My lord." A man with dark hair jogged over and bowed. Ilara gawked at him. Were his eyes…gold? Not just a warm amber, but the color of gold polished to a shine. "I'm sorry to interrupt, but a cockatrice broke through the thin place at the waterfall, and Daven and Captain Cael can't banish it."

Did he say cockatrice? Ilara pressed a hand to her aching head.

Domhnall sighed. "So that's what I felt." He brought Ilara's fingers to his lips. "I'll be back shortly, my flower." With that, he turned back to the man. "Let's go."

Ilara watched them stride through a conjured doorway, her eyes widening at the glimpse of men throwing glittering strands of colorful light at a creature that appeared part dragon, part rooster, but the magical opening snapped shut.

"That was…terrifying," a man's voice said behind her. The speaker moved up next to her. "At least he'll be gone for a while."

Another, taller man approached them with an imposing frown. "Are you supposed to be here?"

It took Ilara a moment to realize past her worsening headache that he was talking to the man at her side, not her.

"Yes. I have your lord's permission to entertain Princess Ilara."

If only she could get the buzzing feeling out of her head, maybe she could understand what it was about both men's words that bothered her so much. But her entire being felt indistinct and soft around the edges, and it nearly hurt to think.

"Hm. Very well." The frowning man left.

The other man grabbed her hand and led her onto the dancefloor. "Ilara." He spoke in a low voice, his tone urgent. "We aren't in Talland."

She giggled. "Of course we are. Where else would we be?"

As he pulled her into position, his brows knit, and his gaze wandered over her face before gentle pressure on her back led her into the steps.

"You look so familiar…" Ilara tilted her head. "Do I know you?"

He closed his eyes for a moment, as if pained. She didn't like that she'd upset him. "Yes; my name is Tristan."

Her mind thrashed like someone trying to swim who didn't know how, but knew if they broke the surface, they could make it.

"Tristan?" Like the first gasp of air after nearly drowning, memories rushed in. Her mind and body broke free of the enchantment dampening her senses and holding her memories captive. "Tristan!"

Relief crashed over his face, and he drew her closer—so close her breath hitched. "Flames, I feared you weren't waking up this time. I was terrified about what that might mean."

"I'm so glad you're all right after Domhnall caught you following us." She shuddered, the memory now clear in her mind although at the time, she'd barely understood what was happening. "I can't believe he bought that lie and agreed, though."

"Honestly, me too." Tristan glanced around, then fixed his gaze on her again. In the bright light of the enormous moon, she could make out tiny flecks of green in the brown of his irises. He cleared his throat and moved back slightly, as if he'd realized how little space there'd been between them.

Ilara stifled her disappointment. Maybe she shouldn't *want* some Rethali ambassador holding her close, but…was it so bad that she did?

"Are fae immortal?" he asked, pulling her out of her thoughts.

She frowned. "I think so. They don't die of old age but can be killed, I think."

"At least there's that. But that proves my men right. Halkon called me mortal. That's not something you call someone unless—"

"You're immortal," she said at the same time as him.

"Exactly." Tristan looked miserable over the confirmation, and Ilara didn't blame him. "At least he's not at full strength, since last night it seems everyone thought he *should* have sensed me, but he didn't, and tonight he mentioned waning abilities."

Ilara nodded, a bit of exuberant hope rising as they swayed around the meadow. "It's hard to keep the memories straight when they come back. They feel…tangled. But he's mentioned something about needing to be king of Talland or he'll lose his power, and something about threats from his enemies, and that he's running out of time."

"At least if we have to face a fae lord," Tristan said quietly, leaning close, "we get to face a weakened one." She knew it was just for secrecy, but his nearness sent a warm rush through her all the same.

"Unfortunately, he's also desperate," Ilara said, mostly to get her mind off of how close Tristan's face was to hers. "Desperate people can be wild and unpredictable."

Tristan laughed. She wasn't sure she'd heard him truly laugh before—not a bitter, ironic sound, but an actual laugh. "Because fae are generally predictable and tame, are they?"

She chuckled. "Fair enough. Still. He's…" A shiver cut through her as Byron's screams echoed in her mind. "I've seen him torture another fae just for coming here uninvited. You need to be careful."

Tristan paled. "I'll do my best."

She leaned in closer, breathless with her daring, and hoped he could read her sincerity. "But this is more than we've known in weeks, and you've helped me remember, even at home. Thank you, Tristan."

"Oh, um. You're welcome." He spun her around, and the strange large skirt of the dress Domhnall had given her swished around her legs. As Tristan pulled her back in, his gaze was fixed on her wrist.

"Staring at my tattoos?"

He tore his gaze away as a bit of red crept along his cheeks above his beard. "Apologies. Tattoos aren't common in Rethalyon. Do…they mean something?" He searched her face, his expression earnest and curious.

Ilara smiled. "They symbolize my womanhood, my rank, and my values. Tallanders get wrist tattoos when we turn sixteen. The interlocking solid and empty triangles symbolize the crown and the responsibility of the throne. The thick line near my hand symbolizes strength. And the three fine lines on my forearm represent determination, because laid flat, they would look like a target." She glanced at her tattoos with a melancholy pang. "I got that one because it matched my mama's. To honor her memory."

"That's lovely," Tristan murmured.

"So you don't have *any* tattoos?" Ilara asked, unsure what to say after mentioning her late mother again.

He chuckled. "No. Wait, are you saying you have more?" His gaze swept over her bare arms and neck before momentarily darting over her dress.

"You'd best not be imagining tattoos anywhere scandalous."

Tristan's entire face went scarlet. "No!"

Ilara threw her head back and laughed. "No, I don't have any other tattoos. Maybe someday, but no, not yet."

"Ah." Tristan nodded. Then, still dancing, he pulled his hand free of hers and reached toward her waist.

She held her breath, heat permeating her cheeks as she tried to determine what he was doing as his fingers brushed against her dress near her hip.

"How did you manage to get Nika's fur on the fae gown?" He flicked long strands of fur out of his fingers, then took her hand again.

A chuckle burst out of her, a frantic attempt to cover the fluttering in her stomach from his gentle touch. "Nika sleeps in my room. The dress was in my room. Doesn't matter how often I brush her or wash and brush off my clothing and bedding, the fur is always there. I think the white fur lies in wait to attack my dark clothing in particular."

Tristan's laugh rumbled in his chest. "Admittedly not a struggle of owning a dog I'd given much consideration."

"Oh, the worst is when you're trying to sit still in a very serious meeting and a single dog hair has worked its way through your clothing to jab directly into your ribs and make you itchy. I recommend if you ever spend much time around a sled dog to check your clothing before attending any events where you need to look dignified."

He snickered. "Noted."

They danced a few minutes more, from one dance into another, in comfortable silence. Finally, Ilara decided she wasn't going to waste a perfectly good opportunity to learn more about him.

"Your knights…is it just me, or do they not really respect you?"

Tristan's expression hardened. "I *told* that idiot," he muttered under his breath.

"Which one—" Noticing a tall figure with flowing blond hair making his way through the dancers toward them, she cut off. "Moonset. Domhnall's coming."

"That can't be good." Tristan's fingers tightened on hers, and he pulled her in closer.

"Ilara, my dear." Domhnall plucked her hand off Tristan's shoulder, but she jerked free of Domhnall's grip.

"I'm not your dear." She prodded Tristan into continuing to dance, but he moved more stiffly than before.

Domhnall's lips thinned. He grabbed the back of Tristan's tunic and yanked him back, putting a hand on Ilara's shoulder to separate them. "Enjoying yourself with the Rethali?"

"Maybe I am." She crossed her arms and glared up at Domhnall.

Tristan ducked his head, but not before Ilara caught his surprised smile.

"Baron Carbrey," Domhnall ground out. "Why don't you take a break?" He shoved Tristan aside, but Tristan didn't move to leave. "At *my* permitting, boy."

Tristan worked his jaw, then, with an apologetic look at Ilara, bowed. "I'll withdraw for a moment."

Domhnall watched Tristan elbow his way between the other dancers with an expression like a storm cloud. But when he turned back to Ilara, he wore a warm smile. "If you can dance with the

boy while not enchanted"—he tugged her into the dance position—"you can dance with me."

"A key difference is Tristan hasn't kidnapped or drugged me,"
Ilara snapped, although she followed his lead.

"I wouldn't have had to do either if you'd simply agreed to
marry me in the first place." Domhnall motioned with his head at
their surroundings. "Isn't all this lovely?" He spun her around,
then pulled her close. "Wouldn't you like to be queen of all this?"

"Queen? Are you the king, then?"

"Of a sort, yes."

"Well, I have my own kingdom to one day rule, so I don't
need you to become a queen. I'm content with my kingdom. Perhaps you should learn to be content with yours." She attempted
to pull her hand away, but Domhnall wouldn't let her go.

"But your kingdom is struggling, isn't it?" Domhnall pressed.
"Food shortages? Ice storms? With my full power, I can help. All
you have to do is marry me."

Her breath caught, and she almost asked how he could help
before she remembered what he was. Lying, trickster, cruel—these
were the characteristics nearly forgotten childhood stories had at-
tributed to the fae. She pushed against his chest and stumbled out
of his arms.

"Never, you fae knave."

Domhnall stared at her, then huffed a dismissive laugh. "Finally puzzled that out, did you?" He clapped mockingly. "About
time. Although, in a way, I'm impressed you figured it out at all."
He waved his hand and a gold strawberry materialized between his
fingers. "I must be losing my touch." He held out the strawberry.

"I don't seem to be hungry. Excuse me." She headed away
from Domhnall, but he grabbed her shoulder and spun her back
around.

"Now, don't be rude." He shoved the strawberry between her lips and pressed her jaw closed. "Eat."

Ilara's traitorous mouth chewed of its own accord. Her memories faded, and the only thing she was aware of was the beautiful music and Domhnall's brilliant smile.

31

Tristan stood in the light of a lantern hanging from a silver tree, scowling as Ilara and Halkon talked. A golden strawberry gleamed in Halkon's outstretched hand, but she turned away, her expression indignant. The fae lord grabbed her shoulder and spun her around before shoving the fruit into her mouth and forcing her jaw closed.

As his fists clenched, Tristan's fingernails dug into his palms. Ilara's countenance lost all of its ferocity. Her soft smile looked beautiful in the silvery light, but he missed the determined flash of her eyes, the challenge of her squared shoulders. This enchanted version of Ilara was lovely, but the girl who lifted her chin to glare at the fae lord was breathtaking.

What was he thinking? He forced his hands to relax at his sides and released the tension from his shoulders. No falling for another princess. He didn't deserve someone like her. He didn't know the right way to treat a woman, let alone a princess. But he could learn, couldn't he? He could try. Would that be enough? He desperately wanted to find out.

For a moment, he entertained a vision of sitting in front of a fire in the Great House with Ilara, both of them wrapped in a single blanket, her head on his shoulder as they listened to rain pelt the window. Or perhaps she might curl against his chest to ward off the cold as snow fell outside…

He sighed. Maybe he could be a good man for her, but he couldn't change his status. He'd still be a Rethali baron and ambassador, not a prince or duke worthy of a crown princess. And besides, how could he think himself better than Halkon? The fae lord had enchanted Ilara, but Tristan had considered enchanting Raelyn.

At least I didn't go through with it. I knew it was wrong.

Wait. Why *didn't* Halkon cast a love spell and force her to love him? Perhaps there were limits to fae power. And if Halkon's magic truly was weakening…maybe he *couldn't* cast an enchantment strong enough to force love. He paced at the edge of the meadow, watching Halkon and Ilara dance as they appeared and disappeared between tall fae couples.

But if Halkon couldn't cast a love spell because of his waning magic and ruling Talland would somehow fix that, why didn't he just kill Onak and seize the throne? Tristan stilled.

Unless Halkon needed to have a rightful claim to the throne. Henry had been crowned because he was a hero, the last king's brother-in-law, had royal blood—however diluted—and was recognized by the Court of Lords. Domhnall Halkon was an outsider with no legitimate claim. If Halkon required a crown that was rightfully his, not stolen, perhaps he had to become king through marriage. And maybe, by whatever laws bound the magic of the fair folk, if he cast a love spell, that wouldn't be considered a rightful claim. But if he was running out of magic, he might try other, more extreme methods to convince Ilara.

He resumed pacing. Why *hadn't* Halkon just put a knife to Ilara's throat and forced her to marry him yet? It was what Henry would have done, and Halkon had the same nature—murderous and uncaring about who he hurt to get what he wanted. Selfish.

You're selfish, too, a voice whispered. That might be true, but he was still going to help. If he could do this, maybe he could finally forgive himself.

Selfish, the voice accused. *You don't care about her. You care about your guilt and the fact you'll die if you don't help.* He clenched his teeth. He cared about Ilara. More than he dared admit. But then another thought invaded.

Because you want to love her yourself. Selfish again.

Tristan withdrew into the shadows and leaned against a gold tree. Would it be selfish to love her if she wanted him? Would it be so wrong to find out if she could love him?

Wait, when had he started thinking about love? Ridiculous. He shook his head, as if he could dislodge the notion. Halkon bowed to Ilara and left the dancers. After waiting a moment, Tristan made his way to her as a new song began.

He tapped her shoulder. "May I have this dance?"

She spun around and her eyes cleared, and her smile widened. "Of course!"

"Are you all right?" he murmured as they danced, gliding over the trampled-down grass in time with the lilting beat of the flutes and strings.

"Annoyed, but fine." Ilara huffed. "He admitted he's fae. At least he didn't try to kiss me."

Anger and shame both flared through Tristan's core. "He's tried to kiss you?"

"A couple times." She shrugged one shoulder. "It made me— well, wake up, for lack of a better term, so he stopped."

Tristan forced himself to stop looking at her mouth. "Speaking of which, I was thinking about why he hasn't used a love spell on you."

"Do you think he can do that?" Worry flashed over her face.

"If he could, surely he would have already." He twirled her

around and was momentarily distracted by the way her silky hair with its crown of braids and leaves caught the moonlight. He had the urge to run his fingers through it, but he returned his hand to where it belonged on her back.

Ilara nodded thoughtfully. "Maybe it's because of this wager he has with another fae that he can convince me to marry him without violence or threats thereof…but no, if magic counted as violence, he would've already lost."

Ah, so that explained the lack of threats at knife-point. Interesting.

She gasped and clutched his hand. "Wait. He mentioned vows. I think he needs me to vow to be his wife of my own volition, even if encouraged by magic or threats."

Tristan was relieved when she eased her pinching grip on his fingers. "Makes sense. You can't deny a love spell. Vows taken under duress or while magically susceptible to suggestion wouldn't be real consent, but you'd still have the ability to say no, technically, which might be enough for fae magic. If he needs you to agree, hopefully that and this wager mean we have more time."

"Not much, though. He said he'd rather lose his wager by resorting to violence than by failing to marry me." She tilted her head, looking up at him with curiosity and…that couldn't be concern. Could it be she cared about him? "You came back to dance again. Aren't you afraid that he might hurt you if you keep interfering?"

It wasn't as if Tristan had any other choice, but he couldn't tell her he was helping her to avoid execution. Even if he could, he didn't want to when she was looking at him so earnestly, her dark eyes fixed on him as if the ethereal meadow and attractive fae surrounding them didn't exist. Not when he was thinking he would willingly risk his life if she would just keep watching him—a lowly foreign ambassador she had no reason to care about—like he was someone worth paying attention to.

"Honestly, I'm trying not to think about it," he said, and forced a chuckle. "I don't want to spend the rest of my life as a daisy or something."

"Daisy?" Ilara laughed. "Daisies are far too common and wild. You'd be some exotic flower that people stop to stare at and smell."

He couldn't hold back his smile. "Are you saying I'm attractive and smell nice?" Immediately he wanted to take back the flirtatious words, but before he could apologize, Ilara spoke.

"I meant you're foreign and confusing." She moved closer as they twirled between other dancers, and Tristan's breath hitched. "But what you said wouldn't be a lie."

She…found him attractive? Tristan's heart threatened to race right out of his chest, and he knew his grin probably looked ridiculous, but he couldn't wipe it off his face.

"I rather think you would be some hardy variety of rose," he said, his gaze fixed on hers as they glided to the music. "Beautiful, but guarded with thorns."

"Are you saying I'm prickly?" She pursed her lips, but there was laughter in her eyes that encouraged him.

Tristan gripped Ilara's waist a little firmer and leaned in close to her ear. "I'm saying you're gorgeous yet strong and won't be pushed around without pushing back. You're…enthralling and alluring."

His heart raced as he waited to see if she would accept his flirting, if he had a chance—

"Moonlight, Tristan." Ilara's breath tickled his neck. "Since when are you so forward?"

He eased away to increase the space between their bodies. *Stupid, stupid Tristan.* "Apologies, Your Highness. I'll stop."

"No, don't start that again." She sighed and gave a little shake of her head. "I can't understand you. Do you want to flirt with me, or don't you?" She smiled, and for the first time, she looked almost shy. "You're kind of good at it, you know."

"Raelyn would disagree." What had gotten into him? What was it about Ilara that made his mind get disconnected from his tongue?

Ilara's expression turned distant. "You still care for Raelyn."

"No!" Tristan sighed. "It's not that. It's just... I wonder, sometimes. Would she have liked me? I didn't love her, although I'm sure I would have with time. But things went so wrong. *I did things wrong.*" He stared at the delicate laurel wreath on her hair, avoiding her eyes. "I'm afraid I will again. I don't want to be that man. But can I be separated from what I did?"

"I don't understand." Distrust crept into Ilara's voice, and it slashed into Tristan. "I mean, I can see how bringing the man she loved in as a prisoner to stand trial and possibly be sentenced to death would be difficult and how the situation with the love spell wasn't exactly a bonding moment, but...what did you do that you're so ashamed of?"

It took him a moment to get his tongue to work. "I was...selfish." He spun her for the excuse to increase distance between them for a moment.

"In what way?" Ilara pressed as soon as they were back into frame.

I thought she belonged to me. His stomach roiled. It had been easier to omit details when he wasn't flirting. But now he had crossed that line, and Ilara deserved the truth; but then she wouldn't look at him the same. She wouldn't trust him. Where would he even start?

"It turns out, my f—" He choked and grunted with frustration. "Um, someone I knew gave poor advice on how marriage works. On all of life, actually. Poor example, and worse advice."

His hands felt clammy, which made him self-conscious, as Ilara was holding one of them. "I was told a wife is a subject whose only goal is to serve and please her husband." The words rasped out of his tight throat.

Ilara's face scrunched up. "And…how did you interpret that with Raelyn?"

He stared down at the gold vines glittering on Ilara's skirt, shame burning a hole through his stomach.

"As crown princess, I command you to tell me the truth."

Despite the ice in her voice, he almost laughed. She wasn't his princess. She couldn't command him to do anything. "You'll think less of me," he said quietly, his heart aching as he realized after this, he'd have no chance with her.

She stopped dancing, bringing them to a halt in the middle of the dancers, and tightened her grip on his hand. "What did you do?"

Tristan dropped his other hand from her back, wishing the earth would open up and swallow him. "To Raelyn specifically, or in general?"

"You—you said you hurt many people. Moon-cursed winter, what did you do?"

He couldn't look at her as he spoke the words that would destroy her opinion of him. "After his curse broke, while he was mourning the death of his friend…I nearly killed Alexander. Then I cut open his back in my anger and jealousy. I made him walk barefoot for four days. And Raelyn… Raelyn was my betrothed. My future wife." His mouth felt like it was full of sawdust.

"According to Henry, that made her mine—mine to touch, mine to command. When she disobeyed me, I had her bound and treated her as a prisoner." His face burned as he pressed on. "I ignored her revulsion and kissed her and held her against her will because it hurt Alexander, not even realizing how much it was hurting her. My own betrothed said my affection felt like punishment and looked at me with fear, and I was so focused on myself, it took me too long to realize it."

Ilara wrenched her hand out of his and stepped back. "You're a snake."

"I know," he whispered, hanging his head. "I only kissed her, and when I realized—"

"I don't care. No wonder they sent you here." Ilara's sharp words stung like ice blown into his face by a cold wind. "They probably hoped you'd freeze out here."

He felt nauseated. Maybe Alexander did want him to freeze to death, despite declaring his forgiveness. Raelyn somehow had forgiven him, but Ilara was right. He didn't merit their forgiveness.

"It would be less than I deserve if I did," Tristan said, then bowed. "I'm sorry about the flirting. I'll keep my distance, Your Highness."

He dodged fae couples as he hurried away. How could he have been so foolish as to think that the man he had been in the mountains could ever be worthy of her? Of anyone? Maybe Masarik was right, and he was a villain like his father, and there was no escaping his nature. Even as he had danced with Ilara, he was lying to her face, concealing why he was truly there. And he had acted out of selfish interest, flirting with her when he knew he was a bad match for a future queen.

He stopped in front of one of the refreshment tables. What was he doing there? But as he reached toward the array of gold and silver fruit, he knew exactly why he had approached the table. Maybe it would numb the self-loathing he felt. He plucked a golden grape off a bunch and turned it in the bright moonlight. All it would take was a bite, and he'd go into that blissful, ignorant trance the princesses did every time they ate the fae food.

Bothersome wetness pricked at his eyes. The possibility of a night of peace, of not hearing his errors over and over again, might be worth being under the fae's power. He closed his eyes, his hand shaking as he raised the grape toward his lips.

A hand covered his, forcing his hand back down. "Don't," Ilara murmured at his side.

Tristan's eyes flew open as he sucked in a deep breath, but he stared ahead into the forest, unable to bring himself to look at her.

"You might forget to follow us back." Her hand slid off of his.

What did it matter if he returned, anyway? Tristan looked at her, but the question that tumbled out of his mouth instead was, "What does it feel like?"

Ilara studied him for a long moment, her lips pinched. At last, she picked up a gold wedge of orange and scrutinized it. "Like forgetting. Like nothing. It's a kind of warm, pleasant happiness that feels hollow and somehow detached, almost as if nothing is real. I know who I am, but at the same time…it's like my life is a dream that's fading from my memory."

Tristan rolled the grape between his fingers. *Forgetting.* "That doesn't sound so bad." Moonlight made the gold skin of the grape glow. It beckoned to him, promising a reprieve from his shame and loneliness.

"You really regret what you did, don't you?"

He felt like he had to force his lungs to breathe. "Every moment. I wish I could go back and do things differently, but you know what scares me? That if I did, I'd do the same things, anyway. Or do something worse, like use that cursed stone. I know it would have been wrong, and yet there are times I've wished I did." A broken laugh escaped him. "What does that make me, if not the villain?"

Ilara took the grape from his fingers. "When was the last time you wished you had used the love spell?"

He frowned, considering. "I…don't know, actually."

"So you know what you did was wrong. You regret it and don't want to repeat it. And you've let go of wishing you could take Raelyn back. Is that right?"

"Yes. And I've apologized to Alex and Raelyn and Gareth and Alex's friends. Over and over." Tristan shook his head. "But my apologies and desire to never hurt people like that again don't undo the terrible things I said and did. I can't make the scars on Alex's back or Raelyn's wrists disappear. My regret doesn't make Raelyn comfortable around me. It doesn't change that Masarik and who knows how many others think I should have been executed and that they aren't even wrong." His voice broke, and he cursed himself for his weakness.

"My mother used to say you can't give up on people when they realize they've made a mistake. Otherwise, they'll never improve." Ilara chuckled. "She was talking about Meelah when she apologized for breaking my favorite doll, but still."

Tristan glanced at her. "Do snakes deserve a second chance, too?"

Ilara squeezed the grape until the skin split open, then tossed it aside. "Hmm, probably not."

He winced and snatched up a silver cherry. "I agree."

"Snakes don't feel regret, Tristan."

He paused with the cherry halfway to his mouth and met Ilara's eyes. Genuine understanding reflected in her gaze, and his heart squeezed. "What I did was wrong; I know that. And I can't stop hating myself for thinking I was right." Hope that she could help him find his way forward prompted him to lower the fruit. "How did you forgive your sister?"

"I just did." She shrugged. "But it wouldn't have meant much if Meelah hadn't accepted my forgiveness."

She rubbed the tattoos on her wrist, her gaze downcast. "After my mama died…I struggled to forgive myself. I thought if I had gone with her or asked her to wait for me that she wouldn't have died. I was supposed to be with her, and it felt like it was my fault. But one day Ryn told me that hating myself wouldn't bring her back, and she reminded me that my mama always believed in forgiveness and love. And just like I wouldn't want Meelah to keep avoiding me and beating herself up with guilt after I forgave her, Mama loved me even when I was imperfect, and she wouldn't have wanted me sulking and blaming myself. I couldn't undo the past, but I could choose who I was moving forward. So I chose to be there for my papa and my sisters and friends and my kingdom. I chose to see people the way my mama did—as people worth loving."

She lifted her eyes back to Tristan's, and the kindness reflected in them nearly made him break down in front of her. "Who we are isn't determined by our pasts. Who are you going to choose to be, Tristan?"

He wanted to be someone who could hold his head high, someone worth loving, but he wasn't certain he knew how to do that.

"What if you're wrong?" he whispered, still holding the cherry. "I want to be good, but what if that's…not me?" The words sounded like a plea.

Ilara shook her head with a soft chuckle. "Oh, Tristan." She cupped her hand to his cheek, and he nearly stopped breathing. "What is a man who is willing to admit he was wrong and is determined to change, a man who is risking his life to help strangers, if not a good man? I know you can change. You already are."

The cherry slipped from his fingers. She thought he could be good. She thought he was *already* good. Tristan didn't know if he wanted to cry or kiss her, but he drifted toward her upturned face. He blinked. What was he doing? Being a good man didn't mean he deserved Ilara—doing the right thing still didn't mean any woman owed him anything.

He cleared his throat. "Thank—"

A shadow fell over them, and Ilara paled, her hand slipping off his cheek. Tristan looked up into Halkon's face. His heart seemed to fall to his toes as he took in the cold rage in the fae's eyes.

"You're about to learn the consequences of lying to me, Reth-ali."

32

"$\mathcal{L}$ ying?" Tristan grimaced as his voice cracked.

"You're not trying to win the princess's trust to convince her to marry me." The fae lord's upper lip curled in distaste. "You're wooing her for yourself."

Tristan liked the idea, certainly, but it was an impossibility. He shook his head, his pulse racing. "No, not at all—I'm only an ambassador. I'm in Talland serving my king—"

Halkon grabbed his neck and lifted him off the ground, crushing his windpipe. Flames, why did no one warn him fae were so strong? "We had a deal, Carbrey. And yet my people tell me they overheard you and Ilara discussing what sounded suspiciously like plans to thwart my goals. You've broken our deal." He squeezed Tristan's throat, and black spots danced in Tristan's eyes.

"You're killing him!" Ilara shouted. "Stop!"

Halkon cried out in pain, then released him. Gasping in air and coughing, Tristan fell to his knees. Halkon rubbed his shin. "Kicking isn't very ladylike!" He waved his hand and vines shot out of the ground and wrapped around Ilara's wrists and ankles, holding her still.

"Stop that." Tristan's voice croaked. He gingerly touched his aching throat.

"Stop that," Halkon mocked. "Mortals are so annoying. After

I marry Ilara and am crowned king, my realm will overtake pitiful Talland. Once my realm is properly anchored, my strength will return. Then I will enslave all of you weak, ridiculous mortals."

"I'll die before I marry you," Ilara spat.

"Fine, but then I'll wed Meelah." Halkon shrugged. "Not my first choice, being so young, but I'll make do."

Ilara's jaw trembled. "No. You won't touch her."

Halkon caressed the top of Ilara's head. "I won't have cause to if you marry me, darling."

Finally able to breathe again, Tristan shoved to his feet, but Halkon turned toward him and punched his abdomen. Tristan doubled over, choking on his pain. The fae pushed him to the ground, then kicked the same spot he'd just hit.

"Your wager!" Ilara cried. "Are you—"

"*He* isn't Tallander. I can do anything I wish to him and not have lost my bet." As if to prove his point, he kicked Tristan again. Tristan curled into a ball, holding his arms protectively in front of his face as his eyes watered.

"Leave him alone!" Ilara pulled against the vines.

"Dearest, I really don't like it when you try to tell me what to do." Halkon plucked a grape off the table, squeezed it until its skin split, and pushed it against Ilara's lips.

Tristan stumbled up and reached for the fae, his gut still burning. "Don't—"

Halkon elbowed Tristan in the forehead. Tristan reeled back, his head pounding as Ilara's lips parted enough for Halkon to shove the grape into her mouth. Her furious expression softened. The vines shimmered and vanished from her wrists.

"Go dance and have fun, my flower." Halkon gave her a gentle push toward the dancers.

"All right…" Ilara swayed along with the music, and Tristan watched with helpless sorrow as a fae man drew her into a dance.

"Now." Halkon stood and grabbed a fistful of Tristan's hair, making his scalp burn and his eyes water. "How shall I punish you?" He tossed Tristan backward.

Tristan slammed into the ground. *Can't…breathe…* All at once, his lungs opened up again, and he sucked in air desperately.

Halkon leaned over him and pushed his knee against Tristan's chest. "I said I'd use you, but you weren't a cooperative tool. Let's make you more compliant." A gold plum appeared in his hand. "Open wide, mortal." He pinched Tristan's cheeks, prying his jaw open, then shoved the plum in and forced Tristan to bite down.

Impossibly sweet and flavorful juices flowed over his tongue. A pleasantly numb and warm sensation spread through him.

"Care for more?" Halkon stood and offered the rest of the plum.

Tristan was reaching for the fruit before he'd consciously considered his actions. *Wait…* He struggled to think as he pulled the plum toward his mouth. *I shouldn't eat this.*

"Eat," Halkon commanded. "All of it."

Tristan did. Everything faded away except the music and a listless happiness and the delicious juices dribbling down his chin.

"Now forget everything," Halkon said.

Tristan wiped his chin with his sleeve, feeling…at peace. And why shouldn't he? His mind was blank. Blank of everything. *What's my name?* he thought frantically. But then even his name seemed unimportant.

"Stand, mortal."

Tristan stood, and the pit fell from his fingers.

Halkon nodded approvingly. "Follow."

He obeyed, feeling oddly weightless. Was this a dream? It was a pleasant dream. Couples in brightly colored clothes danced nearby. He caught sight of a girl he vaguely recognized, but he followed his master. Wait, his master? *Yes, my master.*

Master sat on his throne of vines. "Be my footrest, mortal."

Servant knelt on all fours before the throne, and Master propped his feet on his back. Some niggling sensation in the back of his mind rankled at the indignity. But...why shouldn't he obey? Master made him happy.

The couples danced; the music played. Sometimes Master left and returned. Sometimes he gave Servant food, which dulled the ache in his arms and torso. The sky began to lighten. Master left again and gathered three girls as the other dancers slipped away into the trees. The girls looked vaguely familiar. Master said something to the tallest of the group, and the pleasant smile on her face melted into indignation. How dare she be angry with Master.

The girl looked at Servant. "Tristan!"

He blinked. *I'm Tristan.*

Master—no, not Master. Halkon. Halkon laughed and materialized a goblet and forced Ilara to drink. Rage burned the fog from Tristan's mind as Halkon traced a large circle in the air with his palm. The air rippled with multicolored light, and the fae lord led the princesses through the magical doorway.

Tristan forced himself to stand. He still felt strange, but he could think more clearly. He ran after the princesses. Slipping through the portal, he found himself in the dark, windowless room. He dropped and slid under the nearest bed.

"Farewell, princesses, until tonight." Halkon strode back to his realm, and the lights vanished into darkness.

Tristan crawled out from under the bed.

"What..." Meelah groaned. "You'd think by now it wouldn't surprise me. But I keep hoping I won't wake up in my clothes and shoes."

"I...there's something I need to remember." Ilara sounded miserable. "Something happened. I can feel it."

"You're not wrong," Tristan said, rubbing his aching neck. The girls gasped.

"Tristan?" Ilara asked.

"Yes." He wished it wasn't pitch dark and he could see something.

"Wait, I remember!" Ilara exclaimed. "I remember…" She groaned. "It's so foggy…oh, my head hurts. What do you remember?"

Tristan found he couldn't recall, either. Something about second chances vaguely tickled his thoughts, but what did that mean? "I…" He paused, trying to sort through the muddle of memories. "I remember Halkon using me as a footstool." His nose wrinkled.

"What?" Ilara gasped. "How…he made you eat the food?"

"That's right," Tristan said, nodding as his full memories rushed back in, making his head pound. "But he spoke to you just before leaving this morning, and you got angry, and you shouted my name, which helped pull me out of the trance I was in. But then he forced you to drink something to enchant you again. It made me furious, and I remembered who I was. I…" Horror filled him. "I forgot who I was."

Somewhere close by, one of Ilara's sisters giggled. "Aw, you saw her and fought off the sorcerer's magic! That's *adorable*."

Tristan was glad the dark hid his burning face.

"Not sorcerer," Ilara said, a sour quality to her tone. "Fae."

"Wait, what?" Kiri's voice squeaked. "What do you mean, he's a fae? The fair folk aren't real."

"He admitted it," Tristan said heavily. "They're all fae. That's why the food affects you—us—the way it does." He cringed, wishing he could forget waking up and realizing how he had let Halkon order him around.

The door opened and pale sunlight flooded the room around

the outline of a man. Tristan squinted against the bright light as King Onak strode in.

"Well?" Onak demanded.

Tristan bowed. "I know how to stay awake, Your Majesty."

"Finally, some progress." Onak stomped over to Ilara's bedside table and lit the lantern, further illuminating the room. "I was beginning to fear you were hiding something."

"Papa," Ilara chided. "Tristan has risked his life to help us."

Onak only grunted, and Tristan shifted uncomfortably. In the hall, Masarik and Sharland peered in, curiosity on their faces. Tristan motioned for them to leave. Masarik frowned, and Sharland had to drag the big blond away.

"It's the food," Tristan explained. "Domhnall Halkon isn't a sorcerer from Kilkreth; he's a fae. He's using fae food and wine to enchant the princesses into going to his parties in the fae realm, and he's cast some kind of enchantment on your food so that everyone sleeps. I didn't eat any Tallander food yesterday or the day before, and both nights I stayed awake."

Onak sank onto Ilara's bed. "So…we're just supposed to not eat?"

"No, Papa." Ilara sat next to her father. "All of Talland isn't falling into enchanted sleep, so if we bring in food from far enough away, maybe prepare it in separate containers, the guards will be able to stay awake."

Onak ran toward the door, bewildering Tristan. "You there!" he shouted at someone in the hall. "Tell the guards—tell everyone, but especially the guards—if they haven't eaten yet, *don't*, not until I tell them they can! That's an order! Go quickly!"

Tristan nodded. Hopefully some guards would get the message in time.

"Many of them will have already eaten." Onak sagged against the doorframe. "And fae…how do we even fight the fair folk?"

"Iron, according to my men." Tristan strummed his fingers on his leg. "If we can have some weapons and chains of iron made and have the guards who don't eat in here, maybe—"

"We don't know if it will work," Onak interrupted.

"Domhnall admitted that he's a fae," Ilara said. "So—"

"And did he tell you his weakness is iron?" The king straightened. "I don't like it. If the guards *do* stay awake and are counting on the iron working and it doesn't, what then? Or what if the guards fall asleep and Halkon arrives to find a room full of sleeping guards armed with iron and is furious? Halkon might decide he's waited for a peaceful agreement long enough." He wrung his hands. "We must be certain."

Tristan gulped. Onak had given him three days. Today was his last day. Tomorrow he would die. He didn't have time for testing. "How can we know until we try it?"

Onak shook his head. "We can test the food. But the iron…"

"I can test it," Ilara said quietly. "Domhnall will take us again. I can see if the iron affects him."

"How?" Meelah protested. She reclined on her bed, her pillow propped up against the wall as a backrest, watching them. "He has us change. You can't hide an iron dagger in your dress or something, and how will you even remember?"

Tristan shuffled his feet. "If I can sneak in again—"

"That's not a good idea," Ilara cut in. "He made it clear he won't hesitate to hurt you. Maybe…I can wear the iron. Like iron rings, so when I take his hand to dance, it will either affect him…or it won't."

"No." Tristan's fingers twitched as he resisted the urge to grab Ilara and shake her. "You said yourself, he's growing increasingly desperate and near giving up on his plan to convince you without harming you. If you anger him—"

"Let the Rethali test it," Onak agreed.

Ilara thrust a hand toward Tristan. "Domhnall might kill him! He might hurt me, but he needs me. He won't kill me."

Tristan recalled Halkon threatening to turn his attentions to Meelah but judged it best not to mention that in the hearing of Meelah or their father.

"But that doesn't answer the problem of remembering," Kiri said. "You've only started recalling anything since Tristan has come with us."

"She's right," Meelah said. The look she sent Tristan was full of teasing, and he felt his face going red again.

What *did* it mean that Ilara was only remembering things when he woke her up? He shoved that thought aside. It wasn't important. It couldn't be.

Onak hummed, a low, displeased sound. "Then we'll let you test it, Ilara, but Carbrey will have to follow you again to watch."

"Papa, you don't understand." Ilara stood. "He almost didn't make it back—"

"But he did." Onak nodded. "He can stay out of sight. It's the best plan we have."

"He's right." Tristan shrugged.

"But he caught you following him!"

Tristan fought to keep his calm façade in place. "I'll have to be faster and quieter. If you're wearing new iron jewelry, perhaps he'll be too distracted by it to notice me. I'm doing this, Your Highness."

Ilara harrumphed and crossed her arms. "Fine. But I don't like it."

"Good," Onak said impatiently. "I'll get the smiths working on making iron items, starting with rings for you. Maybe bracelets and a necklace as well. I'll look into how far away people aren't falling asleep at dusk and send for food to be brought in for the guards to try. We'll keep anyone who eats food from outside far away from your rooms, so Halkon won't suspect anything." He sighed. "It's not enough. But it will do for now."

Panic tightened around Tristan's lungs. It wasn't enough if he wanted to keep his head tomorrow—assuming he even made it back from the fae realm again. He cleared his throat. "Your Ex—Majesty? Might I have a word in private?"

Ilara stepped up next to him and fixed him with a questioning stare. "Why?"

"It's not about you or the plan." Tristan forced a smile. "I just…need to speak with your father alone. If you'll excuse us?"

Ilara regarded him with suspicion, but she nodded.

"Your Majesty?" Tristan asked, turning to Onak with a bow.

The king grunted again and went into the hall. Tristan closed the door behind them. To his surprise, Onak went only a few steps, then stopped to face him in the hallway. "What is it?"

Tristan had hoped for more privacy, but he was too nervous to press the issue. He lowered his voice. "This plan…the testing means more time. We won't be able to free the princesses tonight, only see if we've found Halkon's weakness." He gulped. "But we have a decent plan, yes? And once we know if it works, I'll help, but I can't do that if tomorrow morning…if tomorrow you…" He couldn't bring himself to say it, nor could he stop desperation from leaking into his tone. "I'm doing everything I can, Your Majesty."

"What? Oh. Right. You have an extra day." Onak nodded, but his expression was preoccupied.

Tristan's breath hitched. He had hoped to have the execution threat lifted entirely. Did he dare risk asking? "I promise you I'll help—"

"Then it won't be a problem, will it, Baron Carbrey?" Onak's golden eyes flashed with irritation. "If this works, tomorrow night we will end this fae miscreant. You will help us, and if Halkon escapes, or if anything happens to my daughters, I'll hold you responsible."

Sweat formed on Tristan's brow. "Yes, Your Excellency," he said weakly, realizing he'd slipped again into Rethali address. Maybe it was wise to be extra flattering, though, because even if he couldn't save himself, he had to ask for one more thing. "I know I'm in no position to ask anything of you, but if I may—my men. Regardless of how this goes and what happens to me, please, can you promise me they won't be harmed? They haven't made any deals and are good men. Their fate shouldn't be tied to mine."

Onak squinted. "Do you have no faith in the plan?"

Tristan steadied his breathing. "I think it can work. But I could be wrong. I promise you, I'm doing everything in my power to help your daughters. I don't want to fail. But if I do, my men don't deserve to die. Please give me your word you won't execute them alongside me."

"Execute?" Ilara's voice intruded behind him.

Tristan's stomach dropped to his feet as both he and Onak turned toward the princesses' door. How had he not heard it open? Had he not closed it all the way? It didn't matter. The damage was done. Ilara stood in the hallway, her mouth hanging open and eyes wide. Meelah's head poked out of the door.

"Ilara…" Tristan gulped, his mouth suddenly dry as his mind emptied of anything to say.

"What is he talking about?" Ilara looked at her father with indignation that made Tristan quail.

Onak reddened. "Nothing—"

"Because you know what it sounds like?" Ilara said, every word like the crack of a whip. "It sounds like you're forcing Tristan to help us on threat of death."

"I believed he could help," Onak argued. "He has experience with magic! Do you know he arrived the day after the full moon?

It seemed like a sign. I was failing, and he walked in. Perhaps it was the moon's guidance or intuition or desperation, but I was certain he could help; however…he was reluctant. He needed motivation. I gave it to him."

Tristan's face flushed. He wished he'd volunteered to help, that it hadn't taken a threat for him to do the right thing.

Ilara glanced at Tristan before turning her attention back to Onak, her mouth pinched. "Shame on you, Papa. Is this how the monarch of Talland treats foreigners who come in peace? Was this the action of a just ruler with pure intentions?"

Onak seemed to shrink under the weight of Ilara's judgment.

"The good news is you were right. We might have a chance because of him. Even if he did it only to save his own life." She turned her attention to Tristan, and the hurt in her eyes stung more than he would have imagined it could. "You're under no obligation to stay. You may take your men and return to Rethalyon immediately. I'm sorry I convinced him to see you. It seems you would have been better off without my intervention."

Tristan was shaking his head almost before he realized it. "You need my help—"

"I don't need the help of someone who doesn't want to be here." Ilara stared past him, like she didn't want to look at him, and a small fissure opened in his soul. "Papa, tell him he's free to go."

Onak sighed. "I agree with my daughter's wishes. I won't send men after you if you leave. I never planned to actually do it, anyway."

Tristan wasn't sure if he believed that last part, but he did believe Ilara wouldn't let her father kill him. For a moment, he considered fleeing. But he looked at Ilara and knew he couldn't. The man he wanted to be wouldn't run. She was worth saving, and he refused to abandon her—even if staying cost him dearly. He regretted saying no last time, when he'd had a choice, and he wouldn't repeat that mistake.

"I made you a promise, Ilara. I will see this through."

Her lips parted, but then she shook her head. "You swore on your life because your life depended on it."

"Well, it doesn't now." Tristan bowed. "I will do all I can to help you, Your Highness; I swear it on my life."

Ilara was silent. "Why?" she said at last.

"Because he *likes* you," Meelah said in a singsong voice. She flashed a saucy grin as Tristan wished he could melt into the floor.

"What?" Onak demanded.

Tristan backed away from the king, holding up his hands. "No, it's not like that; I only want to do the right thing—"

A scream from the princesses' room cut him off. Meelah disappeared back inside, and Ilara whirled around, her features going ashy. Tristan rushed to her side and looked into the room, and his blood went cold.

33

The last bit of swirling red and gold light vanished, leaving a seething Domhnall standing in the center of the room. Ilara's heart beat faster, and she clenched her fists, her anger rising as she saw him in her home without any of his magic dulling her mind. Why had he returned already? Behind him, Kiri clutched her blankets and pressed against the wall at the head of her bed, her eyes wide. Meelah backed into a corner of the room.

"*You.*" Domhnall pointed through the doorway at Ilara—no, next to her, at Tristan standing by her side in the hallway, his face deathly white. "How did you escape?"

Tristan's throat bobbed, but he lifted his chin. "What, your fae lordship? Were you outwitted by a mere mortal?"

She hated how attractive he looked when he was confident. She'd been so stupid, thinking he was flirting with her, sacrificing for her, when he was just avoiding execution.

Domhnall's face took on a purple hue. "You remember? How?"

"I suppose your magic isn't as strong as you think." Tristan crossed his arms. "I stared down a dragon; you don't scare me with your flowers and fruit."

Ilara remembered the blinded fae spy and could hardly breathe. He had more than flowers and fruit—but could he do that here?

Domhnall sneered and stalked out of the room until he stood in front of them in the corridor. "I need my footstool back."

Affronted fury overpowered her fear. "Return to your own realm!" She swung toward Domhnall's nose, but he intercepted her fist. So she did something she wished she had done a long time ago—she kneed him in the groin. As Domhnall howled, she smirked triumphantly.

"I'm getting tired of you." Domhnall wrenched her arm aside, making her cry out, then shoved her backward so hard she tripped. Arms caught her before she hit the floor, and Tristan leaned over her, his chest close to her face and hands gripping her tightly. Her skin flushed.

Domhnall huffed. "Maybe I *will* just kill you and try for Meelah."

Ilara's heart jammed into her throat.

"No!" Papa fell to his knees and held up his folded hands. "Please."

"Give Princess Ilara to me as my wife." Domhnall peered down his nose at Papa, and Ilara cringed.

Tristan placed her back on her feet and whispered, "Stay behind me." He guided her backward and stood in front of her—shielding her as if *she* were the one Domhnall had come looking for, not him. Maybe his flirting wasn't fake.

"Don't do it, Your Majesty," Tristan said. "Swear you'll never give him any of your daughters. He needs a legitimate claim to the throne, and if you refuse to recognize his marriage to any of them, he can't take your throne and bring his realm into ours."

Ilara edged to the side to see around Tristan, uneasy with his boldness. She hoped it would pay off.

Domhnall blinked. "How do you know…" He growled and looked back at Papa. "Fine—"

"Wait." Papa shook his head. "As king consort, you couldn't

claim the throne, anyway."

"The title of king and marital connection to the ruler are enough for my people's magic to take effect. I didn't choose Talland without research." Domhnall rolled his eyes. "Give me Ilara's hand in marriage, now. Or would you rather have two dead daughters? Because that's what you'll have if you defy me. One more night. If by tomorrow evening you have not agreed, sweet Meelah and little Kiri will pay for it with their lives."

In the room behind him, Kiri started to cry.

"But *you*." Domhnall pointed at Tristan. "No one escapes me, boy." A vine shot from his sleeve and wrapped around Tristan's wrists, binding them together.

With a sharp yank on the vine, Domhnall dragged Tristan forward, making him stumble toward the doorway.

"No!" Unsure what else to do, Ilara seized the vine and pulled. "Leave him alone, you treacherous, vile son of a flea-infested hog!"

Domhnall snorted, the corner of his lips puckering with amusement. Her blood boiled. He would *not* push her, threaten her sisters, try to capture her friend, and then laugh at her. "Let him go, or I'll knee you again!"

"Careful, princess." The fae's eyes darkened as his mouth turned down. "I've already lost my wager, and I'm nearly out of mercy."

"Kidnap someone from my realm," Ilara shouted as she and Tristan both strained against Domhnall's pull, "and I'll never marry you!"

"So dramatic. And untrue, I'm sure. But fine."

The vine vanished from Tristan's wrists. With the resistance gone, Tristan and Ilara tumbled backward, Ilara landing on Tristan's lap in a heap of fluffy pink skirts. Before she could react, Tristan wrapped his arms around her, drawing her close and angling them away from Domhnall, so he was shielding her. Again.

"Interesting." Domhnall tilted his head, his expression calculating. "The Rethali appears to have *feelings* for you, princess. If you don't want to see Ilara suffer, boy, I recommend convincing her to marry me." He raised his hand and vanished in a swirl of colorful light.

For a moment, no one moved. Tristan still held her against his firm chest, and Meelah edged out into the hallway, looking horrified. Papa was frozen in place on his knees, staring at where Domhnall had been.

Tristan's arms loosened. "Are you all right?" he whispered.

"Me?" Ilara shifted so she could meet his eyes. "Are *you* all right?"

"Fine…" He cleared his throat and released her. "Sorry…" He leaned back and rubbed the side of his neck.

Before Ilara could scold him for apologizing again, movement in the doorway captured her attention. Kiri crept forward, the color drained from her cheeks and her pillow squeezed against her chest.

"Am I going to die?"

"No," Ilara choked out at the same time as Tristan.

Papa still knelt on the floor, his gaze unfocused.

Ilara extricated herself from Tristan's lap, fighting the multilayered skirt, and they both stood.

"Papa?" Her voice came out quiet and trembling. "We need to—"

"My girls…" Papa hid his face in his hands. "I'm sorry. I'm so sorry."

Inside, Ilara felt as frightened and helpless as her father sounded, but she couldn't break down. She'd been the strong one when Mama died, and she could do it again. "We have a plan, Papa." She went to him and held out her hand. "We just need to stick to it."

After a moment, Papa nodded and took her hand, and she helped him to his feet. "I'm sorry…" He pulled her into an embrace. "I'm your father. I'm supposed to protect you and I can't—" A strangled sob cut through his words.

Ilara squeezed him. "I know you're doing all you can, Papa." He released her, and she turned to Tristan but couldn't quite bring herself to look at him. Domhnall's comment replayed in her mind. *The Rethali appears to have* feelings *for you.* Yet Tristan had protested that he didn't.

"You should leave," she said quietly. "Domhnall—"

"Would have taken me if you hadn't intervened." Tristan tapped his hand against his leg. "I won't return that by leaving."

"You don't owe me anything, Tristan."

His shoulders heaved with a slow breath, and then he bowed. "All the same. If I can be of service, I will. It's the right thing to do."

The butterflies that had stirred in Ilara's chest quieted. It wasn't about her, but about his guilt and longing to be a good man.

"And you like her," Kiri whispered over the top of her pillow.

Ilara hoped she wasn't blushing.

"N-no!" Tristan's face turned a deep shade of scarlet, and Ilara had to fight a laugh. He cast a nervous glance toward her papa. "I, no, I—I barely know her, and I'm trustworthy—that is—"

"I don't care what your motivation is right now," Papa said wearily. "I won't turn down any help."

"I'll try to follow you again tonight." Tristan glanced at Ilara but quickly looked away, his face still red.

Ilara started to protest, but Tristan held up a hand.

"I'm not letting you go alone."

She sighed. "Very well. Papa, can you see about the food and the guards? I'll visit the blacksmith—"

"Ilara, you need to rest." Papa put a hand on her shoulder. "I'll take care of it."

"I'm too on edge to sleep right now." Ilara took his hand and kissed the back of it. They'd need to discuss what he'd done to Tristan later, but she knew he wasn't in the frame of mind for that conversation yet. "We'll stop him, Papa."

34

As Onak left and Meelah and Kiri went back into their room, Tristan's heart finally slowed to its usual rhythm. He could still hardly believe Ilara had stood up to the fae lord—for him. Not for herself or her sisters, but for Tristan, a man she barely knew. That fact was doing nothing to extinguish the steadily growing affection he had for her, and neither was her sisters' teasing or Halkon's unsettling observation about his feelings. Unfortunately, she clearly didn't return the sentiment after discovering the true reason he had agreed to help. A relationship had been a fool's dream, anyway—

"Baron Carbrey."

Tristan startled, his gaze flying to Ilara. *Baron Carbrey.* As if he needed any more proof that she wanted to distance herself from him. A confused frown wrinkled her expression.

"Would you accompany me to the blacksmith's?" she asked. "I'd like to speak with you. It's a request, not a command, and I understand if you would rather sleep."

A knot formed in his throat. What could she want to tell him? Whatever it was, it couldn't be good, but he probably owed her an explanation. "Of course…Your Highness."

"I'm going to go by my room and change first." Ilara gave the fluffy skirt of the fae dress an irritated pat. "You may meet me in the front foyer in a quarter hour." She hesitated. "I'll understand if you're not there."

"I will be," Tristan assured her.

Ilara nodded and headed away from him, down the hallway toward the stairwell in the back of the Great House. Tristan trudged the opposite direction and up the front staircase, his entire body weighed down by his heavy heart.

Was Ilara angry? Disgusted? Would she renounce her claim that he was changing and becoming a better man? Just the thought of Ilara saying that made him feel sick to his stomach. Or maybe that was his hunger.

He pushed his worries away. Soon enough, he would know what the princess had to say, and in the meantime, he needed to update his men.

Sharland was the only one in the sitting room when Tristan entered. He stood as Tristan kicked the door closed, his thick eyebrows knitting together. "That bad?"

Tristan collapsed onto the couch. "What do you mean?"

"You look...miserable."

Tristan sighed, unsure he had the energy to speak with his men, let alone to Ilara. But he should. "Where's Masarik and Remy? I need to talk to you all."

"Remy went to get us breakfast. Masarik is bathing."

Tristan sat up straighter. "Breakfast. You haven't eaten yet?"

"No..."

"Good. Don't." Tristan slumped back on the couch again. "I stayed awake. The king is going to have food brought in from outside the Great House's lands to see if that works."

Sharland shifted from foot to foot. "Good. But...tomorrow..."

Tristan relaxed further, allowing his tight muscles to release some stress. "The good news is, Onak has lifted the threat of execution. And guaranteed you three won't be punished. That's why I wanted to talk to Remy and Masarik."

"Truthfully?" Sharland asked. At Tristan's nod, the knight sank into an armchair, his eyes briefly closing as he released a breath. "That is good news. Why?"

"Ilara found out and put a stop to it. She wasn't happy." Tristan grimaced. "She wants to meet soon. I think she's angry with me. In the fae realm, we…we danced. A lot. And we talked, both in her room and in the fae realm. We flirted. I flirted."

He should stop talking. He knew he should stop talking. But the words kept coming out of his mouth. "She's so kind—she didn't know my past, and she didn't look at me with disgust. Then I told her, and she said I deserved a second chance. She didn't hold it against me. She…called me good," he whispered.

"But now she knows I was helping her because her father threatened to execute me if I didn't, and I know she must realize now I'm *not* good and I'm selfish and…" He cut off with a groan and hung his head. "Just like my father said. Worthless."

"You are *not* worthless." The force in Sharland's voice stunned Tristan. He raised his head. Sharland sat forward on the edge of the armchair, his face pinched. "And you aren't selfish. You near starved yourself to stay awake and knowingly ran into a fae realm to try to help them, but even if we don't count that, you were willing to send us home, leaving you without help or defense, alone in Talland. Yes, you've been selfish in the past, but we're all selfish sometimes."

"Do you know everything I did?" Tristan asked. His tongue felt thick and dry. "When Ilara first heard, she called me a snake, and she was right. She told me snakes don't feel regret, and that was a sign I'm changing, but what if she's wrong? What if my father was right that I'm a mistake—"

"No." Sharland's jaw ticked. "We all make mistakes, but that doesn't have to define us. People *make* mistakes, but *people* are not mistakes."

Tristan's chest shuddered. "But some people are wicked, like my f—" He choked, and Sharland started out of his seat, but Tristan held up a hand. He stopped choking, and the knight settled back into the armchair. "I heard Masarik. In Kilkreth. What if he's right…and I'm doomed by the blood in my veins?"

Sharland opened his mouth, his eyes flashing, then closed it. "My lord…" He took a deep breath. "Can I tell you a story?"

Tristan scratched his neck. "I need to meet Ilara soon—"

"I think you'll want to hear this story, Tristan."

The use of his first name gave him pause. He hesitated, then nodded.

After taking another breath, Sharland sat back. His thumb tapped his thigh as he began to speak. "Once upon a time, there was a young noblewoman."

Tristan frowned. A fairy tale? He didn't have time for this. But for some reason, he didn't interrupt.

"She was sheltered, treasured by her parents, and hidden from a lot of the world's evils. But after she turned eighteen, she begged her parents to let her spend the winter at the royal court. They agreed, and off she went."

Sharland stared at the carpet. "She hadn't been at the castle long when she met a charming man. He was older than her, handsome, and the queen's brother. He was kind and thoughtful, then flirtatious, showering her with gifts, and he quickly became forward. She fell for him, sneaking kisses in dark corners. The man asked the young woman not to tell anyone about their relationship. He told her he loved her and was trying to protect her from a cruel court that loved to gossip and would make her life miserable."

Tristan couldn't imagine why Sharland thought a tale of young love was important right now, and he glanced at the door. Maybe he should tell Sharland to pass on the news to the others and leave to find Ilara.

"After several days, he took her to a secluded part of the palace, got her drunk, and when she was too incapacitated to disagree, he slept with her, and convinced her she'd agreed."

Tristan started, his attention back on Sharland.

"She didn't feel like she'd agreed. But he was charming, and told her how much he loved her, that he was going to marry her, and argued that she wanted it. He persuaded her to keep sleeping with him—she had already; why stop? But he instructed her to keep their trysts secret until he was ready to wed her, which he promised would be soon. It was for her own good and because of how much he cared about her, he said. And in her naivety and desperation, she believed him."

Whatever the point of this story was, Tristan didn't like it. His stomach lurched. Sharland wasn't comparing him to the villainous man in this tale…was he?

"One day, the man left the palace abruptly, leaving her a note that he'd return quickly, and when he did, he would marry her." Sharland chewed on his lower lip, the muscles in his neck cording. "But later that day, the young woman overheard the court gossip—the man she thought she loved had left to attend his wife's funeral. She had been on her deathbed for nearly three weeks after giving birth, and he had known, and had been sleeping with the young noblewoman."

Tristan was going to be sick. It didn't help that a woman dying so soon after birth reminded him of his own mother. For a man to wrong two women so horribly at the same time…

"The young woman returned home to her parents, heartbroken," Sharland continued. "But a few weeks later, she discovered she was pregnant. She wanted nothing to do with her lover, didn't want him to have anything to do with their child. Her father arranged a marriage to another man, and that man raised her illegitimate son as his own. The noblewoman's son didn't even know his father wasn't his sire until he was in his teen years. But meanwhile, the man who had impregnated her rose in power. The boy heard about this man's cruelty…and stories of how he mistreated his son, the child of his wife who had died."

Dread twisted in Tristan's chest.

Sharland dragged his gaze up to Tristan's. "That noblewoman was my mother. And my sire was Henry Carbrey."

For a moment, Tristan just stared at Sharland. His hands started to shake, and his skin went cold.

"That's why I never went to the palace before," Sharland said, his voice strained. Unshed tears glinted along his eyelashes. "My mother wouldn't let me anywhere near Henry, even though my grandfather made Henry swear he would never bother her or me. And that's the real reason I volunteered for this mission. I wanted to know you. Being Henry's son *can't* mean you're destined to re- peat his sins or that you're tainted, because if that's true of you, it's true of me."

Tristan raised a trembling hand. He needed Sharland to stop talking. It was too much to process. "I…" His chest constricted, the air squeezing from his lungs. "I can't breathe," he wheezed. *The curse.*

But it wasn't the curse—nothing was strangling his throat. He just couldn't make his lungs draw in air. *I can't breathe. I can't.* His hands curled into fists as he choked on nothing, his body betraying him.

"Listen. Tristan, look at me!" Hands grabbed Tristan's shoul- ders, and Sharland's face appeared in front of him. "Look at me. You can breathe. You can. You're sitting on a couch, you're not in danger, and you *can breathe.* Look, breathe with me. In. Out."

Tristan wheezed and shook his head, his vision going blurry.

"No, Tristan, come on." A hand grabbed his and forced his palm flat against something warm and solid. "Breathe in." The thing swelled behind his hand. "And out." The thing went down. "In. Out. In."

Tristan drew in a ragged breath and stared at his hand on Sharland's chest, his skin pale next to Sharland's brown one holding it in place.

"Out. Come on, Tristan, breathe out. And in. Good. In, and out."

Slowly, Tristan's nerves unwound. He managed to breathe in time with Sharland until his racing heart steadied. Sharland released his hand and straightened.

"I'm sorry. I—I didn't mean to upset you."

You told me my father violated a young woman while my mother was dying. The words stayed locked behind Tristan's teeth. After several deep breaths, he asked, "How do I know you're not lying?"

He knew it was unlikely. That wasn't a story anyone would make up. But part of him hoped it wasn't true, as if he could cling to some last shred of belief that his father wasn't entirely terrible— even though there was no reason he should want to defend Henry.

Sharland fidgeted. "Why would I lie? But I also have a letter Henry wrote, dis…" He swallowed. "Disowning any child resulting from my mother's pregnancy and promising never to bother my mother or her offspring."

Tristan nodded, feeling numb. "So…you're…my half-brother."

A small smile relaxed Sharland's expression. "Brother." He shrugged. "My sisters and other brother are all half-siblings, technically, but we grew up thinking we were full siblings, and by the time we found out, it didn't matter. Family is more about who you choose and who chooses you than how much of the same blood is in your veins. You can share blood and not deserve a familial title, and you can share no blood and be family. That's what my father—the man who raised me—told me when he explained that he might not be the man who sired me, but I'm still his son…and that Henry might have sired me, but that didn't mean I had to think of him as my father."

"Then why…" Tristan gulped. "You have no reason to care about me."

His half-brother's expression fell. "Why not? What if I want to choose you as my brother? What if I want to help you, to know you? I admit I was worried that when I met you, I'd discover you'd already hardened your heart and had no interest in redemption or family, but it would be your choice to stay there. I was overjoyed to learn that wasn't true. You're not someone I would be ashamed to call brother—if you are willing to accept it." He hesitated. "Not that you have to. I'm sure this is…a lot. I understand if you don't really want a brother."

Tristan sat frozen on the couch, too stunned to respond. But he latched onto one thing.

"Not ashamed," he said slowly, his voice scratchy, "to call me—" He shoved to his feet, barely stopping himself from breaking down into tears right then and there. "I need some air."

He stumbled toward the door and wrenched it open, not bothering to close it behind him. Tears stung at his eyes, and he wasn't even sure why. Was he hurt by more revelations about Henry's villainy? Angry that Sharland had told him—or that he had waited so long? Afraid he would let Sharland down? Sorrowful? Or maybe it was just…relief.

Relief that he had a living family member who cared, who didn't hate him.

Tristan barely avoided colliding with a servant as he rushed down the winding stairs, his vision blurred. He needed to get away before he completely fell apart. The door to the front foyer squeaked as he shoved it open, and Tristan skidded to a halt as two figures turned toward the sound.

Ilara and Ryn faced him, letting the partly opened front door fall shut behind them. Nika yowled, looking between the door she had been about to go through and her mistress.

Tristan blinked rapidly, trying to hide his weeping, and internally cursed himself. How could he have forgotten?

"I thought perhaps you'd fallen asleep." Ilara took a tiny step toward him. "Is something wrong?"

"What?" The word came out in a croak, and he cleared his throat. "Sorry, I…no, I just was sidetracked. Apologies, Your Highness." He bowed lower than was necessary, hoping it at least somewhat hid his hand as he wiped his tears. With a steadying breath, he straightened. "Shall we?"

35

ristan approached them, but Ilara noted a heaviness to his steps. And he'd probably believed he was hiding it, but she'd seen him wipe at his eyes.

A horrible thought occurred to her. Had Tristan been so relieved to have the threat of execution lifted he had gone to his room to weep, then dragged himself down to meet her? Maybe her instincts and her sisters and Domhnall and Ryn were all wrong. But then why was he still here?

"It's all right." Ilara smothered her disappointment and reached for the door again. "You can go rest. I don't really need your help at the blacksmith's."

He stopped a few steps away, his expression momentarily flinching before it smoothed into stoic calm. "If you don't need me, why did you ask me to come?"

Beside her, Ryn poorly covered a snicker with a cough. The only acknowledgment Tristan gave the sound was a flick of his eyes toward Ryn before focusing on Ilara again.

Ilara sighed. She'd determined to ask him, and now it was like an itch she had to scratch, or she would lose her mind. "I do want to speak with you. But not right here. Come on." She shoved open the door and headed outside. Misting rain fell from a slate-gray sky, instantly clinging to her hair and wool dress. At least it wasn't far to the blacksmith's, but Tristan still wore the thin fae clothes, so Ilara walked quickly.

Nika rubbed against Tristan's legs, and he stroked her back, his cold demeanor easing.

"Do you have a dog?" Ryn asked.

The way Tristan's wide gaze snapped to Ryn, he almost seemed frightened by the query. "No." His face shuttered as he gave Nika a pat on the side, then straightened. "Another thing Henry—my father—didn't see any use in." Unmistakable hurt seasoned his words. How was she supposed to ask her question after that?

They walked in silence to the blacksmith's building, Nika weaving around them and begging scratches off of all three of them. The rectangular wattle-and-daub and wood-reinforced structure was partly the blacksmith and his family's home and partly the connected forge. Its triangular-shaped roof rose at a steep angle and extended down past the walls, reducing the strain from heavy winter snows. The wide double doors that made up most of the wall of the forge to allow in cool air when necessary were currently closed against the rain.

"This is it." Ilara motioned to a smaller entryway, but Tristan turned aside and stood in the shelter offered by the roof's awning. The rain had soaked into his clothes so that they clung to him. He wasn't sinewy the way some of the warriors were, nor was he as thin and lithe as Lorik, but he was fit and strong, and she had to forcibly stop herself from staring.

He sighed. "Please, Your Highness, whatever you wish to say, just say it." He didn't look at her, his exhausted gaze unfocused as she stepped under the awning with him. "I'm sorry for deceiving you, but your father forbade me from telling you. I..." His stoic façade cracked, and sorrow passed over his face as his posture sagged. But then he squared his shoulders and his expression turned impassive again.

After he'd insisted on staying, she'd thought her fear that he hated her on account of Papa's actions was unmerited. Looking at him now, she wasn't so sure.

"First, I apologize for my papa, as his daughter and formally as crown princess. He never should have…" For a moment, words failed her. She was still in shock over what Papa had done.

"He's mired in the dread and pain of loss." Admitting this was uncomfortable, almost painful, but she needed him to understand. "After my mama died, he was trapped in darkness, but over time, he worked to get better. He eventually fought his way out of the crushing anger and helplessness. I was proud of him."

Ilara stared at the wet grass. "But he's slid back. I know he can climb out again, and I know he'll regret what he did if he doesn't already. I believe he wouldn't have executed you. However, none of that excuses threatening you, and I'm truly sorry. A king should do better, even in distress. He handled his fear and shame and desperation poorly, and what he did was wrong. Please don't think that's a representation of Talland and our values."

Tristan's throat bobbed, the only indication of any emotion. "Your father loves you a great deal. At least he acted out of love, not selfishness, like my…" A shiver went through him. "I can't hold a father's love for his children against him, and I certainly don't hold it against you or Talland."

Ilara relaxed a little, even as the undercurrent of hurt toward his own father broke her heart. No mother, a cruel father, a cousin who'd sent him away…had Tristan ever truly felt loved?

"He should have loved justice more," she said. "And it wasn't love—love motivates you to stand by your principles, not abandon them."

As he looked at her, his expression softened. "You're going to be a remarkable, good queen." He cleared his throat, and that blank, stony mask slid back into place. "And second, Your Highness?"

"Why are you still here?" It wasn't what she'd meant to ask, but she was confused by his turning toward warm and affectionate and then going so cold.

He looked away. "I promised to help you. And I want to do the right thing."

That was noble, and it should have satisfied her, but it didn't, not when she hoped there was more. "And that's it?" Her voice shook, betraying her.

"What do you want me to say?" Tristan asked irritably. "That I care? I do care, Your Highness; I have cared since that first morning I failed and saw how upset you and your sisters were. It's not right, what Halkon—"

"But that's all?" Ilara moved into his line of sight, and he frowned at her. "You're only still here because of moral duty?"

He worked his jaw, gazing over her shoulder. "I know it started selfishly, to protect myself. Fine, that oath was partly because I knew I had no choice but to protect you with my life. And I know you're angry I made you think I volunteered—"

"What?" She shook her head, sending tiny beads of water flying. "With you? I'm angry with my papa, not you. I need to know if it's only chivalry, nothing personal?"

Tristan crumpled. "Why?" he whispered.

"Look," Ryn said impatiently, "do you care about Ilara or not?"

Tristan cast a quick glance at Ryn, then dropped his gaze. "I care about you and your sisters and think Halkon is a villain who needs to be stopped, and I want to finish what I started."

"But Ilara *personally*," Ryn insisted. "Because everyone thinks you are…fond of her."

Ilara fought a blush.

"I…does it matter?" Tristan slumped against the side of the blacksmith's house and raked a hand through his wet hair. "Can't you just accept my help? I have no selfish goal, no ulterior motive, no trick I'm trying to pull or reward I'm seeking; I'm only trying to do good. Can you believe that?"

"So you have no feelings for me?" In Ilara's attempt to keep her hurt out of her voice, the words came out harsher than intended. "Because when we danced, it seemed like there was more. Like you *liked* me. Just…" She huffed. "Tell me the truth."

"Is that a command as princess?" The corner of Tristan's mouth curved upward, a bit of playfulness creeping into his tone, but it vanished quickly.

Ilara tossed her hands heavenward. "Yes! Fine, yes, it is! If you're going to stay here, I want to know where we stand, and if I have to command it as princess, then—"

"Yes!" Tristan leaned his head back against the shop, staring up at the awning. "I care about you personally. I might even be falling in love with you."

For someone who had just confessed his love, Tristan didn't look pleased. He looked like he was in pain.

"When you're under Halkon's influence, you aren't yourself," he said. "I hate it. Because when you wake up and glare at Halkon with all the strength and fire I was told a woman couldn't possess, you're radiant."

Ilara held her breath, wanting to reach out and touch him but afraid to interrupt him now that he was talking.

He closed his eyes, his countenance pinching. "I loved dancing with you. I find you utterly attractive and captivating, even though I know I shouldn't. I'm sorry. So call me a snake; tell me I'm selfish and whatever else you have to say." Emotion bled into Tristan's voice, something like despair. "I swear I only want to help, but if you want me to leave, tell me to go back to Rethalyon, and I'll go."

Ilara gaped. He feared she would be angry that he was falling for her? She peeked at Ryn, but Ryn appeared equally perplexed. Ilara couldn't even enjoy knowing that Tristan thought her attractive—radiant, even—because of how broken he seemed.

"Tristan…why would you think I'd call you selfish for liking me?"

"Isn't it?" At last, Tristan looked at her, aching sorrow reflected in the depths of his eyes. "If I'm falling for you and I help you, doesn't that mean I helped only because I liked you or wanted you? Isn't it better if I don't care for you or know I can't have you and help anyway?"

Ilara blinked, unsure where to even start with that.

"I know you don't owe me anything." He scuffed the toe of his boot into the grass, staring at the ground. "And if I have been too forward or made you uncomfortable, I'm sorry. I don't want anything from you. But I care. As a friend, and yes, maybe more than that. I'm sorry."

"Stop apologizing." Ilara sighed, taking in Tristan's hunched shoulders. How deeply had he been hurt that he thought loving someone made him selfish? That he expected his attempts to help to be met with disdain? "You haven't done anything untoward, and I'm not upset with you."

Ryn nudged Ilara's side. "You did sound irritated. But not for the reason you think, Baron Carbrey."

Tristan's forehead wrinkled under messy locks of wet hair. Ilara had the urge to smooth his hair back, but she managed to keep her hands firmly at her sides. She didn't want to spook him.

"I *like* you, Tristan. And after the flirting…" Ilara felt her cheeks heat. "When I overheard you talking to Papa, I feared I'd misread you. Then you were cold and distant again, and that hurt, because I think I'm falling for you, too." She ducked her head, suddenly shy.

Tristan's lips parted as he stared at her.

"Falling; you're both head over heels." Ryn rolled her eyes.

"After…" Tristan hesitated. "Everything…what I did in Rethalyon, why I started helping. You—you…"

Ilara smiled, although inside, her heart was breaking—no longer because she feared Tristan didn't care for her the way she cared for him, but now because he couldn't seem to believe her.

Tristan slid down the wall until he was sitting on his heels. Nika trotted over to him and licked his face, and Tristan chuckled. "Thanks, girl." He buried his hands in her fur, and some of the tension eased from his frame.

"That's it?" Ryn demanded. "She admits she likes you, and you sit down and talk to the dog? No offense, Nika."

Nika cocked her head at Ryn, panting through a large dog grin.

With a sigh, Tristan stood, his expression smoothing to something frustratingly neutral. "I'd be lying if I said I was displeased, Ilara. But I can't…" He shook his head. "You're the future queen of Talland. I'm a Rethali ambassador and not worthy of you in so many ways." A hint of regret flickered in his eyes. "It's why flirting was always selfish of me."

"You're allowed to want happiness for yourself." Ilara stepped forward and rested her hand on his arm. "Wanting love isn't selfish."

His jaw quivered. "We should see about the iron." With that, Tristan pushed past her and yanked open the door into the blacksmith's shop, striding inside without waiting for her.

Ilara turned to Ryn, but she couldn't even phrase her question. She just shrugged helplessly.

"I have no idea." Ryn frowned. "Maybe it's because I'm here?"

"Maybe." Or maybe it had something to do with why Tristan had been crying.

Whatever the reason, Tristan was right—they had another reason to be there, even if it was one Ilara didn't need him for. After instructing Nika to wait outside, Ilara went inside. The forge was blazing hot, but Horden wasn't tending to the bellows; he was standing in front of Tristan with his burly arms folded over his sooty apron.

"—a dagger, at least," Tristan was saying to the blacksmith. He glanced at her as she entered with Ryn on her heels. "But the princess's accessories are more pressing." He stepped aside, deferring to her.

Horden, the royal blacksmith, bowed to Ilara, the light of a hanging lantern glinting on his bald head. His dirty white shirtsleeves had been pushed up as far as his bulging muscles would allow. Soot had already worked its way into the wrinkles on his forehead. "Your Highness. This young foreign man tells me you wish me to make you…jewelry of iron?"

"We think it might help stop the sorcerer."

Horden's questioning look hardened into determination. "In that case, I swear it shall be done. Tell me everything you wish made, and my son and I will get started right away."

Ilara explained the pieces she wanted made, and Tristan added some requests, but as he spoke, his foot tapped the dirt floor. The moment they were done, he bolted out the door. Ilara ran after him, ignoring Nika's greeting as she hiked up her skirt to avoid stepping on the hem.

"Tristan, wait!"

The rain had stopped, leaving in its wake tendrils of fog. Tristan slowed, then halted, his jerky movements making the fog dance away from him. He turned partway back but didn't face her. Ilara came to a stop a couple paces behind him and found that she didn't know what to say. For a moment, they stood there in silence while birds called and servants and farm animals moved through the fog in the distance.

"We should sleep," he said. "We'll need rest before tonight."

"Wait!" She reached toward him, her hand hanging in the emptiness between them. "Will you come to our room shortly before dusk?"

He hesitated. "I don't need to be in your chamber to follow."

"Please?" She needed to talk to him before they went to the fae realm again, and he was more open when it was only the two of them.

"All right." Tristan strode away toward the Great House, leaving Ilara in the fog with Nika whining at her side.

"I don't know, Nika." She patted the dog's head, her heart heavy. "I just don't know."

36

*T*ristan took the stairs two at a time. His head pounded, his left eye ached, and he wanted nothing more than an entire pitcher of water—and to sleep for a solid week.

"Wanting love isn't selfish."

Ilara's hand on his arm and her gentle words had been too much. He'd nearly broken again, and he wasn't about to cry in front of Ilara and Ryn and any servants that happened past.

He hadn't realized how accustomed he'd become to being alone. Once, he'd longed for companionship beyond the surface-level relationships with courtiers and the distant relationship with Henry. But now that he had a half-brother who wanted to treat him like a brother and an amazing woman who cared for him, he found the prospect frightened him. He didn't know what scared him more: being forever unknown, unwanted, unloved…or being known and, somehow, still wanted and loved.

Tristan rammed the door to his suite open, jumping when the door smashed into Masarik's outstretched hand on the other side. The knight yelped and shook his hand.

"Sorry…" Tristan couldn't get his mind to give him anything more than that. They stood there staring at each other while Masarik held his jammed fingers. Tristan sighed. "Can I enter my own suite, Sir Masarik?"

"Oh. Right. Sorry, my lord." Masarik stepped aside, holding the edge of the door to keep it open. "So…"

Tristan groaned. He wanted to collapse into bed and sleep, or perhaps cry and then sleep—maybe if he could get these tiring emotions out in private, they'd stop threatening his composure in public. Massaging his aching forehead, he turned back. "Yes?"

Masarik eyed him in a way that reminded Tristan far too much of someone inspecting a purchase and checking for flaws. "Allyre said he told you. I'm just…curious."

Tristan stiffened. "He told…you?"

"I told Masarik and Remy," Sharland's voice said behind Tristan.

He whirled around. His half-brother stood in the doorway to the knights' room, leaning against the doorframe with his arms folded casually over his chest.

"I hadn't planned to tell them before I told you, but they volunteered to stay after I did…" Sharland shrugged. "They deserved to know the full truth about why I was staying, even if I wasn't convinced you were ready to hear it yet."

"Oh." Tristan managed a nod, too drained for anything else. "I'm going to bed. Please tell Remy—"

"Yes, my lord?" Remy popped out of Tristan's bedchamber, overwhelmingly attentive as ever.

"…to wake me two hours before dusk and have a bath prepared," Tristan finished. "Please." He proceeded to his room, barely registering Remy's serious promise to do so, but stopped at his door. "Allyre?"

It was the first time he had called Sharland by his given name, and it felt odd, like he had crossed some boundary. Allyre simply looked at him expectantly. Masarik tarried in the doorway to the corridor as well, but Tristan ignored his obvious eavesdropping.

"I—I have questions I'd like to ask. Eventually. If you're open to it. Informally, as…" Brothers was too much to say right now, and he couldn't force the word past his taut vocal cords. "Friends," he said instead. Even that felt unreal. "Perhaps tomorrow?" Assuming he didn't die in the fae realm tonight, but he pushed that thought aside.

A smile crinkled Allyre's face. "Certainly."

Tristan nodded, then paused at the threshold. "Oh. Did you all eat?"

"Remy," Masarik said, "our hero of the hour, caught wind of the plan to eat food from outside the Great House's lands. More, he managed to snag some. We'd barely finished eating when you returned."

"There's some on your bedside table, my lord."

Whatever Remy was getting paid, it wasn't enough. "Thank you. You can take it, though—I can't risk it not working."

Remy's pleased expression collapsed. "But—"

"Tristan." Allyre's quiet voice held a startling firmness. "We're out of Rethali food, and you barely ate the last two days. You look terrible. You need to eat."

All three of his men stared at him, and the silent pressure in the suite added to his headache. "Right," he mumbled. "All right."

In his room, he downed the cup of water sitting by the food, stripped off his clothes, and went to sleep without touching the meal.

"My lord."

Something shook Tristan's shoulder. Light streamed over his face, blinding him.

"My lord."

Tristan squinted at Remy and groaned. His feet ached, his

body was heavy, and his head still hurt. Holding the candle responsible for assaulting Tristan's vision, Remy straightened as Tristan sat up.

"You didn't eat anything." Remy's mouth twisted down, and if he hadn't been so tired, Tristan would have chuckled at the disapproval radiating from his manservant.

"Don't tell Allyre." Tristan rubbed sleep out of his eyes. "I just can't hazard it."

Remy sighed. "I refilled your cup with water, and your bath is ready, my lord. Also, an iron dagger arrived for you. It's on the table in the common room."

"Thank you." He gulped the water, hoping it would help the heaviness in his bones.

"So…" Remy picked up the tray of untouched food. "You're calling him Allyre now."

He attempted a casual shrug. "Felt right, I suppose."

"It's good to have friends." Remy shook himself and ducked his head. "Anyway, your bath is going to get cold."

After a bath that Tristan wished he could have stayed in forever—and that eased some of his aching—he dressed, this time in his own clothes. He picked a deep green long-sleeved shirt and a pair of black trousers, hoping they would help him go unnoticed lurking in the woods of Halkon's realm. Gold might have worked better, but dark colors were what he had. He slipped the iron dagger into his boot.

Remy stood as Tristan exited his room. Allyre and Masarik looked up from the table.

"We'd accompany you," Masarik said, "but we've been ordered not to go near the princesses."

Allyre frowned. "If we stay awake, King Onak doesn't want Halkon realizing."

"Oh, of course." Tristan nodded. "I'll see you in the morning, then." *Hopefully.*

"Be careful, my lord." Remy bowed as Tristan passed.

It didn't make sense how loyal they'd become to him—but he was grateful all the same.

To his relief, Ilara was asleep when he stole into her room. Or, at least, she didn't stir or say anything when he entered. He hesitated. She wouldn't know if he left and waited in one of the rooms adjacent to her private chambers upstairs. Ah, well, he was here now. He felt his way over to her bed and started to crawl underneath it.

"Trying to get out of talking to me with all this sneaking about?" Ilara asked, warm amusement in her tone.

Tristan sighed even as his lips twitched against a grin. "Trying not to disturb your slumber."

"Disturbances are unwanted. Like Domhnall." He could imagine her nose wrinkling with disgust. It would be cute if he could see it. "You're not unwanted, Tristan."

He went still, awkwardly half under her bed. Part of him wished to slip the rest of the way under and hide before emotions overwhelmed him again. She shouldn't desire him—no matter how much he wanted her, or how much he wanted her to want him.

"I don't know what's going to happen tonight," he said quietly. "And you still hardly know me."

"What don't I know?" There was a bit of challenge to Ilara's voice. "I know your father was a horrible person. I know your mother died when you were an infant. I know you think you don't have friends—although since Ryn tells me your knights were *not* happy about being commanded not to help you tonight, it seems that's untrue. I know you're too hard on yourself and keep punishing yourself for past mistakes when you don't need to. I know everything you did…unless there's anything you left out?"

Tristan crawled out from under the bed, considering as he sat against the wall. There was one more thing, and she ought to know the full truth. "I'm the reason Alexander's best friend is dead." The words came out brittle and quiet.

After a moment, Ilara murmured, "Explain."

He took a steadying breath. "When I found Alexander, he was human, mostly. But I decided to kill him anyway. My hunters attacked; he transformed into a dragon, and I prepared to fight him. His friend, Lucas—a boy, I think he was no older than sixteen, maybe younger—came out with a sword to defend Alex." Tristan shook his head in the dark. "He put himself between me and a towering, fire-breathing *dragon* to give Alex a chance to escape without bloodshed. I moved to attack; Alex knocked me aside…and one of my archers killed Lucas. They'd grown up together after Alex was cursed. Alex treated him like a brother."

As he spoke that word, he thought of Allyre and Remy and even Masarik. He hadn't known them long, but if one of them were killed, he would want to hurt the one responsible. His throat caught, and it took him a moment to continue.

"Because of my actions, Lucas died in pain while Alex and Raelyn and Lucas's parents wept. My choices killed him." He drew his knees up to his chest and wrapped his arms around them. "I killed him."

"No," Ilara said gently, "you didn't loose that arrow—"

"I might as well have," Tristan interrupted. He wouldn't let this go any further—it would only make it hurt worse when it ended. "I could've given the order to stand down. I shouldn't have tried to kill Alex again right after Lucas died. I shouldn't have harmed or mocked him and never should have treated Lucas's grieving parents as prisoners."

"But you've—"

"You don't understand," Tristan hissed, his heart like lead in his chest. "There were moments I enjoyed seeing the pain and hatred in Alex's eyes, because it felt like justice for everything I'd suffered. Henry always compared us…it's stupid now. I blamed Alex for my father—" He choked. *Flaming curse.* "Anyway, when the woman I thought would help me feel less alone fell in love with someone else, it was easy to blame Alex for that, too."

Saying that out loud made him sound so weak and selfish, and he hated himself for it.

"Tristan—"

"I know none of it was Alex's fault. He didn't make my father what he was." Thinking of Allyre, he clenched his jaw. "I'm far from the only person…*he* hurt." He sighed. "But I chose to take out my pain on Alex and Raelyn and Gareth and Alex's friends. On innocents. There's nothing I can do that will undo the damage I did. If there were," he said as a tear he had no right to cry slipped down his cheek, "I'd do it. No matter what it cost me."

"Then maybe it's time you stopped trying to repair a burned-down house and started building a new one."

Tristan wasn't sure if he was glad he couldn't see Ilara or wished that he could. She didn't sound disgusted. "What do you mean?"

Something poked his shoulder, then a hand squeezed his upper arm. "You can't move on until you forgive yourself, Tristan." She released him. "Alex didn't blame you in his letter. He said he had complete trust in you and spent more ink describing your defiance of your father and your willingness to serve him than your misdeeds. That doesn't sound like someone who is holding onto resentment. I know you want to change"—she yawned, her words slurring together—"but you have to let go of the hurt and shame in your past, forgive yourself, and let people care about you in order to move forward. You can't heal a broken heart without love…"

She trailed off, her breathing deepening into slumber.

Tristan slipped beneath the bed. She made it sound easy, letting go of his guilt and pain and accepting love, but he felt as much in the dark about how to do that as he was in that windowless room. And yet…Allyre, Ilara, and Remy all knew who he was and what he'd done, and they weren't turning away. Even Masarik was becoming friendly. Maybe she was right.

Maybe the way forward was to stop wallowing in shame, as if hating himself enough would absolve him of his wrongs, and instead try to forge something new. Something like a friendship with Allyre…and perhaps even a relationship with Ilara, if their respective stations would allow that. He was so preoccupied with his thoughts, he barely registered Halkon's arrival, and he followed the fae and princesses almost by rote.

Ilara walked out of her bedroom in a fae dress, this one pale blue with a bodice covered in white flowers that trailed down onto the darker skirt that surrounded her like a tent. Her presence snapped Tristan back to his senses.

Halkon frowned. "What's this? Jewelry?" He reached for the wide necklace that rested on Ilara's collarbones. "Why—" He hissed as his fingertips grazed the metal and jerked his hand back, his expression contorting into a snarl. "You ungrateful, miserable *wretch.*"

Ilara blinked and withdrew a tiny step. Triumph lit her face. "Don't you like my *iron* jewelry, your fae lordship?"

"Iron," Halkon spat. He took a menacing step forward, leaning over Ilara. "You—"

"Stay away from me." Ilara shoved against the fae's chest, and where her iron rings pressed against his tunic, whisps of smoke curled.

Halkon grabbed her wrists and screeched, jumping back and staring down at his palms as his fingers curved like claws. When he looked up, the vitriol in his eyes made it difficult for Tristan to remain crouched at the top of the stairs and not rush to Ilara's defense. "That is *it*, princess."

Ilara lifted her chin, her eyes glinting with defiance. If that look could be captured in a painting, it would be a masterpiece, and Tristan might never stop staring at it.

Halkon raised his hand and conjured a portal in the hall. Ilara moved to dart away, but he seized her and shoved her through the portal so hard she fell to the grass. Anger flaring, Tristan started up. Halkon strode forward, and a rope-like vine shimmered into existence in his fist. The vine whipped around Ilara's waist as Halkon continued through the woods.

"Come along, dearest. We need to get you some food and then get those *accessories* off you."

Tristan raced up the hallway as quietly as possible. Meelah and Kiri hadn't emerged from their rooms yet, but Halkon sped down the crystal-lit trail. Ilara stumbled to her feet, the vine-rope dragging her after the fae lord. If Halkon had forgotten about the younger sisters, that was for the best.

As if confirming that Halkon was too preoccupied to bother with the other princesses, the enchanted door shrank. Tristan dove through, his lungs seizing when the magic nearly closed on his foot. He didn't care to find out what would happen if it shut on a body part. Dusting himself off, he cut into the deep shadows of the silver and gold forest toward the meadow.

37

The layered skirt of the fae dress kept tripping Ilara as she struggled to catch up to Domhnall. The vine encircling her waist tugged her forward, hardly giving her a chance to get her feet properly under her. She glanced over her shoulder and saw a dark shape jump through the closing portal and roll across the grass. *Tristan.* Part of her was relieved to see him, but another part wished that, like her sisters, he was safely back in Talland.

"You cursed mortal girl!" Domhnall fumed as they reached the meadow. He whirled to face her. "I picked Talland for two reasons; do you know what they were?"

"You felt like ruining my life in particular?" Ilara guessed, stopping far enough away that the vine wasn't taut, but also no closer than necessary. It was taking all of her mental power not to think about what else Domhnall could do with vines.

He rolled his eyes. "First, because I needed a legal claim to land in the human realm. There is no unclaimed territory left in your realm thanks to you mortals' insatiable greed, which means I'd have to purchase, barter for, or conquer land or marry into lawful ownership. I don't have the time or resources for a true conquest, and I have nothing a human would ask for land that I would be willing to give, so I deemed marriage the most attainable method. I couldn't settle for some small lordship; no, if I was going to do this, I wanted an entire kingdom. You were the only eligible female in line for a throne that I found quickly."

"Lucky me," she said in a flat voice.

Domhnall ignored her. "Three hundred years ago, when I was young and stupid, I fell for a human. Unfortunately, she no longer trusted me after I revealed to her what I am." Grief flashed in his eyes for a brief moment. "Fae don't have much of a heart to break or love in the human sense, but if we love a human enough, we can choose to become mortal. I told her I would make that sacrifice for her. In return, she attempted to kill me—so I killed her."

Ilara would have drawn back if it wasn't for the vine still around her middle. "If this is supposed to make me feel sorry for you—"

"Oh, not at all." Domhnall's smile reminded her of a viper. "I just want you to understand. Any heart I had, I buried with Yrene. I returned to my realm hating humans, and your antics and stubbornness are testing my benevolence. So when I tell you I didn't pursue you lightly and that you will either marry me and become fae or you and your loved ones will suffer, I'm deadly serious."

Ilara gaped. Become fae? "What do—"

"However," he interrupted, "the second reason I chose you specifically is that fae haven't been active in Talland in centuries, and before that didn't visit often. Fae lore isn't as common there as in some other kingdoms." His lips pinched. "Unlike Eynlae with its beloved tales of Sir Roderick, including the story about the fae…" Realization dawned on his face. "Which made it into neighboring *Rethalyon*. This was that Carbrey boy's idea, wasn't it?"

Ilara tried to keep her expression unbothered. "The iron? Yes. The jewelry? That was mine."

"Next time I'm in your realm, he'll pay dearly for his interference."

She thought of Tristan making it through the portal just

before it closed. Hopefully he would stay hidden, and Domhnall wouldn't realize he was there.

"Unless…" He looked around the forest and glanced at the dancers behind him. "He didn't follow us again, did he? Unlikely he made it in, but if he did, that would be excellent. Perhaps I'll feed him fae food until he vomits, then amuse myself by making him do whatever ridiculous thing I can think of until I get bored, then I'll use him for archery practice."

Ilara felt the blood drain from her face. She fought to keep her voice steady as she said, "Good thing he had the sense not to come back here, then."

"You think you've outsmarted me?" The fae laughed. "I'm five hundred years old. You know nothing." Vines shot up from the ground and ensnared her arms, avoiding the iron bracelets, and dragged her to her knees. The vine on her waist vanished.

Her chest heaved, but she refused to show her fear. Instead, she focused on her rage as she glared at him.

"Now." Domhnall knelt in front of her and conjured a silver date. "Eat." He reached for her, and she tried to pull away, but the vines held firm. He forced her mouth open, making her jaw ache, and pushed the date into her mouth. Then he pressed her jaw closed.

Tears lined her lashes, but less from the pain than from realizing she couldn't stop this. The date tasted tarter than most of the other fruit, but still rich and sweet. Her anger dulled, and as Domhnall kept feeding her dates, a pleasant fuzziness settled over her. Something released her. Had something been holding her? No, that didn't make sense.

"Here. Drink." Domhnall held out a goblet. The dates had made her thirsty, and she drained the wine from the goblet.

"Take off your jewelry," Domhnall said gently.

"Jewelry?" She blinked.

"Yes, my flower." He pointed. "The rings, the bracelets, the collar. You look better without them. They don't match the dress."

"Oh." Something deep in her mind protested as she pulled the rings off one by one and dropped them. No, she should leave the bracelets. But she was already pulling them off. And the collar…that should stay. Go. No, stay. She frowned, feeling sick to her stomach.

"Look at me," Domhnall soothed. "Take off the collar, lovely. For me?"

Suddenly taking off the necklace seemed like an excellent idea, so she dropped it to the ground. Domhnall stood and helped her to her feet.

"Shall we dance, my sweet?"

Ilara giggled despite the disorienting feeling she didn't want to be there. He pulled her into the meadow with the other dancing couples. Silver moonlight and dulcet music surrounded them. Domhnall's captivating emerald eyes held her gaze as they twirled over the grass, her layers of skirt swishing about her legs.

"See? Isn't that better?" He spun her around. "With those gone, I can do this." He ran his fingertips over her throat. She shuddered, but why? She liked Domhnall, didn't she?

"Now." He pulled her in close, and his breath brushed over her cheek as he leaned down. "Kiss me, Ilara."

Kiss…that didn't seem right. She blinked, trying to think.

Domhnall smiled, but his grip on her hand tightened. His lips pressed against hers. She stiffened. No…yes? *No.* The enchantment on her mind cleared with a jolt, and she shoved him away. "Get off me!"

Domhnall sighed. "See? This is why I need your mortal kingdom. Too many years of drifting have sapped my magic. A couple hundred years ago, you would have said yes and gladly taken your vows the first night. I require an anchor, a tether from my court in the infinite fae realm to your finite one. Most fae lords have them because it makes our courts stable—it's also what causes the thin places where humans can wander into fae lands. After Yrene betrayed me, I foolishly cut my tether—and then my court started draining my energy to remain stable. Now I can't even keep one mortal boy from escaping! And if the other courts realize how weak I've become, they will tear me apart." His gaze darted around as he muttered, "If my own subjects don't do it first."

Ilara felt her bare wrists and neck, unimpressed with Domhnall's sob story. At least she knew the jewelry worked, but Domhnall possessing enough power to convince her to surrender her best defense against him made her want to retch. Hopefully Tristan had seen and would get back all right, because Domhnall would never allow her to remember.

"Yes," Domhnall said. "I made you remove your jewelry." His upper lip curled. "I could have made you remove more."

Ilara jerked backward, bumping into a fae couple that shot her a glare before spinning away. Domhnall seized her hand and drew her into another dance.

"But then," he said, "every time I push you to do something you really don't want to, you break free. I've been patient, trying to wear you down without breaking you. Once you marry me, things will be easier.

"When you're my queen, imbued with the magic of the fair folk, your vows will bind you to me, and me to you, which might reduce your desire to resist me."

A tremble went through Ilara. She needed to control her fear and revulsion and trust Tristan and the plan. "What if I don't want to be a fae?"

Domhnall laughed. "You don't have a choice, my dear. You marry a lord of the fae, here in my realm, and you become a fae.

And you either marry me, or I'll turn your sisters into rabbits and let the foxes chase them down while you watch."

Her skin went cold, and she tripped, falling against his chest. She pulled away as if burned. *Meelah and Kiri…* If they couldn't stop Domhnall, she didn't know what she would do. She couldn't watch her sisters die.

"As I suspected." He nodded. "If I hadn't drunkenly made that bet with Eldrich and had been able to threaten a terrible death to your sisters from the start, you would have already married me. Hubris, I suppose, thinking I had the charm and power to enchant you into doing my will."

He brushed her hair behind her ear. "But then, you have an unusually strong will of your own. Stronger than most mortals I've encountered. Certainly stronger than the annoying boy. He'll do anything I tell him to."

Not Tristan. She glanced up at Domhnall, then quickly looked away, cursing her stupidity.

"What's this?" He pinched her chin and turned her head toward him. "What's the Rethali's name, again? Not Carbrey, his given name, it's…Tristan?"

She glared at him, trying to disguise her fear. By the slow smile that spread over Domhnall's face, she hadn't succeeded.

"So his affections *aren't* one-sided." He laughed as he released her. "Oh, I'm going to enjoy tormenting Tristan after we're married."

Ilara's lower lip quivered. It wasn't enough to threaten her family if she *didn't* marry him, but he would still torture the man she loved if she *did* marry him? "You'll leave him out of it. He's not even Tallander."

"Why should I care what mortal kingdom he calls home? He will be in my domain, and I will crush him." His features darkened. "Do you know, when fae make a deal with each other, there's a magical binding, and we sense when the other has broken it? After I threatened to kill your sisters this morning, I returned to find a gloating Eldrich waiting to collect his winnings. I've been in a sour mood ever since. But the thought of torturing Tristan after all the trouble he's caused…it's enough to lift my spirits."

She pressed her eyes closed and hoped to the moon that the guards who had eaten food from outside the Great House's grounds had stayed awake. They had to stop Domhnall—as soon as possible. Tristan was right. They should have attempted it instead of delaying for testing.

Tristan. She was finally getting through to him. He was opening up to her, and now…she'd have to send him away. If Domhnall hurt him because he was angry with her—

"Ilara."

She opened her eyes as a tear escaped near her temple.

Domhnall wiped away the tear with his thumb. "Why don't you beg me to spare him?"

Ilara wrenched her hand free and turned her back on him, her arms crossed. She would not beg.

"So be it. What do you think of this plan? First, I will turn him into a frog and place him in a glass jar in the sunlight until he's dry and shriveling. Then I'll turn him into a goldfinch and clip his wings so he can't fly. I'll keep him in a cage, and every day, I'll pluck a few feathers. And once every feather is gone, I'll turn him back into a man, so you can see the look on his face and hear his screams as I slowly kill him. Death by a thousand cuts, maybe?"

She swallowed back the bile pushing at her throat and clenched her teeth so hard they ached.

"Unless you beg me to have mercy on him. Right now. Last chance."

What if their plan failed? What if Domhnall realized Tristan was in the woods? Even without having all the details, she knew

Tristan had already suffered enough at the hands of his father and from his own self-loathing. He deserved a chance to be happy—he didn't deserve to bear Domhnall's viciousness. Her pride crumbling, Ilara faced the fae. "Please."

"Please what?"

"Spare him."

Domhnall crossed his arms. "Spare who?"

"Tristan," Ilara whispered. "Please. Spare him."

"I don't know…"

She clenched her fists, battling the urge to punch him. "I'm begging you. Please."

"This is you begging?" He laughed and shook his head. "I'm unconvinced. Try harder."

She should have strangled him when she was still wearing the iron rings.

"You know what I haven't done in, oh, two hundred years?" Domhnall snickered. "Flayed someone to death. Or, I could break every bone in his body—"

"Please." Ilara shuddered and fell to her knees. Anger and humiliation burned her skin. She forced herself to look up at him as she raised her clasped, trembling hands. "Spare Tristan. Please. I beg you."

Domhnall grabbed her hands and hauled her up. "I will spare his life. On one condition." He yanked her against him and cupped the back of her neck in his hand. She went rigid, her breathing shallow. "Marry me right now, and the boy lives."

"Leave her alone!" Tristan's voice rang out over the music.

Oh, no.

38

The musicians went silent and the meadow full of dancers stilled. Tristan shoved aside a woman standing in his path and stormed past a table covered in metallic fruit. "Stop!"

"Oh, look. It's my pet goldfinch." Halkon's smile reminded Tristan of a hungry fox. "Here in my realm, too. Maybe I'll make him perform, then turn him into a frog."

He had no idea what Halkon was talking about, but he didn't care. Ilara's eyes were wide, and she quaked as the fae lord's arms held her trapped against his chest. "Let her go. Can't you see she's terrified?"

"You say that like her fright doesn't amuse me. Nothing makes you feel as powerful as making someone quail with fear. Especially someone as defiant as the princess." Halkon eyed Tristan. "You strike me as someone who understands the rush of seeing your enemies fall to their knees before you."

Tristan stilled. "It turns out that feeling fades quickly and leaves you hollow. It's not worth the guilt."

"Guilt?" The fae lord laughed. "A pitiful human emotion that dampens enjoyment and makes life miserable. I have no use for it. Pleasure, I have use for." He removed his hand from the back of Ilara's neck to motion at the stalled party surrounding them, then traced his fingertips around the edge of her face. She flinched away, and Tristan's fingernails dug into his palms.

How could he ever have behaved like this? But he wouldn't fail Ilara the way he had failed Raelyn.

"Power," Halkon continued as he looked back at Tristan, "is also worth my time." He wiggled his fingers, playing with shimmering threads of gold and purple light. "But guilt? I'd need a heart for that, and as I recently explained to Ilara, I cut mine out. Metaphorically."

"Release her." Tristan stalked forward, bending down to pull the iron dagger from his boot.

Halkon scoffed. "You forget where you are, mortal."

Tristan rushed Halkon. Vines erupted from the grass and tangled his feet, and he fell. He caught himself on his hands, but more vines pinned him to the ground, knocking the dagger out of his grip. Halkon released Ilara and moved to stand over Tristan, kicking the blade beyond his reach.

"How slowly shall I kill you—"

"Please," Ilara said, her voice shaking. "Stop. I beg of you. Please."

Halkon grinned, wolfish. "How sweet true fear sounds."

"You—" A vine wrapped around Tristan's throat, silencing him. He choked and tried to move his hands, but the vines held his arms in place.

"If you harm him, I will never marry you!" Ilara stepped up next to Domhnall.

Domhnall snorted. "You've already sworn you won't marry me before, and I believe I have all the power in this situation, dearest. You're going to have to give *me* something."

Tristan strained to look up at them as he fought for air. He met Ilara's gaze. Fear and heartbreak reflected in her tense expression, and he hated himself for the momentary feeling of joy at realizing how deeply she cared. He shook his head, as well as he could with the vine strangling him. *Don't do anything. Not for me.*

It meant he would die. He still wasn't ready, but if he had to die, at least it was while doing the right thing and trying to help someone. Someone he cared about—maybe even loved.

Ilara's lower lip trembled, but fire flashed in her eyes. She turned to the fae lord. "Don't kill him, and I will *consider* marrying you. I'll dance with you tonight, unenchanted, and be polite, and consider any argument you can make for why I would choose to marry you, and I'll give you my final answer tomorrow night."

It was more than she should be willing to do for him, but he doubted it would be enough to appease Halkon. To his shock, however, the vines binding him dissolved.

Tristan gasped and rubbed his sore neck, taking a moment to breathe. *I'm alive.* And he had a chance at staying that way—because Ilara had made a sacrifice to save him. *Am I truly worth that?*

"All right, my flower." Halkon stroked Ilara's hair, and although her expression twitched into disgust, she didn't pull away. "I agree to the deal. I won't kill him, as you have requested."

That had actually worked? Masarik had mentioned fae usually kept their word. As his breathing normalized, Tristan pushed himself up.

"But that isn't quite the same as letting him go." Halkon spun away from Ilara and grabbed Tristan's hair.

Tristan yelped as Halkon strode toward the trees, dragging him across the ground. The strain on his scalp caused his eyes to water. He grabbed Halkon's wrist and tried to get his legs under him, but the fae's pace made it impossible.

"What are you doing?" Ilara shrieked, chasing after them.

Halkon stopped and tugged Tristan to his feet. Hating the tears that rolled down his cheeks from the stinging pain, he glowered up at the fae. Releasing his hair, Halkon waved a hand. Vines curled around Tristan's wrists, digging into his skin, and yanked his hands up. They tied themselves to the branches of two silver trees on either side of him, leaving him bound with his arms spread above his head.

"You can't harm him!" Ilara grabbed Halkon's arm. "I know I only said kill, but do you really think I'll let you touch me after watching you hurt him?"

Tristan didn't dare speak. His heart pounded in his chest.

Halkon yanked his arm free without acknowledging Ilara and conjured a small bunch of silver grapes. He broke one off and held it up to Tristan, close enough that if Tristan leaned forward, he would be able to bite it.

"If you want to forget your fate, boy, eat. If you wish to stew on it a while yet, forego the fruit. But know that come tomorrow night, when I wed Ilara, I will make you my slave. You will wait on me hand and foot, eager to please, willing to endure any indignity, even acting as a log for me to walk across a muddy path. And whenever I'm bored, I'll think up new ways to torment you, breaking you and healing you so I can break you again."

His fear forgotten in his anger at the thought of Halkon marrying Ilara, Tristan bared his teeth. He wished he could pull off Alexander's intimidating snarl. "You'll never wed Ilara."

The grapes vanished in a blink of light. "Suit yourself." Domhnall flicked his fingers, and the vines drew up further, straining Tristan's shoulders. He stifled a cry of pain.

Ilara stepped between him and Halkon. "You can't—"

"I promised to spare his life," Halkon interrupted. He lifted one shoulder in a noncommittal shrug. "I made no promises in what condition."

Something pricked at Tristan's wrists, and he looked up in horror as large thorns grew out of the vines, stabbing into his skin. A pathetic whimper caught in his throat. He turned his face away as Ilara spun to face him.

"Tristan? What's—he's bleeding!"

"So he is." Halkon slipped his arm around Ilara's waist, pressing his chest against her back. "Now, are you going to come dance with me, or shall I add further torments?"

Ilara gently turned Tristan's face until he met her eyes again. "I'm sorry," she murmured.

"It's not your fault. And…" He forced himself to continue. "You don't need to worry about me."

Ilara's brow furrowed, her gaze searching his face.

"I'm doing a terrible job of helping you," he said, his mouth dry. *And even if I were doing better, I still wouldn't deserve your affection.*

"Yes, you are." Halkon gave a derisive sniff. He stepped back and turned Ilara toward him. "And you have a promise to keep, my flower."

Ilara leaned away from Halkon and looked over her shoulder at Tristan.

A thick vine—thankfully one without thorns—wrapped over Tristan's mouth, gagging him. What could he say, anyway?

"Are you breaking our agreement?" Halkon's tone held a challenging edge.

"No," Ilara said quickly. She cast one more apologetic look at Tristan, then placed her hand on Halkon's shoulder, and they danced away.

The night dragged on, each hour slower than the last. Tristan's shoulders screamed in pinched agony, and sticky blood oozed down his forearms, adhering his shirt to his skin. Ilara danced or talked with Halkon while watching the other dancers. Sometimes his countenance darkened, and he said something that made the color drain from Ilara's cheeks.

Pink crept into the sky, and fae dispersed, many casting amused, disgusted, or intrigued glances his way as they passed.

Tristan watched with tired fury as Halkon forced Ilara to eat something and she settled into dreamy oblivion. Then Halkon came and stood next to Tristan, observing Ilara dance with one of the few remaining fae.

"I'm letting you return with her."

Tristan darted a confused look at him.

"You will have one last day of freedom. Once I marry Ilara and bind my court to Talland, there will be no escape for you. I will keep you as my slave and torment you until I grow bored, and then I will throw you in a lightless hole to live out the remainder of your mortal days." With a snap of his fingers, the vines restraining Tristan turned to dust.

Tristan coughed out dirt and groaned as his aching arms fell to his sides.

"However," Halkon said slowly, "Ilara's fight has increased since you arrived." He adjusted his sleeves. "Leave Talland. Go home. It will take time for my magical dominion to spread to the borders after the marriage and coronations are complete, so if you depart soon, you should be able to escape before then. Even if you don't make it in time, if you run, I will not come after you."

"Why?" Tristan's voice came out like sand scraping over rocks. He cleared his throat. "Why?"

"I suspect it will wear down her resistance. Don't get me wrong, I will marry her either way." The fae crossed his arms. "But she will fight me less with you gone. Heartbreak is…a terrible thing. It saps your will and crushes your hope. Even more so for mortals, I imagine. Besides, what do you have to lose? If you stay, she will marry me, and you will be my prisoner."

As if to emphasize his point, he kicked the back of Tristan's knee. Tristan collapsed with a grunt, and Halkon bent over him and grabbed his face. His fingers clawed into Tristan's cheeks and jaw and forced him to look up. Tristan glared, but his arms were too sore to come to his aid.

"If you depart, you'll go free, along with any other Rethalis you brought with you. I give my unbreakable vow. Abandon Ilara to her fate, leave Talland, and you'll be free and unharmed. Stay and try to help her, and you will beg me for death and the end of your pain. And any Rethali friends you might have will become my slaves as well." Halkon released Tristan's face and patted his cheek. "Understand?"

"Understood," Tristan muttered.

"Good boy." Halkon straightened. "Come along."

Begrudgingly, Tristan followed Halkon as he got Ilara and created a portal. Halkon kissed Ilara's hand.

"Until our wedding, my dear."

Ilara's expression pinched as the fae ushered her into her room. Tristan started to follow, but Halkon seized his shoulder.

"Remember. Abandon her and flee." He shoved Tristan through, and the portal vanished, leaving them in darkness.

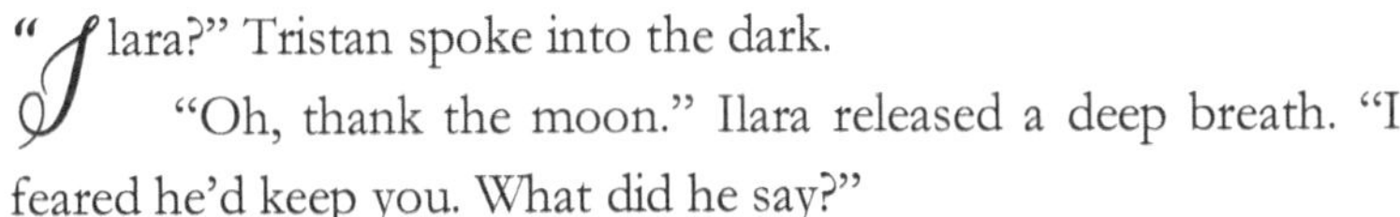

39

"*I*lara?" Tristan spoke into the dark.

"Oh, thank the moon." Ilara released a deep breath. "I feared he'd keep you. What did he say?"

Before Tristan could decide how much to disclose, the door was thrown open. Three figures crowded the entryway, early dawn light filling the hall behind them.

"They're both here!" Masarik exclaimed. Tristan actually smiled, but then he remembered Halkon's threat, and his amusement vanished.

"Ilara!" Onak rushed to his daughter, pulling her into a tight embrace.

Someone crossed to Ilara's bedside table and lit the lamp. Candlelight played across Allyre's dark face.

"The food worked?" Ilara asked, taking the words out of Tristan's mouth.

Onak released her. "Yes! Everyone who ate food from outside the Great House's lands was able to stay awake. Or be awakened if they dozed off. But…" He rubbed his daughter's arm. "Kiri and Meelah woke up, too. They were here all night. I was so worried—I didn't know what it could mean—"

"The iron works," Ilara said. "Domhnall was furious. I think he simply forgot about them."

Tristan nodded. "He was more worried about making Ilara take off the iron than about Meelah and Kiri."

"Good." Onak smiled, and Tristan wondered if he'd seen the man smile before. "At least that's good news—"

"Oh!" Ilara clapped her palm to her cheek. "Papa, we need the healer—"

"Healer?" Onak stepped back, looking her over. "You're hurt?"

"No, Tristan—"

"I'm fine." Tristan waved dismissively but winced with the movement.

Allyre dodged around Onak, holding the lantern. "You're wounded? What happened? My lord," he added.

"The fool was supposed to stay hidden and didn't; that's what happened." Ilara stepped over to Tristan, arms crossed. "I appreciate the protective instinct, but—"

"It didn't help; I know." Tristan bowed his head. "I'm sorry I made things worse."

"No, that's not what I meant." She uncrossed her arms. "I'm upset because you were hurt, and I'm sorry that happened."

Tristan's heart pushed into his throat. "I couldn't stand by while..."

"I know." She gently lifted his right hand. "I keep trying to tell you that you have a good heart. When someone you love is suffering, it hurts you, too. That's why I couldn't let him kill you..." She trailed off as the lantern light fell on his wrist.

Tristan blanched, staring at the blood plastering his sleeve to his lower arm. Seeing the evidence made his arms feel achy and the punctures sting all over again. Even with the distraction of his wounds, his mind was stuck on *love*. Had Ilara just implied that she'd saved him because...she loved him?

Masarik joined Allyre and cursed under his breath. "What'd

they do to you?"

Ilara turned Tristan's hand, observing the damage going all the way around. The punctures were hidden under dried blood, but as she rotated his arm, he had to clench his teeth against the pain.

"Domhnall bound his hands above his head with vines," she explained, "and the vines had thorns… Tristan, I'm—I'm so sorry."

"We'll patch him up, Your Highness," Allyre said. "If it's bad enough, we'll ask for your healer. But we'll take care of him. Don't worry."

Ilara glanced at Allyre, then looked back at Tristan with a ghost of a smile on her face. "I thought you didn't have friends, Tristan?"

Somehow, he managed a weak smile of his own. "It seems that's changing."

"Good." She lightly squeezed his hand.

Onak faked a cough. "After your wounds are treated, Baron Carbrey, come speak to me. I would appreciate your help with forming a plan for tonight."

Tristan gave a small bow. He'd rather have gone to sleep after seeing to his injuries, but he didn't have that luxury—they needed to plan, and he should be part of that. "Of course, Your Majesty." He stepped forward to leave, but Ilara didn't release him.

"Wait."

He looked back at her, confused.

"I…I want to talk to you. Meet me for lunch?"

Tristan frowned. "But you should—"

"I'll meet you in the library," Ilara said without meeting his eyes, and he had the strange feeling that she was hiding something. "We need to discuss our plan for tonight, anyway."

"…all right."

"Good." She let go of his hand. "Go get your wounds seen

to." She started to turn away, but then abruptly went up on her toes and kissed his bearded cheek.

Tristan flushed. He hunched his shoulders as he passed Onak, following Allyre and Masarik out of the princesses' room—although Kiri and Meelah weren't there. They must have slept in their own chambers for the first time in a while. *Good.*

Masarik chuckled as they walked down the corridor. "I've heard that being wounded is a good way to win a lady's concern and affection."

"I'm quite certain she liked him before he was wounded," Allyre said. He glanced at Tristan, a deep line between his brows, and his mouth turned down. "We have food for you."

"Oh, thank goodness."

"I'm still angry you didn't eat yesterday, though."

Tristan groaned. "That traitor! I told Remy not to tell you."

"Ah, but you didn't tell Remy not to tell me," Masarik said triumphantly. He wagged a finger at Tristan. "I didn't realize keeping you alive was going to include making sure you don't starve yourself to death."

Allyre cast an annoyed glance at Masarik. "For my part, it's more brotherly concern than our mission. Which is also why I'm not letting you go back to the fae realm. This"—he stopped and snatched up Tristan's arm, halting their progress—"is not 'fine,' Tristan. How am I supposed to protect you if we aren't even in the same world?"

Tristan barked an incredulous laugh. "I don't think you, as my knight, get to stop me from doing anything—"

"Fine, but if you go back there, I'm coming with you."

"Allyre—"

"Don't argue."

"Sir Sharland!" Tristan pulled his arm free. "The plan is to catch Halkon here, tonight. If all goes to plan, there will be no returning to the fae realm. But if the plan goes wrong…” He sighed. “You three have to get out of Talland. Immediately. This time, it’s an order.”

Allyre crossed his arms. “No.”

“No?” Tristan blinked. “Excuse me?”

Allyre waved in Masarik’s direction. “Masarik and Remy can do what they want, but I was hired to protect you, and I plan on doing that. More importantly, you’re my brother, so I’m going to look after you.”

Tristan worked his jaw, then turned and headed up the stairs. “You know I’m your *older* brother, right?” He hesitated. “I’m not…used to this. But doesn’t that mean *I’m* supposed to take care of *you*?” He glanced behind him at Allyre and Masarik. “Right?”

“He might have a point, Allyre.” Masarik shrugged. “I want to know why you want us gone, though.”

Allyre cocked his head, a smile tugging at his lips. “It’s funny, I never really considered before that you’re older. That is, I knew that—only by about nine months, but still older—I just never thought about it. I’m used to being the oldest. And I’ve spent years wishing there was some way I could help you.”

Tristan stumbled up the steps. “Help…me? Years?”

“I’d always despised the injustice, but after I learned the truth, protective brother instincts flared every time my father relayed a new rumor or reason to suspect Henry wasn’t treating you well, or even just noted how cold you grew as you aged.” Allyre scratched the back of his neck. “I felt guilty we had the same progenitor, but I got two loving parents, and you got…”

“Henry,” Tristan finished drily. “As I’ve told someone before, I wouldn’t wish my family on anyone.” He gave a wry smile. “Not even on family.”

“You still haven’t said why you want us to leave,” Masarik interrupted.

"I'll explain when we have Remy, too, but basically…I seriously angered the fae lord. Anyone associated with me will be in danger if he wins. I don't understand how, but if he succeeds in forcing Ilara to marry him, his realm will combine with Talland. I can't guarantee you'll make it out in time, but at least you'll have a chance."

They left the stairwell and headed down the hallway toward their rooms.

"So what I'm hearing," Allyre said, "is if things go well—which is more likely with help—we'll be fine. If things go wrong, we might be stuck in Talland even if we *do* run. Also getting the feeling this fae will hurt you far worse than he already has if given the chance."

Tristan winced. "To put it mildly. But—"

"I'm staying." Allyre gave a sharp nod, as if that settled it, then wove around Tristan to open the door to their chambers.

Tristan sighed. Remy was pacing in the middle of the room as they entered, and he stopped so abruptly he nearly tripped over his own feet.

"My lord! You're…" Remy's eyes bugged. "Hurt! I'll get water, and we'll need bandages—"

"There's some in my bags, Remy. Should be a needle and some thread, too, in case we need it."

Within minutes, Remy and Allyre had Tristan sitting at the table and were working together to clean and bandage his wrists. Remy prepped bandages and cloths and a bowl of water while Allyre cut and peeled away Tristan's blood-encrusted sleeves. It felt like ripping off his skin. After the fabric was gone, Allyre started wiping the remaining dried blood with a wet rag.

"Ow!" Tristan yanked his hand away as fresh blood seeped out of his injuries.

"Infant." Masarik sniffed from his seat on the couch.

Tristan slumped down in his chair, wishing his hair were long enough to hide his face. He sheepishly offered his wrist back to Allyre. "Sorry."

"Pain is human, not something to be ashamed of." Allyre resumed cleaning, and Tristan flinched. "These are bad. What did you do to anger Halkon?"

"Interrupted. Defied him. But I think it's mostly because—" He sucked in a breath as Allyre scrubbed. "Because Halkon believes Ilara and I are…I don't know. In love, I suppose."

Masarik snorted. "You are."

"Fine, maybe I am, but why would Ilara love *me*?"

Remy switched out Allyre's blood-soaked rag for a clean one. "Because you're brave and selfless and kind?"

Tristan opened his mouth, but Allyre cut him off.

"If that's an argument, save it, Baron Was-Supposed-to-Stay-Hidden-but-Risked-Himself-to-Help-and-Was-Tortured." He frowned at Tristan's wrist before pressing the wet cloth against it. "Hold that, Remy." While Remy obliged, Allyre threaded the needle, breaking off the end of the thread with his teeth. "Have you been stitched before?"

Tristan nodded, and Allyre bent over his wrist. Remy pulled the cloth away while Tristan stared at the wood-paneled wall. The needle poked into his skin and Tristan ground out a curse.

"Thought you'd done this before," Masarik said with a hint of amusement.

Tristan made an irate face at the knight. He needed something to distract him from the pain in his wrist, so he returned to his argument. "If I were selfless, I would force you all to leave. Halkon thinks my leaving will break Ilara's heart. I don't know if that's true—she was upset when she believed I didn't care for her, and she mentioned…love. But I don't know. Either way, I'm not leaving her, but Halkon promised a lot of pain to me and anyone serving me if I stayed. So you should finish patching me up and go."

"You're a blind fool if you think Ilara wouldn't be heartbroken by you leaving," Allyre said without looking up from his work.

A bit of heat crept into Tristan's face, and he was thankful that a painful prick of the needle stopped him from asking "Really?" like a lovesick boy.

Allyre finished off the suture and met Tristan's gaze. "As for me leaving, if I felt guilty that I couldn't help you as a youth, do you really think I could walk away now?"

Tristan shook his head. "You don't owe me—"

"Flames, it's not about owing or deserving." Allyre sat back in his seat, his expression almost pained. "It's barely even about any shared blood. It's about doing the right thing, and helping another person, and the fact that even though I've only known you a few weeks, I care about you! I'm not only working for you; I think of you as a friend. How can you refuse to leave Ilara and not understand someone not leaving you?"

"Because I'm not like Ilara!" Tristan snatched the red-tinted rag from Remy and pressed it to a bleeding mark on his wrist. "I'm not like Alexander, or even you! I'm not innocent or—or worthy. Even aside from the terrible things I did, I've never been the person anyone stayed for, so there must be something *wrong* with me!"

Allyre frowned. "What are you talking about?"

"I had a tutor and nurse as a child that I loved, and my…you can guess, he sent them away for 'making me soft.' None of the others were kind to me or stayed long." Tristan tried to tell himself the tears blurring his vision were from the sting of his wounds. "*He* rarely spent time with me, and when he did, it was usually to tell me what I'd done wrong or what I could do better, or to give advice, all of which turned out to be wrong. Because of him, I judged the love and kindness and mercy and selflessness I saw in my aunt and uncle and in everyone from servants to lords, even though they seemed far happier and better than I felt, because *he* told me those things would make me weak.”

“But you’ve learned better—”

“Do you know,” Tristan interrupted Allyre, “I only ever had one friend as a child, because I wasn’t allowed to get close to any- one. Then the other boys were afraid to be too casual with their prince. *No one* has ever cared about me, and no one should, be- cause how in flames would I know how to care for them when the only person I ever thought loved me, cursed me? For all I know, he wondered if his other offspring would have been a better son, because *anyone* would have been better than me!”

Allyre’s mouth hung open.

Tristan slumped forward, letting his hair partly obscure his face as he pressed his eyes closed and tears dripped onto his lap. The room was deathly silent. Every breath shook his shoulders, and he remained hunched over, his eyes still closed, as if he could block out their stares. All this not eating and barely sleeping and fearing for his life needed to end before he said or did anything more embarrassing.

“I care,” Allyre said quietly. “You’re someone, mistakes and all. You’re a person, and that’s all you have to be, and I’m sorry you were made to feel like you weren’t enough. No one is perfect or completely innocent. I know you’re not perfect. I still care. I won’t leave.”

A tremble went through Tristan, but it felt like a weight he’d been carrying for so long he’d forgotten it was there had shattered and fallen from his shoulders. Still bent over, he covered his face with his hands, ignoring the ache in his wrists as Allyre’s ac- ceptance flowed like water through his soul, washing away years of stains left by Henry’s words and his own self-doubt. But like cleaning a wound, it hurt—it left him feeling raw and with a pounding behind his temples.

If this was love, why did it scare him? If this was acceptance, why did he still want to hide?

Masarik cleared his throat, breaking the moment and drawing Tristan's mind back to the room. "Well." There was an awkward stiffness to Masarik's tone that made Tristan not want to know what he'd say next.

"I know." He released a shaky, humorless laugh. "I'm acting like an infant. Weak, pathetic, worthless, embarrassing; I've heard it all before. Honestly, I'm past caring."

"I'm sorry."

Of all the possible things to come out of Masarik's mouth, that was the last one Tristan would have guessed. He lifted his head and looked at the big knight. Masarik usually looked completely at ease, the way a man does when he knows he's the greatest threat in the room. But right then, he looked downright uncomfortable.

"I misjudged you, and I've been harsher than necessary. I…" Masarik's heel tapped a rapid rhythm on the rug. "I'd swear on my life—you're not the cruel man you may have been in the past. You're not your father. And you're not weak or pathetic, either. What's more, I'm staying, too. Not because it's my job, but because it's an honor to serve someone who has shown as much integrity as you have in the last few days."

Another shudder cut through Tristan. He wasn't sure how to respond—a thank-you, a promise to live up to that—but any words he might have spoken lodged in his throat. He wiped away hot tears, wishing he could stop crying or get out of there. He glanced toward his bedroom door.

"No." Allyre got off his chair and wrapped his arms around Tristan. "You're not running away this time."

Tristan stiffened. Henry had never embraced him. The closest he'd had to a hug in years had been playful tackles after training from the sons of noblemen who suddenly realized whom they were touching and moved on. Allyre's arms tightened on him, and Tristan hesitantly returned the embrace. Something inside him cracked, and it took every ounce of his self-control not to break down sobbing again. He released his brother, afraid he wouldn't be able to keep it together any longer, and Allyre returned to his own seat.

Next to Tristan, Remy smiled, but Tristan thought he detected some wetness at the corners of Remy's crinkling eyes. "You know," Remy said, "just because someone doesn't appreciate you, that doesn't make their opinion of you true."

"Wise words," Allyre said as he returned to cleaning Tristan's wrist. "Where'd you learn that?"

"From all of you." Remy shrugged. "At home…my siblings said I was in the way all the time and too stupid to figure things out on my own. But you all think I'm useful and capable." He fidgeted with the bandages. "I hoped I could be more than they said, and I took this job to prove it, but I didn't truly believe I could do this until you told me I was an exceptional manservant, my lord. It made me realize you and my siblings couldn't both be right. So I had a choice who to believe, and I didn't see any reason why I should choose the words that hurt."

"You—" Tristan bit back a curse as Allyre started suturing another spot. "You're definitely useful and capable, Remy, and I'm grateful to have you here."

Remy's grin held mischief. "So if I tell you that you're valuable and selfless and admirable and I'm honored to serve you, you can't argue, right? Otherwise, I might just think if your father was right about you, my siblings were right about me…"

"I'm feeling very cornered, and you're all in trouble." Tristan had meant it to come out stern, but his voice cracked as he wavered between a sob and a laugh.

"So," Allyre said while he wrapped bandages around Tristan's wrist, "who was this childhood friend of yours, and why aren't you friends anymore?"

Tristan leaned back in his chair. "Oh, simple, really. A certain blood relation turned me against my only friend with lies and mockery and manipulation, then turned said friend into a dragon. Then my friend-turned-enemy reappeared, married my betrothed, and reclaimed his crown."

"Oh." Allyre gaped at Tristan before taking his left wrist and cleaning it. "That's...rough."

Tristan shrugged and turned to Remy. "Say, now that I have one free hand"—he waved his bandaged wrist—"might I have some food?"

40

*I*lara watched Tristan close the door behind him with a soft smile. Whatever differences he and his men may have had when they first arrived, they appeared to have sorted them out.

Papa sighed. "Be careful with your heart, Ilara."

She turned toward him. "Hm?"

"The Rethali ambassador. Be careful. That letter was missing details, and he must have made some bad decisions regarding his cousin's return, or he wouldn't be here."

"He's told me." She shrugged at Papa's surprised look. "Tristan is an honest, selfless man who repented of his wrongdoing and is respectful and caring and trying so hard. Mama always said we judge people on how they behave now, not on mistakes they've owned and apologized for."

Papa winced at the mention of Mama. "I know, sweetheart. I just don't want you to get hurt, and he's not who I would have picked."

Ilara bristled. "Maybe you should have thought of that *before* you forced him into spending time with me. And perhaps you shouldn't judge him for any bad decisions after what you did. How could you?" The words came out jagged and broken.

Papa's expression crumpled, and he moved to sink onto her bed. "I'm sorry."

"I'm not the one you need to apologize to. You abused your power, treated a man unjustly, and risked war with Rethalyon. What if the House Heads had learned of it?" She heard her scalding tone and saw the pain in his eyes too late. She stepped closer. "I'm sorry—"

"No. You're right." He hung his head. "Except it wouldn't have risked war. Even Baron Carbrey didn't argue that his cousin and their Court of Lords wouldn't care about his death."

Ilara's heart twisted.

"I wouldn't have killed him, either. That doesn't make it right, and the moon knows your mama would be ashamed of me." A tear streaked down his cheek, glistening in the lantern light. "But she's not here, and I can't lose you and your sisters, too. It would break me. I can't."

Even though she was still upset with him, she ached for the grief and emptiness he was experiencing. She sat down and put her arm around him.

"I've been thinking about it since yesterday." Papa's shoulders rose and fell with a deep breath. "You were right," he said hoarsely. "Every word."

She winced, fighting the part of herself that wanted to apologize for the pain her words had caused, regardless of whether they were true.

"I will apologize to Baron Carbrey before the meeting." He rubbed his temple. "Even without knowing about this, the Heads have lost faith in me."

"Papa, no—"

"I see the doubt in their faces every time I speak to one of them. And after this…they're right." Beneath her arm, she felt him tremble. "When I was crown prince and courting your mama, I promised her I'd be a strong, just, merciful king. But I thought I'd have her to support me in that. I've failed her." A sob squeaked from his throat. "I've failed you, I've failed Talland, and I'm sorry. I'm so sorry."

Ilara rubbed his arm and leaned her head on his shoulder, wishing she knew what to say. Papa took several deep breaths and wiped at his face.

"I'm considering ceding the throne to you."

Ilara sucked in a breath and straightened. "Papa, that's not a decision to make in the middle of a crisis and when you're discouraged."

"No, not yet. I'd wait to announce it until after Halkon is dealt with and you've had time to rest and recover."

"We should wait and *discuss* it after things have settled."

Papa turned so he could see her face. "I'll be there for you, like you've been there for me. You'll be a better monarch than I am. I trust you completely, far more than I trust myself." He smiled. "Which is also why, if you love the Rethali boy…I'll agree."

"Thank you, Papa." Ilara wrapped him in a strong embrace. "But we're discussing your *potential* abdication again before you make any announcements, all right?" Deep down, she knew it might be time, and it wouldn't be a role she was unfamiliar with. She also had too many tangled thoughts and emotions to know how she felt or to want to tackle that decision just yet.

"All right." He squeezed her back and placed a kiss on the top of her hair, easing some of her tension.

Someone knocked, and Ilara and Papa parted.

"Ilara!" Ryn opened the door and entered with Nika.

Papa patted her shoulder and stood. "I'm going to eat. Get some sleep."

She murmured agreement as he left, but she had far too much to talk to Ryn about before she could consider sleeping.

"So it's true?" Ryn asked. "Meelah and Kiri stayed here?"

Ilara nodded as Nika shoved her head onto her lap. "Domhnall was so angry about the iron burning him that he forgot to take them. Tristan made it in, though." She scowled. "And then he tried to stop Domhnall from touching me, and oh, Ryn, it was awful. His wrists—"

"I saw." Ryn held out her hand. "Come on, let's get you changed out of…whatever this monstrosity of a dress is. But do I ever have gossip for you."

"Oh?" Ilara lifted a brow as she took Ryn's hand.

Ryn pulled her to her feet, then linked their arms and led her out of the room. "I was walking down the stairs when I heard voices coming up. I realized it was Tristan and his knights…so I may have hid around the bend after the second floor landing and made Nika wait so I could listen and see them pass."

"You eavesdropped?" Ilara clicked her tongue. "I wish I could say I was surprised."

"Oh, but you'll never guess what I overheard."

"Something about me?" Ilara asked as they headed up the stairs.

Ryn shook her head. "His knight was talking—the dark-skinned one, not the big, scary blond—and said he felt guilty they had the same progenitor, but he had loving parents while Tristan had Henry."

"The same…" Ilara paused and gawked at Ryn. "They're *brothers?*"

"That's what it sounded like." Ryn tugged her back into motion. "So I was right; you didn't know. Why would Tristan hide that? I don't like the thought that he's lying to you, Ara."

"Tristan said he didn't even have friends…"

"Maybe he's not as trustworthy as you think."

"No," Ilara declared without reservation. "Tristan has told me his darkest secrets. If they're brothers, he hasn't said they aren't, and he must have a good reason for not telling me."

Nika shoved past Ilara's wide pink skirt and bounded into her bedroom as Ilara opened the door.

"Oh, moonlight. What if he was afraid Papa would threaten his brother, too?"

"I hadn't considered that." Ryn frowned. "Still. I'm worried."

"I know; you don't want me to get hurt. Can you help me out of this dress?"

"Of course." Ryn began unlacing the back of the gown.

"I know you haven't spent much time with Tristan, but you should have seen him last night, Ryn. The fire in his eyes as he stood there, armed with only a dagger, facing down a powerful fae lord, demanding Domhnall let me go. And..." Her stomach flipped. "You didn't see the look on his face when Domhnall had a vine choking him. He was dying..." Her throat caught.

Ryn paused in her unlacing and rubbed Ilara's shoulder reassuringly. Nika licked Ilara's arm, as if sensing her mistress was upset.

"He was dying," Ilara repeated. "And he shook his head. He didn't want me to save his life if it meant promising Domhnall anything."

"What did you promise Domhnall?"

Ilara glanced back at Ryn. "I didn't say I did."

Ryn smiled sadly. "Tristan isn't dead, and I can hear it in your voice. You love him, don't you?"

"I think I do," Ilara whispered. "No, I know I do. I can't help it." The dress fell to her ankles, and she stepped out of it. "All I promised Domhnall was that I would dance with him and be polite and consider any argument he could make for our marriage."

She wandered over to her wardrobe and withdrew an outfit, ignoring Nika padding after her. "But moonlight, Ryn, if Domhnall had pressed me... I don't know what I would have done to save Tristan. I couldn't watch him die. It hurt." She choked on her swelling emotions. "Watching Tristan suffer hurt like a knife in my chest."

Ryn helped her pull on her underdress, and Ilara turned toward her with a broken smile.

"You're trying to make sure I don't give Tristan my heart in case he doesn't deserve it, but he already has it."

Ryn smoothed Ilara's hair, her touch gentle. "I suppose I should ask him if he is aware of marital cuffs, then, so I can be certain he knows what he's doing."

Ilara laughed, and the release from the tension of the serious moment passed. "Oh, I already had to explain that to him. He thought they were related to titles."

Ryn huffed a laugh. "I admit I'm curious if the fae had any good arguments for your marriage."

"It was mostly 'power' and 'beauty' and 'immortality,' but…he does claim he could grow normal food, magically." She took a dark blue wool overdress from Ryn. "But there were also threats. And I don't trust him."

"Then what's the plan to stop him?"

"I honestly don't know. Papa and Tristan are meeting about that after Tristan's wounds are tended to, and I suppose Tristan will fill me in when we have lunch."

For a moment, Ilara considered telling Ryn about her conversation with Papa. Although she trusted Ryn, had even told her about Papa's threat against Tristan because she knew her friend wouldn't tell, it didn't seem right to secretly inform the daughter of one of the House Heads that their king was considering transferring the crown. Papa might still change his mind. She would deal with the complicated emotions of Papa relinquishing sovereignty to her when it happened. No need to add that to everything else yet.

"In the meantime," she said instead, "I'm going to check on Kiri and Meelah, and then take a nap. Maybe ask Kiri to do my braids before lunch."

"You mean before you declare your undying love to Tristan?"

Ilara gave Ryn a playful shove, eliciting a disapproving whine from Nika. "Something like that."

41

By the time the conference with Onak and the captain of his guard was complete, Tristan was even more astonished that Ilara had been spending the night in Halkon's enchanted wood and then joining meetings. He felt more ready to sleep than meet with her for lunch. The fly that had kept buzzing around his head the whole meeting hadn't helped matters. He wouldn't dream of letting Ilara down, though, so tired as he was, he asked a servant for directions to the library.

When he arrived, Ilara wasn't there yet. He thought he'd grown accustomed to the smaller scale of things in Talland's Great House compared to Rethalyon's palace, but he was still surprised by the room. Where the Rethali palace's library had towering walls of books in a cavernous hall with floor-to-ceiling windows, the chamber the servant showed him to looked more like a study.

A couch with a pile of cushions sat near the single narrow window. In the middle of the room stood a desk and chair, the desk clear of any clutter except for a lantern and a set of flint and steel. The left and right walls were covered in shelves with not only books, but various objects—a bust of a man, a vase with a lid that was a particularly breathtaking example of Talland ceramics, a...what was that? Tristan bent closer to look. An antler had been carved into an entire herd of miniature elk. As he straightened and crossed over to light the lamp, a faint buzzing made him pause. If that fly had followed him, he was going to lose his mind.

The humming ceased, and he shook himself. He really needed to sleep.

He'd just set down the flint when the door to the library opened and Ilara entered, a basket in hand. She wore a dark blue wool dress over a pale green long-sleeved underdress that looked more comfortable than Halkon's fancy gowns. The top half of her hair was pulled back in multiple intricate braids, the rest flowing over her shoulders. A brilliant smile split her face, and Tristan's tiredness evaporated.

"Hello." He barely contained his grimace. Hello? That was all he had?

"Hello," Ilara said softly as the door clicked shut behind her.

He searched for something else to say. "Where's Nika?"

"Oh, outside. She hates being cooped up all day, and she'd spend the whole time arguing she needs scraps and attention."

Tristan chuckled. "Arguing?"

"You should hear her when she gets needy. She makes the most ridiculous sounds, like she's trying to talk." She held out the basket. "Anyway, I have food. Obviously I have food; I invited you for lunch…" Her cheeks reddened.

Tristan swooped forward and took the basket. "Excellent, thank you. Strategy meetings make me hungry." He met her eyes, dark as rich, freshly tilled earth, and stilled. She was so close… He stepped back. They were close when they danced; why did he have to get all flustered now?

"We can sit on the couch." Ilara breezed past him. She shoved cushions to the floor, making space for them to sit in the bit of sunlight coming through the window. She took the side near the wall and looked at him expectantly.

Tristan set the basket next to her and sat on the other end.

Ilara removed the cloth covering, revealing two bread bowls filled with steaming lamb stew. The aroma made his mouth water. They were quiet for several minutes as they ate, but Tristan didn't mind. It wasn't the quiet that had occurred at his meals alone with Henry—that silence felt like waiting to see if a wild animal would flee or charge. This quiet as they sat together in the library, eating a stew that made Tristan want to melt into the couch, was peaceful.

All the same, he wasn't disappointed when Ilara spoke. "How are your wrists?"

Self-consciously, Tristan touched the edge of a bandage poking out from under his sleeve. "They sting and pinch, but they're not bad."

"Good. Did my papa apologize to you?"

"Yes." He stirred his spoon through his soup. "I've never seen such humility and sincerity from a king. He seemed relieved I forgave him. I understand better now what it was like for Alex and Raelyn, because I won't claim it was easy or that I feel comfortable around him yet." He lifted one shoulder, trying to appear nonchalant. "But I sympathize with making mistakes in times of stress that you later regret, and I'm willing to give him another chance."

He couldn't bring himself to admit that he mostly forgave Ilara's father for her sake and because he might be unsure if he trusted Onak, but he knew he trusted her.

Ilara released a deep breath, her posture easing. "And how did planning go?"

A mouthful of stew-soaked bread delayed his response, but Ilara didn't appear to mind. "We plan on separating Kiri and Meelah to prevent Halkon gaining any leverage, with guards with them just in case, but we'll be waiting with you in the room on the first floor. We'll also put an iron bear trap in the area where I saw him appear. More iron jewelry is being made for you."

"Will you be hiding under my bed?" she asked teasingly.

"Heh, no, not this time. I need to be able to get to him quickly." He wanted nothing more than to drive his sword through Halkon.

"As long as you're there." She focused on her bread bowl. "What's my role?"

Tristan shrugged. "Be your usual defiant self, don't let him bully you, and use the iron jewelry if necessary." He smiled at his soup. "So you're already perfect at your role."

There was a pause, then Ilara placed her empty bread bowl in the basket between them. "Tristan… Are you certain you want to stay?"

He turned toward her. "No—I mean, yes, I want to stay." He returned his attention to his food. "Unless…you want me to go."

Ilara fiddled with a serpent-shaped ivory brooch pinning one strap of her overdress in place. "I want you here. I like having you close, Tristan."

"I like being close to you." He quickly shoved another spoonful of stew into his mouth.

"But I'm also afraid for you."

He nodded, although she wasn't looking at him. "I understand. My men refused to leave. I'm worried they'll be injured or worse, and yet…I'm glad to have them. I've never had people who cared before. They know the risk, though, and they made their choice. So have I."

She met his gaze. "I'm sorry you've gone so long without people who love you, but I'm pleased you have them now."

Tristan hesitated. Did he dare tell her? He deposited his bread bowl in the basket. "Can I tell you something? I…learned new information. Unrelated to Halkon, that is. And I don't entirely know what to do with it. It's confusing and kind of difficult." He blew out a breath. "But you have enough on your mind—"

"No, please." Ilara moved the basket to the floor on the other side of her feet and shifted closer to him. "If something is weighing on you, I can listen. You don't have to carry things alone."

He rubbed his beard. It was uneven and needed to be trimmed again, but he didn't have the time or energy. "My knight—you've seen my knights. You know the tall one with dark skin?"

Ilara sat up straighter, her expression oddly intense. "Yes, I met him briefly. Sir…Sharland, I think?"

"Yes. Allyre Sharland. He… Yesterday, he told me…" Saying the words aloud was difficult. As if by speaking it, it'd be revealed as false and would destroy one of the few good things in his life. "I'm still trying to comprehend it. I had no idea…" He forced the admission out in a rush. "Allyre is my half-brother."

She didn't say anything, just watched him, clearly interested but not pushing.

He focused on his hands. "I mentioned my mother died within weeks of my birth. Allyre is younger than me. By about nine months."

It only took a moment for Ilara to understand. "Moonless winter. Tristan—I…I'm so sorry."

"It gets worse." He blinked, annoyed at the tears threatening his eyes. "She was dying, and he wasn't even at home. And…Allyre's mother, it—it wasn't… She didn't know he was married, and he lied to her and manipulated her and—and forced her and called it love."

Ilara laid her hand on Tristan's forearm, and he shuddered with suppressed emotion.

"At least she left him, and was able to marry, and Baron Sharland has been a good husband to her and an admirable father to Allyre. He has a loving family." His voice cracked, and he clenched his jaw. He wasn't going to cry again, not in front of Ilara.

"Oh, Tristan." Before he knew what was happening, she had

her arms around him and pulled him close. "Henry was cruel to you long before Alex returned, wasn't he?"

He nodded against her shoulder. "I want to tell you. I need to tell someone. To—to have someone who fully understands." He worked his throat. "I'm tired of it hurting. I can tell you all the terrible things I've done that I wish I could take back, and maybe you won't see me any differently—"

Her grip on him tightened. "I know the worst, don't I?"

He gave a mute nod, his beard catching on her dress.

"I've told you," Ilara said, her tone thick with emotion. "I care more about who you are now and the choices you make going forward than what you did in the past. You aren't your worst moments. I don't want your guilt or shame, Tristan; I want your love and your honesty."

His love? A panicked part of him protested he wasn't sure how to give that, but at least he could try.

"But I can't give you my honesty." His voice scraped over his vocal cords like gravel. "You said I don't have to carry things alone, Allyre says talking helps, but I can't speak my hurt aloud. I can't even say how much I hate—" He choked, which was unfair, because he was only going to say *him*. Tears he could no longer withhold fell onto Ilara's shoulder. He pulled away. "I apologize—"

"No. Moonset, Tristan. It's all right to cry."

He glimpsed Ilara's tear-streaked face as she hugged him back to her chest. Her fingers stroked his hair, her other hand rubbing his back. Without thinking, he wrapped his arms around her and leaned into her soft form. Something inside him broke, like a weakened dam finally giving way, and he wept onto her shoulder, too broken and aware of how her arms tightened around him in a comforting manner to be embarrassed.

After a while, his tears lessened, and his breathing slowed.

"Did he hit you?" Ilara whispered. "Your father?"

"Not usually," Tristan hazarded. Nothing happened.

"But sometimes."

He'd said he wanted to tell her, for someone to know, but now shame argued he shouldn't admit to it. He forced his mouth to move anyway. "Yes."

"Yelled?"

"Constantly."

She was quiet for a moment, still stroking his hair. "You mentioned he compared you to Alex. He made you feel inferior to your cousin…even after he was gone?"

"Apparently Alex was a better crown prince as a child than I could ever hope to be. And the insults…" Tristan shuddered. "I don't know how I thought someone who called me weak, embarrassing, and worthless was someone who loved me." More hot tears ran down the side of his nose and along his temple to Ilara's shoulder. "Why did I think someone who didn't let me have friends, who made me beg on my knees for forgiveness for speaking out of turn, who would arrange for me to be beaten in combat practice, loved me?" His voice warbled, but the admission made him feel lighter.

He slipped out of her embrace so he could dry his face on his sleeve. "If I thought that was love, how can I care for you? Or for Allyre? He…he said…" Tristan gulped, wishing for water.

"Henry or Allyre?" Ilara asked softly.

"Allyre. For some reason, he cares. He believes in me. He said I must be more than the blood in my veins because it's his blood, too. I don't understand…"

Tristan shifted, focusing on the strip of muted sunlight cutting across the blue rug covering the floor of the library as he worked through his chaotic emotions. "Allyre knows what I've done, and he knows about what—what was done to his mother, to my aunt and uncle, to Alex, to me. But he's not ashamed to be my brother.

He won't leave, even though he has a family to return to and will be in danger if we fail, and I—I love him for it." More flame-cursed tears trailed down his cheeks. "I'm also frightened by it."

He looked at Ilara. No disgust or pity marked her expression, just sympathy and…affection.

"Same with you," he whispered. "You're still here, you don't despise me, and I…" He couldn't quite get the words *I love you* past his lips. "I'm falling for you because of it. And because of your determination and dedication to your kingdom and courage and kindness…" He dropped his gaze. "But I'm afraid…you'll regret it. You, Allyre, Masarik, Remy; what if—"

"You fear you'll be hurt," she murmured. "That we'll change our minds, or you'll let us down, and we'll react like your father did."

She saw right through him. He nodded, then took a deep breath.

"And if—if anything terrible befalls them because of me…" A tremor went through him. "That reminds me. No matter what happens tonight or what Halkon threatens, promise me you won't make any more deals? Not for my sake."

Ilara sighed. "I love you, Tristan. So I can't promise that."

He nearly sobbed again, both from the euphoria of hearing her say *I love you* and his fear. "I won't see you harmed. I don't matter. I'm not worth any sacrifice—"

"Tristan, I said *I love you*." She cupped his cheeks in her hands, gently turning his face back to her, her expression tender. "You matter; you matter *to me*. Love—real love—is selflessness. It's sacrifice. Love isn't taking, it's giving and demanding nothing in return. It's putting someone else before yourself. Self-sacrifice is love in its purest form."

"Maybe…I—I don't want you loving me, then." He nearly choked on the words. "I don't deserve the kind of love you're talking about." The thought of Ilara loving him as much as Raelyn had loved Alex when she'd leapt in front of Tristan's sword…it terrified him.

"Why not?"

He blinked at her. "Because—"

"Because your father didn't love you like that, so you think you deserve more of the same? Because you did some things wrong?" Her thumbs stroked his cheeks. "What does it matter if Raelyn and Alexander forgive you if you can't forgive yourself? You love your men and me, and we love you. How are you going to let us love you if you refuse to love yourself?"

Tristan pulled her hands away from his face. "What if you're wrong, and I don't deserve forgiveness or love, and eventually—"

"Forgiveness and love aren't earned." Ilara gripped his hands so he couldn't draw away. "Someone withholding love doesn't mean you didn't deserve it. Forgiveness requires admitting some-one hurt you, but choosing not to retaliate or hate them for it. If you do something to earn forgiveness beyond an earnest apology and commitment to do better, that's not forgiveness. You shouldn't have to grovel for it. Real love isn't conditional on being perfect."

He drew in a shaky breath, almost afraid to believe her. "If Alex truly forgave me, why did he send me away?"

"Forgiveness and trust aren't the same thing." She lightly squeezed his hands. "But I trust you, Tristan."

His fingers spasmed in her gentle hold. There was no lie in her eyes.

"You risked yourself for me when you could have left or re-mained hidden. You chose to be selfless. You care about your men, and you're concerned for Meelah and Kiri. You're gentle and sweet with Nika. You're not even bitter toward my papa. You de-sire to do what's right, and I can see you working to change. I know that's not easy, and it's brave to admit you were wrong and strive to be better."

Ilara released one hand and spread her palm on his chest. His heart raced beneath her touch. "You have a good heart. You're just learning how to listen to it after years of being forced to keep it locked away."

Could he truly believe he had a good heart? If he could, and if he made a point to keep choosing to do the right thing…could he deserve Ilara?

His blossoming hope wilted. Even if he could love her the way she deserved, even if she and Allyre were right about him, he was only a Rethali ambassador, and she was the crown princess of Talland.

Ilara's hand pressed against his chest. Sunlight from the window haloed her head. He wet his lips, his breathing going shallow.

"Is something wrong?" she whispered, placing her other hand on his chest.

His tongue too tangled to speak, Tristan stumbled off the couch and away from her. A wrinkle formed between Ilara's brows as she followed him.

"Are you all right?"

He backed up until his thighs bumped into the desk, and Ilara stopped in front of him.

"Tristan—"

"Please…step back." He curled his fingers around the edge of the desktop as he fought the desire to touch her hair, to hold her, to kiss her.

Hurt flashed across her face, and he hated that he'd put it there. He'd known he'd hurt her eventually.

She took a small step backward. "What's wrong?"

"I don't…trust myself." His gaze flicked to her lips, and he leaned his head back and stared at the ceiling, his entire body as hot as if he had a fever. "I should go."

"Tristan—"

Still staring upward, he shook his head. "Ilara, please. I don't want to hurt you."

"Hurt me? How?"

He forced himself to look at her. Her head tilted to one side as her dark eyes studied him, concern pulling at her pink lips. One curvy hip slightly thrust to the side as she stood with her arms crossed over her middle. He wanted to take her into his arms and kiss her until he forgot all his worries and failings and believed everything she had said.

"Flames. Why did King Onak have to have a beautiful daughter?" Heat burned his ears as he realized he'd spoken aloud. "I—I—"

Ilara laughed, and the sound felt like a refreshing spring rain. "You're adorable." She stepped closer and put her arms around his neck, making his legs weak. "And handsome." Her eyes drifted closed as she rose up on her toes.

Fighting his own overwhelming desire, he grabbed her waist and moved her back instead of drawing her nearer. "I can't. Right now. I don't know if I'm—ready. I doubt your father will let this happen, anyway." He winced. *Or Alex, for that matter.*

She smiled and shook her head. "My papa gave his blessing."

"He did?" Onak and Ilara had already discussed it? His shoulders caved. "It doesn't matter. Tonight could go wrong, things are uncertain, and…I'm still a Rethali ambassador. I shouldn't do anything I'll regret."

Ilara's hands slipped off his shoulders and her confident posture crumbled. "Why would you regret it?"

"I didn't give my heart to Raelyn, not really. And losing her still hurt."

Ilara deserved the truth, even if it meant he had to voice feelings he knew had the power to destroy him.

"If I kiss you now, my heart will be completely, irrevocably yours. I don't want to know how much it would hurt to lose you."

Sorrow overshadowed Ilara's countenance, and Tristan was its cause, and he didn't know if he could fix it.

"The thing about love," she said quietly, "is sooner or later, it always hurts. Real love is choosing it anyway." She hurried out of the library, leaving Tristan feeling wretched and alone.

He leaned back against the desk. Maybe he didn't need to change first to love. Maybe loving could change him instead. He headed for the door, determined to go after Ilara and say the words he'd been too much of a coward to speak.

"I admit," Halkon drawled behind him, "I'd forgotten what good drama you mortals provide."

Spinning around, Tristan nearly knocked over the lantern on the desk. Halkon reclined on the couch, one ankle slung over the opposite knee. The fae waved with a mocking smile.

"When did you get here?"

"Oh, after the stunt with the iron, I suspected a plot was forming. I also didn't trust you to do the smart thing and run, so I've been *buzzing* about most of the day." He winked. "I'll be more than prepared for your little trap tonight."

Tristan's tongue felt thick, like it wanted to choke him. Would it do any good to warn the others?

"But, in the meantime"—Halkon stood—"I plan on having some fun." He rolled his shoulders. "It's been a while since I've done this, so give me a moment, and I apologize if it's not right at first. Noses sometimes elude me."

Bright light swirled around Halkon as Tristan frowned. Was it a rule that fae had to speak nonsense? He looked toward the door, considering making a run for it while Halkon was busy do-ing…whatever it was he was doing in that cloud of vibrating, glowing color.

"Hm," Halkon said. "Inelegant fingers. A bit short; don't care for that."

Tristan glanced back at Domhnall and stopped dead. Slowly, he turned around, a sick feeling in his stomach. He wasn't looking at Domhnall. He was looking at…himself.

"What do you think?" Halkon's voice came from the duplicate Tristan. No, not an exact replica. His irises were emerald green. Green-eyed Tristan cocked his head. "What is it? What did I miss? It's the nose, isn't it?" Halkon felt his nose. "Seems appropriately square and ugly. Ah, it's my eyes, isn't it?" He snapped his fingers, and his irises turned brown. "Say something."

Tristan swayed as the world tilted. He squeezed his eyes shut, but when he opened them again, the other Tristan still stared back at him. "What are you doing?"

Halkon cleared his throat. "What are you doing?" he said in an imitation of Tristan's voice. "I told you. Having fun. I do love to play a good game with mortals' hearts."

Tristan bolted for the door, but something tripped him. A tan-gle of vines had replaced the carpet, and they lashed around him, pulling him down. He cried out as the blessedly thorn-less vines tightened on his injured wrists. Ignoring the pain, he attempted to thrash free, to no avail.

"Why—" A vine wrapped over Tristan's mouth, gagging him.

"Don't worry, the vines won't kill you, but they should hold you long enough for me to cause some mischief and then come collect you." Halkon in Tristan's body stepped on Tristan's hand as he strode past. He paused with his hand on the doorknob. "I forgot how much fun it is to dabble in your pitiful existences."

Halkon walked out, and the door closed with a loud click that cracked Tristan's heart open.

See him for who he really is, Ilara.

Please.

42

The hunting trophies and weapons and carvings on the walls rushed by Ilara in a blur as she headed for the rear stairwell, where she was less likely to run into any members of the court in her emotional disarray. She ached for the love Tristan was too afraid to give her, for the self-doubt in his soul. He'd been vulnerable with her, only to push her away again. Why, oh why, did her foolish heart fall for someone like that? A man so scared of himself and of rejection that he struggled to accept her love.

It killed her that Tristan saw only his shadows and none of his light. Moonless winter take Henry Carbrey, wherever he was, for how he'd treated his son. She would give anything for Tristan to see himself as she saw him.

His reckless bravery, his determination to improve, his intelligence, the way his hand was so steady and sure on her back, how protected she felt when he pulled her close—Tristan had stolen her heart. Ilara wanted him to be present to hold her like that for the rest of her life, wanted to feel his lips on hers, to hear him say *I love you*. Not *I'm falling for you* or *my heart will be yours*. She wanted him to *be* hers, right now, but he clung to his battered heart, unwilling to trust her with it. She couldn't blame him, but it still broke her. Tristan was so afraid of getting hurt, he didn't realize she was already hurting.

"Ilara!"

Her breath caught as Tristan's call echoed in the hallway. Almost reluctant to hope, she turned back. He reached her, panting, and stopped so close it made her stomach flutter.

"I'm sorry." Tristan bit his lower lip. "I need to tell you the truth." He hesitantly reached out and stroked her hair as he whispered, "All I do is hurt people. I'll hurt you."

She took his hand. "There are always risks in relationships. I know you'd never hurt me on purpose."

He met her eyes. "I…"

Tristan leaned down and kissed her. It took Ilara by surprise, but as joy unfurled in her chest, she held the side of his neck and kissed him as if she could kiss away all his doubts. But then his lips abruptly left hers. His hands dropped to his sides as he moved back.

"Hm." He wiped his mouth. "Disappointing."

His words hit her like an icy wind. "What?"

"Please." Tristan rolled his eyes. "Did you genuinely believe I was enamored with you?" He sneered. "That I could find you desirable? Short. Plump. Small chest. Drab. Raelyn is an angel compared to you. I honestly don't know what Domhnall sees in you, but then, maybe you'll be prettier as a fae."

Her lower lip trembled as his criticism carved into her. She opened her mouth to yell, and all that came out was a sob. She turned to run, but Tristan grasped her wrist and yanked her back.

She blinked against tears. "Let go."

"No." He shoved her against the wall, and her head slammed back with a crack against the wood, making her skull throb. He pinned her wrists above her with one hand, malice contorting his expression.

"What are you doing?" Her voice shook.

"Are you frightened?" He leaned forward until his nose nearly touched hers. "You're trembling. Pitiful."

"This isn't like you." What had come over him? This wasn't the Tristan she'd fallen for. "Let go or I'll scream."

Tristan chuckled, the sound dark and menacing. His free hand encircled her neck. Her lungs shuddered with shallow, panicked breaths.

"Scream," he whispered close by her ear. "I dare you."

This couldn't be happening. This had to be a nightmare, but she could feel Tristan's hands crushing her wrists and pressing against her throat, see his face inches from hers. Ilara squirmed, trying to push him off. She might as well try to fight the wall at her back. Anger burned up her face and over her scalp.

"Get away from me, you cretin! Was it all an act? The tears, your father—"

"I did warn you." He let go of her neck.

She slammed her forehead into his mouth.

Tristan's head whipped back, but his grip didn't loosen on her wrists. Wrath twisted his lips before he laughed. "Such a spirited princess. You'll make an excellent fae queen."

She stilled, her jaw quivering. "What are you talking about?"

"Oh, I made a deal with Domhnall." He sneered. "You didn't seriously believe I stayed for *you*, did you? Because I *care* so much? After your father threatened me? You're not worth enslavement and torture. I relayed the plan to Domhnall, and I won't help you tonight, so he'll spare me."

"No, you...no! You could have run. You didn't have to— to—" Ilara strained against him as another sob pushed out of her throat, but she only succeeded in pinching her wrists. She wanted to strangle him or lie down and cry as she tried to gather up the shattered pieces of her heart. "Why are you telling me this? Why now?"

Shame flickered over his countenance as he looked away. "He ordered me to break your heart. To make you think I loved you, and then…do this. I could hurt you and be free, or he could torture me. I'd apologize, but I told you—self-sacrificing love isn't for me. It was an easy choice."

Every word he spoke was like an axe striking her and ripping away a chunk of her heart.

"No…" She searched his face for any sign of enchantment, any indication that Domhnall had forced him to eat that moon-cursed fae food and was controlling him. But Tristan's green-flecked brown eyes were clear as they watched her without pity or remorse.

"How long?"

"Last night. While you were enchanted and dancing and I was hanging from my wrists in agony," Tristan snarled. He ran a finger down her cheek. "I admit I was…growing very fond of you. But I love my own life more."

She sagged against the wall as tears slipped down her cheeks. "I loved you."

"A terrible mistake." Tristan snorted. "I told you I'd hurt you." He released her and stepped back. "You're a naïve fool. Domhnall can have you."

"You were right," she said, sorrow and rage crackling through her. "There's nothing good or redeemable in you." She punched toward his nose, but he dodged it.

His expression turned menacing, and before she could run, he grasped a fistful of her braids. "Try that again," he snarled, yanking on her hair so her head snapped back. A cry of pain escaped her lips.

"Stop—"

"Your father"—he seized her chin and dug his fingers into her cheeks, still tugging on her hair—"shouldn't have threatened me. Now you're paying for his error."

He tossed her backward, and she slammed to the ground. The

impact jolted up her arms and sent a stab of discomfort through her right wrist.

"I hope your fae husband enjoys kissing you more than I did." Tristan jogged down the hallway and disappeared around the corner at the rear of the Great House.

Ilara cradled her aching wrist and stifled a whimper.

How could he have lied so flawlessly? What kind of monster could cry on her shoulder, all the while knowing he was betraying her? He'd manipulated her and then laughed at her pain, all to spare himself. Perhaps that shouldn't surprise her. It was why he'd helped her in the first place, after all.

And her kiss was disappointing? She shouldn't have cared about that in the midst of his greater betrayals, but she did.

Ilara screamed the anguish she couldn't find words or logic to explain. Tears blurred her vision and ran into her mouth as sobs wracked her chest. Footsteps thundered in the corner stairwell and down the side hallway behind her. Guards asked what was wrong; was there a threat? She couldn't answer past her choking cries.

Someone grabbed her shoulders, then pulled her into an embrace. "What happened?" Meelah asked.

"Is it Domhnall?" Papa asked above her. "Was he here?"

Ilara shook her head. She attempted to speak, but her throat was too tight to form words.

"Tristan," she said, but it was a whisper that barely reached her lips.

Three guards clustered near Papa, looking anxious without a threat to confront.

A door crashed open, and footsteps ran toward her. "Where's Ilara?"

Tristan.

How had he already made it all the way around the Great House and returned to the library without her noticing? And why?

She didn't care. Wrath curled her hands into fists and dried her tears. She sucked a breath into her aching lungs. How *dare* he come back after what he'd done? What sick game was he playing? She pulled away from Meelah and pushed to her feet even though her legs trembled.

Wide eyes looked at her from a pale, worried face. What an immaculate actor. "Ilara—"

"Traitor!" She swung with every ounce of her fury and heartbreak. This time, he didn't dodge. Her punch slammed into his mouth, and he stumbled back. Pain throbbed in her fingers, but she ignored it. She drew back her fist again, but Meelah grabbed her arm and held her back.

"What are you doing?" Meelah cried.

"Ilara, wait!" Tristan fell to his knees as blood beaded from a cut on his lower lip. "It was—"

"Guards!" Ilara yanked her arm free and pointed at Tristan. "Arrest him for—" A hiccupped sob broke through her words. Be strong, she had to be strong. "He betrayed us!"

Tristan looked up pleadingly as two of the guards flanked him. "Ilara—"

"Liar!" She flexed her fist and winced. The skin on a few of her knuckles had split. She held her shaking hand against her stomach. "How dare you come back here after…"

"What is going on?" Papa bellowed. "Did he harm you?"

"Yes! He attacked me, hurt me, and he's working with Domhnall!"

Tristan grew paler. "No," he whispered. Tears ran into his beard. Mocking her.

"Take him to a cell." Papa put his arm around Ilara's shoulders. "Tell the executioner to prepare the block."

"No!" Tristan strained against the guards as they hauled him up. "It wasn't—" One of the guards punched him in the gut, and he doubled over with a groan.

"Silence!" The guard looked at Tristan with disgust.

Tristan wheezed, but still he struggled. With one hand free, he tried to shove the second guard. Bright red blood showed through the bandage wrapping his wrist. Strange, she hadn't noticed the bandages when he'd slammed her into the wall—

"You have to listen," Tristan pleaded. "Halkon—"

"Get him out of here," Papa snapped.

"What is—" A man cursed behind Ilara. Metal scraped against leather. "Release my lord."

Ilara whirled. Past Papa and Meelah, Allyre stood with his sword in hand and a dangerous glint in his eyes. The third guard drew his own weapon, and the men stared each other down.

Papa folded his arms over his chest. "You dare draw your sword on me? Your *lord* assaulted the crown princess and conspired with our enemies. Sheathe your blade, and I'll consider not executing you alongside him!"

The pucker between Allyre's eyebrows was the only sign of his confusion. He didn't sheathe his sword. "What exactly happened?"

Ilara tried and failed to keep her voice steady. "He made a deal—"

"No!" Tristan cried out. "I didn't—"

"Stop lying!" She turned back toward him. "Just…stop. Please."

Hair whipped around Tristan's face as he shook his head. The guards dragged him away, unmoved by his protests. "He stole my face! Halkon stole my appearance and voice! It wasn't me! Please believe me!"

Ilara gaped. Stole his appearance? It wasn't Tristan at all?

Tristan jerked in the guards' grip. One of them kicked the back of his knee, and he collapsed. The other guard pinned him down, pressing his knee against Tristan's spine as he drew a long dagger from his belt.

"Ilara!" Tristan looked up, eyes full of tears. "Whatever Halkon did, it wasn't—" He cut off with a sharp inhalation as the guard pressed the edge of the dagger to the side of his neck.

Halkon. But when he'd attacked her, he'd said *Domhnall.*

"Wait." Ilara pulled back her shoulders and tried to look commanding. "Let him speak."

The guard dragged Tristan to his knees, but he rested the dagger on Tristan's shoulder.

"I'd never hurt you on purpose." Tristan's intense gaze stayed focused on her. "I feared I'd disappoint or fail you, but I'd never lay a hand on you. After you left, Halkon was in the room; he was watching the whole time. He transformed himself to look like me, then bound and gagged me with vines and went after you." He hung his head. "I tried to fight free. The vines faded; his magic didn't last as long as he thought it would. I'm sorry. But it wasn't me." He jerked his head up. "But Halkon knows everything. We need a new plan!"

Horror squeezed at Ilara. Her vision clouded, and she swayed. Meelah steadied her. Tristan had been…Domhnall? She'd almost had Tristan killed for no reason.

Bile pushed against her throat. It wasn't him. He hadn't betrayed her, hadn't hurt her. The lies were all Domhnall's. She started to laugh with relief, but another thought made her already queasy stomach churn. *I kissed Domhnall.*

"Ilara?" Tristan asked weakly. "Please believe me. Please. I love you. I love you."

She nearly began crying again. *He loves me.* Tristan watched her, his ghostly face pinched with fear and…heartache. The blood staining his lips and chin stood out in sharp contrast.

"Allyre," Tristan said. "Put it away."

Allyre still stood behind her with his blade at the ready, his attention fixed on Tristan. She could see in the knight's eyes that he believed his lord—his brother. He sheathed his sword with obvious reluctance.

"Ilara." Tristan's voice wavered. "If you don't believe me, at least believe this—Allyre had nothing to do with it. Let him go. Please. *Please*."

That was the Tristan she knew and loved.

"He looked and sounded just like you." Ilara worked her throat.

She'd known it made no sense, had even considered Domhnall's influence…and his wrists hadn't been bandaged. Hating herself for falling for the fae's tricks and doubting Tristan, she took a steadying breath.

"I should have known. I'm so sorry. I believe you. Release him."

The guard sheathed his dagger and stepped aside. Tristan closed his eyes as he exhaled heavily.

"Aw, a pity." Domhnall's mocking voice turned her blood to ice. The other Tristan rounded the corner at the far end of the corridor, behind the real Tristan. "It was unfortunate the vine spell faded so quickly. I'd planned on taking him during the inevitable 'hunt down Tristan' party so you'd think he'd fled, but this was better. I really thought you were going to execute him. I would have had so much fun gloating."

Her Tristan leapt to his feet and spun around, shielding her with his body. "Don't touch her."

"Oh, I will, but not right now." Domhnall's voice coming from Tristan's twin's mouth was nearly more than Ilara's roiling stomach could bear. Multicolored swirls of light encircled the second Tristan, then dissipated, leaving Domhnall behind.

Two guards drew their swords and started toward Domhnall, but with a wave of his hand, vines erupted out of the wood and ensnared them, lashing them to the walls.

Allyre darted past Ilara to position himself next to Tristan with his sword raised. The remaining guard stood near Papa and Meelah, his blade quivering.

"Get out of my home," Papa warbled.

A lazy smile slithered across Domhnall's face. His emerald eyes swept over them.

"Part of me is tempted to act now." He waved his hand, and three confused foxes appeared in the hallway. "I could turn sweet Meelah into a rabbit right here. But, since the youngest isn't here…" The foxes disappeared in a flash of light. "Besides, it's amusing to give you a glimmer of hope. Let you think that in the next few hours you'll be able to come up with a way to defeat me." He chuckled. "Mortals are so predictable."

Tristan stepped forward, his fists clenched at his sides. "Get. Out."

"Are you going to make me?" Domhnall drawled. Allyre matched Tristan's advance, and Domhnall's attention shifted to the knight, his gaze sparking with interest. "So you're the brother? Similar eyes and jaw, I suppose."

Tristan visibly stiffened.

Domhnall laughed. "Is he a pressure point for you, Baron Carbrey? How fun." He looked between Tristan and Allyre at Ilara. "I'll see you tonight, my queen." Then he vanished in a swirl of color.

43

*T*ristan stared at the spot where Halkon had been. Panic clawed at the edges of his mind, but it was dulled by the overwhelming throb of heartbreak. Allyre's sword slid into its sheath with a dull scrape, but Tristan couldn't make himself move.

It'll be fine. Ilara hates you now, but there's still a chance to save her. And Allyre. That will be enough.

Allyre touched his arm. "Tristan? Are you all right?"

He wasn't, not even a little bit, but he nodded. After a steadying breath, he turned toward Ilara. He was afraid to look at her, afraid of what he would see. Fear. Uncertainty. Maybe the scalding hatred that had burned in her eyes when she punched him. His mouth still ached, and blood had dried on his chin. He must have a particularly punch-able face. Finally, he dragged his gaze over to her. She blinked against tears, and his heart snapped.

"I'm so sorry."

Whatever Halkon had done while wearing his body, it'd been bad. He hated the fae for hurting her, for making her cry. But what right did he have to offer her comfort or support? Ilara would view him as an aggressor now. Halkon had ripped out her heart as Tristan, and Tristan would pay the price—either because she would see Tristan as the one who attacked her, or she would realize that he'd once hurt others in a similar fashion. The candle of hope he'd allowed to ignite of a shared future, a shared love, died a gasping, shuddering death. Despite the bleeding wound in his soul, he still loved her. And he would still help her.

So he bowed to Onak. "Your Majesty. We need a new strategy."

"We can't win." Hollow defeat sounded in Onak's voice, chipping at Tristan's resolve.

"I'm not giving up without a fight." A muscle throbbed in Ilara's temple, and her eyes were red, but her raised chin and straight back shouted her defiance. "I refuse to give in and willingly hand over Talland."

Tristan could never deserve her, but he would have loved to spend his life trying. *Selfless, Tristan. Focus on helping her regardless.*

"I have an idea." He dropped his gaze to the floor. "But it *is* risky."

"Any idea is risky at this point," Ilara replied. "Doing nothing is a far greater risk."

"I'm with you," Allyre said, quiet steel in his voice.

Tristan nodded, then forced himself to meet Ilara's eyes. "We can't be certain Halkon won't overhear us, question someone, or in fact *be* someone involved in the plan."

"That wouldn't be any worse than the current mess we're in."

He winced at her frustration. "I suppose you're right." He drew a steadying breath and explained his idea, answering questions and adapting it with input from Ilara.

Once they finished, the guards left to start preparations. The king departed without a word. His distant expression and slow, heavy steps proclaimed he had abandoned hope. Allyre patted Tristan's shoulder and said he'd be in their quarters before he headed upstairs, leaving Tristan with Meelah and Ilara.

"You should both sleep, princesses." Tristan bowed without looking at Ilara and turned to follow Allyre.

"Wait."

He paused and braced himself for whatever she would say.

"Can you walk us back? I…" The slightest tremor sounded in her voice. "That way I know you're—you."

Tristan had assumed she'd prefer to get far away from him as quickly as possible. Honestly, he didn't want to be around her. As his joints had strained and his wrists bled afresh from his struggle against the vines, he'd realized that he would do anything, *anything* to protect Ilara. He still would, but he had been right.

Losing her was the worst pain he'd ever experienced.

Where his heart should be, he felt an aching chasm. He forced his expression into the impassive mask he'd learned to wear as crown prince before facing her.

"Of course." He bowed, avoiding meeting her gaze. "Lead the way, Your Highness."

Meelah pushed off the wall. "I'm actually going to meet a friend, so I'll go on my own. You two need to talk." She breezed past Tristan and up the rear stairs.

For a long moment, they stood there, the silence in the hall deafening as Tristan willed his splintering emotions to go numb. Finally, he couldn't take it anymore. "Are you sleeping in your bedroom, or—"

"Yes. I want my own bed." Ilara looked up at him and winced. "I'm sorry I hit you. Does it hurt a lot?"

He touched his swollen lip, and dried blood flaked away. "I've had worse." He gestured weakly at her hand. "Is your hand…"

"Oh. Fine."

Another moment of silence, then Tristan cleared his throat. "Shall we?" He led the way to the front stairwell without looking back, but her steps behind him assured him that she followed.

In front of her bedroom, he bowed again. "I'll see you tonight—"

"No, come in." Ilara jostled open her door and motioned him

inside. "Please? There's water on the vanity; you can clean up."

She wanted him in her *room*? Alone? Maybe things weren't as bleak as he feared. He hesitated, then slipped inside.

In awkward silence, Tristan used the washing bowl and vanity mirror to clean the little trail of blood out of his beard. The cut on his lip didn't look bad, and the pain had already lessened, so he hoped it would heal quickly. But his wrists throbbed, and crimson marred the bandages. Allyre wouldn't be pleased.

When he turned around, Ilara had closed the door and was standing in the middle of her room, watching him with an unreadable expression.

"Are you all right?" Tristan asked weakly. Part of him wanted to ask what Domhnall had done, what he'd said. Part of him absolutely didn't want to know. He couldn't see any bruising or wounds, but that didn't mean they weren't there. "Did he hurt you badly?"

Ilara shook her head. "Mostly my heart." She sighed, and when she spoke again, her voice was so quiet, Tristan had to move closer to hear. "It felt so real. He looked and sounded exactly like you. The things he said at first seemed like things you'd say."

He gulped against the knot in his throat. She trusted him enough to be alone with him, but she appeared more uncomfortable than ever before. Why had he let her leave the library instead of being courageous enough to confess his true feelings? Why did he always mess up everything, even when he was trying to do the right thing?

"I kissed him," she whispered. "I thought he was you, and I kissed him."

The abyss in his chest opened wider.

"He said…" Ilara sobbed a tiny, strangled-sounding whimper.

Tristan took a half step toward her. He wanted to comfort her, to hold her. But he didn't dare, and if he couldn't console her, he wished he could cover his ears and hide the sound of her pain. He stared at his boots, wishing he knew what to do.

"He was insulting and crude and vicious," she murmured. "Then he said you were working with Domhnall to spare yourself, and that loving you was a mistake."

Maybe it would be. He tried to unstick his tied tongue. "I'm sorry."

"It wasn't you. You can't apologize."

"You believed it could have been."

"No."

Tristan glanced up in surprise. Ilara's cheeks were red as she fiddled with a thin braid near her ear.

"That is…it *was* you, and you didn't appear enchanted." She paced back and forth, chewing at her thumbnail. "I couldn't disbelieve my own eyes and ears. I couldn't understand how you could say and do those things and hurt me. But it was you—except it wasn't, and I'm so angry with myself for not realizing. *I'm* sorry."

How was he supposed to respond? Accepting her apology felt wrong. He fixated on the dressing screen behind her. "You really should sleep—"

"Tristan, look at me, please."

The corner of her lips turned ever so slightly up. And flames, her gaze—gentle, open, and kind—pierced right through him. His throat tightened.

"Is loving you a mistake?" Ilara asked quietly.

He hoped not. If given the chance, he would try so hard to do right by her. He would probably fail, but she was good enough she would forgive him and help him be better. She wouldn't only be his equal, she would be his strength, his inspiration, his home. He would learn what love meant at her side.

Even if they succeeded, he was still only a foreign ambassador and disgraced former prince, and Alex might not approve. He felt like drowning in the emptiness in his heart.

"I don't know," he admitted at last.

"Explain." She said it softly, like she was trying to coax the truth out of him.

"I can't guarantee I won't make a mistake—"

"Of course not. You will make many mistakes and let me down, everyone does. You can't live in fear of making a mistake." Ilara stepped close to him. "Let me in, Tristan."

He plucked at a frayed edge of the bandage on his left wrist. "You should be with someone who can love you as perfectly as you deserve."

She. *Laughed.*

Did she have to mock him?

"Oh, Tristan." She giggled and placed her hands on his chest, and his breath caught. "I'm in love with an idiot."

Torn between offense and reckless joy that she still loved him, he dared to lift his gaze. Their eyes met, and this time, he couldn't look away.

"No one is perfect or loves perfectly," Ilara said. "You think I'll love you perfectly? I punched you in the face!" She winced apologetically. "It's not whether you fail or make mistakes, because we both will. It's whether you own your mistakes and learn from them and keep living, keep striving to do better. Lady Dersa—Ryn's mother—is always saying a good marriage isn't about finding a perfect person, but about being committed to growing together.

"I don't need you to love me perfectly because no one is capable of that. I just need you to love me in return and let me in."

"I do." The words pushed out in a whisper. "Flames, I do. I love you. I love you. I'd give anything to spend the rest of my life proving it." Stone-cold determination settled into his stomach. "We're going to defeat Halkon. I swear it."

"You swear it?" Her hands slid up to his shoulders, overwhelming his senses, as she angled her face up toward his. "A solemn oath?"

"Yes." Tristan nodded as his whole body heated. She was so close—her lips were so close. But he couldn't make the first move—

"Seal it." A mischievous smile pulled at her mouth.

He frowned. "What?"

"You swear to protect me." That teasing smile widened, and there was sweet, tantalizing danger in the look in her eyes. "Seal it with a kiss."

Tristan's fingers twitched at his sides. Should he? Flames, he wanted to. But then an idea for a little mischief of his own occurred to him. "All right."

She closed her eyes, and Tristan gently kissed her forehead.

Ilara's eyes flew open, and he grinned at her indignant huff. "You're impossible." Seizing his tunic, she pulled him down.

As her lips met his, his eyes drifted shut, and an exhilarating tingle shot down his spine. He kissed her gently and rested his hands on her sides, fighting the urge to pull her in close and kiss her with all of the heat burning over his skin.

Ilara had no such reservations. She released his tunic to wrap her arms around his neck as she deepened the kiss. That was it. Tristan gathered her into his arms, lost in a moment of senseless bliss. When they finally stopped for air, he didn't loosen his grip on her, and Ilara didn't move away.

"Blessed moonlight," she breathed.

"Warn me next time," he murmured, his eyes still closed. "You nearly stopped my heart."

"You…liked it?"

Tristan opened his eyes, and they separated enough that he could see her clearly. His hands dropped down to rest on her hips, but Ilara's usual confidence faded as she watched him uncertainly.

"Liked it?" Confused and a little hurt, he forced a smile. "Did…you not?"

"I did." Ilara snuggled against him, and it was all he could do to remain standing and not melt to the floor. "It's silly, but when he was in your body, he told me my kiss was disappointing. He said I was undesirable."

"He's a cad and a liar." Tightening his hold on her, Tristan leaned his cheek against her head. "Flames, Ilara, sometimes I look at you and can't breathe because you're so beautiful."

"Tristan?"

"Hm?"

"If we make it past tonight, you'll stay…right?"

He started to smile, but his joy faltered. Even if Onak didn't rescind his blessing…Alex might forbid it. Tristan would prostrate himself and beg if that's what it took. Alex and Raelyn were kind; surely they would agree…yet at the same time, who would allow a potential rival to marry a foreign sovereign's heir? Ilara had enough to worry about, and Halkon might yet kill him anyway, so he kept that fear to himself.

"You're sure your father is all right with me? What about your court?"

"If any in the court object, they'll get over it. And I'm certain he'll give you my hand."

That made Tristan smirk. "What if I don't want your hand?"

"Excuse me?" She pulled back with an affronted expression, but Tristan caught her hand and drew it up to his lips.

"What would I do with just your hand?" He kissed her palm. "It's a nice enough hand." He pressed a kiss to her fingertips. "But I think I'd prefer all of you."

She rolled her eyes. "I take back anything I ever said about you being good at flirting."

He winked. "I'll work on it."

44

If it weren't for his aching wrists, Tristan would have lingered in Ilara's room much longer. She lightly shoved him out the door with a laugh, threatening him with her severe disappointment if he didn't tend to his wounds. As he walked down the hallways, the high of kissing Ilara faded and his exhaustion and worry crept back.

When he entered their suite, Allyre, Masarik, and Remy were sitting on the couch talking, and they fell silent. Suspiciously silent.

Like they were trying to act normal and failing.

Tristan kicked the door closed and slumped against it. "What?"

"Well? What happened?" Remy asked.

Tristan looked to Allyre, too tired to explain. "You didn't tell—"

"No, with the princess." Masarik winked. "You walked her to her room, and…what?"

Embarrassment flamed over Tristan's face. He opened his mouth to snap that it was none of Masarik's business but found he didn't want to return to that relationship.

"We talked, we kissed." He waved a hand, cutting off the men's questions. "That's all the details you're getting. Allyre, would you help with my—"

"Bandages?" Allyre guessed, already halfway to his chamber. "Would have forced you to let me if you hadn't asked."

Tristan sat at the table. "Allyre explain the new plan?"

Masarik nodded. "Where are we going to be assigned?"

"Patrol," Tristan said without hesitation. "Third floor north."

"No." Hands full of supplies, Allyre stomped back into the sitting room. "I want to be stationed with Princess Ilara and you."

Every muscle in Tristan's body tensed. "No."

"Because I'm…a pressure point?" Allyre asked as he took the chair next to Tristan.

Tristan's mouth went dry. "Possibly."

"If it came to a choice between me and Ilara, I know who you'd choose." Allyre grabbed Tristan's right hand and began unwrapping the dirty bandage. "So I won't jeopardize the mission. This isn't a request, Tristan. I'm insisting on it as your bodyguard."

"I don't want to have to choose between you and Ilara!" Tristan groaned and stared up at the ceiling.

Masarik snorted. "Is that even really a contest?"

Remy appeared at Tristan's shoulder with a cup of water, which Tristan gladly accepted. "I don't know. I'm not close to my siblings. A couple of them I don't particularly like. But I still wouldn't want to see them hurt."

"You ripped out the sutures," Allyre chided as he inspected Tristan's wrist.

"At least that explains why it hurts so much."

Shaking his head, Allyre pulled bits of broken thread out of Tristan's wounds. "You're hardly in shape to fight; you know that, right?"

"With any luck, I'll only have to do minimal fighting." Tristan ground his teeth as Allyre restitched a puncture closed.

"Then my presence shouldn't be a cause for concern." Allyre shot Tristan a smug smile.

Tristan glared back. "Fine! But—ow!"

"Sorry, bad angle." Allyre rotated Tristan's wrist before continuing to mend Tristan's skin like it was a torn shirt. "I'm glad you and the princess worked things out. I was worried you'd be too mired in shame and fear to let her in. She's good for you."

Tristan winced as Allyre tied off the thread. "Too good for me."

"Enough of that." Allyre gave Tristan a chastising look, then wiped away the blood. "Your beliefs about yourself affect who you are. Don't worry about letting her down. Embrace that she loves you and love her back with every part of you. Then even when you do fail, you'll be motivated by love and not shame to apologize and do better."

"How did you become so wise, anyway?" Masarik inquired.

"A flawed but patient father who modeled empathy and an imperfect but passionate mother who demonstrated unbridled love." Allyre briefly met Tristan's eyes. "Just passing on their wisdom, because it's never too late to learn."

Tristan chewed on the inside of his cheek. "Do…do you think Al—King Alexander will let this happen? What if he says no?"

Allyre paused in wrapping a fresh bandage around Tristan's wrist. "Ah. I hadn't considered you'd need his approval and release from your oath of fealty to marry a foreign crown princess."

Fear wheedled back into Tristan's heart. "He won't allow it." The words slipped out in a whisper. "Will he?"

"How should I know?" Allyre motioned for Tristan's other arm. "But our king seems fair, honorable, and kind. You have a good chance."

"If I survive the night," Tristan muttered.

"All right," Masarik said, "with that attitude, I'm going to insist I accompany you as well."

Tristan made a face at the knight, feeling less annoyed than he should have been.

Masarik chuckled. "Not losing my money now."

"I wish I could help." Kneeling on the couch, Remy folded his arms on the back and rested his chin on his overlapped hands.

"Are you kidding?" Tristan smiled. "Keeping us fed and clean and ensuring I'm up on time? This mission would have failed without you, Rem."

"Ah." Masarik crossed his arms. "So it's Rem and Allyre now? No nickname for me? I see how it is."

"Everyone calls you Masarik," Tristan quoted with a poor attempt at a frown. "You made it sound like you didn't *want* to be called anything else."

The knight pointed at Tristan. "Correct! All right, we can keep him."

"Oh, excellent, thank you," Tristan said, his tone dripping sarcasm.

After Allyre finished dressing his injuries, Tristan went to bed, and exhaustion quickly sent him into a deep sleep. Remy woke him too soon, and it took a few minutes for Tristan to pull himself out of a confused haze.

After he freshened up, changed, and ate some food Remy brought for him, he found Masarik and Allyre waiting for him in the common area.

"Last chance to run—or at least take a safer posting," Tristan said as he passed them.

"Don't insult me." Masarik sniffed.

Allyre cast a disappointed look at Tristan. "We're with you."

Tristan gave an exaggerated sigh and shake of his head, but as they headed down to the Great Hall, he couldn't deny he was glad to have Allyre and Masarik at his back.

45

$\mathcal{S}$leep eluded Ilara. After Tristan left her room—and she might have begged him to stay longer if not for the blood staining his bandages—she lay awake, her emotions churning.

Her thoughts kept returning to kissing Tristan, the real one. The way he'd been so gentle at first, so tentative…and then he'd kissed her until her knees felt weak.

And, oh, moonlight, when he kissed her hand, so slow and tender…it was probably a good thing he was injured and had to leave, or she could have whiled away the rest of the day kissing him.

Eventually, exhaustion conquered her storm of emotions, and she slipped into dreamless slumber.

Papa woke her with a gentle shake of her shoulder. "Ilara?"

"Mm." She rolled over and stretched, knocking her hand against a corner bedpost. "It's time already?" It didn't feel like she'd slept for long.

"I'm afraid so." In the orange glow of the lantern in his hand, Papa's face looked weary. "Are you certain you don't want me to stay?"

Ilara sat up and rubbed at her eyes. "Tristan's right. It will be safer."

Papa's lips thinned. Along with a couple guards, Papa, Meelah, Kiri, and Nika would ride hard from the Great House. Domhnall wouldn't hesitate to leverage her family against her, and they needed to take away as many advantages from him as possible. The fae lord could find them, of course, but it had taken him until an hour after sunset to find them the time they'd tried to hide away from the Great House, so they were counting on catching him before he even knew they were missing.

Soon, guards armed with iron would pretend to be the princesses in the three beds in the windowless room on the first floor and in the princesses' real beds. Hopefully, Domhnall would check there first and might be killed or weakened before he found her in a spare room.

"I'm so sorry I didn't listen to your concerns and turn Halkon away," Papa said.

Ilara shook her head. "There was no way of knowing this would happen. But we're going to end this tonight."

She was done being Domhnall's plaything, done watching her sisters cry and Papa's spirit break, done fearing for her loved ones, and done seeing Domhnall's schemes affect Talland. Additionally, she couldn't be with Tristan as long as Domhnall was around. By the moon, she was going to keep kissing her ambassador if she had to cut out the fae lord's heart herself to do so.

"Your mama used to get that look," Papa said softly, his eyes moist. "You're so like her." He leaned forward, cradling the sides of her head, and kissed her hair. "Moon guide and protect you, my precious daughter."

"And you, Papa."

Kiri, Meelah, Ryn, and Nika were all waiting for them in the corridor. Kiri tackled Ilara in an embrace the moment she emerged from her room.

"I wish I could help," Kiri said as she squeezed Ilara's ribs.

Ilara hugged her sister, trying not to think that if tonight went wrong, she might never hug Kiri again.

"Just stay safe," Ilara whispered. "Moon protect you."

Kiri slowly released her. "We'll be home to see you first thing tomorrow morning." She gave a sharp nod, as if she could will their victory over Domhnall into existence.

Ilara smiled. Healthy confidence never reduced one's chances. "I'll see you then."

Meelah embraced Ilara next, a quicker exchange, but just as strong. "Did you kiss him?" her sister teased as she stepped back.

Papa coughed, and Ilara fought to keep her expression neutral.

"What, kiss Tristan?" Kiri asked.

A smile broke free as Ilara recalled Tristan's kiss.

Kiri squealed and pointed at her. "Moon-blessed summer, you did!"

"Ha." Meelah and Ryn nudged each other with smug expressions.

Ilara rolled her eyes. "All right, enough swoony nonsense!"

"Yes, more than enough," Papa said drily. "You're *all*"—he cast a defeated glance at Ilara—"too young for such things."

"What?" Meelah smiled innocently and batted her eyelashes. "Kissing? Ilara had her first kiss around my age."

"Meelah!" Ilara hissed as her face went red.

Ryn hid her laughter behind her hand. Kiri peered at Ilara with curiosity, but Papa stared at her, looking positively scandalized.

"You really need to be going." Ilara knelt down and rubbed Nika's fluffy neck. "You take care of Meelah and Kiri and Papa, Nika."

Nika just panted with a dopey grin. Ilara gave her dog's head one more scratch and stood. This felt painfully like goodbye.

"It's going to work," Meelah said, as if reading her mind.

Kiri put on an overly innocent expression. "Tristan is probably very motivated—"

"All right, let's go." Papa placed a hand on both young girls' shoulders, steering them down the hallway. "We'll see you first thing tomorrow, Ilara."

Ilara nodded, her throat tight even as she smiled. "Until then, Papa."

"Come on, Nika," Kiri called.

Nika started forward but stopped when Ilara didn't join them. Ilara sighed and scratched behind Nika's ear, then motioned after her departing family. "Nika, go with Kiri."

After a moment's hesitation, Nika bounded after the others, disappearing with them down the stairs. With her father and sisters gone, Ilara slumped and looked to Ryn.

"You're staying safely in your quarters, right?"

"Yes."

Taking a moment to steel herself before heading downstairs, Ilara stared at the floor. Ryn rubbed Ilara's shoulder but didn't say anything. Reassurance would have felt hollow, anyway. But she didn't have time to waste in fear. She gave her friend a hug, then squared her shoulders.

"See you in the morning."

Ryn blinked back tears. "In the morning." She left for her own room.

"Ilara?"

She turned toward Tristan's voice. He stood at the top of the stairs at the end of the hallway. Clean bandages poked out beneath the sleeves of a green tunic in the Rethali style with embroidered fasteners down the front, and dark circles marked his eyes. It was past time they stopped Domhnall before he caused any more suffering.

"Are you ready?"

Ilara stepped forward, but suspicion stilled her. "Are you really Tristan?"

Tristan's mouth twisted to the side. "Hm. Oh, I know how I

can prove it. Halkon knew about my condition, but not what it does. My father is a despicable villain."

Had he just…

"Wait." His eyes went wide. "Henry Carbrey is a villain?" He tugged on the stiff collar of his tunic. "Henry cursed my cousin, Alexander, and lied to me. My father tried to make me enchant Raelyn and—and struck and cursed me when I didn't." Tristan sagged against the wall near the stairs. "I'm…free?"

Now assured that he was her Tristan, Ilara went to him. She rested a hand on his shoulder, her chest tight for some reason. He laughed, the sound both pained and relieved.

"I'm free," he whispered. "Henry doesn't have any hold on me anymore." A stricken appearance came over his face. "This isn't Halkon's doing, is it?"

Ilara smiled and laced sarcasm into her voice. "I can't think of anything that happened today that often breaks curses in stories…"

No understanding reflected in his expression. "I'll remind you my father forbade me fairy stories."

Now it was a little embarrassing for both of them. "Oh, right. But surely you've heard of true love's kiss?"

"True…" Tristan reddened. "I—I mean, yes, of course I have, I just… Flames, come here." He looped his arm behind her and pulled her in, stealing her breath away with a passionate kiss.

"As much as I enjoy that," she said when they separated, "we should get downstairs."

"Right." Tristan took Ilara's hand, his fingers weaving be-tween hers, and led her down the stairs. Despite the fear still scratching at the back of her mind, she was beaming the entire way.

They went to the great hall first. Passing guards bowed to them, and a few cast narrowed glances at their clasped hands. In the main hall, Horden, his son, and a couple men Ilara didn't rec-ognize were busy handing out iron weapons and shackles. Tristan's knights joined them as they approached the tables. Horden presented Ilara with a new set of rings and a dagger, while his son gave Tristan a shackle and another dagger. The other men equipped Tristan's knights.

As Ilara slipped the last iron ring on her thumb, two Tallander guards joined their group. One, a lithe man not much taller than Ilara, carried a spear with an iron head. The other held an iron sword. They bowed to her and nodded to Tristan.

"Ready?" Tristan asked her.

Ilara murmured her agreement, and Tristan led the group out of the hall.

46

As soon as they entered the spare room on the second floor, Tristan sent the men to their places. Allyre hid in the empty wardrobe and accepted his orders to remain hidden unless and until everyone else was incapacitated with a surly countenance.

Masarik stood inside the washroom, ready to jump out the moment Halkon appeared. The Tallander with the spear took up position behind a changing screen in the corner, while the other Tallander bravely assumed his role as the visible guard and first line of defense in the open. Ilara slipped her dagger under her pillow and pulled up the covers as if sleeping.

Nervous anticipation thrummed through Tristan. If his plan worked, they'd face a weakened Halkon, slowed by the guards in the other rooms. He hoped Halkon would be more intent on finding Ilara than on killing the decoys. If all of those men died…he didn't want to think about it.

The red sunlight coming through the narrow window faded, the darkness growing deeper. It was time.

With one final glance around the room, Tristan leaned over Ilara on the bed. He brushed his fingertips over her black hair spread against her pillow, the iron shackle clutched in his other hand. She peered at him in the gathering dark. His throat was thick, making it difficult to speak, but if this was his last opportunity to say it, he had to take it.

"I love you," he whispered. "With every imperfect part of me."

A soft smile played on Ilara's face. "I love you—every imperfect part of you. With every imperfect part of me."

He pressed a desperate kiss against her lips, then pulled away quickly. Hands sweaty, he crawled under the bed and drew the iron dagger from his belt.

Please let this work.

This wasn't going to work.

Halkon would destroy them all. He was going to slaughter the guardsmen, kill Allyre, torture Tristan, take Ilara…

His breath wheezed down his throat, and the shackle rattled faintly in his fist. His heart beat like it was trying to escape his chest. *I have to calm down. I can't! Why can't I just relax?* He couldn't panic, not now, not when Halkon could arrive at any moment—but he couldn't fight the feeling of doom pressing against his ribs.

What had Allyre done? *You can breathe.* Tristan released the dagger and shackle and pressed one hand flat against the wood floor, splayed the other over his sternum, and focused on slow breaths. He thought of Ilara, counting on him, loving him, of Allyre in the wardrobe and Remy probably pacing in their quarters and Masarik standing nearby, all believing in him—all helping him.

He wasn't alone.

Gradually his heart slowed, and his shaking stopped.

Faint shouting and banging sounded from upstairs, and Tristan snatched the shackle and dagger back up. Above him, Ilara's breath caught. Silence fell again, the sound of his own heartbeat filling his ears.

Multicolored light exploded near the visible Tallander guard, and three figures crashed through a portal into the chamber. The guard swung his sword at the closest figure—whether it was Halkon, Tristan couldn't tell from beneath the bed. The guard grunted as he was thrown into the wall. His body slumped to the floor, but Tristan had no idea if the man was dead or just unconscious. The portal faded and was replaced by a teal glow from a floating orb that illuminated the entire room.

"I know you're awake, Ilara," Halkon snarled. Three pairs of boots stomped closer, and Tristan readied himself.

"Surprise!" Masarik leapt into action, sword swinging. "I'm awake, too."

Someone screamed.

"You're next," Masarik taunted.

Halkon made a growling noise, then a flash of purple-blue magic slammed Masarik backward. A loud crash came from the washroom, followed by a low moan. At least Masarik wasn't dead.

Another burst of indigo flew past Ilara's bed. A clatter sounded, then a dull thunk. Tristan's stomach dropped. That would be the other guard down.

Shiny black boots stopped in front of Tristan. He slammed the shackle around the fae's right ankle. The fae staggered backward, and Tristan scrambled out from under the bed. Leaping to his feet, he readied the dagger to strike.

But he wasn't facing Halkon.

A male fae with dark red hair gaped at Tristan. He wielded a thin, curved sword, but seemed to have forgotten what to do with it as he limped back. Behind the redheaded fae stood Halkon, his face twisted with fury. Tristan shoved the redhead aside and lunged at the fae lord.

"There you are." Halkon held forth his hand and silvery threads of light surrounded Tristan. The strands pinned him in place as if he'd been turned to stone. He remained frozen mid-step, his outstretched right arm still pointing the iron dagger at Halkon's chest. Only his eyes moved at his command.

To his right, the redheaded fae poked the iron shackle with the tip of his blade, his expression horrified. Another fae lay unmoving near the door to the washroom. One Tallander guard sat slumped against the wall, his body motionless and unseeing eyes open. If Tristan hadn't been frozen, he would have hung his head.

He had failed.

But sweat beaded on Halkon's brow, and his chest rose and fell with each labored breath. If Tristan could have moved his mouth, he would have smiled. Halkon was weakening. Ilara still had her dagger and rings, and Allyre was still hidden, waiting for the right moment—at least Tristan hoped that was true and he hadn't missed something.

"My lord…" the other fae gasped.

"Yes, yes." Halkon scowled and shot an explosion of light at the shackle, wincing as if in pain when his magic hit the iron. The metal shattered, and the redhead breathed a relieved sigh.

The plan hadn't gone perfectly—Halkon was still standing, and Tristan was stuck—but it was working. The fae was wearing down.

Tristan just needed to get free of this magical trap.

47

*I*lara sat up, staring at the silver light twining over Tristan's body and holding him in place. A lump formed in her throat as she found the hilt of the iron dagger under the pillow.

Was it her imagination…or had Domhnall winced as his magic touched the iron shackle? Maybe things weren't as bad as they looked.

As Domhnall strode past Tristan toward her, Tristan rotated like a top—still frozen, just magically turned around. Even his face was locked in a hard, focused expression, but his eyes… His eyes moved to hers and filled with worry.

"Show me your hands." Domhnall crossed his arms, looking down his nose at Ilara.

The wardrobe doors across from the bed burst open, and Allyre leapt out. Ilara held her breath as Allyre's iron sword arced toward Domhnall—

The fae lord spun around and a golden surge of light shoved Allyre back. The knight slumped against the bottom of the wardrobe and shook his head before stumbling to his feet. Ilara blinked. What was she doing? Domhnall's back was turned and his and the other fae's attention was fixed on Allyre. She steeled herself and stabbed at Domhnall's ribs—and where she hoped his heart was.

At the last second, he pivoted, and her blade plunged into the side of his upper arm. He shrieked and stumbled back, leaving the bloody knife in Ilara's grip. Ilara had hunted many times, but this…this was different. Her stomach flipped as she dropped the dagger and it clattered to the ground.

The teal light Domhnall had cast over the room glinted off the blood running down his sleeve as he pressed a glowing hand over the wound. The magic binding Tristan vanished, and he stumbled forward, catching himself just before he fell onto the bed. Allyre swung, the blade aimed at Domhnall's neck.

With a curse, Domhnall directed another blast of magic at Allyre with his free hand. Dark spots danced in Ilara's eyes from the intensity of the flash, and she blinked them away. When her vision cleared, the redheaded fae had his sword to Tristan's throat, and Domhnall had dropped his hand from his shoulder.

"Well played." Domhnall inclined his head. "I underestimated you. But I'm not yet so weak I cannot heal a flesh wound, even one inflicted by iron."

Maybe he could, but it looked taxing. He stood with less ease than usual, sweat coated his forehead, and his hand quivered. She glanced at Tristan, standing stiffly and glaring at the fae restraining him. His dagger lay useless by his feet.

They'd weakened Domhnall, but it hadn't been enough.

"Rude to stab me before our wedding, though, my flower." Domhnall's expression turned dark. "You're going to pay for that—actually, no." A vengeful smile cut across his face, and his attention fixed on Tristan. "The boy is going to pay for that."

Ilara's heart nearly stalled. Tristan's countenance betrayed little emotion, that stony façade he wore so often firmly in place. Domhnall crossed to Ilara and seized her upper arm.

She could punch him with her iron-ring-decked hands, but what would be the point? Tristan was in danger, and if the dagger hadn't stopped Domhnall, her rings would only anger him.

"I was going to give you fae food, boy, so you would be an obedient little servant at our nuptials," Domhnall said. "But you would have been oblivious, so I will withhold the food and make you watch. Then I'll think of a suitably painful way to torment you until the very sight of me makes you wet yourself."

Ilara shuddered as Domhnall dragged her to her feet. If she could contrive something to distract him, maybe—

"There's only one problem." Tristan's cocky expression was reminiscent of a child with a secret. "You can't marry her because she's already married to me."

Ilara's mouth fell open. Unless she had slept through her own wedding, they weren't married. Rethalis didn't have some illogical custom about kissing signaling marriage, did they?

Domhnall's face twisted. "Fine," he snarled. "I'll kill you—"

"No!" Ilara choked out. "You promised not to kill him!"

"I did." His nose wrinkled, but then he brightened. "But there was no mention of not *ever* doing so. In fact, that agreement was really only about last night. We had a deal—I didn't execute him last night and you danced with me. The deal is complete."

A snort came from Tristan. "Unfortunately for you and your trickster ways, that won't help you. According to Talland law, a man or woman whose spouse has died must wait a minimum of sixty days before remarrying, or the new marriage is void."

That definitely wasn't a law.

He was stalling.

Domhnall made a sound rather like an angry bull. "I kill Ilara and marry—"

"Nope." Tristan's tone could only be called smug, and Ilara didn't understand how he looked so calm while lying through his teeth with a sword pressed to his neck. Especially when her heart was threatening to race right out of her chest. "Meelah is not of marrying age according to Talland law, and any marriage to her would not be legally recognized, and as you would not *legally* be her husband, you would not have any right to the throne."

Ilara didn't want to know what Domhnall would do if and when he realized not a thing Tristan was saying was true.

"Well that's a lie," Domhnall hissed. "You're not even married, are you? I can't imagine why, but you're stalling."

The lump in Ilara's throat grew. She glanced down at the bloody iron dagger not far from her feet. If she touched Domhnall with the rings, could she get to the knife and kill him before the other fae could murder Tristan? She didn't like her odds.

Tristan shrugged. "It's the truth. Don't believe me if you want, but don't be surprised when you can't properly meld your realms or whatever it is you need to do."

Domhnall's fingers dug into Ilara's arm. "Is what he says true?"

Oh, moonless winter. Lying was not something she had prepared for.

Ilara lifted her chin and tried to look confident. "Every word. We outwitted you. Now get out of my kingdom."

Domhnall studied her for a moment, his emerald eyes smoldering like a fire. "And if I start cutting off his fingers, will it still be true?"

Her hands went cold. "Yes."

"Hm." Domhnall's gaze caught on something behind her, and he peered over the top of her head. A wicked grin curled his mouth. Before she could twist around to see what he was looking at, he shoved her toward the bed and stomped past.

48

An unsettled feeling twisted Tristan's gut as Ilara fell on the bed and Halkon stalked toward the back of the room. What was he doing? Tristan risked a glance at the washroom. He'd hoped if he stalled, the guard and Masarik and Allyre would recover. Halkon was almost finished; Tristan was sure of it. But they'd need the others' help—

"Wake up," Halkon said as he bent down. There was a sharp slap, then Halkon stood. Tristan's chest spasmed as the fae pulled a dazed Allyre up. "I'll save torturing you, Carbrey, for revelry after my wedding. But this one…Allyre, isn't it?"

Allyre scowled at Halkon and jerked his arm free.

Halkon laughed wickedly. With a snap of his fingers, vines bound Allyre's arms to his sides. The fae lord shoved Allyre forward, closer to Tristan.

"Not sure what you're trying to accomplish," Tristan said, fighting to keep his voice steady and expression impassive. This was exactly why he hadn't wanted Allyre in the room. "Dragging him into this won't nullify my marriage to Ilara."

Chuckling, Halkon pushed Tristan's brother to his knees. A knife glittered into existence in his fist, much slower than when he'd conjured things previously. He placed the edge against Allyre's cheek. "But his screams might convince you to tell the truth."

"Torturing him won't do you any good!" Only the cold edge of the blade against his skin kept Tristan in place as he watched his brother squeeze his eyes shut, as if bracing for the pain. "If I tell you I lied, all that means is I told you what you wanted to hear to get you to stop."

Fury twisted Halkon's expression. "Fine! I didn't want to have to do this."

He held out his hand and stepped around Allyre as he slowly conjured a silver grape. The redheaded fae removed his sword from Tristan's throat to place the tip against his back. But as long as Halkon was focused on him, Ilara and Allyre were safe. He needed to keep the fae's attention on himself.

Tristan slapped the grape off Halkon's hand and lunged, aiming for his throat. As predicted, Halkon pointed his palm at him. Tristan dropped to the floor and snatched up his dagger. Halkon's purple and gold burst of magic passed over him, ramming into the other fae and tossing him onto his back.

Halkon snarled. "You little—" His words cut off with a pained grunt.

"Tristan!" Ilara cried, sending Tristan's heart racing again.

But when he jumped up, Ilara was holding a squirming, panting Halkon by his upper arms from behind. Tristan smirked as he met Halkon's eyes—and slammed the blade into the fae lord's chest.

This time, Halkon didn't scream. He pulled in choking gasps of air as the brilliant green faded from his bulging eyes, leaving the irises a dull gray. The golden tint receded from his long hair, the strands turning brittle and the brownish color of a rotting apple. His entire body spasmed so violently Tristan nearly lost his grip on the dagger, but he pressed forward, keeping it embedded in Halkon's bleeding chest. Movement in his periphery put Tristan on alert, but it was only Allyre, free of the vines.

"Curse…y—" Halkon's eyes rolled back as he twitched again, and his skin turned gray. All at once, a blast of air erupted from Halkon's writhing body. The dagger was ripped from Tristan's hands as he was thrown backward. The fae's body collapsed into a heap of dead brown leaves.

Half fallen and clinging to the side of the bed, Ilara gawked at the pile of leaves with all the confusion and concern Tristan felt mirrored on her face. Allyre pushed off the wall and crept toward the mound of leaves, watching it like it might contain a viper. Tristan stood, every muscle tense as he waited for some last trick, some final show of power.

A groan sounded from the washroom doorway. "What is *in* that fae magic?" Masarik moaned as he cradled his ribs.

The Tallander who had been behind the dressing screen clambered to his feet, his gaze darting around as if looking for danger. "One moment, I'm attacking; the next, I'm waking up and the fighting is over." He looked around and frowned. "Why are there leaves?"

Allyre nudged the pile with the toe of his boot. "It's…the fae?"

Ilara stood and peered at the dead foliage. "He sort of…turned into leaves."

"Where are *you* going?" Masarik strode forward, and Tristan turned around as Masarik grabbed the tunic of the redheaded fae, who was crawling in the direction of the door. Tristan nearly slapped himself. How had he forgotten about their remaining opponent?

The redhead held up his hands. "I have no quarrel with you. I was following orders. I just want to go home."

"How?" Ilara demanded.

The fae stared at the floor. "There's a temporary thin place in the woods where I can pass through. It will be less stable with

Lord Domhnall dead, though, so I need to go—"

"And the other fae in his court?" Tristan interrupted. "What will you all do now?"

"There will be a fight to determine the next lord." The fae fidgeted with his hands, glancing at the leaves-that-were-Halkon. "That lord will need to find somewhere to anchor the Gilded Court, and quickly. After this debacle with Halkon's failure and your killing of our court's most powerful fae, they'll avoid Talland. You're unlikely to see any fae here again in your mortal lifetime." He made a sound almost like a whine. "So you can let me go. No trouble."

Tristan frowned. That seemed like a bad idea, but before he could tell Masarik to kill him, Ilara spoke.

"Let him go," she said quietly. "Enough. Just…go. And you'd better be right. Any fae seen in Talland will die. I swear it as princess heir."

The redhead nodded vigorously. With a huff, Masarik released the fae. He scrambled to the door and pressed his hand against the wood. A pale green light spread out from his palm, opening a doorway into the woods behind the Great House. The fae only let it get big enough to tumble through, then the magic shimmered closed behind him.

49

For a moment, they all stood in silence. Ilara's heart broke as she took in the dead body of one of her guardsmen. Were there more bodies in the other decoy rooms? It was difficult to enjoy their victory when it had come at such a cost.

She kicked at the pile of decaying leaves. They scattered harmlessly, the bottom of her shoe brushing against the dagger Tristan had stabbed Domhnall with. He was really gone.

The nightmare was over. They were free.

Ilara wasn't sure she could even remember what it was like to go to bed when she chose and wake up after a night of undisturbed slumber.

"What now?" Sir Masarik asked.

Allyre shrugged. "We…go to bed?"

Tristan laughed as he turned to his knights. "Oh, yes, please. I haven't had a good night's rest in ages. I might sleep straight through tomorrow, too." The broad smile on his face brought one to Ilara's lips. He'd never looked so genuinely happy.

Unfortunately, as much as she liked the idea of going to bed safe and unworried after weeks under the curse, she couldn't yet. "Baron Carbrey, you and your knights are relieved. Thank you for your help. You may retire, with my blessing."

Tristan's smile faded.

"That was…very…" Allyre floundered. "Official?"

"Sorry." Ilara blushed, realizing it had probably sounded like a complete dismissal. "My papa isn't here. I'm regent in his absence, which means I have to be official." She looked at the guardsman's body with a twist of sorrow. "It also means I need to check on the other knights and guards and ensure that the bodies are properly cared for until they can be buried."

"I'll accompany you," Tristan said quickly, his expression earnest.

His readiness to stand by her warmed her heart. "Those were some clever lies, by the way."

Oddly, fear flashed across Tristan's face. "I—I just thought of it in the moment. I didn't mean anything by it. I wasn't trying to trap or trick you, and I wouldn't lie to you—"

Ilara couldn't help her laugh. "Oh, I know. It was a good idea. Although it did remind me you should learn our laws if you're going to be king consort—wait, you do at least know you'll be consort only, right?"

Tristan nodded. "I think I'll make a better consort than king, anyway, especially since I'm still getting used to how different Talland is compared to Rethalyon." He blushed. "Do you think a lifetime will be enough time for me to learn?"

"Well," the blond knight said as he headed for the door, "we've been officially dismissed, so I'm going to go rest my aching head and avoid this lover nonsense."

Tristan slapped the big knight's shoulder as he passed. "Thank you, Masarik. For everything."

Masarik nodded. "Aye, my lord."

"I'm turning in as well, unless you require my help." Allyre gave a small bow to Tristan.

"No." Tristan frowned. "I'm tempted to say I told you so, though."

"Except I'm fine, and so are you, so *I* was correct."

Tristan opened his mouth, closed it, and glared rather unconvincingly. "I can't argue with you right now."

"That's what I was counting on." Allyre winked and left with Masarik.

The guard cleared his throat, startling Ilara. He'd been so quiet she'd nearly forgotten he was there. "Your Highness? What would you ask of me?"

"Accompany us, if you would?"

The man bowed, and the three of them checked on the other rooms. The fae had killed two more of Ilara's subjects. Four men were injured, one of whom didn't look like he was going to last the night.

Ilara oversaw getting the wounded to the physician and made sure to personally thank all of the survivors. Then she supervised moving the bodies into the windowless room at the back of the Great House and covering them until their families could be notified and their honorable burials planned.

Through it all, Tristan stayed by her side, offering help when he could, but mostly just following her lead and providing silent support. His steady presence meant more than he could know as she witnessed the hurt Domhnall Halkon had brought on her people. The sorrow and sympathy in his eyes made her love him even more.

After the guards were seen to, Tristan escorted Ilara to her room. Despite the exhaustion weighing her down, she lingered in front of her door. Tristan didn't seem in any hurry to leave, either. He simply stood there, holding a candle in one hand and looking at her like he was afraid he'd miss something important if he looked away even briefly.

"You should rest," Ilara murmured.

"I may actually sleep peacefully for the first time since before Alex returned." He stepped closer and gently caressed the side of her face. "Not just because Halkon is gone and we're safe. But because you—well, you and my men, especially Allyre—you've helped me believe I can be more. I'm ready to let go of the past and my shame, to love and be loved. I know I'm not perfect, and tomorrow this all might appear more difficult than it does right now, but…I feel more whole than I have in a long, long time."

She caught a damp glimmer in his eyes before he pressed a soft kiss to her forehead.

"Goodnight, Ilara," he whispered against her hair.

"I love you, Tristan."

She could hear his smile in the warmth of his voice as he said, "I love you, too." He kissed her forehead again before stepping back. "I'll see you tomorrow. Sleep well."

"You too." Reluctantly, Ilara entered her room and closed the door. The flickering light of the candle momentarily lingered in the hallway, then Tristan's soft footsteps faded away.

Domhnall was gone. Tristan loved her. Ryn and Lorik could get married without the curse interfering, and Ilara would be able to fully enjoy the wedding. She could work with Tristan on a trade agreement with Rethalyon and secure the food her people needed.

Her only concern as she drifted to sleep was that Papa would want her and Tristan to have a long engagement.

50

When Tristan awoke, only a little sunlight filtered through the window. He rolled over, considering going back to sleep until the sun fully rose—after all, he more than deserved it—but laughter from the common area drove the last bit of sleepiness from him.

"What's all the laughter about?" Tristan asked as he shuffled into the main room, rubbing grit from his eye.

Masarik, Remy, and Allyre looked up from some game with dice on the table. Remy bounded to his feet, catching his foot on a table leg in the process. Masarik and Allyre laughed again, and Remy blushed through a smile.

"Masarik thought we wouldn't notice him trying to cheat," Allyre said as he leaned back in his chair. "He's not nearly as sneaky as he thinks."

Remy bowed. "What can I get you, my lord? Are you hungry for supper?"

Tristan started. "Supper?"

"Yes?"

Masarik scooped dice into a rough wood cup. "You slept all day."

"Oh." Tristan rubbed at his short beard. "Why didn't you wake me?"

Allyre snorted. "We weren't about to do that without good reason after all you've been through." He cast a sly look Tristan's way. "Your princess came by to check in on you, and she also ordered us not to wake you."

"We couldn't disobey a direct order from a princess, now could we?" A self-satisfied grin settled on Masarik's face.

"You seemed to need the rest," Remy added.

Tristan couldn't disagree. He felt much better, and it was the most untroubled sleep he'd had in weeks, maybe years. Even if he was a little embarrassed, he was grateful.

He took the seat Remy had vacated next to Allyre. "Supper would be excellent, Rem. Masarik, could you let Princess Ilara know I'm awake and would like to see her after I eat?"

Masarik wrinkled his nose. "Do I look like an errand boy?"

Tristan stilled. Weren't they past these rebellious antics? He rubbed his temple. "Sir Masarik…"

"I'm just fooling." Masarik stood. "I'll gladly let your lady love know you're awake."

"That's hardly an appropriate way to speak about her," Tristan protested, but Masarik was already headed out the door with Remy.

Tristan sighed and looked at Allyre. "I was wondering… I have a question."

Allyre nodded. "I thought you might."

"When… After you told me, when I…panicked, I suppose." Tristan shifted, avoiding Allyre's gaze. "How did you know that would work? To calm me down?"

"Oh. Not a question I was expecting." Allyre rubbed at a nick in the tabletop. "My uncle, my father's—well, Baron Sharland's brother—had a run-in with some bandits when I was really little. They kidnapped him, and he fought his way out with his bare hands. For years, he'd have these moments where his mind went back to that place of manic fear, and he'd just freeze. It was the only way my father found that helped bring him back."

"Well…thank you." Tristan cleared his throat. This brother relationship—even just a friendship—was still new. "What did you think I was going to ask?"

Allyre shrugged. "Something about my mother or family. You know, I'm certain they'd love to meet you." He nudged Tristan playfully. "Assuming you're ever in Rethalyon, since you're finding a life here."

Tristan's spirts fell. "I'll have to go back to report to Alexander and ask his permission to wed Ilara."

"Ah, right."

They both fell quiet. Finally, Tristan asked, "How *did* your parents get married? After…you know."

"More what I was anticipating." Shifting into a more comfortable position, Allyre folded his arms. "Baron Sharland—well, at the time, Lord Sharland—had asked my grandfather for my mother's hand before she went to the palace. They hadn't even courted, just talked a few times, but Lord Sharland said he knew she was the woman he was going to marry." He chuckled. "My parents have a disagreement if that was terribly romantic or ridiculous, but since they did get married and they love each other now, my father insists he was right all along."

"But your mother wasn't convinced," Tristan guessed.

"Oh, not at all. She was young and had only just gotten her parents to agree to let her spend the winter at the court, so my grandfather asked him to wait and see if he still felt the same in the spring. After she returned home pregnant, my grandfather explained the situation and asked if he would still marry her. Lord Sharland was furious with Henry, and he married her immediately, swearing to regard her child as his own. Meanwhile, my grandfather made Henry pay a large sum to keep the scandal quiet—my mother didn't want to see him and feared accusing the queen's brother of assault—and Henry signed a statement that he wouldn't lay any claim to…to the child. To me."

It made Tristan queasy to think about his father doing those things, and he would have given anything to grow up with parents who loved each other and loved him—which was why the bitterness in Allyre's voice surprised him. But it only took him a moment to understand.

Their father, who should have loved them, was a monster who hadn't wanted either of them. He'd ignored Tristan as a newborn and scorned him all his life, but he'd discarded Allyre. The circumstances were different, the wounds different, but they both had their own pain.

"Your father sounds like a great man who loves you and your mother," Tristan said, wanting to say something.

"He is, and he does." Allyre smiled. "My mother once told me that when they wed, she was grateful, but she wasn't certain she'd ever love him. Then, when I was born, my father picked me up. She said, 'He looked at you with stars in his eyes, like he had never seen anything so beautiful, and whispered, "I'm a father. I have a son."' That was the moment she fell in love with him. If I fail in everything else but have half the heart my father does, I'll consider my life a success."

"Considering you believed in me when no one else did…" Tristan fiddled with the cup of dice Masarik had left on the table. "I'd say you've succeeded."

"No one? Don't discount Remy like that." Allyre winked, and Tristan laughed.

"Never discount Remy."

As if summoned, Remy entered, carrying a covered tray. The aroma of venison wafted through the air, and Tristan's mouth watered.

"How did you get back before Masarik?"

Remy set down the tray and whipped off the cloth with a flourish. "I knew where I was going, and I'd asked the kitchen to hold a meal for you. Masarik probably can't find Princess Ilara. Would you like me to prepare a bath?"

"Oh, yes, thank you." Tristan looked from the steaming food to Remy. "I don't deserve you."

"It's my honor, my lord." Remy bowed and scurried off.

As he picked up his fork, Tristan turned back to Allyre. "I'm glad for you. I'm sorry Henry wronged your mother and you, but…I'm grateful one of us was safe and happy."

Allyre crumpled like a puppet whose strings had been cut. "I'd worried you'd resent it. I'm sorry I couldn't help you—"

"Flames, taking care of me wasn't your responsibility. If you'd gone to the palace and tried to befriend me, Henry wouldn't have let it happen. You might have become another Alex for him to compare me to, or who knows what he might have done if you'd walked into his hands once he was king. Your mother was wise to keep you away." He poked at the roasted asparagus on his ceramic plate. "I'm glad to have you now, though…brother."

Allyre nodded, then clasped Tristan's shoulder, the firm, reassuring gesture conveying more than any words could have.

Tristan was halfway through his meal when Masarik returned.

"I have either good news or bad news," Masarik said as he plopped onto the couch. "I'm optimistic, though."

With his mouth full, Tristan raised an eyebrow at the knight and waited for him to explain.

"The princess wants to see you. And…" Masarik winced. "So does the king. They asked that you meet them in the great hall in half an hour."

"Half an hour?" Tristan choked. He still needed to finish his dinner, and Remy hadn't even finished filling the bath yet… Ah, well. No time for a relaxing soak, anyway.

He shoveled down a few more bites, then bathed in the half-filled tub. The waves of his damp hair brushed against the top of his tunic's stiff collar as he headed downstairs. Allyre and Masarik had offered to accompany him, but Tristan had no idea if this meeting would be official or personal in nature. If it was the later, he didn't want them there.

Steward Dessen showed Tristan into the great hall. A table had been pushed in front of the thrones, which didn't seem like the setup for an official hearing. Ilara and Onak were examining parchments and scrolls scattered across the table, but they looked up when Dessen announced him. Ilara's entire face lit up with a breathtaking smile. Beside her, Onak straightened, his expression regal and unreadable.

Tristan stood across the table from them and bowed. "Your Majesty. Your Highness."

"I hope you really came here to discuss trade," Onak said without preamble.

Tristan's heart sank. That was the only reason he had been called? His official capacity as the Rethali ambassador? It was his job, so it shouldn't have hurt so much, but he had hoped for more.

"Of course." Tristan inclined his head. "King Alexander desires to increase trade between our kingdoms. Rethalyon's agreement remains in place with Kilkreth, allowing safe transportation through its borders, but trade has fallen, regardless."

Onak frowned. "I'm aware. Our merchants have been largely unable to make the trek. We don't have enough food. We need the Rethalis to bring grain and preserved foodstuffs here—we can provide our goods at exceptional value to accommodate the trek. Lumber, furs, ivory, antlers, wool, our artisans' products, including woodcrafts and pottery—we mostly have material things we can offer in trade at this time. Gold and silver payments can only be partial."

That made sense and would be feasible, given Alex's instructions. Even though this wasn't the conversation Tristan had hoped to have, he was relieved that he would succeed in his mission.

"Papa," Ilara interrupted, her voice almost pleading.

Onak glanced at her. "However, we can discuss particulars later. We have a more…personal matter we must discuss." He tugged on the ends of his sleeves and smoothed his tunic before clasping his hands behind his back. "What exactly are your intentions toward my daughter, Baron Carbrey?"

The challenge in Onak's tone nearly stole Tristan's poise. But Ilara sent him a reassuring smile, so Tristan squared his shoulders. "I am formally asking you for Princess Ilara's hand in marriage, King Onak."

"Why?"

Tristan's brow furrowed. "Because I love her." He looked to Ilara. "And she loves me."

Onak stared Tristan down as if waiting for him to break. Tristan returned his gaze, spine straight.

"Papa?" Ilara touched her father's shoulder. "You said—"

"I know." Onak sighed. "My daughter loves you—and more importantly, she trusts you. Her account of your behavior is impressive, and I've not found fault in you. I can't thank you enough for helping my daughters and killing the fae Halkon. But I don't wish it to appear I'm giving my daughter to you as a reward."

"Certainly not," Tristan said quickly. "I did what I believed was right and because I cared about Ilara. I love her, but I would never demand her. A woman is not a reward for services rendered. If I'm allowed to wed Ilara, she will be mine to love and support and serve."

Stars seemed to glitter in Ilara's eyes as she gifted him an adoring smile.

"And how do you feel about Talland and Tallanders, Baron Carbrey?" Onak tilted his head. Even Ilara sobered at that, likely recalling his admission he hadn't wanted to come.

"Tallanders are brave and noble from what I've seen," Tristan said, considering his words. "Talland itself has a wild beauty. I would dedicate my life to Ilara, and she is dedicated to her kingdom, so I will learn to love and serve it as she does."

The smitten look Ilara gave him as she pressed her hands over her heart made him itch to kiss her.

Slowly, the king relaxed. "A noble answer. Baron Tristan Carbrey of Rethalyon, I would be honored to have you as my son and Princess Ilara's consort. I gladly give my permission. However," he added gravely, before Tristan could savor his delight, "it is not solely my decision."

Ilara rolled her eyes. "Obviously I want—"

"Not you, my dear." Onak gave his daughter a quick, sad smile. "You are not free to make this union, Baron Carbrey, are you?"

Shoulders bunching, Tristan released a slow breath. "No."

Ilara started as if he had slapped her, and his heart plummeted. He should have explained already. Everything had happened so quickly and been so uncertain…and he had been a fool. No excuses could change that he'd made the wrong choice in waiting. Now he had Onak's permission and Ilara's agreement, but how could he ask her to wait for him when Alex might not permit him to return?

"Tristan?" Ilara's voice quivered as she leaned against the table. "You aren't…promised to another…right?"

"Oh, no!" Tristan shook his head, hard. "Nothing like that. I'm sorry. I should have told you. I'll need my king's permission to marry a foreign crown princess."

He stared at the floor, unable to look at her as he continued. "I must return to Rethalyon and give my report, deliver the trade agreements, and ask King Alexander to release me from my oath of fealty and grant me leave to wed you."

He hated that Alex held his future in his hands, even though he knew he shouldn't. No, it wasn't hate so much, really… It was fear that Alex would be tempted to deny him this happiness, either out of distrust or revenge.

Soft footsteps sounded as Ilara made her way around the table and stood in front of him. "Tristan, my love." Ilara stroked the side of his face, her touch soft on his beard. "I'll wait."

It was more than he would dare ask for. "Are you sure? I'll be gone for weeks, and he might not agree—"

"I'm choosing to believe he will." Ilara went up on her toes and gave him a quick kiss. "I love you. But travel quickly, because I'll be waiting impatiently."

Tristan's knees went weak. "Trust me, I'll be just as anxious to return."

"You should leave as soon as we finalize trade details," Onak said. "I want to get as much food into Talland as possible before winter. Of course, I will write a letter of reference and explanation regarding the marriage." The king tapped his chin. "Actually, I'll even make trade contingent on the union."

Tristan blanched as Ilara moved to stand at his side. "Respectfully, Your Majesty, King Alexander might interpret such a condition as evidence of treachery on my part. I don't want to give the impression there's any motivation other than my love for Ilara. Nor do I want to come between Tallanders and the supplies they need."

"Hm." Onak nodded. "Very wise. But my report of you will be excellent."

"Thank you, Your Majesty."

Taking Tristan's hand, Ilara said, "I'll write King Alexander as well. If he's as good as you say he is, surely he'll listen."

Tristan's anxiety eased. It was true—Alex was good. And Raelyn was kind. If nothing else, perhaps he could convince Raelyn. One way or another, he had to.

Over the next several days, Tristan, Onak, and Ilara drafted a new trade agreement to present to Alexander and the Rethali merchants. He was also introduced to the House Heads, all of whom had their own suggestions for the trade agreement.

In between preparing to depart for Rethalyon—including sending word ahead to Alexander that Onak was sending him back to discuss an important matter in person—Tristan spent every spare moment with Ilara. She told him about Talland's customs, and they learned more about each other and their likes and dislikes between kisses.

Ilara also informed Tristan that after they married, he would be king consort sooner than expected. Onak wished to retire from his role as monarch, and they had agreed on a gradual transition until a formal transfer of the crown in a year and a half—which would give Ilara and Tristan some time to adjust to being a married couple before adding the pressure of reigning.

Tristan sheepishly approached the blacksmith, Horden, and asked for aid with fashioning an engagement ear cuff. Horden laughed and explained jewelry was not his trade, but he knew enough from making his wife's cuff to help, and he approved of Tristan respecting their customs and making it himself. It took four tries before Tristan had a rough silver ear cuff he was happy with, composed of three connected, downward-pointing chevrons.

"I got you something," Tristan told Ilara a couple days before his planned departure.

They were sitting on a blanket in a sunlit patch of grass in the forest, enjoying a sunny and warm day. Nika gnawed on a large stick nearby, and Ilara was partly reclining on the basket they'd carried their food in.

She sat up as Tristan pulled a small pouch out from under his belt. His hands were sweaty, and he fumbled with the drawstring. At last, he reached in and pulled out the cuff. It wasn't as shiny or the lines as straight as he would have liked, but he thought it looked pretty good.

Ilara gasped and snatched the cuff from his fingers. "Oh, Tristan!" She moved it closer to her face, inspecting it. "Did you make this?"

He rubbed the back of his neck. "Is it that bad? Horden told me he wasn't a jeweler, but I knew only him, so he showed me what to do—"

She threw her arms around him, cutting him off. He pulled her close but tensed when he realized she was crying.

"Ilara?"

Her arms tightened around him as she sniffled. "It's perfect, Tristan. I didn't think—but you remembered, and you did it, and it's perfect." She pulled back and kissed him, the salty tang of her tears on her lips, then she pushed the cuff onto the outside curve of her ear. "How's it look?"

"Beautiful," Tristan breathed.

She gave him another quick peck on the lips. "Now you have to come back."

He swallowed hard. "I'll do my best. I intend to replace that with a proper marriage cuff."

Ilara reclined against his chest. "Good."

When he left with his men, he kept twisting in his saddle to look back, watching Ilara fade into the distance.

He would return to Talland.

He had to believe that he would.

❧401☙

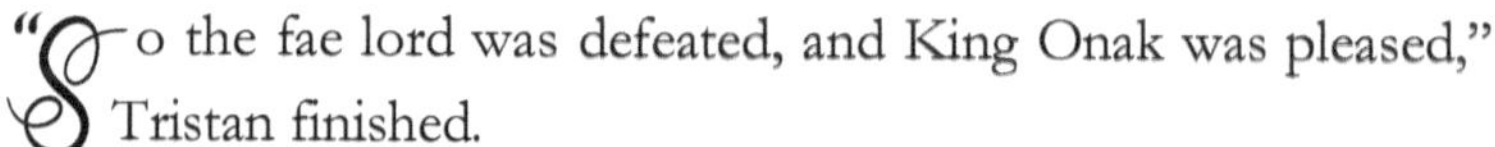

51

"So the fae lord was defeated, and King Onak was pleased," Tristan finished.

His voice sounded small in the cavernous silence. Why had Alex and Raelyn decided to see him in the Great Hall? Between Alex receiving Tristan when he first arrived for just long enough to accept the letters from Onak and Ilara and then dismissing him to give his full report later—what turned out to be three days later—and choosing this location, it was like Alex wanted to remind Tristan he had no power here.

It didn't inspire much hope of getting a favorable answer to his request. At least Alex and Raelyn had let him stand instead of kneeling to give his report; that was a good sign. Still, by the time he finished, Tristan was sweaty, and his nerves wound tight. He pictured Ilara's smile and pressed on.

"But in the process…" He stared at Alex's chin, unable to maintain eye contact. "As you must know from King Onak's and Princess Ilara's letters, Your Excellency, Princess Ilara and I fell in love. I wish to marry her." He bowed, afraid to see Alex's reaction. "I humbly beg your permission to be released from my oath of fealty to you and to marry Crown Princess Ilara of Talland, my king."

Terrible silence. Tristan remained bowed despite his trembling legs.

"You truly love her?" Raelyn inquired, her tone gentle.

Tristan didn't trust himself to straighten. "Yes, Your Majesty. I have changed, I swear. I have treated her honorably, and I love her. Please, I'm not the same man. I have learned and I am striving to be deserving of her. She—and Allyre and Remy—believed in me, and that gave me the strength to be a better man." He licked his lips. "Please. Allow me to wed Ilara."

"No."

Tristan jerked at Alex's flat response. He lifted his gaze to the king's impassive face. "Your Excellency, I promise I will never act against you or Rethalyon. This isn't about power."

Alex's stoic expression remained unchanged.

All Tristan's hope slipped out of his grasp, as if he were desperately trying to catch sand poured into a river. "I mean no disrespect or threat to your rule. I fulfilled my ambassadorship as honorably as I could. I returned out of loyalty. And I would only be a king consort after her coronation. Please, Alex." He winced. After that blunder, he probably had no chance. "Your Excellency, I apologize. I ask humbly—"

"My answer is no." Alex's stony countenance remained unchanged, as if he had no intention of being dissuaded.

Tristan's entire body quivered. He'd clung so tightly to the thread of hope that Alex was good, Alex was just and a romantic, he wouldn't say no. Now that thread snapped. He looked to Raelyn. Surely she could change her husband's mind.

"Your Majesty, please…" Words failed, the pain in his chest too acute for him to string together a coherent argument.

Raelyn pursed her lips, something like pity in her eyes, but she shook her head.

More because his legs wouldn't support him than from a conscious decision, Tristan fell to his knees. His heart cracked. He blinked to stop the emotion threatening to break through.

"I beg of you—"

"You claim to be loyal," Alex said, his tone icy, "and then you make this request? And you argue when denied?"

Tristan struggled to breathe. Everything in him wanted to argue. But here, in this throne room where Henry had often humiliated and degraded him, he could not. Alex's gold crown glinted on his dark hair, a declaration of his authority. Tristan had sworn an oath, and he would not break it.

Defeated, Tristan bowed his head. He couldn't go to Talland in defiance of his king without threatening the trade Talland so desperately needed. Jeopardizing his own safety he would do, but he couldn't risk being the reason Tallanders starved that winter.

I'm sorry, Ilara. He would write to her and explain and promise to make his request again as soon and as often as he dared, whatever the consequences of such insolence might be. But, for now…

"No, I won't argue." The words came out strained. "As it pleases Your Excellency. I am your servant and will obey." Head pounding, he pressed his eyes closed. Under no circumstances would he weep in front of Raelyn and Alex. "What task—" His voice broke, and he had to clear his throat. "What task would my king ask of me?"

Please, say you don't know yet and dismiss me. Tears burned at his eyes. *I can't hold it together much longer.*

"Is that sufficient for you, Alexander?" Raelyn asked softly.

"Yes," Alex said. "I think you've more than proven yourself. Stand, Baron Carbrey."

Tristan looked up, confused.

Alex smiled. "Stand, Tristan."

Tristan wobbled to his feet, glancing back and forth between

Alex's smile and Raelyn's watery-eyed grin.

"The Tristan who left here a couple months ago would not have wept over a woman," Alex said. "Nor would he have accepted a ruling that clearly hurt him without any sharp taunts. The Tallanders' letters did speak highly of you and confirmed a marriage was desired by all parties. Perhaps more convincingly, I spoke with Sir Masarik and Sir Sharland."

He had? Tristan hadn't known that. Allyre had even wished him luck before this meeting, and he hadn't mentioned it.

"They praised your character and assured me the love between you and Princess Ilara was true." Alex sighed. "But letters can be forged, and men can lie or be deceived. Many in the Court of Lords already think me weak and foolish for not having you executed or banished, and my wisdom in sending you as an ambassador was harshly questioned. This will be difficult to explain to them. I needed to be certain this wasn't a plot, and that you genuinely love her." His smile turned melancholy. "I'm truly, deeply sorry for putting you through that. It is…excruciating to think you have lost the one you love."

Tristan's breath came in gasps. "What are you saying?" He wouldn't hope. He didn't dare—

"I release you and give you permission to marry Princess Ilara of Talland, Tristan Carbrey." Alex's smile broadened.

Raelyn beamed. "We were already inclined to give a favorable decision, but some things are hard to forget. Please forgive us for our distrust and that cruel test. I wish you all happiness, Tristan, truly."

Tristan tried to speak, but all that came out was a squeak. His chest heaved as he collected himself after a whirlwind of emotion. "This is your final decision? I can return to Talland and marry Ilara?"

Alex gave him a confused frown. "Yes. Were we unclear?

Again, I apologize for my harshness in refusing you, even temporarily. Now that it's clear your love is true, I wouldn't dream of hurting you like that."

Peace flowed over Tristan. "Thank you." He gave another bow, hoping it conveyed the depths of his gratitude and forgiveness. "Thank you, Alexander."

"Stop fidgeting," Allyre whispered.

Tristan forced his hand away from the violet sash tied at his waist over his Tallander-style turquoise tunic with a scooped neck and loose, long sleeves trimmed with embroidery. The crowd filling the great hall was staring at him, and he was about to lose his mind waiting for Ilara to appear.

According to Tallander tradition, they hadn't been allowed to see each other for the past three days, and Tristan had spent most of the previous night receiving marriage advice from old men he didn't know. Now he stood on the dais with Ryn and Onak to his right and Allyre on his left. The wolf fur trimming his white cloak tickled his ears, and he just wanted to see his wife.

Wife.

Ilara was going to be his wife.

At that moment, the small group of Tallanders standing off to the side began to sing. Everyone turned toward the far end of the hall as the right-side door opened.

Ilara stepped into the hall, a radiant smile on her face and a bouquet of wildflowers in her hands. All of her black hair was intricately braided, and her silver circlet set with a large pearl glittered in the torchlight. Her matching fur-trimmed white cloak partly covered her violet wool overdress and turquoise linen underdress, both trimmed with intricate embroidery.

She had never looked more beautiful.

His grin threatened to split his cheeks, and he held back tears of joy as Ilara approached him—too slowly and somehow also too fast as he both longed to get through the ceremony and kiss her and wanted to stand there and stare at her. Ilara handed her bouquet to Ryn and faced Tristan.

"Moonlight, you look good in Tallander clothing," Ilara murmured as she took his hands.

"You're breathtaking," he whispered back.

Between them, Onak cleared his throat, and Tristan thought he heard Allyre smother a laugh. Ilara winked at Tristan, and Tristan had to stifle his own chuckle. Now that Ilara was standing in front of him, her hands clasped firmly in his, the stares of the crowd didn't bother him.

Onak gave a speech about love and duty, sacrifice and growth, but Tristan had difficulty concentrating on anything his new father-in-law said; he was too distracted admiring Ilara. He repeated the vows Onak recited, pouring every ounce of fervent devotion into the words as he promised to cherish, protect, and be loyal to Ilara for the remainder of his days. As Ilara echoed the vows back to him, he was nearly delirious with joy and amazement. His excitement was a jittery energy coursing through his veins as he took the marriage cuffs from Allyre.

First, he removed Ilara's engagement cuff, tucking the silver cuff in his sash, then tried to ignore his clammy palms as he replaced it with a cuff of smooth gold wires that curled up and down, ending in delicate flowers, and set with a single small diamond. He bent down so Ilara could work a gold band with a geometric design over the middle of his ear.

"I, King Onak, note these vows and the symbol of the cuffs binding these two to each other." The king motioned to the couple. Tristan forced himself to remain calm and dignified. "May the moon bless this union, and may the moon forever hide its face from the one who breaks these vows." The tiniest sigh escaped Onak. "You may kiss your spouse."

That was all Tristan had been waiting for. He wrapped his arms around Ilara and tugged his wife in close as he kissed her. Ilara's hands went to his neck, her fingers tangling in his hair as she matched the passion that burned through him. As he gradually became aware of the sounds of cheering and whooping, he reluctantly released his wife.

He shifted so only one arm held her waist, and they both turned to face the gathered crowd. Tristan rolled his eyes as Masarik pumped his fist in the air and winked. Next to Masarik, Remy was applauding hard enough to hurt himself.

Onak's voice boomed behind them, "I present Crown Princess Ilara and Prince Consort Tristan. May their lives be long and moon-blessed."

Another cheer went up from the crowd, Allyre's enthusiastic shout loud at his side. Tristan couldn't be more thankful that Allyre and Masarik had consented to provide his escort back to Talland, and especially that Allyre had so readily agreed to stand by his side as the witness required by Tallander law. Allyre had also been amused to learn his responsibilities included finding and dragging Tristan back if he tried to run instead of either going through with the ceremony or formally breaking the engagement.

However, Tristan was sorrowful that they would be returning to Rethalyon in a couple of days. At least Remy had agreed to remain as Tristan's manservant—actually, he had begged Tristan to keep him on. It was going to be hard to say goodbye to Allyre. For now, he pushed the sting of the forthcoming loss of his friends away, focusing instead on the overwhelming joy of being Ilara's husband.

Around them, the hall descended into chaotic activity as

guests helped servants rearrange the hall for the wedding feast. Even Onak left to help maneuver his throne into position at the head table that was being moved from along the wall. Tristan took advantage of the distraction to kiss his wife again.

"How long do these feasts usually last?" he murmured into Ilara's ear.

She leaned against his chest. "Late. Very late. Tallanders love a party."

Tristan bit back a groan. Ilara's laugh vibrated against his body as she reached up and stroked his short beard.

"But it's common for the bride and groom to sneak off early," she murmured with a teasing lilt. "Thank the moon, because it is *very* tempting to kiss you senseless right here."

Tristan hummed and tightened his grip on her waist. "You're going to break down my sense of decorum if you say things like that."

"Mm, but you see…" Ilara ran her fingertips over his chest. "I like when you're improper and lose your decorum."

"Is that so?" He grinned down at her, and she looked up at him with a soft smile.

"You're more yourself when you aren't wearing that proper mask you learned to wear to please Henry," she said quietly.

Tristan's throat caught. He'd never explicitly told her that, but he didn't need to. She saw him, all of him, and understood, and loved him—mistakes, wounds, and all.

"I love you so much," he whispered.

"And I love you." Ilara pushed up on her toes and gave him a gentle kiss.

Whatever pain his past held, whatever challenges his future would hold, it didn't matter. He had someone to love with all his heart, and someone who loved him with all her heart, and they would fight to support and better each other for the rest of their lives. After a lifetime of feeling like he could never be enough, he finally understood it was all right that he wasn't perfect, and that he didn't have to be.

Who would have known that in cold, distant Talland, Tristan wouldn't just find beauty and healing and love…

He'd find a home.

The End

Thank you for reading!

Reviews on any retailer or review site are greatly appreciated.

Read book three now!

A Fated Quest

The quest was simple: retrieve the stolen firebird. The prophecy Prince Gareth stumbled into is complicated.
A prince who would rather be a knight teams up with a talking fox to help a captured female knight and stop a witch intent on vengeance in this story inspired by The Golden Bird and Tsarevitch Ivan, the Firebird, & the Grey Wolf.

Make sure not to miss out on future Miraveld stories by subscribing to my newsletter at:

SelinaRGonzalez.com/Newsletter-Subscription

… (Acknowledgments)

Acknowledgments

This book has been a while in coming and I've worked on it—and had to take a break from it—through a lot of highs and lows over the year and a half or so it took to get this book to the point of publication. I don't know that I recommend writing a book about a character struggling with low self-worth while in the midst of a depressive episode—heh—but I do recommend being willing to admit when you're not okay and seeking support.

So I'd like to thank my support system first. Everyone who has listened or offered encouragement or understanding, thank you, especially my mom, Becky, my therapist, the ladies in the "Coffee Group" on Facebook, Jenni, and Alexis, for helping me through some rough emotions both author-related and life-related. Not sure I would have finished this book or had the courage to put it out in the world without you.

A big thank you to Dani—if you hadn't seen the potential in Tristan before I did, this book probably wouldn't have been conceived.

Kelly, thank you for both pointing out the weak points to improve this story and for helping me regain some lost confidence in my story-telling abilities.

Thank you to all of my outstanding alpha and beta readers for your feedback, encouragement, and suggestions.

Mom, thanks for reading this book almost as many times as I did.

Thank you, Micheline, for making my cover dreams come true a second time.

To the folks at Deranged Doctor Design, thank you for your beautiful work on the title and text design on the cover and for your flexibility.

Kate, thank you for being my proofreading and comma- and hyphen-fixing fairy (and catching some continuity errors!). If any incorrect commas or hyphens remain, it's probably because I'm stubborn. Also thank you for all the random lexicography, lynx, and *Rebels* messages. I do not regret giving you my number, lol.

To everyone who has helped with this launch through ARC reviews, cover reveal, or other shares or posts, thank you!

A huge thank you to you, my dear readers! I literally can't keep publishing books without you. Thank you for every book purchased, every review written (and copied over to other review sites), every message about how much you loved a book or moment or character, every social media post, every time you recommend one of my books to your friends—you not only make pursuing my author dream possible, you make it worth the hard parts and the discouraging days. You rock.

No thank you to Rex, who firmly believed kibble was more important than these acknowledgments and kept head-butting my hand away from the keyboard because he and Bear were clearly *moments* from starvation at exactly 5 o'clock. You're both lucky you're so cute and fluffy.

Finally, all thanks and praise to the divine Author of my story, who called me worthy of His love and His sacrifice when I had done nothing to earn it, who keeps loving me when I make the wrong choice or when I feel alone, whose wings protect me even when I feel lost in dark valleys, and who has promised me an eternal Home.

About the Author

Selina R. Gonzalez is a Colorado native with mountains in her blood and dreams that top 14,000 feet. She loves chocolate, fantasy, costumes, bread, history, superheroes, faux leather, things that sparkle, medieval Britain, snark, dogs, and Jesus—not in that order.

She loves to travel and has driven coast-to-coast in the US, visited Britain three times, and has a list of places to go as long as Pikes Peak is tall, but always comes back home to Colorado.

Get a free ebook, bonus short stories, book playlists, early announcements, and make sure you don't miss any exciting news or Selina's future books by subscribing to her newsletter at:

SelinaRGonzalez.com/newsletter-subscription/

www.ingramcontent.com/pod-product-compliance
Lightning Source LLC
Chambersburg PA
CBHW030355200726
48286CB00014B/1425